The Chronicles of Anuru

Lark's Kiss, Volume 4:

The Sack
of
Arx Cervus

by

D. Alexander Neill

Contents

◆

For more original art by J. Gagnon,
to purchase a print, or to request a commission,
contact **jgagnon999@gmail.com**

◆

For more information about my writing, please visit:

...my Facebook page: **https://www.facebook.com/DAlexanderNeill/**

...or my website: **http://www.alexanderneill.com/**

...or contact me at **dalexanderneill@gmail.ca**

◆

**This book contains intense depictions of violence and sexuality.
It is not suitable for children.**

◆◆◆

The story thus far (and a little history)

The Sack of Arx Cervus is the fourth book in a series of tales collectively entitled 'Lark's Kiss', chronicling the adventures – and misadventures – of Alauda Volo.

If you have not yet read the first three by now, you've missed a great deal of the story. Each of these tales is intended to stand alone, of course, and of course there's nothing inherently wrong with beginning a story *in medias res* – but at this point you're two months and several hundred pages behind. The present volume necessarily assumes that you know something of the protagonist's character and proclivities, her recent past, her family, the history and culture of her people, and something of the wider world in which she lives. In the absence of this preparatory narrative, it may be a little difficult to keep up with the present story.

Briefly, Alauda is an elf; her name means 'lark' in that most ancient and lyrical of tongues. A young lady with one foot over the threshold of womanhood but still decades short of legal majority, she is a citizen of the oldest continuous polity in the known world.

A little nomenclature might be helpful at this point. That polity, which its denizens call 'the Realm', and which folk from other nations term 'the elf-realm' or 'Elvehelm', its proper name, is located in the south-central region of a land mass – a continent – called Erutrei. Erutrei, along with the islands to the east and west, and the semi-continental land mass of Jarla to the far north, are the only known inhabited places on the world of Anuru.

The origins of the name 'Erutrei' are obscure; those of the name 'Anuru' are not. It is an amalgam of two of the most ancient words of lore, common to all tongues no matter how disparate. According to legends shared by all of the folk of Erutrei, the origin of things began in the far-distant and trackless past, with a dispute between two opposites: Ana, the light; and Uru, the darkness.

In those days, of course, there was neither any actual light, nor any absence thereof, for the world had not yet come to be. It's easiest to think of Ana and Uru as philosophers do: as the antipodes of good and evil.

Ana and Uru existed in the chaos of the Void – perhaps with others of their kind, though this is not, and indeed cannot be, known. Desiring some means of determining which of the two might claim primacy of place, they joined their powers and hived off a portion of the Void, fencing out its roiling chaos with walls built of order, the foundations of which were laid upon an agreed compact: that the new space would serve as a field of contest between them, and that the walls that defended it should endure until their dispute was decided. This was the beginning of the World Made, so-called because it was differentiated by form and structure and solidity from the unmade, endlessly mutable pandemonium that lay beyond its shielding walls.

Ana and Uru then set about crafting vessels for their will, to carry out their contest. By agreement each made seven servants. Ana made the Anari, the Powers of Light; and Uru the Uruqua, the Powers of Darkness. The Anari consisted of three sisters: Bræa, Vara, and Tian; and four brothers: Hara, Esu, Nosa and Lagu. All were mighty, each in his or her own way, and incomparably beautiful; but Bræa, their chieftess, was the most beautiful of all. The Powers of Darkness were led by Bardan, and counted among their number Zaman, Ekhalra, Morga, and diverse others. All were as terrible as the Anari were wonderful, rife with might, and hungry to dominate and destroy.

Fearful that battle between such titans might sunder the walls they had built and bring the newly-wrought World Made crashing down in ruin, Ana and Uru forbade the Powers from engaging in direct combat. The Anari and the Uruqua were therefore given leave to create minions of their own, to serve as warriors in the contest between the darkness and the light. The Anari created brilliant beings of skyfire and glory, wrought in their own image, and Bræa called them the *Sarvaloka*, the Host of the Light. The Uruqua, by contrast, crafted monsters inspired by their own horrific dreams, spawning grotesqueries that crawled from hidden places to sow terror and destruction. Among these were the dragons, who call themselves First-Born; the giants; and the fiends, towering monstrosities of venom and frost, iron and flame.

A battle requires a battlefield, and so Ana and Uru crafted a firmament whereupon their offspring might contest for mastery: a land in the heart of the World Made that they called Anuru, meaning 'the place of light and darkness'. Then they withdrew to hidden places within the outer realms, on the very lip of the World Made above the seething ruin of the Void, to see how their battle might play out. Thus was Anuru from its very inception wrought to be a charnel house; an arena wherein the darkness and the light might strive for eternity, each seeking to undo the other.

These origins, some say, explain why so much of the history is writ in blood.

To distil thousands upon thousands of years of that history into a few pages is no easy task. Briefly: the Powers and their servants fought for an age with no clear outcome. No one knows how long, for when all are immortal there is no need to mark the steady march of time. The warriors of the Sarvaloka fell in their thousands, and when they died, their bodies became the stars in the sky. The minions of darkness perished likewise, becoming the stones of the earth, and thus both earth and sky grew immeasurably as the age of battles went on.

At length, seeing no clear resolution, Bræa conceived a new understanding: that because all that lay within the World Made was the creation, balanced and deliberate, of Ana and Uru, victory could never be achieved by hewing solely to that which lay within the boundaries of the walls. The thousands upon thousands of servants, divine and profane, could fight and fall forever, but could not win or lose; for they had been crafted according to their will of their makers, and could not exceed their limitations. All of them, even the Powers themselves, were nothing more than tools.

And so Bræa reached beyond order's walls and seized a pinch of the chaos of the Void; and with it, and the four elements of the world Made, she crafted new beings to do her bidding. From the high and graceful winds she made the Elves; from ravenous, mercurial fire she made Men, who make and destroy in the same breath; from swift-flowing water, that evades every obstacle to go where it will, she wrought the Halflings; and from stolid and incorruptible stone she carved the Dwarves. And within the *sielu* of each of them she placed a seed, the tiniest of motes, of the Void, so that each of them, and all of their descendents, might be able to grow beyond the designs of their maker. These kindred children were granted a gift never before known: the power to choose the light or the darkness. This was Bræa's great gamble: her hope that her children might one day upset the contrived and artificial balance of the World Made, and thus grant a final victory – *the* final victory – to one side, or the other.

The making of the Kindred brought new life to Anuru, and it was prolific, and expanded wonderfully over the whole of the known world. Bardan, unable to comprehend what Bræa had done, seized many of her new children and warped them into beings better suited to serve his dreadful ends. From men he made ogres, and from elves, orks; tormented dwarves became goblins, and Halflings, gnomes. But his fell designs went awry. All that he achieved was to change their form and poison their hearts and minds; each of them, descended from wilful forebears, still carried within their *sielli* the shard of chaos that granted choice. Thus even the goblins, orks and ogres could, if they chose, turn away from the Ender to serve the light instead of the darkness, and further upset the balance of the World Made. His plot miscarried in another way, too; for the irrepressible joy of the Halflings was so ingrained that the gnomes, crafted to be Bardan's servants, quickly tired of his dark designs, and abandoned him altogether, turning as one to the light.

Bræa's plan succeeded...for a time. At length, though, just as the gnomes turned away from darkness, so did many among her children turn away from the light, lured by the blandishments of the Uruqua. Power and fortune, glory and pleasure and knowledge, are all heady wine. Elves, men, and even dwarves abandoned her to cast their lot with Bardan, lured thither by the prospect of unlimited license.

When she saw her creations abandoning her to chose the foe, Bræa at last comprehended the folly of her great gamble, and in a rage, she raised her hand to strike down her children, every one of them. Ana halted her; and in punishment for so terrible a betrayal Ana reft away Bræa's power, casting her from the company of the Anari and leaving her little more than a mortal, so that she might live as her own children did, and comprehend their frailty and their fears, and in time come to understand the why of the choices that each had made.

From Bræa's power Ana wrought a great light, placing it in the sky above Anuru and setting the world a-spin, to grant light to the foes of darkness, and forever remind Bræa of her crime. The rising of Bræadan – Bræa's Lantern – was the first dawn, and the beginning of the march and measure of time.

Bræa, outcast and in grief, wandered among her children for an age, taking many forms: a young girl, a warrior, a priestess, a slave, a princess, an old sage, a thief, a skald, a cripple, a king. She lived with the *elvii* in the forests, and with men in their fortresses; with *dwéorga* in their caverns, and gnomes in their hillside homes, and even with the *halpinya* in their impermanent riverside camps. She had many guises, but in each of them she was accompanied by two guardians set by Ana to observe her penance: two wolves, or two dogs; two falcons, or two ferrets; two ravens, two great cats, two swift foxes, or two lumbering bears. Thus although she contrived to hide her face and form, she was ever known to all with the wit and wisdom to see the truth behind her diverse disguises.

Her brothers and sisters – especially the twins, Vara the Merciful, and Hara the Wise – begged her return to them, and live once more as one of the Anari, even a lesser one, for they loved her, and missed her company and leadership; but she refused their entreaties. She had learned regret for her attempt to destroy her children, and grief, and sorrow; but she had not yet learned the truth of their hearts. Wisest of all beings, she knew that she yet lacked that essential wisdom. Everywhere she went she remained apart from her creations, retaining the last vestiges of her divine power like a cloak and a shield, until at length she understood Ana's final lesson: that to truly comprehend the lot of those that she had made, she had to truly become one of them.

And so Bræa gave up the last of her divine power and took on a *manu*, a mortal form, and went to live among the *elvii*, the first and oldest of the people she had made. She doffed her disguises and confessed who she was and why she had come, and begged them to allow her to live among them. She had not, however, considered the effect of her appearance on them; for Bræa, even in mortal guise, was yet the most beautiful creature ever to exist within the walls of the World Made. Thus it should have come as no surprise that the *elvii* fell at once enamoured of her. Cîarloth, the Elvenking, claimed her at once as his bride, and wed her with great and glorious ceremony. He sired many sons and daughters upon her, and she bore them as all mortal women have done before and since. Thus did Bræa at last gain the last true measure of wisdom, learning for herself the joy and sorrow, the glory and the agony, that her children had known ever since she had woven them from earth and water, wind and fire and the void, in the far-distant and long forgotten past.

Yet even this selfless act was not without terrible consequence; for while it had been Ana's intent that Bræa should learn how her children suffered, Ana had not intended that Bræa should mingle her divine blood with theirs. Nor did Ana foresee that Wise Hara, desperate to convince his beloved sister to return, would imitate her in every wise, discarding his divinity like a cloak, taking on a mortal *manu* as well, and siring children upon a princess of the elves.

Thus were the *elvii* by their posterity divided into the different peoples that have come down through the ages. The children of Bræa and Cîarloth, and all their descendents, became the First House; and those who came from the union of Hara and his bride, the Second. Most troublesome were those of the Third House, the children born from the mingled blood of the First and the Second, for within them ran both the fire and creativity of Bræa, and the wisdom and serenity of Hara, and these divine traits were ever at war within those whose lineage included two gods rather than one.

It was from the Third House that the greatest kings, the most powerful magi, and the strongest warriors were destined to come. Tior the Mighty, the first High King of all the elves, and his brother Dior Fell-Handed, were Bræa's grandchildren. Tior gave his people wisdom and power, and brought them to the pinnacle of understanding of the Art Magic; but he also gave them unending grief in the shape of his son, Xiardath the Usurper, who stole his father's crown, and cast Tior beyond the Walls of the World Made, into the Void. Xiardath in his turn fathered Biardath Ill-Born, Tior's grand-son, who turned the Realm into a charnel-house. Their line numbered also Mærglyn, called The Kin-Slayer, who was Tior's great grand-daughter, sired by Biardath upon a demon of Bardan. Mærglyn summoned an army from the darkness of her fiendish mother's blood and set the Realm aflame from the mountains to the sea. Her otherworldly hordes were defeated only when Bræa herself, armed and armoured as a warrior of the light, took up spear and shield to lead the host of the *Sarvaloka* one last time, casting Mærglyn down from Mighty

Tior's throne, exiling her to darkness, and cleansing the Realm.

The defeat of Mærglyn ended Tior's line and brought the line of his brother Dior to the forefront, and with that change came hope. Dior's descendents did not traffic with fiends, study under the malevolent eye of ancient wyrms, or otherwise meddle with the Art Magic; they brought rectitude, wisdom and war-craft to the throne. As War Chief, Dior had penned the Codex that gave law to the Realm. His mate Anyalla, cool and formidable, had established the law that governed right conduct between husband and wife, parent and child, servant and master. And Yarchian, their grand-son, rebuilt the Realm after Mærglyn's defeat, and so was called *Renovator*, The Renewer. His reign endured for long years of peace and prosperity, until at the last the Realm was called to war against the massed hordes of Bardan himself. The war lasted for decades, and despite the deeds of innumerable heroes (two of whom loom large in the pages that follow), in the end the Realm was crushed. The Age of Wisdom, which had begun with Bræa's marriage to the Elvenking and which had lasted almost fifteen centuries, came to an end, and the Eon of Darkness descended upon the world.

The empires of men, the dwarves in their deep cities, and the Halflings in their hidden vales did not perish; indeed, they flourished in the Darkness. The Realm of the elves, its borders besieged, did little more than endure. Yarchian was dead; the dragons of light, who had betrayed Bardan to rally to the Elvenking's banner, had been all but wiped out. Bræa, immortal but lost in mourning, had faded into obscurity, with scarcely a shadow of her once immense power remaining to her. Hara was gone as well, his *manu*, like the dark and fearsome body inhabited by Bardan during the war, abandoned like a husk. They had been sealed away from the mortal world by a compact among the Anari and Uruqua that prohibited the Powers from intervening directly in mortal affairs; the gods would never again touch the earth.

The Darkness did not end until the Argent Three – a trio of dragons led by an ancient wyrm who had fought at King Yarchian's side in the last of the Realm's great battles – brought word of the Powers of Light to the elves in the form of a book that rekindled their faith. A thousand years of prosperity followed, for elves and men alike; their kingdoms waxed and grew strong.

Another that grew strong, unfortunately, was a mage of unknown origin, who called himself only *Rex Ombris*, the King of Shadow. He had learned – or re-learned – a powerful magic, and having mastered it, he marched against the empires of men. He was defeated, but not without great cost; for in a last act of defiance he raised his hand and split the land of Erutrei in twain, sundering the northern kingdoms of men from those of the south, shattering one of history's greatest empires to ruin, and drowning the greater part of its lands, and its capital – Yl of the Towers, a city of wonders unparalleled in all of history – beneath the icy northern sea.

The elven Realm was largely untouched by the depredations of the Shadow King; its folk went their own way while the kingdoms of men struggled back from the ashes of the sundering. Seven hundred years later, the Realm lives in uneasy friendship with its nearest neighbour and greatest rival, Ekhan, an empire peopled almost entirely by men. Strong in arms, waxing in numbers, muscular in policy, and optimistic – perhaps overly so – about its destiny, Ekhan represents the new world, and is beginning to rub up against the old. Rubbing causes friction, and friction, heat. Supplied with tinder, heat may become an all-consuming flame.

Now, history and myth are all well and good, and they do provide a substantial backdrop to help flavour and explain contemporary events; but this story is not about gods or ancient heroes. It's about a girl. Let's get back to her, shall we?

Such is the world into which Alauda Volo, sixty years ago, was born. From her perspective, it is a world of danger, promise, possibility – and difficulty. The Realm is stable and secure, but it is also stultifying, particularly for folk who look to change their status and their stars. Its nobles, the Duodeci – the so-called 'Divine Twelve', the noble houses who can trace their lineage back to Dior, and who have the wealth and influence to maintain their claim – jostle continually for position and for power. Allegiances are explored, formed, exploited and betrayed so swiftly that it can be difficult to know at any one moment who is aligned with, or against, whom. As a famous elven poet once put it:

The throne is but a fickle seat; it changes in a trice –
to rule, a King must lie and cheat, as he would at bowls or dice.

The king at the time of Alauda's tale is Callaýian Æyllian. *Domus Æyllianus* – House Æyllian – has held the throne for almost two thousand years. This is the longest that any of the *Duodeci* families has maintained control since the days of Tior himself, and is entirely down to their cultivation of alliances, their wealth, and their utter ruthlessness. Callaýian inherited the throne from his elder brother Sîarahalla, who'd succeeded their father, Allarýchian *Rex Rectus*, the Upright King, who fell in battle with the Shadow King at the gates of Yl more than seven hundred years earlier. Allarýchian's father, Artakanzallon, who had been known as *Rex Primus Æyllianus* – the first Æyllian king – had seized the throne from his predecessor, a king of House Drývanteum.

Artakanzallon's rebellion took place more than a thousand years before the rise of the Shadow King, so far in the past that men hardly remember it. And yet in all that time, only four kings had sat upon Dior's golden chair. Elven memories are long, so long that men can scarcely comprehend them. When Artakanzallon came to the throne, for example, the land of Ekhan had not yet been settled; four Elvenkings later, it was, in geographic extent and military might, the greatest empire in all the world.

With only four kings in the span of nearly eighteen hundred years, elves inevitably view the march of time very differently from men.

This difference in perspectives accounts for much of Alauda Volo's restless spirit. Like all of her people, she views the passage of centuries with equanimity. All other things being equal, if she is spared the consequences of war, pestilence, and her own folly, she might very well expect to live for a thousand years or more. At the same time, however, she is young, impatient, and plagued by the eagerness and arrogance of immaturity, things that we who have left childhood behind can no longer truly comprehend. She has left schola in her life's wake, and is ready to embark upon something new, but does not yet know what that might be. She is an adult in every physical sense, if only just, but still a child under Dior's ponderous law, obliged to spend another sixty years – as many as she has lived thus far – under her father's roof, his supervision, and his command. More to the point, she is fated to spend the coming six decades under the watchful eye of her well-meaning but formidable mother.

Alauda, in a word, is infected with that most lethal of maladies: restlessness. She is fed up with *being*; she wants to be *doing*.

In the story thus far, her father's house – the house to which she is bound until, on the one hundred and twentieth anniversary of her birth, she will 'pass without the walls' – is on the move. Kampat and Alyssa, her sire and dam, have left their home in Corymbus, in the north of the Realm, to make a new life in the free city of Portacaminus, the so-called Fire-Gates, a bustling trading town on the verge of the northern wastes. The wastes are the physical remnant of the ancient wars of the Powers; a dire, blasted land where nothing grows save storms, and where creatures of havoc and terror flit and roar amid the ruins of long-vanished civilizations.

Porta', outside of the mountain-wall that encircles and defends the Realm, lies upon the Great Road that spans the breadth of Erutrei, connecting the lands of the west to those of the east, a vast artery carrying the commercial lifeblood of kingdoms and empires. It is here that Alauda's parents hope that they, and their increasingly fractious daughter, will find their place.

Such a move is not without its hazards. Descending through the mountains, Alauda managed to lose herself in a snowstorm, and was saved from death only by luck, and by the good offices of Clan Raven. The *Suku Gagak* are a tribe of wild elves – the sole remnant of the ancient *elvii* as Bræa made them, whose blood was never exalted (or tainted, as they would say) by that of Bræa and Hara, and who never joined Tior's ancient compact, preferring to remain bound to native glory and majesty of the Green. Rescued by Jantun Langu – Singing Heart, the tribe's huntress – Alauda ended up spending some weeks with the clan, learning more about the ways of the woodlands than a lifetime behind city walls could teach her (q.v., Book 2, *The Huntress*). She also learned some disturbing things about the Forest Gods, including Hutanibu the Forest Mother, and Cernunnor the Horned God, to whose service all of the women of her family have been bound by a pact forged centuries ago by Elspina, Alauda's great-grandmother (q.v., Book 1, *The Horned God*). Finally, she learned some disturbing things about herself, the origins of her peculiar and unreliable abilities – and the strengths, and weaknesses too, of her own heart.

At the melting of the snows the clan returned her to her family, and Alauda's journey continued. The mountain pass met the Great Road at Vitrafoss, a town quite literally in the middle of nowhere, equidistant between the two great market towns of Porta', a hundred leagues to the east, and Gaudium, a hundred leagues to the west. Claimed by both the Realm and the Empire, Vitrafoss had always been something of a diplomatic hot coal, a situation that was complicated by the presence of a scheming member of House Cælestis, one of the Realm's wealthiest Duodeci families. Alauda's arrival, coinciding as it did with that of a mage-lord from the Empire of Ekhan to the west, and of a Cortina of Disciples of the Maiden of Blinding Beauty from Zare in the east, put tinder to the coal. By the time the conflagration died down some days later, Alauda had rescued the Disciples; been invited to join their number as an acolyte; assisted the mage-lord in dealing with a religious schism within his own ranks; been appointed a Knight-Aspirant of his most august chivalric order; and unmasked, and contributed to the defeat of, the principal antagonist, Lady Kalanna Cælestis, earning thereby her undying enmity – no small thing, should Alauda or her family ever intend to return to the Realm (q.v., Book 3, *The Mummers*).

Following the uproar at Vitrafoss, Alauda, her family, and the caravan of which they were a part continued their slow progress eastwards, still aiming for Portacaminus. As the present tale opens, they have just reached Buckhill, a small tin-mining town whose fortunes have recently begun to improve with the discovery of a rich vein of silver. The sudden influx of wealth has summoned all manner of ne'er-do-wells, necessitating the despatch by the Empire of a warlord and his mage-trained wife to reopen an ancient elven stronghold in order to provide security for the town and Road.

The gleam of coin has also attracted a migrating village of Halflings from the distant east. Alauda, a devout student of the vagaries of language, knows that bats congregate in a colony, ducks in a flock, partridge in a covey, and herrings in a shoal – but to date no one has ever taught her that any group of more than two Halflings is, somewhat disparagingly, called a 'bother'.

She is about to find out why.

While all of these developments make for a volatile mix, it is the ancient fortress – and more particularly, the storied hero to whom it once belonged – that attracts Alauda's interest. This results, through a series of rather improbable coincidences and events, in Alauda Volo – a girl barely out of school – leading a cabal of reivers in breaching and pillaging one of the oldest citadels ever raised upon the borders of the Realm. As she will later justify it to herself, every individual event, and every decision that she took in response to them, made eminent sense at the time. It is only when you line them up end-to-end – say, in the context of a story – that the sum total looks like an unstoppable juggernaut of outright lunacy.

Alauda would argue that in addition to logic, she was following her heart, even though together they were to lead her into the uttermost depths of catastrophe. Some might call that a serviceable explanation for all of mortal history.

♦

One

It was the thirtieth day of Forars, the year's third month, and the last day before the first of Greenspring. Alauda, rocking back and forth in Perda's saddle, soothed almost into sleep by the mare's easy stride and the warmth of the afternoon sunlight, found herself reflecting on, of all things, the oddities of mensural conventions.

It seemed peculiar to her that the elves, who were conspicuously jealous of their ancient tongue in nearly every other imaginable respect, were content to employ the month-names assigned by the men of Ancient Esud in eons past. The month-names, moreover, reflected man's irritating willingness to be comfortable with linguistic inconsistency. The names they'd chosen were based on the Travelling Tongue, which was itself a jumbled hotchpotch made up of bits and pieces of other languages, and contained words from the *dwéorgaspræc*, the dwarven tongue; the old Esudi language; the *nordmannir* speech that was still in use in places like Jarla; the speech of the beast-folk, Orkana; and even the odd phrase from the wyrms' tongue. The result was a quilted mishmash of a lexicon that had taken her long years of study and practice to master. She still found it confusing – and, therefore, irksome.

The trouble, she decided, was that people were too lazy to be bothered with fixing something that was so obviously broken. The fact that folk were accustomed to a bad business was no reason to be content with it.

(She'd been feeling peevish all day; month-names were not the first topic to attract her ire. Tonlees, her best friend, had already felt the lash of her tongue. She'd even quarrelled with her mother. This was proof positive that she was out of sorts; in her right mind, she'd never have dared to beard that particular dragon.)

It was nonsensical. The elves, the humans, the dwarves, and everyone else called the winter months Jule, Efterjule and Wintersdyb. The months of spring were Forars, Greenspring, and Sáning; the summer months were Er-sommer, Heitsommer, and Firstreap; and autumn consisted of Heitreap, Lastreap, and Ars-waning. She'd once, years ago, asked her mother to help her translate the twelve months into *elvii*. Together they had managed to come up with 'Celebration', 'After-Celebration', 'Deep-Winter', 'Spring', 'True-Spring', 'Sowing', 'Near-Summer', 'High Summer', 'First Reaping', 'Great Reaping', 'Last Reaping', and 'Year's-Waning'.

"If we know what they mean," she'd asked, deeply frustrated, "then why don't we use our own words, instead of that foreign drivel?"

"Because the whole world uses that foreign drivel, and is comfortable with it," Alyssa had – infuriatingly – replied. "There are many matters more worth our time, dear. Don't fret yourself into a lather trying to fix things that aren't broken."

It had taken Alauda more questions to induce her mother to offer a more effusive explanation. Human month-names were used, the girl had learned, because humans had been the first to establish regularized principles for the passage of days and moments. This, Alyssa theorized, was because the humans had also been the first to venture out for long periods upon the sea – and also, she'd added wryly, the first to engage in complicated and extensive wars of conquest. Both activities required a more detailed approach to time-keeping than that which the ancient elves had found satisfactory for their purposes of hunting, gathering, and minding both their own business, and that of the forests.

"Just imagine planning a military campaign," Alyssa had chuckled, "and telling your allies that the attack was to begin a week before your shaman usually said it was the right time to plant oats, or on the morning of the eighth day after the first Morbannen blossoms appeared. Or on the sixth night after the celebration of the deeds of one of your tribal heroes who went to wind a century ago."

"Fine," Alauda grumped, "but how did the humans decide to divide the year into twelve months, and that every month should have the same number of days? I thought the day and night, and the seasons, and the length of the year, were fixed by the rising and setting of the Lantern?"

"They are," Alyssa replied. "The facts of the natural world determine the shape and span of our measures, dear. We call a day a day because that's the time between two sunrises. One-twelfth of that span is a stick because it's a convenient length to cut incense for meditation and ceremonies of faith. Did you think it was more likely that the course of Bræa's Lantern across the sky was fixed seven thousand year ago by Ana coming to earth, determining how long a stick of incense burns, and then deciding to make the Lantern move just fast enough to complete a single circuit in twelve such spans?"

"Of course not!" Alauda exclaimed. "I understand that part – we choose the length of our own measures, obviously. What I wanted to know is, why does a year take exactly three hundred and three-score days?"

"It doesn't, dear. It's a tiny bit longer than that."

Alauda, swaying in Perda's saddle, smiled as she recalled that her reaction to that alarming revelation. She'd sat bolt upright in her chair, squealing, "*What?!*"

When Alauda had pressed her, her mother had explained that she had read of a place in the royal palace at Starmeadow, a stone tower and frieze built thousands of years ago by Tior Magnus himself, where the light of the Lantern, piercing an eye high up on the roof of an arch, was supposed to illuminate a carving of Tior's crown, the *Laurastralis*, precisely at noon on Bræa's Dawn – the first day of Forars (or "Spring", as Alauda grumpily insisted on calling it). " 'Supposed to'?" she'd asked.

"It doesn't," Alyssa had replied. "Not anymore. That's how Tior built it, but it's been changing over the centuries. Now the Lantern's light falls upon the crown on the seventh day of Forars, in the evening."

Alauda had been taken aback by that tale. "I thought Tior was infallible. He was the wisest man who ever lived!"

"He was gifted, certainly. Immensely so. But infallible – certainly not. After all, he gave us Xiardath the Usurper, and Biardath Ill-Born, and Mærglyn Kin-Slayer, no? Not to mention the *Ars Anecros*, so that fools drunk on their own magic may make the dead rise and walk again. He was *not* infallible.

"But," she mused aloud, "his understanding of the skies and the stars was said to be without peer. What I think, dear, is that it simply means that things change. Nothing is eternal – neither the stars above our heads, nor the earth beneath our feet. Change can be a good thing, sometimes; without it, we could not learn, or grow, or aspire to greatness.

"And if Mighty Tior erred," she added with a grin, "proving that he was something less than omniscient – then that too is a good thing. At least in my opinion. It proves that he was a man, and not a god, as so many folk have claimed. It comforts me, in my fumbling incompetence, to think that even *he* could make a mistake."

These memories occupied Alauda's thoughts as Perda's relaxing steps carried her along the grassy verge of the Great Road. She'd been thinking about dates, and ancient Tior too, because the next day – the first day of Greenspring – happened to be Tiorsday. And by ancient tradition, the first Tiorsday of Greenspring was a holiday throughout the Realm. The common people called it 'Second Spring', and it signified that a month had elapsed since the grand festival of Bræa's Dawn – the day thousands of years ago when Holy Bræa had closed her eyes in the celestial realms, and had opened them again in a mortal body upon the hilltop of the *Lucum Sacrus*, the Sacred Grove of ancient Morbannen trees at the heart of Starmeadow.

Today, Starmeadow was the greatest city in the world, most ancient, and most beautiful. Not the largest; that title was held by Norkhan, the imperial capital far to the west. Back then, though, Starmeadow had been little more than a collection of camps; the small confederation of *elvii* tribes that had joined under the banner of a war chief. Holy Bræa, who had made the elves and all of the kindred races many thousands of years before, had come to earth, the better to know the children that she had brought into the world, and later had attempted to destroy. She'd woken in mortal guise, inhabiting a *manu* of peerless beauty, and had captured the heart of Cîarloth. Guided by her wisdom he had united the elves and became their king; and upon her, he sired the semi-divine children whose descendents would one day found the great houses of the Realm.

Bræa's Dawn was traditionally a day of thanksgiving, calm, and reflection. It was also a day when many life-mates chose to make or renew their vows, in honour of the vows taken by Bræa and Cîarloth more than five thousand years ago. Second Spring, by contrast, was a different sort of holiday – a glorious effusion of gratitude and joy that winter was at last at an end, and that the work of harrowing and sowing, planting and spading, and all of the labour of creating new life was about to begin in earnest. It helped that the Morbannens usually flowered about that time; the heady scent of their gold-and-silver blooms dominated the festivities, figuring in decorations, ladies' scents, and even the cuisine. Nor was it only the earth that was tilled; in the months that followed the revels of Second Spring, many elven ladies found to their delight (or chagrin) that more had been planted than just wheat and corn.

Alauda had talked about Second Spring with old Akaryah, the Clan Raven singer. Her adoptive clan-mates, the folk of the *Suku Gagak*, would be holding Morbannen-fuelled revels of their own – an uninhibited Bacchanal, according to the old woods-walker, the likes of which were unknown among the more civilized cities of the high elves. She'd expressed sorrow at missing it, and he'd laughed, telling her that it was better that she return to her own people. Amongst the clans, girls like she, unmated but of marriageable age, were highly sought-after by the tribe's unattached warriors on the eve of Second Spring. As a rule, such demozels awoke the following morning bleary-eyed and aching, and tended to throw their first cub some ten moons later, in the first weeks of Deep-Winter. Such, he'd explained, was the effect of Morbannen blossoms on anyone of *elvii* descent. Though the wild elves lived much closer to their ancient roots than Alauda's folk, the so-called high elves, he'd warned, were no less susceptible to the blandishments of the flowering forest. So had the Holy Mother made them.

Even here in the north, on the Realm's outskirts, the mighty trees were in flower; Alauda could smell their intoxicating fragrance, carried on the winds from the mountainside far above. Akaryah's account of Second Spring among the clans definitely intrigued her, and she would have liked to have witnessed it – but as an observer, not a participant. Her instincts, inclinations and desires notwithstanding, Alauda was still a maid, and the notion of giving herself over to a night of unrestrained passion with a score or so of her erstwhile clan-mates, though exciting in the abstract, in reality posed so many potential practical problems that she was glad that the opportunity was going to pass her by.

All the same, she was looking forward to the festival, largely because it would be a chance for her to spend the night on Alacer's arm. Second Spring featured music and dancing, and while her silver-haired beau was not the most graceful creature ever to be dragged through his paces, she was confident that between the two of them they ought to be able to avoid knocking into too many other party-goers or stepping on too many toes. It would also be an opportunity for her to renew her acquaintance with him; after the events in Vitrafoss the previous week, he'd been a little stand-offish. At times it felt as if he'd been avoiding her. Alauda wasn't entirely certain what was going on; perhaps he was as nervous as she at the prospect of their first formal outing as a couple. Whatever the reason, she was certain that, given the opportunity and a few quiet moments alone, she would be able to pry some answers out of him.

She also couldn't wait to don her gown – however horrid it might be; that was a whole different nightmare – and put her head on Alacer's shoulder; to feel his heart beating against her cheek, and to chat and smile gaily the whole night long. That, and to spend the evening gloating like a miser at the envious faces of the caravan's other eligible females – especially the older ones who still treated her like a child. Alacer's good looks and sunny disposition had attracted more than one pair of doe-eyes on the long journey from Astramicor, from girls even younger than Alauda to mated dams older than her mother. And yet, in spite of all temptations, he had chosen *her* – and she hadn't had to 'wink and whisper' him into it, either. She hadn't done that to him since before the snowstorm. He loved her, and that was a fact.

The thought of showing him off to the rest of the caravan was so enticing that the deficiencies of her gown worried her not at all. Although far too circumspect to crow openly about her conquest (she didn't care a fig for discretion, but she could feign it readily enough when circumstances demanded), Alauda had discovered that there was something immensely satisfying in having landed such a splendid specimen of manhood where the rest of the caravan's genteel demozels – slavering, loose-kneed harpies, the lot of them! – had tried and failed.

Tonlees was looking forward to the party as well. Alauda knew this because her friend was sitting behind her, sharing Perda's generous saddle – a snug fit. Toni had spent the better part of the morning babbling incessantly about the anticipated glories of the coming festival, and dropping broad hints about what might happen after the last keg was empty and the last torch burnt out. The endless flood of giggling speculation had driven Alauda to distraction, to the point that she'd goaded the mare into a canter, hoping that the clattering pace might still the tide of chatter. It had worked, to a point; her auburn-haired passenger had been forced to grit her teeth and hang onto Alauda's waist as they clip-clopped their way carefully between the wagons, making for the head of the caravan.

When they reached the vanguard and saw Captain Rettik riding easily with a handful of his men – more were riding further ahead as scouts, Alauda knew, and the bulk were deployed at the rear of the wagon-train, as insurance against bandits picking off stragglers – she slowed Perda's pace. Her mother had told her that she could ride anywhere within the span of their escort, but that she was not to fall behind, nor to ride too far ahead. She knew that this wasn't capricious advice; the Great Road was dangerous. A troop of mercenary horsemen was a costly extravagance. Rettik would not have been there had the situation not warranted sharp eyes, and sharper swords.

She reined Perda in, falling back to a walk a few horse-lengths behind the officer's stallion. "What was...that about?" Tonlees asked, gasping.

"I just felt like a bit of a gallop."

Her friend patted the horse's rump affectionately. "Perda couldn't gallop if her arse was on fire."

"Not with this much cargo aboard. That's for sure and certain."

"What's *that* supposed to mean?"

"That notwithstanding the alleged and myriad privations of a long mountain journey," the younger girl said with a rueful grin, "we've both of us somehow managed to become a little more matronly in the fundament. Or at least I have."

"You have a lovely backside," Tonlees giggled, slapping Alauda's hip; the younger girl jumped, scowling. "And so have I. It just means you've travelled a little further along on the path to womanhood. And about time, too – there's no better moment for you to start showing your curves, 'Huntress'!"

"If you say so," Alauda sniffed. Privately, she agreed with her friend; one of the biggest problems with the dress her mother was frantically altering for her was that Alauda didn't have much to stuff into it.

"I do say so!" Toni crowed. "Between the two of us, we're going to absolutely *murder* every boy at the party tomorrow night. You just wait; the sound of hearts breaking will drown out the drums!"

Alauda scowled. "What does a breaking heart sound like, exactly?" she wondered aloud.

"Like this!" Tonlees put the back of her hand to her forehead. "Oh, woe!" she cried. "Woe unto me, for mine innocence is sped, and my fair knight captived by a beauteous treacher's false and faithless smile! Oh, woe!"

Alauda turned and goggled at her friend. She burst into appalled laughter. Toni followed suit.

Rettik and his two outriders turned to glance at the giggling girls. Alauda flushed mightily, embarrassed at having been caught tittering like and infant. Toni didn't; she merely smiled gaily, and waved.

One of the horsemen made the mistake of waving back. Rettik barked at the man; he stiffened in his saddle, his eyes snapping back to the road ahead.

Alauda glanced back over her shoulder. "Promise me," she snickered, "that you will never, *ever* perform on stage."

"Why not? You did!" her friend reminded her. "Just last week! I was there, remember?"

"That was singing, not acting!"

"You *could* act, though," Tonlees chided. "Easily. It's just like lying, and I've seen you lie; you're the best. You could talk your way out of a noose." She shook her head. "I wish I could do that; it might save me another switch-"

Her voice trailed off suddenly.

Alauda didn't miss obvious cues; she could feel Toni's arms tense about her waist. "Another what?" she prodded. "Another *switching*? Is that what you were about to say?"

"What if it was?"

"Tsk-tsk. What'd'ye do to earn that, *heya*?"

There was a pause. "I was late getting back to the wagons," Tonlees replied after a moment. "Mother'd sent me on an errand, and I lost track of time. She didn't really do much; it was just a swat. She hasn't whipped me in years. Wouldn't matter if it did; she doesn't put her heart into it." She poked Alauda in the ribs. "Not like *your* mother."

"Hmm," Alauda grunted. "Yes, they must teach it at the College, along with illusions and fireworks and such. That, or she practiced by beating carpets.

"Though to be fair," she added, "it's been a long time for me, too. Maybe I'm just getting better at hiding my sins. Thanks be to Wise Hara, and may that blessed respite continue."

"It's been a long time since you gave her reason," Tonlees

remarked. "The last month doesn't count. It's not like you tried to get lost in a snowstorm, after all. And you certainly weren't looking to get wrapped up in that business back in Vitrafoss."

"I *did* try to break into Lady Kalanna's castle, though," Alauda reminded her, shivering a little; the memory of being swept downriver toward the roaring mist still woke her at night. "And I succeeded. I thought I was in for it that time."

"Oh, come on!" the older girl chided. "Not even your mother would whip a girl who'd survived a tumble over a waterfall, and ended up being named a hero of the Empire by someone like Lord Trivinako!"

"I wasn't all that concerned about my mother, to tell the truth," Alauda said quietly. "It was my neck I was worried about, not my backside. When Renvig and I were chained up in that tower, I was certain that Kalanna was going to kill us. Or that she'd have that cretin Laws do it for her."

"That woman makes my blood run cold."

"Are we still talking about Kalanna?" Alauda forced a laugh. "Or are we back to my mother?"

"Either," Toni shivered. "Or both."

Alauda snickered.

"It's too bad your mage friend didn't set Ring Castle alight, and cook Kalanna to a turn." Toni brightened. "Still, your mother can't be *too* angry with you; she's letting you wear your sword." She flicked a fingernail against the scabbard.

"Hmm," the younger girl nodded. She glanced down at Lord Trivinako's gift. "This one, anyway. She still won't let me take Jantun's spear out of the wagon."

"Good. You'd look a right savage, dragging that thing around."

"That's exactly what mother said," Alauda sighed.

Alauda's mother, to her daughter's infinite surprise, had managed to dig up an old lady's baldric, complete with hangers, and had helped Alauda properly sling the blade that the Ekhani mage lord had given to her in recognition of her service to his homeland (as he'd put it). The baldric was ancient, of faded silk the shade of a tangerine, and it was too big for her, but Alauda had borrowed hammer and awl from her father and had punched a few more holes in the straps. After trimming their protruding tongues with Elspeth's dagger the thing was serviceable enough – and hey presto, here she was riding about like a cavalryman, feeling every inch the 'Hero of the Empire' that Tonlees had called her.

That the baldric's ghastly colour clashed horridly with her cote and dress bothered her not at all. "I suppose this *is* more ladylike," she sniffed.

"I think it was kind of your mother. At least she's giving you've a chance to act like a lady."

"I suppose. She keeps surprising me." Alauda touched the baldric again. "This was...unexpected."

"I'll say." Tonlees glanced at the other side of the belt. "Where's the knife? The one with the naughty handle?"

Alauda kicked her right foot out of the stirrup, straightened her leg, and tugged at the hem of her skirts. "Boot," she said. "That wasn't even a struggle; when I asked mother if I could keep it, she just nodded and said it saved her buying me a *pugio*."

"I'd've thought the hilt would have put her off," the older girl chuckled.

"Me too." Alauda wrinkled her nose. The dagger had been a gift from Lady Elspeth, the Disciple of Miyaga whose rescue Alauda had facilitated the previous week in Vitrafoss. The hilt was of ivory, carved in the shape of a nude dancing girl. "But she doesn't seem to mind it. Said it was a lovely piece of art, as well as an artefact of an ancient, if somewhat disreputable, faith."

" 'Somewhat disreputable'! That's all she had to say?" Toni sighed. "You should hear what my parents call the Disciples. 'Whores and procurers' was the most pleasant of them."

"I can just imagine."

Toni was quiet for a moment. At last she said, "You're mother's odd, isn't she? It must be a little hard to live with. I mean, she's fabulous and all, and brilliant, and terrifying – but the most terrifying thing about her is that there's no way of knowing what's going to set her off. Is there?"

Alauda shook her head. "There really isn't."

She hoped Tonlees wouldn't ask about the last gift that she'd acquired in Vitrafoss: the jade amulet that Elspeth had given her;, which she kept tucked away beneath her pillow. She'd tried wearing it, but it was too distracting; she could feel its warmth against her skin, and hear the echoing of the music like a distant chorus every time she stopped to listen. She'd spent most of that day fidgeting upon her seat in the wagon, flushed and gasping for breath, until her mother had threatened to dose her with something to ward off ague.

It had taken most of the day, but she'd finally realized that the amulet had been provoking the symptoms. Now she kept it hidden, and only pulled it out at night, clenching it against her heart and feeling the thunder of the drums echo in her belly. The visions imparted by the tiny trinket throbbed in time with her lifebeat, spreading a tingle of heat through her flesh – an exquisite, convulsive joy so potent that it was all but unbearable. Elspeth herself figured in the intimate visions, and not only as a dancer. Renvig and Vidar, the two other members of the lady's Cortina, were usually with her, but not always. Sometimes, Elspeth was dancing for

Alauda alone. Those were often the very best of visions.

Even thinking about the violet-haired Disciple provoked a tingle in her belly that made her squirm restlessly in the saddle. She hoped Tonlees didn't notice *that*, either.

Toni, apparently, did not. "Sword and dagger both; how martial!" the older girl was saying with an approving nod. "You should dress like that tomorrow night; you'll look quite the brigand."

"If I really wanted to cause a stir," Alauda laughed, "I'd dress the way I did when I was feasting with the *suku Gagak*: loincloth and feathers, beads in my hair, stag's blood for rouge – and nothing else!"

"That'd cause a stir, all right," Tonlees smirked, poking her again; "a stir in every man's trousers!" She hesitated a moment, then asked, "What of Alacer? You said you were going with him. You are, aren't you?"

Alauda nodded. "We spoke about it a few weeks back, just before the storm. He hasn't asked me yet, but he's been especially busy the last few days."

"I know," Tonlees grumped. "Mistress Faradin's been driving all the boys like a mad thing. He's been busy checking hooves, greasing axles, shifting cargo and what-not. I've hardly seen him either."

"I'll make a point of it tonight," Alauda said firmly. "If I corner him, that'll give him the chance to ask me. I might even get a kiss out of it, too." That had become an increasingly sore spot for her; in the six days since leaving Vitrafoss, she'd seen Alacer frequently at a distance or in passing, exchanging smiles and waves, but had only spoken to him a handful of times. They hadn't been able to find any time at all to be alone together; he was always either working, or off on some errand for the drovers, or abed. Their all-too-brief interludes at the standing stones, in various fields or upon convenient river banks (and for that matter, beneath the bed of his parents' wagon), seemed like dreams of a distant and scarce-remembered past.

"Good luck with that," Tonlees murmured.

"Who're you going with?" Alauda demanded. "Please tell me you haven't asked Welferic!"

"No," her friend sighed. "As you pointed out – repeatedly! – he's too old for me. I haven't found anyone yet."

Alauda's jaw dropped. "What? How's that possible?" There was a limited number of boys of eligible age about the wagons, and an equally limited number of eligible girls – and Tonlees was, in Alauda's biased opinion, the prettiest of them all, herself included. "How has nobody asked you?!"

"Everyone's been too busy, like you said," the auburn-haired girl shrugged. "It'll be fine. I can come with my parents."

Alauda hesitated only an instant. "Bugger that!" she exclaimed. "If none of the gutless shovel-swingers in this mob can manage to work up the spunk to ask you, then you can bloody well come with Alacer and me!"

The arms about her waist tightened momentarily. "Thank you," Tonlees murmured. "But I wouldn't want to...to get in the way. Like you said, you haven't had much time together lately."

"Don't be stupid," Alauda said bluffly. Having already made the most painful part of the decision, she decided not to indulge in half-measures. Toni was her friend, wasn't she? "It's supposed to be a rite of passage, after all; 'first loves bloom with the flowers of spring', or whatever it was Ceorlinus said. I'm sure you'll catch *someone's* eye."

"Are you feeling well?" Tonlees snickered. "Did I just hear you misquote a Ceorlinus lyric?"

"I can't remember them all," Alauda said crossly. "The man wrote over two hundred plays! Regardless, Second Spring is important for girls our age, so, you're coming with us. It's settled. We'll all dine and dance together."

"Dance?" Tonlees smiled. "With three?"

"It can be done, believe me," the younger girl said, recollecting the images imparted by Elspeth's jade medallion. Then she recalled again the images that came *after* the dancing...and her treacherous mind subconsciously replaced Elspeth's, Vidar's and Renvig's faces with those of Tonlees, Alacer – and herself.

She swallowed past a sudden knot in her throat. A shiver of – of what? *Revulsion*? *Anticipation*? – shot through her.

"Cold?" Tonlees asked.

Quite the opposite, Alauda thought, her jaw tightening; she felt warm, too warm. "No, I'm fine." She squinted; the Lantern was high, and she'd caught a glimpse of something in the distance; a glint of sorts, against an outcropping of stone. "Can you see that?" she asked, glad for a distraction.

Tonlees leaned to one side. "A sparkle? On the mountainside?"

Alauda kicked her heels into Perda's flanks, spurring the mare into a canter.

"What're you doing?!" Toni exclaimed.

"Telling Rettik," Alauda snapped. "It might be an ambush."

"Ambush?" The captain chuckled when Alauda mooted the possibility. "Good instinct, ladies. Always best to be cautious, and I'm glad to see that you're growing the right sort of eyes."

"Alauda saw it," Toni piped up.

Rettik rolled his eyes. "Of course she did. Well, sorry to disappoint you, but that's not an ambush. Not this time, anyway." He nodded in the direction of the glint that they had observed. "That's Arx Cervus."

"Arx what?" Alauda asked.

"Cervus." The one-eyed soldier pointed at the glint. "It's right there, perched right on the knees of the mountain."

Tonlees was beaming. " 'The hearthstone of fearsome Fineleor'!" she exclaimed.

Alauda turned to frown at her friend. "What in the World Made are you babbling about now?"

Tonlees straightened in the saddle, lifting her chin, and setting her gaze on the far-off hills. She tried to clasp her hands before her middle, but there wasn't enough space between her belly and Alauda's back, so she settled for raising them in a grand gesture, palms out like a skald addressing an elegy to someone's throne, and declaimed ringingly:

By the crystal fall, 'neath the mountain wall
On the path trod only by lonely deer
Arx Cervus stands to defend our lands:
The hearthstone of fearsome Fineleor!

The two horsemen riding alongside Rettik applauded enthusiastically. Tonlees bowed awkwardly from the saddle, beaming.

The pair desisted as the captain turned a gimlet eye on each. He snapped a command, and the two spurred their horses on.

"Ha!" Tonlees exclaimed. She spat a puff of air into Alauda's ear; the younger girl squirmed. "And *you* said I couldn't walk the boards!"

"I said 'shouldn't', not 'couldn't'," Alauda noted somewhat waspishly. "Any addled drunkard can stumble across a stage. Besides, that wasn't acting, it was singing – if you want to call it that."

Toni swatted the back of the younger girl's head.

"Fine," Alauda sighed, "I take it back; you *can* carry a tune. Even one that doesn't have handles nailed to it."

"Oh, thank you!" Tonlees swatted her again. "Pay heed, all! The hero of Vitrafoss, the huntress of the Sucky-Gaga – *she* says I can carry a tune! Such praise, *heya*, from one so lofty and so wise!"

"*Taceo!*" Alauda hissed, mortified. "You lunatic! I'm sorry, all right? You sang it well. You just surprised me. I've never heard that one."

"That's because it's a soldier's song," Tonlees grinned. "They don't teach us those in *schola*, love. I learned it from old Petruvio, the silversmith my mother used to visit in Corymbus. He was a High Guardsman once, and taught me a load of their marching songs, whenever he thought she couldn't hear him." She winked elaborately. "That's the only decent one, by the way. The others are all full of blood and wine and bosoms and such."

Rettik, who was riding near enough to overhear the pair, suppressed a snort.

"Bosoms, eh?" Alauda chuckled. "I don't doubt it. Is there more to it?"

"Gods, yes. Verses and verses."

"I want to learn it." Alauda had a passion for anything even remotely musical, doubly so when there was history involved. Fineleor Orkarel was of particular interest to her; after all, the ancient general had been betrothed to Anja Antaíssin, the heroine and progenitrix of her eponymous house, whose surname Alauda bore as part of her own.

The manner in which Anja and Fineleor had met their end was one of the Realm's most cherished legends. They had stood in the high mountain pass northwest of Arx Vespertinus, and together they had halted an invading army long enough for their own outnumbered troops to escape. Their courage had cost them their lives, of course; but that, to Alauda's mind at least, was what made their tale so compelling. That, and the fact that, though betrothed, they had never found the time to wed, and had never sullied their unspoken vows.

As a consequence, Anja and Fineleor were hailed throughout the Realm as symbols of pure, selfless sacrifice; unrealized passion; and stern, uncompromising obedience to morality and the law. Alauda couldn't comprehend such self-abnegation, but she could at least admire it – in others.

Tonlees sighed. "I knew you were going to say that. Look, I'll try to remember it all today, and we can practise tonight or tomorrow. Accord?"

"Accord. Of course," Alauda added, reaching behind to poke Tonlees in the ribs, "we could just ask Captain Rettik, here. I'm sure he knows a few soldiers' songs. Do you know that one, Captain? About 'fearsome Fineleor'?"

"Sorry, ladies," the soldier grunted. "I only know the name. I was in the Imperial Army of Ekhan, not the High Guard at Starmeadow. Humans have different tunes." He glanced back at them – then, improbably, winked with his sole eye. "They're still all about blood, wine and bosoms, though. I mean, soldiers are soldiers, pointy ears or no. *Nec*?"

Both girls burst into laughter.

♦

Two

"The old fort had been there for centuries by the time Fineleor took it over," Rettik explained. "It was his for centuries, and he's said to have put a lot of work into it. Even brought some dwarves in for some of the finer masonry. Look there, to the left of that tower; can you see the difference in the colour of the stone?"

The girls' jests had sparked his volubility; or perhaps he was simply bored. They were passing below the cliff-side castle; a spur from the Great Road wound up the hill, switching back and forth as it climbed. The old fortress – Alauda could see its age; it was weathered, dreary, and moss-covered, so that it looked like part of the mountain's granite flank – squatted on a hill-top next to a straight-sided, jagged peak from which a crystalline waterfall tumbled.

The cloud of spray reminded her forcefully of the waterfall at Vitrafoss. She shuddered with the memory; the coloured spray looked a lot prettier from the outside.

Her eyes followed the tumbling water up, and up...and up. There would be no surviving a tumble over *this* waterfall, Alauda thought with another shiver. It exploded from a cleft high up in the mountainside, tumbling hundreds of feet to splatter into a stony bed behind the castle proper. Bulked with spring melt-water, its runoff furnished the bulk of the headwaters of a river that ran away eastwards, following a line betwixt the foothills and the road.

Rettik pointed up at the cliff behind the ominous heap of grey-black stone. "There, too; you can see the transition between the two structures: the gatehouse where the bridge terminates, the great hall, and everything to the right of it are all newer. The old keep – the triangular bit there, with the round tower nearest the road – that part dates from Tior's day, a thousand years before Fineleor and Anja got their hauberks punctured by Gryshgranax and his lot."

"What about the walls below the old keep?" Alauda asked, shading her eyes with a hand. The Lantern was lowering at their backs, but the day was still very bright. "Or are they walls at all? They look like...I don't know. Terraces, or something."

"Lower outworks, I suppose," the captain shrugged. "Look there, past the one on the left, beyond the old keep – that's a chapel, I'll wager. It's new, too."

" 'New'?" Alauda exclaimed. "That's an odd way to put it. The 'Old Keep' was built five thousand years ago, and the rest only – only! – four thousand."

" 'Newer', then," the soldier shrugged. "The difference is the dwarfy stone-work. Their craft wears better; always has. That's their work, all the way back to the old gatehouse there. Can you see the bridge on the left, and the barbican beyond, high up on the mountainside?"

Both girls nodded.

"That's the mountain road from the song," Rettik explained. "'The path trod only by lonely deer'. It used to lead past the waterfall there, and up into the mountains. It was another one of the passes that led through the peaks of the *Armanix*, into the Realm."

" 'Was'?" Alauda asked.

"It's been closed for seven hundred years. Ever since the Shadow King cracked the world. The mountains shook and fell; stones filled the vales. No more pass meant no more road." He cocked his head. "And no more road meant no more threat of invasion. That's why nobody's bothered occupying this place. It was abandoned shortly after the sundering. Without the pass, and the traffic into and out of the elfy lands, there's nothing special hereabouts. Just another lonely outpost, an empty castle on the Great Road."

"But then Buckhill opened up," Tonlees interjected. "Right?"

"Yes, but only a wink ago by your lights," Rettik nodded. "Forty years, give or take. At first it was just stannum for pots and bronze and such; that was enough to merit a mining camp, with all of the glories, good and bad, that such places bring. Mostly bad." He hawked, leaned over, and spat. "I first saw it twenty years ago, and it was a rough enough place back then.

"Couple years back, though, some miners cutting a new drift came upon a vein of silver – and that, my ladies, really brought in the trade. Silver means money, and money means merchants, taverns, skalds, and...ah, entertainment." He gave them a broad wink. "And all of those things mean cut-purses, costers, confidence men, bandits – and worst of all, nobles. And as soon as there're nobles poncing about, the next plague to arrive is always soldiers. Formed troops, I mean."

Alauda's eyebrows climbed. "Are there troops at Buckhill? I haven't seen any on the road."

"None from your Realm; not yet, anyway. And the place isn't big enough to warrant an imperial garrison, though if it keeps puffing up like a boil it won't be too long before it does." He scowled. "Of course, that doesn't mean that the Empire doesn't care what happens here. It's thirty leagues back to Vitrafoss, and nearly eighty to Porta'. That's too far for succor once the swords, the spears and the torches are out. Also, there's the small matter of this orky bint, the one supposedly building an army in the east. Her reivers have been seen in the hills hereabouts, according to the foremen here."

"By 'orky bint'," Alauda said frostily, "I assume you mean Morgat

Karkea, the ork chieftess."

"Who else?" Rettik snorted. "And don't jump salty with me, little miss. It's said she has a special place in her heart for ladies of the Third House. If half of what I've heard about her is true, then you'd best hope you never cross her path. If that happens, you'd do well to take that knife out of your boot, and put it to your pretty throat."

Alauda's retort was on her lips when Toni slapped her shoulder. "Look!" she exclaimed, pointing at the castle. "I see smoke!"

"I was getting to that," Rettik said. "As I said, between the money pouring out of Buckhill and the troubles on the road and in the hills, it was inevitable that someone would take steps. As of last autumn, Arx Cervus has been open for business." He pointed at the lower part of the hillside, where the river tumbled down to meet the road. "If you look close, you can see the mill-wheel turning. It's at the bottom of the hill, just below the gatehouse."

Alauda looked. "I see it," she said. "I can also see smoke rising from the chimneys, I think." She squinted. "Not all of them, though."

"I imagine quite a few of them are blocked, or have fallen in," Rettik mused. "The place is old, after all; it predates the Darkness. It'll take a lot of work to put the place in order. But that smoke means that the new master's at home."

"And that is..." Alauda prompted.

"A warlord," the mercenary said, with clear approval. "From Ekhan. Not an army man; he's supposedly a noble who made a name for himself in the wars along their western border, where they've been fighting with Gasparr over control of the Niriam Vale. From what I hear, he was rising in the King's favour when he suddenly shat the bed by taking a Gasparri mage to wife. She's apparently one of the magisters from the College of the Eye, in Illostina. That got him exiled."

"It's 'magistatrix'," Alauda corrected automatically. "Unless this noble fellow prefers shaft over gully, of course."

Rettik's face darkened. "Sorry?"

"In *elvii*," Alauda said, "the feminine of magister is 'magistatrix'. No offence." Her brow furrowed. "Though if he did marry a 'magister' of the College of the Eye, that would certainly warrant exile, from Ekhan anyway. They're a little primitive about that sort of thing, I understand. Did you come across it – no pun intended – when you served with them?"

Rettik glowered at the younger girl for a moment longer. "You've a filthy mouth on you, young lady. I ought to have a talk with your father; perhaps he'd see fit to correct it with a hiding."

"You'd have more luck with my mother," Alauda said calmly. "She's the whip hand in House Volo. Captain, I'm sorry; I didn't mean to seem impolite. We appreciate your stories, truly; both of us."

Toni nodded her enthusiastic agreement. "You seem to know a lot about this warlord fellow," the older girl said brightly. "Tell us, please!"

Rettik glared at the girls for a moment longer. Then he turned his attention back to Toni. "Why not? Well, I've met him. He has a dozen or so guardsmen, retired army all, so as soon as they arrived – last autumn, in Ars-Waning – I paid him a call. His name's Alfaric, Alfaric Plowbrace, and his wife is Lady Nidlo. Magistatrix Nidlo," he added with a narrow glance at Alauda. "She's something to see; just as pale and black-haired and pretty as one of you lot, but tall, with a real woman's figure." He glanced pointedly at Alauda. "No offence."

Alauda glared. "None taken, I assure you."

Tonlees merely tinkled a laugh. "If she's that beautiful – and shapely," she suggested, "then it's no wonder that her husband chose her over his allegiance to the Empire."

"Rumour holds that she bewitched him," Rettik said darkly.

"Ah, rumour," Alauda sniffed. "Of course! I mean, you can see why she'd do that. What woman would want to stay in a filthy backwater like Illostina, Jewel of the Mountains, when she could marry an ape-faced pike-pusher, and live a life of grace and luxury in fabulous Buckhill, along with the pit-rats, whores, money-changers, and mercenaries?" She blew the one-eyed cavalryman a kiss. "No offence."

Rettik cocked an eyebrow. "Your mother ought to exercise her whip hand a little more frequently."

"She'd be the first agree with you, captain," Alauda said. "Why not mention it to her? Maybe she'll let you do the honours."

The one-eyed warrior coloured visibly.

"Captain," Tonlees said loudly, leaning past her simmering friend again, and resisting the urge to clamp a hand over her mouth, "when will we meet Lord Alfaric and his lady?"

"*Meet* them?" Rettik chortled. "Girly, you're not listening. This isn't a social call; every day we dally we risk another delay, and there're bad folk about – the kind that'd kill you and eat you, hopefully in that order. Or worse folk like Morgat. We're not going to the fortress at all, just the town, and we'll be laagering up outside, in an unplanted hayfield. Last thing we need is you young vixens playing tourist amid the whores and pit-rats.

"We'll be here just long enough to rest the draught animals, and get through your 'Second Spring' nonsense. Day after tomorrow, we're off and on the road again. I'm not taking any more chances with you lot. Not with your predilection for meddling in things that are none of your affair. And the small matter of an ork-horde somewhere hereabouts."

"Oh," Tonlees murmured, crestfallen.

Alauda scowled. "You're *that* worried about Morgat and her

thugs? You have a whole troop here!"

"Morgat's got twice a thousand warriors under her sway," Rettik replied. "At least. And more arriving all the time." He spat again. "Forget I said anything. We're not supposed to mention her to you kiddies. Your parents don't want us frightening you."

"Frighten us?" the younger girl bristled. "It's truth. You don't frighten with truth! Besides, I thought you were a free-sword. Who can give you orders, *heya*?"

He shot her a bemused glance. "The people who furnish the coin, girly, your sire and dam among'em." He wrinkled his nose. "Though I don't suppose it'd do much harm; you're not the sort to panic easily.

"Briefly put – Morgat's becoming a problem. She's been prowling the wastes with her band of cut-throats for a couple of years now. She was supposedly working for someone in Porta', but apparently they had a falling out. Last I heard, she'd oathed herself to the dragon."

Alauda's brows rose. Behind her, Tonlees stiffened. "Dragon?" the younger girl asked, suddenly breathless. "Which dragon, the one in Mons Lacrimosa? Shadow-of-Midnight?"

Rettik nodded. "Now Morgat's got an army instead of a single tribe, and the most powerful patron imaginable. She was already a pretty potent shaman, but with the dragon's backing she's become a lot more than that. It's said she can make the dead rise, and follow her. Her people worship her like a goddess." He made a face. "We ought to be safe, though."

"Why?"

"Since throwing in with the dragon, Morgat's left the Great Road pretty much alone," Rettik said. "Her quarrel's always been with the elves – your folk, I mean, the blackhairs – and Shadow-of-Midnight has always been threatening to destroy the Realm. Looks like their interests have aligned." He scowled at her. "Isn't this why the lot of you are moving away? So you won't be in their path when the invasion comes?"

Alauda had never put the two factors together. Now she cursed herself for missing the connection.

"Any road," Rettik went on, "there's not much point in either Morgat or her mistress coming north when their fight's southwards. They'll have plenty to worry about dealing with your army and the High Guard."

"That's stupid," Alauda said automatically. She was starting into the distance. She hadn't previously considered the threat posed by the dragon and the ork-chieftess working in concert, but now she couldn't think of anything else. "Where'd you learn strategy, *heya*?"

"Excuse me?" Rettik's eyes bulged. "Are you teaching me my trade, little girl?"

"Somebody has to," Alauda smiled. "You plan for an enemy's capabilities, not his intentions. What he *can* do, not what he might or might not do."

The captain snorted, shaking his head. "I'll be sure to mention that to the Governor of Portacaminus. I'll be taking wine and sweetmeats with him as soon as we arrive."

"No, you won't," Alauda sighed.

"No, I won't," Rettik agreed. "And neither will you."

Tonlees put her mouth to Alauda's ear. "Shut up," she whispered genially, "before he gets sick of you and stops talking to us." To Rettik, she said, "Will we at least get to visit Buckhill, captain?"

"In suitable company, I don't see why not," he shrugged. "But certainly not alone. It won't take very long; there's not much for ladies like yourself to see or do. It's got shops, markets, and of course no end of taverns, ale-pits, gambling dens, and that 'entertainment' I spoke of." He shot them both a one-eyed glance. "We'll be laagering the wagons in an open field, as I said, well below the plateau. I want your word that you'll not wander about the town itself without one of your parents in tow. Bad things happen to girls in unpatrolled mining towns."

"We're not children, captain," Alauda sniffed.

"No, you're not," he agreed. "That's exactly the problem, you annoying, impertinent little –" he ground his teeth "– lady. Annoying, impertinent little *lady*. To the sort of folk who ply their picks all day and their tankards all night, you're a tasty morsel who might not be offered a chance to say 'nay'. D'ye understand me?" He leaned over in his saddle. "Your word on it, now, the both of you. Stay out of Buckhill! I don't need a repeat of that *kak* at Vitrafoss, and neither do your parents!"

Tonlees raised a hand, her eyes wide. "*Promittimus!*" she squeaked.

"Fine," Alauda sighed, raising her hand as well. "Me too. Now, how much further is it?"

"Two leagues, give or take," Rettik replied. He was squinting at her. "This is not a place for games. You especially, mistress Volo," he grated, "will keep your fondness for meddling, and in particular your overly smart mouth, strictly under control. Accord?"

"Yes," Alauda sighed again.

Rettik stared at her, his one eye narrowed menacingly.

She raised her hand again. "Accord!"

"Better," he growled.

They rode on. Alauda, intrigued by the ancient castle, kept glancing at it over her shoulder. As they rounded the promontory, following the road, they passed the mill-house, whose pond was fed by the frothing cascade tumbling down from the fall beside the keep. Sure enough, the mill-wheel was spinning. From behind the wooden walls, a deep, hollow thumping arose. "What's that?"

"Trip-hammer," Tonlees said at once. "Haven't you ever seen one before?"

"Seen one, yes," Alauda replied. "I've never heard one. But that means someone's working there, no?"

"I suppose," the older girl shrugged. Her face changed. "I wonder if they've found the treasure?"

Alauda looked over her shoulder. "If you're waiting breathlessly for me to ask 'what treasure'," she said, "then you can keep waiting."

Tonlees' grin only widened. "According to legend," she said, affecting a deep and ominous tone, "Arx Cervus is home to a great treasure. Guarded, so they say, by an ancient sorrow."

"They say that, do they?" Alauda sighed. "How can 'sorrow' guard something?"

"It's an *ancient* sorrow!" Toni reminded her. She grabbed Alauda by the rib-cage and tickled until the younger girl shrieked. "They also say that it's guarded by the spectre of Anja Antaíssin herself, all glistening white and misty in the moons-light!"

"Wise Hara give me strength," the younger girl muttered, pinching the bridge of her nose. "Right. First of all, what's your evidence? Who's 'they'?"

"I don't know," Tonlees shrugged. "You know...*they*. Sages and skalds, and...well, they. They all say it."

Alauda rolled her eyes. "It's a good thing you're pretty."

Tonlees slapped the back of her friend's head again, harder. Alauda winced. "It's quite a skill," Toni cried, "to be able to insult me and compliment me at the same time!"

"Well, then, stop prattling on about great treasures and ancient sorrows!" Alauda exclaimed. "And...and misty spectres! According to 'they' – or 'them' – every abandoned pig-sty and shithouse in the world has a great treasure guarded by an ancient sorrow!" She spat angrily. "It's all a lot of *kak*!"

Rettik put a hand to his mouth and coughed to catch their attention.

"Yes, Captain?" Alauda exclaimed.

"Treasure's real."

"See?" Tonlees crowed.

Alauda glared at him. "Indeed, Sirrah? Then what is it, pray? Sapphires? Diamonds? A life-sized golden statue of Bræa herself?"

"Nah," he said at once. "Not gold; silver. And not statues, just coin. A lot of it, though; a king's ransom. A tribute, it's said, that Fineleor had no time to deliver, so he buried it here, at his castle, just before he went off to war."

"Buried treasure," Alauda muttered. "Guarded by an ancient sorrow. Hara's love! And I suppose there's a map?"

"Don't know," Rettik replied. "But I don't think so. Fineleor didn't tell anybody where his bounty was, and nobody's ever found it, though folk've presumably been all over the castle. It's been abandoned for centuries, after all. All anyone knows is the legend: that it's guarded by life and by death." He paused, then added, "And a whole load of hideous monsters, murderous traps, and magic spells. Naturally."

"Naturally," Alauda repeated, shaking her head.

"Ha!" Tonlees prodded the younger girl in the ribs again. "See? Treasure! Told you!"

"And traps." Alauda reminded her. Her fingers tightened until the reins creaked. "Murderous traps, remember? Besides, you said that it was guarded by an ancient sorrow, not by 'life and death'!"

"Monsters are alive, and traps are death," the older girl sniffed. "You're just not thinking like a skald."

"You're not thinking at all!" Alauda expostulated. "You know, Captain, you're being pretty inconsistent."

"How's that?"

"Well, in one breath you order me not to meddle," the girl said heatedly, "and in the next, you tell me tales about a legendary treasure!"

"Heavens, you're right!" Rettik grinned. "That must be terribly frustrating!"

"It might be," Alauda muttered under her breath, "if it wasn't all a lot of steaming, stinking *kak*."

Tonlees sniffed. "Well, aren't you the wet blanket! Where's your sense of wonder?"

"It's working just fine, thank you," Alauda growled. "For example, right now I'm wondering just when it was that all the wits leaked out of your head."

"Says the girl who went over a waterfall...on...purpose!" Tonlees replied, poking Alauda repeatedly in the ribs until the two of them were giggling like idiots again.

They continued along, both girls stealing glances over their shoulders until the ancient fortress fell out of sight around a bend. The river followed the Road, and continued burbling and chuckling alongside them.

"It'd be nice, though, wouldn't it?" Tonlees said, as afternoon slipped gently into twilit evening. "A wagon-load of coin?"

"I suppose," the younger girl shrugged. "What would you do with it?"

"Buy myself a newer dress for tomorrow night," Tonlees giggled. "Something daring, cut low in the bodice. From Starmeadow, maybe."

"A nice dream," Alauda sniffed. "For you, anyway; at least you've got something to show off. Besides, there's an awfully fine line between daring and slatternly, and there's not a couturier in the capital that didn't leap across that line with both feet a long time ago."

"You've never even been to the capital!"

"Mother has," Alauda pointed out. "And she told me how the ladies there dress, if you can call it that. She said they might as well be wearing nothing at all."

"Prude," the older girl giggled. "Tell me *you* wouldn't like something different to wear tomorrow!"

Alauda winced. Her mother, in her wisdom, had pronounced herself delighted that Alauda was going to the Second Spring festivities on the arm of her pretty, silver-haired paramour. To mark the occasion, she'd exhumed one of her own spring-tide gowns and had spent the last several days plying needle and thread in an attempt to fit it to her daughter's smaller stature and meagre endowments. Alauda didn't want to offend her mother or disparage her efforts, but Alyssa, for all her skill as a practitioner of the Art Magic, was a middling seamstress at best. The result of her labours as a couturier was mortifying: a heavy, rustling heap of faded rose-coloured satin trimmed with ancient lace, that required so many complex undergarments – chemise and bloomers, corset and stays, stockings and garters and the gods alone knew what else – that Alauda was afraid that she would spend half the day getting into the thing and half the night getting out of it again, with scarcely time for a single dance and a glass of wine in between.

Meanwhile, all that she could think of was Lady Kalanna's mordant sniff of disdain about wearing her mother's cast-offs. When she mentioned her dilemma to Tonlees, however, her friend was singularly unsympathetic. "I think you'll look grand," she said firmly. "Like a little porcelain doll."

"That's a charming image," Alauda grumped. "Alacer's going to be too afraid to touch me. It'll take him a stick or more to pry me out of it!"

"Oh," her friend replied, frowning. "Ah...thinking that far ahead, are you?"

"I've been thinking of nothing else," the younger girl exclaimed heatedly. "He's been so busy lately that we've hardly had time to exchange greetings, let alone touch. It's maddening. But tomorrow night will be perfect. I can't wait!"

"No, I can't wait either," Tonlees said after a moment. "Especially if we're all going together." She smiled wanly. "So long as you don't outshine us all."

"That should be simple enough," Alauda sighed. "The problem isn't me, Toni, it's you. You could wear a vegetable sack and look beautiful." She waved at her front. "It takes a lot of work to make this mess presentable."

"That's *kak*," Tonlees laughed. "But thank you nonetheless."

"In fact," Alauda went on, wrinkling her nose, "given the choice between the vegetable sack and the abomination mother's thrown together, I think I'd be better off wearing the sack. Alacer likes onions; the smell might help me draw him in."

"I won't tell her you said that," the older girl promised.

"Good," Alauda muttered. "Because I don't think they allow corpses to attend Second Spring."

♦

Three

Alauda, devout student of the poetry of Ceorlinus though she was, was hard pressed to come up with a suitably abject metaphor for the town of Buckhill.

The great skald had once referred to Starmeadow, whose principle urban feature, Greatisle, stood in the middle of the River Lymphus, as 'an emerald eye bound up by fears / and rins'd by a thousand, thousand tears'. No sentiment so grandiose could reasonably be applied to a nouveau-riche mining camp. Rather than lofty towers, Buckhill had shacks, and slag-heaps stood in the place of gardens. Instead of soaring, verdant forests, it had smouldering charcolliers' mounds; and where the Elven capital boasted the flashing eyes, pale cheeks, floral scents and scintillating jewellery of the lords and ladies of the twelve houses of the *Duodeci*, Buckhill's populace was a lumpen mob of grubby pit-rakes – sons of Esu and Lagu, men and dwarves alike, who emerged from their drifts and shafts bleary-eyed and blinking into the sunlight, their faces, hands and clothing homogenized by their craft into the same uniform shade of ochre.

"A bilious, fervid, fest'ring stye," she giggled under her breath, "staining the mountain's nether eye." It was hardly a phrase worthy of Ceorlinus, but it was just as accurate a depiction as his lofty paean to the Realm's royal seat. It would have to suffice, as there certainly were no other points of comparison. The River Whyle, which bathed the Buckhill's borders, was not the Lymphus – though ironically Alauda was familiar with the headwaters of both floods. The Lymphus, after all, had its source in the mountains outside of Astramicor; they'd followed one of its principal tributaries north past Aldeni, and up into Lete Pass in the heart of the Armanix, before descending the snowy range's northern face to meet the Great Road at Vitrafoss. And of course she'd already witnessed the birth of the Whyle in the pool at the foot of great waterfall behind the gloomy heap of Arx Cervus.

The Road had swung southerly, hugging the foothills, but now turned north, reaching wide out into the Waste once more, tracing the outline of the mountain's base. Here some ancient cataclysm, possibly the Sundering itself, had thrust a stony peak up out of the earth, and the mountain's knees lay directly across their path. Those knees, according to Captain Rettik, had given rise to the lode of silver ore that was Buckhill's new lifeblood. The Whyle snaked around the up-thrust stone, cutting a deep furrow that was traversed by a narrow wooden bridge. Across that bridge lay the jumbled squalor of Buckhill.

Even a mile and more away, Alauda could hear the place. The

babble of voices and the setting sun suggested that a shift-change was taking place. She could hear the ring of hammers, too, and the steady roar of bellows.

She could smell the town as well. The reek of the settlement was more potently obvious than its clamour. The evening breeze was out of the east, bringing with it the scent of forge-fire and charcoal, firestone and food, wood-smoke, brimstone, sewage, and the mingled reek of tired, aching bodies. *Definitely a shift-change*, she concluded, wrinkling her nose. Alauda found it difficult to imagine what the place would smell like close up, and her gullet warned her not to try and find out. At the same time, she wanted to look around the place, and hoped that her stomach was as strong as her curiosity.

Toni evidently felt the same. "Gods, please tell me we're not staying there!" she wailed, waving a hand before her face.

"I don't think so," Alauda replied. "There wouldn't be enough room for the wagons; the whole plateau's covered with buildings as it is." She pointed. "Look over there, just around the hook of the river. That field, there, with all the funny tents."

The older girl looked over. "Those tents have wheels. They're wagons, too. Is it another caravan?"

Alauda didn't answer; she was squinting. There was something odd about the distant wagons. They were pretty enough – gaudy, even, decorated with bright, painted motifs, some flowery, some formal. Their canvas covers were likewise embroidered and embellished with scenes and devices of every imaginable hue.

But they looked...peculiar. *Wrong.* Alauda stared, trying to figure out what was bothering her. "Damn," she murmured, "that's peculiar."

"What is?"

"The horses. What's the matter with their horses?!"

"What d'ye mean?"

"They're...short," Alauda mused. "And fat. And hairy. I don't –" She shook her head. "This is making my eyes hurt."

Just ahead of them, Rettik was chuckling softly under his breath. "Something funny, captain?" Alauda asked waspishly.

"You two are," the soldier laughed. "It's not your fault, girl. Distance is playing tricks on you, that's all." He nodded at the distant field. "That's a bother of halpies. *Halpinya.* Been here for months. Arrived just before Jule, in fact."

Halpies. Alauda sighed; that explained it. She wasn't going mad after all.

"Why so long?" Tonlees asked, frowning. "I thought they liked to move around."

"*Have* to move around, more like," Rettik grunted. "Not much point in sticking about after you've picked every pocket and fleeced every fool in the neighbourhood. But I'm guessing it's the mine. So long as it keeps churning out silver, why would they ever want to leave?"

Alauda felt like a fool. That was why their wagons looked odd, and their horses too: the scale was all wrong. In an instant, her eyes had picked out other objects that clarified what she was seeing: fence-posts, and a tower near the river; even the width of the Great Road itself, where it passed the hayfield. The Halflings were using ponies, not horses; and the figures that she could see bustling about the campfires might at best have come up to her chin, maybe her nose. And she was hardly a towering giant among elves.

One of Rettik's words sparked her curiosity. "What did you call them? A 'bother'?"

"Can you think of a better name for a mob of halpies?" the captain scowled.

"They're lovely!" Tonlees gushed. "Look! There's one with dragons! It almost looks alive!"

"I don't think Bardan ever made any orange and purple dragons," Alauda said, dubious. "He might be the epitome of all evil, but I'd like to think that the chieftain of the Powers of Darkness had taste."

All the same, she thought, it was hard to be too critical. From a distance, the Halflings' camp looked charming, like a field of wild flowers. Up close, it would be different; the profusion of colours would likely be painful, even disorienting. Nauseating.

"I think they're pretty," Toni muttered.

"Oh yes, they're pretty," Rettik grunted. "Take my advice, ladies, and give them a wide berth. Ride through that lot, and even at a gallop they'll have every last groat out of your purse, the rivets from your tack, the silver off your spurs and your smallclothes off your arse before you reach the other side. Do it at a trot, and your horse'll have to be re-shoed into the bargain."

"Do you speak from experience, captain?" Alauda asked, all innocence.

Rettik turned his single eye toward her. Without replying, he opened the satchel at his waist, extracted a jingling leather pouch, and made a show of stuffing it into his breastplate, beneath his gorget.

The two elf-girls giggled. Alauda's tittering trailed off first. Laughter was one thing, but coin was another. Rettik had a valid point. There was a great deal of money in Alauda's purse. Ilon, the lad she'd befriended back in Vitrafoss, had managed to sell Bale Laws' harness shortly before the caravan had left town the previous week, and had insisted that she take what he called 'the swell's share' – the one-third of all proceeds that any gang of pickpockets owed to its overlord.

"Or overlady," he'd amended with a wide grin. The stitched vellum bag in the pocket of her dress held five golden Ekhani crowns and twenty-five shillings. That in itself was a fortune the likes of which she'd never known – and her mother's chest held a further forty crowns, along with eleven odder coins: dwarven double-weights. These were square, thick, and heavy. Her mother had told her that they were cast from fine gold rather than stamped from coiner's alloy, and that each was worth as much as four or even five of the elf-realm's lighter *aureæ* – the orries she'd grown up ogling as they changed hands in the wealthier shops of Corymbus.

Alauda liked money, at least in the abstract, but she had never spent much time thinking about it. Now, though, as they rode towards the outskirts of the Halflings' camp, she realized that that was because she'd never really *had* any money before. Mimicking Rettik, she tugged her purse from her pocket, and stuffed it into the bodice of her gown – where, to her dismay, it made a more obvious bulge than what was already there. She was, she realized with a start, becoming a collector. Her corner of the wagon was already cluttered with the sword-spear she'd been given by her Raven Clan-mates, the skin of the lion that she and Jantun had slain (which her mother, unwilling to have the thing stinking up their conveyance, had treated with an alchemical mixture of ash, acorns, and *salpetrum*, until at least it no longer reeked of rotting flesh), and the ruined helmet that she'd kept from Bale Laws' brassy panoply. Elspeth's knife, Lord Trivinako's sword...at the rate she was accumulating plunder she was going to need a wagon of her own, and oxen to pull it. An even more alarming thought was that she could probably afford one now.

That thought led naturally to another: that having her own wagon would give her and Alacer at least a modicum of privacy. They'd managed to spend plenty of quiet time together in the mountains, but on the Great Road there were no trees, no silent springs or glades – and there were many, many more people. She hadn't lied to Tonlees; she and Alacer had hardly managed to find time for a kiss since leaving Vitrafoss, and even on that occasion he'd seemed rushed and nervous. They always seemed to be under someone's eye. Alauda had nearly gone so far as to commit the mortal social sin of calling upon the boy's parents – she'd snuck by their wagon in the dusk, hiding near the wheels, and listening for the sound of his voice.

It was pathetic, really; she was moping about like...well, like a love-sick girl. Alauda shivered violently, cursing under her breath. The very idea! It was repellent. *He ought to be pursuing me!*

"Cold?" Tonlees asked, solicitous. "I have my cloak."

"Hmm," Alauda replied, mentally cursing herself again, this time for being a quivering ninny. In truth, she *was* cold. The Lantern was right on the horizon, and the air sliding down the mountainside was noticeably chill.

She said nothing as the older girl tugged her woolen cloak about her shoulders – and, with her customary solicitude, draped its edges over Alauda as well. "Better?" Toni piped.

"Thank you."

"Can't have you taking a chill. Tomorrow's Second Spring, after all. We ladies have to be ready to prowl and to howl. You can't howl with a raw throat."

Howl indeed! Alauda scowled. It was utterly intolerable that she should be chasing after an empty-headed ox-pusher like Alacer Tiivus. After all, *she* was the one who'd walked out of a snowstorm alive – ridden out of it, actually, atop a giant wolf! *She* was the one who'd killed not one lion, but two; and *she* was the one who'd saved a town by unmasking a traitor, had survived going over a waterfall with nothing but an unconscious round-ear and a couple of inflated oilskins to keep her afloat, and had found Lady Kalanna's hostages when an imperial mage-lord had been stymied.

Hadn't Lord Trivinako made her a citizen of the Empire for it, and given her a sword with his own hands – hands that wielded power enough to slay men by the hundreds, and tear a city wall to rubble? *Bugger howling*, she decided, *and prowling too*. No more chasing after the clod. Alacer could bloody well come to her; all she had to do was wait for him to come to his senses.

Waiting couldn't be all that hard, could it?

♦

Four

Buckhill didn't smell any better close up than it did from a distance, but the complex miasma of odours was subtly different. The reek of burning charcoal was less obtrusive, for example. Presumably, Alauda mused as she passed through the rough gate of peeled logs, her father at her elbow, this was because the various chimneys caused the smoke from the smelters to waft up and away, over the hill.

If that was a blessing then it was a mixed one, because the absence of the choking stench of charcoal and brimstone simply left the olfactory spectrum wide open for other smells to come to the fore. Spoiled food, overflowing privies, unwashed bodies – all these Alauda knew of old.

There was one odour, however, that she did not recognize. When she tried to describe it to her father, he laughed. "What's so funny?" she demanded.

"You've never been to a silver mine before," he chuckled. "Not surprising; there aren't any near Corymbus. If you'd spent some time with the alchemists...well, let's just say, your mother would know what it was."

"Mother's not here," Alauda pointed out. "Why don't you just tell me?"

Kampat glanced around, then pointed at a long, low brick building. It had three clayed chimneys protruding from the slate roof. A thick grey smoke was pouring from the central chimney. "There," he said. "That, my dear, is what you're smelling. A *cupellatorium*."

"I thought it was just another smelter," Alauda objected.

"It is. But it's a special one, used to separate silver from impure ores, mostly galena. Lead."

"I know what galena is, father," she said crossly. "Why does it smell so...*gah!*" she gagged a little.

"It's the lining," he explained. "To separate the silver it has to be baked very hot, nearly hot enough to forge iron, over a bed of roasted limestone, or seashells – or, in this case, bone ash. Bone ash stinks, so it's only used if the other two aren't available." He glanced around at the mountains. "These peaks are granite, mostly, and we're a long way from the sea. But bones are always available anywhere there're animals. Or people."

Alauda mentally crossed 'silversmith' off of her list of prospective trades.

They'd departed the caravan together, leaving Alauda's mother in charge of seeing the wagon the last half-mile to the field that the company had leased. Perda had had no difficulty with the short climb up the hillside to the odoriferous little settlement. They'd left her hobbled outside the palisade; animals, other than draft animals belonging to the mining concerns, were not allowed within. Kampat had given one of the gate guards a brace of coppers to keep an eye on the mare.

They were, according to her father, looking for tanned ox hide to re-spring one of the wagon carriers. Kampat had checked them the previous week, and had announced that one of the straps was fraying, and that unless they fancied riding on the axles and feeling every stone and rut in their backsides, he would have to do something about it.

"Do you think we'll find wagon leather here?" Alauda had asked, surprised.

"Almost certainly," had been his answer. "Miners like a comfortable ride as much as anyone else."

It had been a guess, but a good one. Her father usually guessed right. She glanced up at him, curious – and a little impressed. "Bone ash, eh? How do you know all this?"

"It's my business to know it, dear," Kampat replied. "It's not enough to know money; it's important to know where it comes from. I've put coin into mining operations before, so I thought it would be wise to learn what I could about them. Actually, it was a dwarf who explained all of that to me – Airik Barg, a smith-crafter of Dwéorgámen. That's 'Pleasure-of-Dwarves', the foundry city in the Deeprealm."

"I remember him," she smiled. "Red hair, with braids and a forked beard. He came to the house in Corymbus. It must have been...what, thirty years ago, now?"

"About that," her father nodded. "You were just a nubbin at the time."

Alauda grinned. "He let me ride on his shoulders."

"All around the garden," Kampat nodded. "He could've carried your mother and me as well; the man's arms were bigger than my legs."

They passed the smelter with its belching smokestack. Alauda could hear the hissing and crackling of the furnaces that fed it. "Have you heard from him?"

"He's dead, dear."

Alauda stiffened slightly. "What happened?"

"An accident of some sort," Kampat said soberly. "A cave-in, I think. About ten years or so ago. I found out about it when a contract we'd been working on together was returned unsigned."

"Oh." She was surprised to feel sorrow for the loss of someone she'd only met once, and scarcely remembered. "I'm sorry."

"So am I. He was a good builder."

"Aren't all dwarves good builders?"

"Most of them," her father smiled. "But Airik was also a good man. They're not as common. Among any of the races."

Alauda reached out and took his hand. "You're a good man too, father."

Kampat glanced at her, surprised; she hadn't held his hand in public for years.

They were ambling rather than striding; the foot traffic sped past them on both sides. Folk were polite enough, if busy. The bulk of them seemed to be miners and their families, and there was more than the usual proportion of dwarves. Men – humans – were heavily represented as well, though more often, she noticed, in the garb of smiths, carpenters, farriers and the like, than in the heavy boots and smocks of miners. She even spotted the odd Halfling here and there, though none with a spade or pick over his shoulder. "Why're there so many dwarves?" she asked suddenly. "Is it because they're the better miners?"

"Naturally," her father replied. "Of course, it's as much a matter of inclination as it is of size and shape, and folk can take up any trade that will them to 'prentice; but mining is a business, and business is driven by profit. Humans make good miners, too, but they need more space to swing a pick. A dwarf can work comfortably in a shaft only three-quarters the size of one built to accommodate one of our round-eared cousins. That makes for a big savings in labour over the life of a mine."

"Hunh." Alauda pursed her lips. "I never thought of that. I thought it was because the Powers made the dwarves to be good diggers."

"That's what the priests'll tell you," Kampat agreed. "But it's just as valid to say that the dwarves are good diggers because of their size and shape, without bringing the Powers into it at all."

Alauda grinned to herself. "Why, father," she chided, "that's blasphemy!"

"Don't turn me in," he winked. "Who'd drive the wagon? Your mother doesn't have the patience, and the oxen won't listen to you."

"That's the truth. Seriously, though – don't you believe that Holy Bræa made us differently, so that we can serve different purposes?"

Kampat looked solemn. "Suppose She did," he said. "And suppose, as you suggest, the dwarves were made to be miners. Why were we made as we are?"

"For poetry and song, obviously," Alauda said primly. "Painting, sculpture, tile work, plays...we're artists first."

"Tior Magnus might take issue with that," her father said drily. "Dior, especially."

"Are you suggesting Tior wasn't an artist, father? Or Dior?"

"Not at all. Just that they obviously felt themselves better suited for other trades. Like the Art Magic, in Tior's case – and in Dior's, leadership and the law." As much as he enjoyed talking with his daughter, she had a habit of leading him into rhetorical quagmires. "Since we're discussing your plan for how you, Holy Alauda, would have ordered the universe, what were the humans made for?"

"For war, obviously," Alauda said at once. "They march faster than the dwarves, and they have longer arms. And they can stand daylight, and they...they..." She swallowed the last argument.

Kampat glanced at her, curious. "Go on."

Alauda flushed a little. "They breed faster."

"That they do," he nodded. "Actually – that leads me onto a related subject."

"Oh?"

"Yes, 'oh'." Kampat considered his words carefully. "Tomorrow night is Second Spring. You're going, I take it?"

Alauda grinned. "You know I am, father. Mother's been messing about with that old gown for most of the past week."

"Yes, I've seen her at it. She's pricked her fingers so many times that you're going to look like you've just come from an abattoir."

Alauda giggled aloud. "She's really terrible, isn't she? I wish she'd just let me alter it!"

"She wants to do this for you," Kampat said quietly. "And it's good for her. It helps take her mind off of what happened at Vitrafoss."

Alauda's good humour began to fade at that point. "Father," she sighed, "I've already apologized for –"

The look he directed at her cut her off. "I wasn't talking about what you did," he said quietly, "though that was certainly a part of it. No, I'm talking about Lord Trivinako, and what *he* did. And what your mother almost had to do."

Alauda shivered involuntarily, recalling the horrific butchery of the warcaster's fire at the town square. Hundreds of men had fallen in the space of three breaths. "It was awful," she said. "I'm still dreaming about it. But that was him, not her."

"Yes, but it *could* have been her," Kampat pointed out. "Your mother was trained to do precisely that sort of thing, Alauda. It could've been her at the castle, too – and it very nearly was. She told me that she came within a heartbeat of obliterating Kalanna Cælestis."

"It's a shame she didn't," Alauda snorted. "The world would be a sunnier place without that –" she caught herself "– that *noblewoman* cluttering it up."

"I don't disagree," her father said. "However, it would not be a sunnier place for you if you had to spend the rest of your life under threat of a blood feud with House Cælestis. And it would not be a sunnier place for your mother if she'd been forced to break a solemn vow, and slay someone with magic."

Alauda blinked. "Vow? What vow?"

Kampat looked pained. "You'll have to ask her that yourself. I'd wait a while, though. She's been a little shrill for the past week."

"Yes, I'd noticed."

"But back to my original point," Kampat said briskly. "Second Spring. I take it you'll be going on young Alacer's arm?"

Alauda nodded vigorously, her cheeks colouring.

"I like him," Kampat said. "He's a good lad. A hard worker. And he seems to treat you well." A pause. "I haven't seen him about much, lately."

"He's been busy, father," Alauda sighed. " 'Hard worker', remember?"

He nodded. "The Morbannens will be blooming soon," he said idly.

Alauda's head jerked up. She knew where he was going with this.

"You're going to be feeling things," he went on inexorably, as inevitably as the tide of doom. "Things you haven't felt before. Needs...desires...and sometimes a girl your age may – may feel the urge to, to –"

"STOP!" she cried, her face flaming. "For the love all the gods, father!"

He glared at her. "This is my duty, young lady. You need to be prepared for –"

"*Aiyah!*" she squealed. "D'ye think mother hasn't already given me this speech? And in enough blasted detail that I just wanted to crawl into a hole and *die*?"

Kampat blinked. "She did? When?"

"At least once a week since we left Corymbus!" Alauda cried. Three of the lectures had occurred since her mother had caught her and Alacer at the standing stones. "And twice last year. And once the year before that!" She was on the verge of tearing her hair. "If I have to hear about 'a maiden's favours', and 'no true gentleman would demand' and 'the purity of the body' one more time, I swear I will run myself through with my own sword!"

"Alauda –"

"*Both* swords!" she squealed. "At the same time!"

Kampat's mouth tightened. "I want to be certain you'll be all right," he said. "Young Alacer – he seems like a good lad, but then so did I at his age, and...well, I was anything but. I want to make certain he respects you, and your wishes, too."

"He *is* a good lad," Alauda said stiffly. "Or – a good man. But has it occurred to you that I might not be a 'good girl'?"

"It's certainly occurred to your mother," Kampat growled. "I prefer to think of you as my little Lark, who laughed so hard while Master

Barg was jouncing you about on his shoulders that you vomited out your nose."

Alauda smiled. "Gods, that stung! Father, that *is* me, still. But I'm other things, too. And one of those things is...well, I'm in love with Alacer Tiivus."

It sounded a lot more momentous once it was out in the open and she couldn't call it back. Her father simply grimaced. "Yes, I figured as much. Look, dear, all I meant to say was...Second Spring can be an occasion for joy, and fun, and a little folly. A little folly never hurt anyone. But it can also be a time when irrevocable things happen. Try to avoid doing anything you'll later regret, *heya*?"

Alauda heaved a sigh. "Father, I'll tell you exactly what I told mother: I'm going to go to the party, dance, have a glass of wine or two, and probably eat too many pastries. If there's a decent troupe of skalds, I might even sing a song. I am *not* going to spread my legs for Alacer. No matter how much I might want to."

"Bardan's ball-sack!" the merchant exclaimed, wincing. "Are you trying to stop my heart? There's a reason we use euphemisms, girl!"

"I just thought it was better to speak to the subject at hand, instead of dancing around it," Alauda shrugged. "That's the vow that you wanted to hear, isn't it?"

"Yes!" he roared. "But not in so many words!"

Alauda dimpled. "I know it's difficult, father, but you're going to have to start thinking of me as a woman, because I am one, in every sense that matters. And thanks to bloody Dior Law-Giver, you're going to have to put up with it for another sixty years before you can legally chase me out of your door." She patted his shoulder in commiseration. "Sorry."

"Oh, I do thank him," Kampat growled. "Nightly."

They found the spring-leather at a shop near the plateau's westernmost edge, where, according to the stink of boiled acorns and urine, the effluent from the tanning vats seemed to be dumped over the cliff. Alauda made a mental note to avoid the Whyle downstream of the town. The shop itself was clean and organized, and there were many small and interesting items for sale, but the smell was so overwhelming that Alauda couldn't bear lingering to look at them.

Her eyes were stinging by the time her father finished haggling with the tanner. They left at a trot, Kampat bearing a half-dozen pace-long strips of heavy leather over one shoulder. "Let that be a lesson to you," he growled. "There's nowhere worse to shop for incidental goods than at a settlement with a silver mine."

"Were they expensive?" Alauda asked. She hadn't seen any money change hands; she'd been too busy mopping at her streaming eyes with a kerchief from her sleeve.

"I managed to beat him down," her father replied, "from ridiculous to merely extortionate." He paused – then stopped. "Well, isn't that a stroke of fortune."

Alauda glanced at him, puzzled. He pointed, and Alauda looked. Coming out of a small shop not far ahead was none other than Alacer Tiivus.

Alauda was on the cusp of suggesting that they turn around when the silver-haired boy spotted them. To Alauda's surprise, he appeared to start guiltily, as if he'd been caught with his hand in someone's strongbox. He clasped his hands briefly behind his back – and then, incongruously, waved.

Alauda, keen-eyed student of behaviour that she was, didn't need to be slapped in the face to know when something odd was going on. It helped, of course, that Alacer didn't have so much as a grain of deceit within his soul.

With her father trailing in her wake, she strode across the street, dodging a cart-load of ore and a steaming cow-pat with equal dexterity. Alacer beamed. "My lady." He bowed, one hand still behind his back. "Sieur Volo."

"Young Alacer," the elder Volo said. He extended a hand. "Good evening. What brings you to town?"

The boy changed hands, fumbling something behind his back, before taking the proffered fist and clenching it firmly. Alauda rubbed her forehead. Alacer was absolutely the *worst* conspirator she'd ever seen. She was going to have to work on that.

The lad grinned, too obviously uncomfortable. "Just visiting the shops. Yourselves, sir?"

"Spring-leather," Kampat replied, touching the bundle on his shoulder. "Did you find anything worth your coin?"

"No," the boy replied. "Nothing at all. Just...you know, looking about."

Alauda rolled her eyes.

Kampat glanced at his daughter. "Well, I'm certain Alauda will be safe enough in your company." He dropped her a wink. "I'll see you back at the wagon, dear." Then he turned on his heel, and made good his escape.

Alacer looked both delighted and alarmed at the prospect of being left alone with his light o'love. "Well," he said. "Ah, hello."

"Hello." Alauda gave him a level glance. "Auditioning for the Imperial inquisitors, are we? Perhaps the Lictors of the Dark Queen?"

The boy frowned. "What?"

Thick as a pilaster. "What's behind your back, Alacer?"

His face reddened. "Oh, you...you saw that, did you?"

"You look like you're trying to hide a live weasel," she said with some asperity, beckoning with a finger. "Show me."

"Well, it's not the setting I'd hoped for," he said, "but...all right."

From behind his back he produced a small parcel about the size of Alauda's fist. It was wrapped in an old, overwritten rag of parchment. Alacer handed it to her without ceremony.

Alauda took the thing. It was surprisingly heavy. She unwrapped it...and very nearly dropped it.

It was a rose; a rose of blown glass the size of her palm. Blood-red petals, emerald leaves, the whole encased in a clear crystalline carapace...sudden tears appeared in the corners of her eyes. "Is this for me?" she gulped.

Alacer nodded. "I wanted to give it to you tomorrow night. Is it...do you like it?"

She was nodding furiously. "It's b-beautiful!" Clutching the glass confection tightly in one fist, she threw her arms about his neck and kissed him ferociously.

Alacer put his arms about her – and instantly, everything was all right. All of her megrims, her fears and worries, seemed to vanish in that one instant. They stood like that, their lips locked together, until a passing passel of dwarven miners congratulated Alacer loudly, one of them patting him on the shoulder with a dirty, gloved hand.

Alacer, flushed, was the first to pull his head back. "You really like it?" he repeated.

Alauda nodded. She looked at the thing again – and noticed that there were tiny droplets on the leaves. She had no idea how that had been done. "Alacer, this must have cost a fortune!" she murmured. "How did you ever afford it? I know you spent those crowns I gave you having a new wheel made for your wagon!"

He looked suddenly uneasy. "You, uh...you're not supposed to ask about the price of a gift."

Alauda glanced down at the rose in her palm. Then she did one of the hardest things she'd ever done: she held it out to him. "The truth," she said calmly. "Or you can have this back."

Trapped, the boy bit his lip. "It...ah, it was Toni's idea."

The elf-girl blinked, taken flat aback. "What? What d'ye mean, Toni's idea?"

"Just that," Alacer explained. "She said I hadn't been paying enough attention to you, and she told me how much you were looking forward to Second Spring." He looked uneasy. "I...I know we planned to go together, but I thought you'd forgotten."

"Quite the contrary," Alauda said, eyeing him strangely. "I've been thinking about nothing else ever since we left Vitrafoss."

"That's what Toni said," he replied. "So – we're going together, then?"

Alauda nodded slowly. "Alacer?"

"Yes?"

She held up the crystal flower. "You still haven't told me where you got the coin for this."

His jaw tightened. "Toni paid for it."

She blinked. "And where did Toni get that kind of money? She didn't..."

He was nodding again. "She gave me the two crowns you'd given her at Vitrafoss." He winced visibly. "And her beaded bag, the one her mother made for her. The rose was really expensive."

"Hara's arse!" Alauda exploded. "What's wrong with you two? I don't need trinkets like this!" She waved the glassy bauble under his nose.

"Toni said we should do it."

"Then you're both insane," Alauda snorted. "Well...thank you, I guess. But I'm giving Toni back those two crowns."

"You can't pay for a gift!"

"Watch me," she growled.

He offered her his arm, and they retraced their steps through the town together, making for the main gate. "Your father left awfully quickly," Alacer said after a moment.

"Yes," Alauda chuckled. "And with good reason. He'd just finished giving me the talk. He very nearly discorporated."

"Excuse me?" the boy asked, puzzled.

"*The* talk," she grinned. "You know – the one about Second Spring, and the Morbannen blossoms, and virtuous chastity, and the importance of girls keeping their knees together so they can be wed with honour the moment they pass without the walls. You know." She dropped a broad wink. "*That* talk. It was mostly about you, of course."

"Ah." He nodded, blushing. "Er...yes. Well, he has nothing to worry about on that score. We spoke about this, Alauda. I'm happy to wait for you."

"For sixty years?" she teased.

"For as long as it takes," he replied. He gave her hand a gentle squeeze.

It was meant to be reassuring, but Alauda wasn't reassured; not in the least. Something wasn't right. She stopped dead in the middle of the street. "What's happened to you?"

Alacer jerked to a halt. "What do you mean?"

"I mean, something's changed," she said. "Three weeks ago you couldn't wait to get at my glories. You were even making plans about our wedding, taking our majority through blooding, and going into business for ourselves in Porta', and the Realm and the Codex be damned.

"Since I got back from the mountains and the clan, though...nothing." She scowled. "*Nothing!* So I'll ask again: what's happened to you?"

"Nothing's happened, Alauda," the boy insisted. "It wasn't hard; you made your decision very clear, and I decided I could live with it. That's all."

Alauda was silent for a long moment. Eventually they started walking again. After some time had passed, she said, "That's a very responsible way to look at it."

"If you say so," Alacer shrugged. "From where I'm standing, though, it's the only way to look at it."

She took a deep breath, trying to decide whether to say what had to be said. At last she gave up, and just said it. "I love you," she murmured. "And I want you. You can't even begin to imagine how badly I...I...but even though it's Second Spring, Alacer, we *can't.*"

"I know."

He sounded so damnably complacent that she turned to stare at him again. "Really?" she demanded. "That's all you have to say? I tell you that I can't take you to my bed, like we both want, and all you have to say is 'I know'?"

"What else *can* I say?" Alacer said, a sad smile twisting his lips.

"Well," she began hotly, "you *could* say – wait, did you see –"

"Eh?" Alacer glanced at her sidelong. "Why would I say that?"

What Alauda had seen was a pickpocket in action. A matronly woman – a human – had been ambling along before them, her crumena in its usual station at the back of the broad belt that cinched her gown at her ample waist. Alauda had seen a Halfling lad – a boy no more than three feet tall, with black hair and dark eyes – pass behind her at a quick walk. His hand had been almost faster than her eye could follow – but her eyes were quick. She had seen that hand, definitely seen it, entering the woman's pouch.

What she saw next made her smile. The lad passed another Halfling child a little older, surreptitiously passing something to the new boy. That boy in turn – Alauda quickened her pace so as to keep an eye on him, dragging Alacer after her – passed the pogue to a girl, one who looked far too young to be out without her mother. That discrepancy resolved itself an instant later when the girl delivered the stolen purse to a matronly looking Halfling woman who was standing nearby.

Alauda nodded to herself, appreciative of the speed and skill with which the purloined goods had changed hands. Her self-satisfaction faded a little when the Halfling woman who had received the purse glanced at her, caught Alauda's eye...and smiled.

Alauda's eyes narrowed. She put a hand on the pommel of Elspeth's knife – she carried it everywhere now, at the back of her cincture next to her crumena (which held only her sewing kit; her purse was tucked firmly into her bodice) – and glowered at the queen of the thieves, but the woman merely laughed gaily. She had the temerity to wave; and then she gathered up an impressive brood of bare-footed, curly-haired brats, and began herding them toward the town's gate.

Alauda turned to Alacer, fuming. "You didn't see any of that." It wasn't a question.

The boy shook his head. "What happened?"

Alauda explained what she had witnessed – and was irritated when Alacer's only response was a shrug. "She probably had to feed her children."

"Maybe the woman she stole from had children to feed, too!" Alauda exclaimed.

"Maybe." He put a hand on her shoulder. "You can't right all the wrongs in the world at once, you know. You tried that last week." He kissed the top of her head. "Maybe you should take this week off."

"I'm not sure I can afford to," Alauda said darkly. She patted her crumena, then her pockets. "Bloody Halflings!"

"What is it now?"

She glared up at him. "Somebody took my rose."

Alacer's eyes nearly popped from his skull. "But it was *in your hand*!"

Alauda held out her hands. They were empty. That was when it dawned on her what had happened. "That," she said thoughtfully, "was bloody brilliant."

"Sorry?"

"That whole set-to," the girl explained. An appreciative smile spread across her face. "The pocket-picking was a show. That's all it was, a show. They must have been watching the shop you came out of, waiting to see where the rose went."

Alacer looked baffled. "What are you talking about?"

"Those halpies that rifled that woman's crumena," she said, thinking aloud, "they were all part of a team. They set up and executed a five-man shufty right under my nose. They did it just well enough to ensure that I would be watching them, while another of their number – or more likely, a whole team of them – took your rose right out of my hand." She shook her head, awed. "They're good. They're *very* good."

"The thieving little –"

"Calm yourself," she said. "I'd rather take it as a compliment – sort of. It's almost as if they knew I was good enough to spot their diversion, but not good enough to notice the main event. Odd they could set their tumble so precisely."

"They're obviously professionals," Alacer said, grinding his teeth. "And there's a whole encampment of them right next to our wagon lines. That's excellent. They'll steal the grass right out from under our horses' hooves. They...Alauda?"

Alauda wasn't listening; she was frantically enumerating her possessions once more. Her crumena and sewing kit were untouched, and her purse was still in her bodice. To her vast relief, Elspeth's dagger was still at her belt – though what might have happened to it if she hadn't had her hand on the pommel a moment ago did not bear thinking about.

She tugged the sheathed weapon from her cincture, bent, hiked up the hem of her gown, and jammed the knife back into the top of her boot. It was uncomfortable while she was walking, but hopefully more secure.

Alacer's thoughts were following more or less the same path. "D'ye suppose it'll be safer there?"

"I'd like to think I'd notice if there were a halpie fumbling about beneath my skirts," she said with a narrow smile. "Besides, isn't that *your* job?"

"One of my jobs, maybe," he said darkly. "The other is wandering around that wagon laager with a pick handle, looking for your rose."

"Take Tanju's club with you when you go," Alauda said with a wink. "It'll be more convincing."

"Are you sure that's wise? They might steal it right out of my hand!"

"Doubtful. It's too big for one of them to carry."

He looked pained. "Alauda, you know what I paid for that rose! This isn't funny!"

"No, it's not," Alauda laughed – but it was a bitter laugh. "Except – it is. If I had a hat on, I'd take it off to them. They're very, *very* good."

She said it with forced admiration because it was the only way to hide her rage. *Bloody* Halflings!

♦

Five

Alauda spent most of the evening fuming. She was short with Alacer as he walked her back to her parents' wagon, although she did unbend long enough for a perfunctory kiss before he went on his way. She was snippy with her mother when Alyssa sent her out to the market stalls that occupied the stretch of dirt between the unsown wheat fields to look for bread and vegetables. She was uncommunicative to the various merchants with whom she spoke; and she spent the whole of her abbreviated shopping excursion with one hand on her purse, the other on the hilt of Elspeth's dagger, and a gimlet eye fastened on every Halfling that came within a spear's length of her.

She wasn't sulking; she was analyzing her failure. The halpies had set a snare that had been designed especially for her, and she had walked right into it. She needed to understand why she'd failed to spot the trap in time to avoid it. That took some serious consideration. Alauda knew that she was not a master thief; hells, she wasn't even a novice. She had some native skill at stealth and sleight-of-hand, but most of that was a consequence of her birth, her diminutive stature, and a surfeit of gumption. It certainly didn't come from any special training or experience.

No, where her skills truly lay was in deception and chicanery. She had a facility for falsehood that her friends (and her weary parents) had remarked more than once, and an eye for a swindle that derived from spending decades struggling to outwit her mother. Too, she'd read voraciously since first picking up a book, and had focussed heavily both on histories and on tales of fantasy – cunning roadside robbers fleecing the wealthy, for example, or crooked chamberlains concocting plots to undermine or displace a sovereign. Those were her forte. She could, with a lot of time and the proper tools, work her way around the lock on a door or a coin-chest; but a professional burglar she was not, and she knew it.

That, however, was not how the Halflings had hooked her. They'd caught her just as they might have caught a fish: by dangling the perfect bait in front of her nose, and waiting for her to take it. In her case, the perfect bait had been another petty theft – and a complicated one, too, with the pogue – the purloined goods – being naffled by the pick-pocket, and then handed off through a series of cut-outs until at length it was delivered to the thieves' mistress. Alauda had focussed so much of her attention on trying to follow the twists and turns of the scheme that the thieves had been able to sneak up on her and pluck their true objective right out of her fist.

The bait, she decided, had been the key – and the bait was the scheme they'd laid out for her to solve. Had it been a simple pickpocketing, it would not have engaged her interest; the only reason she'd spent so much attention on them was because of the complexity of the affair. This meant that they were more than mere pickpockets. In order to design a snare for a specific person or type of person, one had to know a great deal *about* that person. In Alauda's case, they would have to have known that Alauda was a lover of conspiracy and skullduggery, but not a master of them.

But how had the Halflings known *that*? It was a puzzler. Somehow, they had managed to learn enough about her to be able to design their scheme specifically to entice her into falling for their deception – or, she thought with a shrug, someone so like her that there was no conceivable difference. She'd observed a similar event in Vitrafoss, of course – an actual theft that had led her to Ilon and his crew of ne'er-do-wells, whom she'd quickly co-opted. But unless the lad had ridden a fast horse and passed them on the road – and he hadn't; whatever else he might be, Ilon was no horseman – there was no one in Buckhill apart from Alauda herself who knew anything at all about that incident. There was simply no way for *anyone* to know about her lust for unscrewing the inscrutable.

Compounding her irritation, of course, was the fact that the wretches had made off with the crystal rose that Alacer, apparently at Toni's urging, had bought for her as a sort of apology-*cum*-reconciliation offering. Beyond its symbolic value, it had been a beautiful example of the glass-blower's art, and Alauda was determined to recover it – and, just possibly, to break the fingers of the miscreant who'd managed to pry it out of her fist without alerting her to his presence. Hara *Sophus*, through his priests, counselled the high elves to attempt to understand evil-doers and to use gentle persuasion to woo them from their ill ways; but in Alauda's experience, gentle persuasion worked best when it was backed up by a hawthorn switch, a horse-whip, or a noose.

She was still pondering the afternoon's annoying events as dinner ended; her mother had to speak sharply to her to snap her out of her reverie and begin the washing up. *It was all about bait*, she thought as she heated water to rinse the dishes. One studied one's mark, learned his strengths and weaknesses, internalized his abilities and frailties – and then, based on these observations, one crafted the perfect lure. It wasn't all that difficult, really; if the lure was good enough, the mark would convince himself that he wanted to be a part of the plot, and would in time come to overlook observations and warnings that conflicted with his perception of the situation. She'd seen that herself, many times, particularly with Tonlees. Her friend was practically the saint of not changing her attitudes to conform to changes in facts.

She would have to keep a close eye on Toni, in fact – and for that matter, on Alacer as well. Neither of her friends was especially sophisticated or worldly, and Alauda was mortally terrified that, with the right enticement, either of them could be drawn into some sort of nonsense that would doom them all.

She spent the period after dinner sitting with her parents in the wagon. The sides had been rolled up, the better to take advantage of the cool but pleasant evening breeze. Alauda was poring over her mother's book, looking for mundane means of detecting falsehood and lies. It seemed like an important skill.

"This is interesting," Kampat said. "What do you think? I got it from the factor, when I paid for our pasturage."

He was tossing a coin idly, and catching it betwixt thumb and forefinger in mid-spin. Alauda had always laughed at that trick, and did so again. Her father's fingers had always been so much more nimble than her own. "Comes from picking pockets," he'd told her once, with an outrageous wink. "A vital skill for any merchant!"

Alauda stifled a snort; it came out as *snrk*. She'd decided not to mention the real pickpockets she'd seen at work in Buckhill – mostly because they'd gotten the better of her. After all, she hadn't seen the best pickpockets; she'd only seen the second-best. And as much as she appreciated the sophistication and sheer artistry of the thieves who'd purloined Alacer's gift, she didn't like being duped. The problem was figuring out what to do about it.

"What is it, dear?" Alyssa asked. She was sitting at her desk, an oil lamp at her elbow, poring over a short, thick volume, and tracing the tiny lines of writing with the tip of a dry quill.

Alauda recognized the tome. Lord Trivinako had given the book to her mother shortly before their departure, and the wizard had hardly closed it since. She was only a quarter of the way through the dense, spidery text. Alauda had asked her what it was about, and her mother's response had been a spate of gibberish that made no sense whatsoever. When Alauda had complained about the excessively technical language, Alyssa had sighed. "It's about how to make your fire hotter."

The girl blinked. "What, our cook-fire?"

"Magical fire, dear."

"Why didn't you just say so?"

"Because," her mother had replied absently, without looking up from the pages, "that's a gross oversimplification. And coo-coo would've hated anyone oversimplifying his explanations."

Alauda snorted a laugh. " 'Coo-coo'? The wizard's name was 'Coo-coo'?!"

"His name," Alyssa said, her voice dripping with frost, "was Kuukyytipoikas. In wyrm-speech, it means Moon-Chaser. He was a brilliant theorist who thought it might be possible to visit Lodan and Chuadan. This was his masterwork."

"Well, why would he mind oversimplification?" Alauda said airily. "Don't dragons live forever? A dragon could afford to spend a year explaining something, couldn't he?" Her mother's words sank in at that moment, and her eyes widened. "Wait, what makes you think a dragon *wrote* it?"

"Because it's written in draconic, by someone using a *sulkakynsi*," Alyssa replied. "That's a talon-quill – an ink-pen on a wide band, designed to be worn over a dragon's claw." She turned a page, thoroughly engrossed. "Also," she'd added, almost as an afterthought, "because the parchment is made from the skins of fire giants. A dragon couldn't very well use ordinary linen paper."

"Well, of course not," Alauda sighed ostentatiously. "What with the breathing fire and all. Why would he want to go to the moons?"

"Why wouldn't he?" Alyssa muttered, her attention entirely on the words before her. "Why wouldn't anyone, for that... matter..."

Her voice trailed off. Alauda gave up. Long experience had taught her that her mother – who ordinarily was able to find time to closely control every mortal aspect of her daughter's existence – could, if given some morsel of arcane lore to peruse, become so immersed and uncommunicative that she might as well have already travelled to one of the moons.

Sighing, she turned to her father. "What's so interesting about the coin?"

He spun it to her. "You tell me."

Alauda plucked the silver disk out of the air. "It's new," she said at once. The silver was bright, and the edges were crisp – and, she noted, deeply fluted. "What's this?"

"The ridges?" Kampat grinned. "That's to keep unscrupulous folk from shaving them. That's good silver, there, and dodgy folk – disreputable merchants, shady money-changers, even the odd king from time to time – have been known to shave the edges of coins. Do it to forty or so, and you've enough silver to make a new coin." He rubbed the pad of his finger across the flutes. "It's called 'clipping'. The ridges make any damage too obvious to conceal."

"Clever," Alauda murmured. "A little elaborate, though, isn't it?"

"Coining is serious business, love," her father pointed out. "If a country's – or a king's – coin can't be trusted, folk won't accept it, and trade crumbles. Counterfeiters get a rough ride, therefore."

"Rough?"

"They're whipped in Starmeadow, and then thrown into the river from the palace gate, bound hand and foot, with their heads tied in a sack of their false product," Kampat said, utterly serious. "The Empire is a little more lenient; anyone who debases their coinage is beheaded, often on the spot." He pointed at the coin. "Which, in a roundabout way, is why this is so interesting. Look at the face."

Alauda looked. The coin's face was a deeply embossed image of a stag with spreading antlers. The obverse was equally simple; it bore a baronial coronet, and the devise 'Alfaric of Eregard, Imp.Gr.Dom.AxCv.'. There was also a year: '737 Æ.Sp.'.

"Any thoughts?" Kampat grinned.

"It's not just new; it's brand new. And the name is obvious enough," she murmured, turning the coin over in her fingers. Eregard, she knew, was the first city over the Ekhani border from Duncala. It lay just across the Bay of Iron from the old tree-town of Ætillio – the place she'd sung of to the unfortunate Bale Laws. "Whoever this Alfaric is, he's from the Empire. Which would make the rest *Imperium Gratia Dominus*...something." She frowned. "Would that be 'Arx Cervus'?"

"That's my guess," her father nodded.

"And it was minted this year," she continued. "Seven hundred and thirty-seven, *Ætas Sperum* – the Age of New Hope." She rubbed the coin between her thumb and forefinger; the etching was very crisp. "It's fresh from the dies. Nobody's even had this in his purse! Not for any length of time. Right?"

"Dead right," Kampat chuckled. "You can see that near the stag's head. The background is flat; there're no scratches. Like it was minted yesterday. Well, I suppose it might have been, *heya*?"

Alauda was still staring at the coin. "Mm-hmm."

"Don't grunt, dear," Alyssa said without looking up from her tome. "It isn't becoming."

"Yes, mother." Alauda couldn't stop wondering. She'd never learned anything of the coiner's art – and now she wanted to. The smooth silver felt delightful against her skin. "Why's it in *elvii*?" she asked suddenly.

"That's one of the things that's interesting about it," her father replied. "If these coins were going west to the Empire, or east to Skywaters or Zare, they'd be marked in the travelling tongue, wouldn't they? Hells, you could even make them with inscriptions in *dwéorgaspræc*, and send them north to the stubbies – though no coiner in his right mind would want to compete with their doubleweights." He pulled a second silver coin from his pocket. "But these are all in *our* language. This silver is obviously going back over the mountains – to the Realm."

"Why?" Alauda frowned.

"That's the question, isn't it?" Kampat said. "I imagine the King would like to know the answer."

Alauda's mother looked up, alarmed. "Kam –"

"Right." He pointed a finger at the girl. "That was an observation, young lady, not an invitation to more mayhem. This is a rough place, and there's not much here in the way of law. You *will* stay out of trouble this time, d'ye hear?"

"Of course, father," Alauda sighed, rolling her eyes. She held up the coin. "Can I go show this to Tonlees?"

Kampat glanced at his lifemate; his mouth opened to ask a question, and then closed it again. Alyssa was staring at the book once more, lost and ignoring them. The wizard's eyes were bright, her lips parted slightly. Her colour was high. "Wish she looked at me like that," he grunted. "Maybe I can find some way to distract her."

"Father!" Alauda hissed, mortified. She knew what he was getting at; she could smell the Morbannens herself.

Kampat slapped her knee. "Off you go, love, and enjoy yourself. There're plenty of torches out. Keep one hand on your purse, and don't put a foot on the bridge to Buckhill. Be back in a stick or so."

He glanced once more at his wife. "In fact," he whispered, with another wink, "don't be back for at *least* a stick."

"Oh, gods!" Alauda muttered. She snatched up Trivinako's sword and fled.

♦

Six

She found Tonlees at her friend's wagon. Toni's parents were considerably less protective than her own, and rather than admonitions about bridges and purses, her friend's mother, *Dos* Shavinta, merely asked her daughter to keep a weather eye out for blue thread. "Azure-sky, not aqua-sea," she specified. She gave Tonlees a pair of silver argies, adding, "One for my thread, and one for something sweet."

"*Kak*," Tonlees groaned as the pair walked toward the stretch of road that divided the two camps. "Errands! It's as though she still thinks I'm thirty!"

"At least she gave you a little glitter," Alauda sniffed. "My mother couldn't be bothered to look up from that bloody book Lord Trivinako gave her. And not a groat to be had, either."

"That's because you're squatting on a dragon's hoard!" the older girl exclaimed. "*Aiyah*! What d'ye need money for?" Her eyes suddenly sparkled. "Ooh, are you going to buy a new dress?"

"Where?" Alauda sighed. "They're Halflings, Toni. Even if I could squeeze myself into one of their gowns, it'd leave me bare from the knees down."

"There's nothing wrong with your knees, is there?"

Alauda slapped her friend's shoulder, flushing. "That doesn't mean I want to show them off at a party! This isn't Starmeadow!"

"Ladies in Starmeadow show off a lot more than their knees," Toni observed, waggling her brows suggestively.

Alauda slapped her again.

The hayfields were split by a rutted dirt track that marked the dividing line between the lands rented by the two caravan parties. The division was little more than a formality. The Halflings had set up a jumbled, confusing bustle of wagons, tables, stalls, booths, tents, and – occasionally – heaps of goods set out on a blanket on the ground. The girls found themselves surrounded by all manner of folk, and spent the next stick or so stepping over piles of wares, bumping into each other, and generally stumbling aimlessly about, all the while giggling like a pair of school-girls.

The babble of the crowd was deafening. After nearly tripping someone with her scabbard, Alauda discovered the trick of gripping the hilt and holding it vertical, so that the long blade lay along her left thigh instead of projecting dangerously to the rear. It only helped a little; the sword was long, she wasn't overly tall, and the chape of the scabbard had a habit of digging into the furrows, threatening to trip her instead of passers-by

She kept her other hand on the flap of her satchel. It was empty; she'd left her purse in her bodice, where it made a secure but somewhat obvious bulge between her breasts. It took some effort to even things out, and even then she wasn't entirely successful.

Tonlees saw her adjusting her undergarments. "You look like you have three tits," she remarked, her teeth flashing in an evil grin.

"Oh, thank you!" Alauda expostulated. "Where d'ye keep your purse, then?"

"I'm not carrying one," her friend shrugged. "Why would I? To store my vast fortune?" She rubbed the pair of coins her mother had given her between thumb and forefinger, then tucked them back into the pocket of her gown.

The girls prowled the market, doing their best not to get lost. It wasn't too difficult to navigate; even Alauda, short as she was by elven standards, managed to keep her bearings by the simple expedient of standing a-tiptoe and looking over the peaks of the Halfling tents. So long as she remembered that the elves' caravan lay in the general direction of Buckhill, which she could spot by the torch-lit smoke from the chimney stacks atop the distant plateau, she reasoned that she would have no difficulty plotting a course for home.

In addition to the various and sundry wares for sale – a profusion of goods that was surprisingly diverse for such an out-of-the-way place – there were stalls that sold food and drink, travellers' supplies, works of art, worked leather, hammered bronze, clay and glass oddments, and even armour and arms. There were games, too – games of skill, and games of chance. She saw dice in play, and some sort of frolic where three men – full-grown humans, miners from the look (and smell) of them – tried to throw woven rings of grass over pegs set in the dirt. The three men were obviously drunk, and so didn't appear to perceive what Alauda spotted right from the off: that the stakes were thicker at the top than at the bottom, and that the inner diameter of the woven rings was smaller than it looked. Not a single ring landed on a peg. None of the men seemed to notice, or if they did, seemed to be bothered by their persistent failure to score. Rather than roar in anger, they simply laughed and tottered away.

She thought about pointing out the obvious deception to Tonlees, but her friend was already moving on, watching another game where a short fellow in a peculiar hat – he was short even for a Halfling, Alauda noticed; the crown of his head scarcely came up to her breastbone – was moving three chipped cups across a painted board with swift, dextrous fingers. Beside him, another halpie – a girl this time, much taller, and devastatingly pretty, with light brown braids that reminded Alauda jarringly of Jantun's knotted, beaded coiffure – was shouting in the travelling tongue, inviting would-be gamesters to place their bets. "*Heya,*

heya, a penny, an argie, a shilling, a crown! Try your luck! Best Fearless Fearghan and master the cups! *Heya, heya –*"

Behind the table, peering intently at the board, was a third Halfling, another boy. He was...

Alauda shuddered to a halt, transfixed. He was *beautiful*. The lad towered over his fellows; he was as tall as Alauda herself, in fact, and even looked vaguely elfin, with pale skin, fine features, and a riot of chestnut-coloured hair. His brows were narrow and arched, and his ears – in stark contrast to the more outlandish adornments of the shorter folk all about him – were no larger than her own.

And he had golden eyes. They were like a hawk's eyes, she thought, so bright that they were almost blinding – and yet they were not the eyes of a merciless killer. They lent his face a gentle vulnerability that made her want to touch it.

He must have sensed her staring, because he glanced up, puzzled, and saw her gazing raptly at him. He smiled –

Alauda gulped, her knees suddenly weak. She seized Tonlees by the elbow, tugging the girl into motion. "Hey! What –"

"Thread!" Alauda squeaked, hustling her friend away from the booth. "You need thread, don't you?"

"Yes, but I was watching that ga –"

"Thread's over there!" Alauda pointed, her finger trembling visibly. She clenched it into a fist, which also trembled. She jammed the trembling fist into the pocket of her apron.

"What in the World Made is the matter with you?" Tonlees grouched.

Alauda accelerated her pace, very nearly yanking the older girl off of her feet.

They found the thread in short order. It was considerably less costly than they'd anticipated, and Tonlees was able to purchase a spindle of aqua-sea and another of azure-sky, and still had one silver argie and a half-dozen groats left for sundries. Alauda bought herself a new sewing-blade – her old one, through continuous sharpening, had been worn away to a sliver – and, by way of apology, bought one for Tonlees as well. "Thank you!" her friend exclaimed.

"We all need one," Alauda shrugged. "Especially in places where knives aren't allowed."

"Or swords," Tonlees reminded her, winking. "Also, unlike a sword, this'd be useful for getting out of a complicated gown in a hurry. Right?" She dug an elbow into the younger girl's ribs. "Right, *heya*?"

"I suppose so," Alauda said with a long-suffering sigh.

The question of getting out of gowns was on her mind when she paused at a stall whose proprietor, a jolly, apple-cheeked halpie woman of indeterminate years (Alauda guessed that the score was somewhere north of a hundred) had an array of delicate feminine sundries spread for display. Alauda was taken aback; evidently there was a good deal more going on under the everyday clothing of the folk around her than she'd ever expected. Curious, she asked the woman if she had anything in other sizes, and was shown a dizzying collection of undergarments of all varieties. One particularly frilly piece caught her eye, and the first thought through her mind was what Alacer's face would look like when he saw her wearing it. "I'll take it!" she whispered, stuffing the silky, insubstantial thing into her satchel, and handing over the gold crown the Halfling woman demanded without even attempting to haggle. She didn't bother to haggle; even in the Realm, silk was expensive.

"Why, thou slatternly beast!" Tonlees cried. "What sort of loose-kneed jade would wear such a thing?"

"Shut up!" Alauda hissed, her face flaming.

"Not a chance," her friend gloated. "This is too delicious. I'm telling everyone. The whole camp'll know what you're wearing – or not wearing, almost! – under your lily-white virgin's weeds!"

The younger girl's right eye was twitching slightly. "Will they?" she asked. "Will they indeed?" Before Tonlees could answer, Alauda dipped into her purse, plucked out another golden crown, and slapped it on the table before the perplexed but smiling Halfling woman. "Have you got another one?" she demanded, pointing at Toni. "Big enough for that chubby arse?"

"I can't believe you did that!" Tonlees gaped as they moved on. She'd stuffed her own item into a pocket. Her cheeks were still flaming.

"It was the only way to shut you up!" Alauda hissed.

"I was just joking," the older girl protested. "A whole crown! And I wouldn't've told anyone. Not really."

"Not even Alacer?"

Tonlees bit her lip.

"That's what I thought," Alauda growled. "Well, the tables are turned now, missy. I'm going to be the one to tell him what *you're* wearing!"

"Then what's to stop me telling him about you?!"

"You won't need to. I'm going to show him myself, the first chance I get."

Tonlees was silent for a moment. The bustle of the market loomed large in their ears. At last she said, "You really do love him, don't you?"

Alauda thought about that; it seemed like a serious question. "Of course," she said at last. "You know I do."

"And he loves you too?"

"Yes."

Another pause. "Has he told you?"

"Yes," Alauda said at once. She recalled her return from the Raven Clan, when she'd taken Alacer to the river, and made him scrub her back, along with other more interesting places. He'd called her a little savage, and said that it was one of the reasons that he loved her. The memory still made her tingle; it had been a pleasant homecoming.

"Well...that's good," Tonlees murmured.

"It certainly is."

The auburn-haired girl was silent a moment longer. At last she murmured, "Do you really think my arse is chubby?"

"Oh, for the love of all the gods!" Alauda hissed. "Are you *really* that insecure? You're the prettiest girl among the wagons; you don't have to keep reminding me of it."

"Do you really think so?"

"Of course! Gods, Toni, I'm still stunned that Alacer picked me over you!"

Toni shot the younger girl a troubled look. Alauda didn't spot it; she was still thinking about the night at the river-bank.

They found a stall-keeper who'd set up a small oven and was selling dark biscuits drenched in honey. He called the confection 'fire-sticks'. The name reminded Alauda that she hadn't replaced the firestick she customarily carried in her crumena, that had (fortunately) failed her when she'd tried to burn Ring Castle to the ground. The name of the pastries became apparent a few moments after the girls had swallowed the last, sticky crumbs. The biscuits were stuffed with a savoury paste the prevalent component of which appeared to be some sort of extremely hot pepper.

When the burning began they gasped; then they coughed. Soon both girls were red-faced and choking. The concerned shop-keeper took them by the hand and hauled them bodily to the next wagon, where another Halfling was selling cider from a keg, at the exorbitant price of a shilling a cup. Alauda was in too much pain to haggle; her tongue had swollen to the point where it was difficult to articulate the words to request two cups instead of one. In fact, each girl managed to drain five substantial bowls of the cool, fruity beverage before the fire in their mouths – and bellies, Alauda noticed with a tremor of anticipation – began to subside. She handed over another crown with a growl at the expense.

"Lucky that *vinarius* was there," Tonlees remarked as they continued through the market. She was red-faced and sweating, still gasping a little.

"Lucky indeed," Alauda said stiffly. He tongue felt as if it had been sanded raw. "It would've been a long run to the river."

The older girl shot her a sidelong glance. "What's wrong now?"

Alauda was doing her best to keep her ire under control. It wasn't working. "Are you simple?" she hissed, her tongue still stinging. "D'ye think it was mere chance that those two were side-by-each? I'll bet you anything you like that they're partners, in league with each other!"

"What you are you talking about?" Tonlees demanded. "There're food vendors and drink sellers all over the market!"

Alauda scrubbed her face with a palm. "Never mind."

They moved among the stalls. Alauda saw a thick blanket of varicoloured wool that she knew her mother would love, and managed to work the seller – a human, to her infinite relief, albeit one with an odd, guttural accent she hadn't heard before – down to only four shillings. She threw it over one shoulder, and they carried on. She found herself having to carefully put one foot in front of the other. The enormous quantity of cider she'd imbibed and the speed with which she'd done so threatened at every step to scythe the legs from beneath her. She was, she realized belatedly, a little drunk.

At Tonlees' insistence, they tried a few of the games. The older girl wasted groats attempting to roll a wobbling wooden ball up a ramp and into one of several holes, and seemed disappointed when Alauda pointed out that the highest-paying holes were almost certainly too small for the ball (which was more ovoid than spherical) to pass through. She didn't let her friend go near the game with the wooden pegs and woven rings. When they found a booth with long bows and blunted arrows, though, and clay jugs balanced on fence-posts only a dozen paces away, Tonlees pleaded until Alauda, sighing, agreed to stop. Toni had a passably steady hand at the longbow, after all.

The booth's proprietor was a stately-looking Halfling fellow. He was dressed like a gentleman, with abbreviated trousers below a long coat of rich blue fabric that was positively festooned with buckles and buttons. He wore shirt and waistcoat, and a scarf of fine silk was knotted about his neck. His most salient feature, though – apart from his eyes, which flitted about, seemingly seeing everything about him at once – was the most magisterial pair of side-whiskers that Alauda had ever seen. They made her wonder whether he had a touch of dwarf in his ancestry.

"Greet the stars, my ladies," he said, bowing floridly. "I am Airy Curmagh of Broadwaters, in distant Dunholm. Who might you be? Maidens of the *Ancillulae*, perhaps? Flowers such as yourselves are worthy of adorning the Elvenking's high court!"

His command of *elvii*, Alauda noticed, was flawless; had he been speaking from behind a curtain, she might've thought him a gentleman of the Third House. She glanced at Toni, muttering, "Keep walk–"

Too late. "Tonlees Havintalla, Sirrah!" Toni was saying, replying to the fellow's bow with a quick curtsey of her own. Alauda rolled her eyes.

Curmagh caught her expression. "And you, pretty lady?" the Halfling pressed.

"No one special," Alauda said.

"Come, come!" he laughed. "Wizard, warrior, wastrel, wench – we all have a name!"

"Alauda," Tonlees interjected. "Her name's Alauda. She's not a wizard. Or a wench." She tittered suddenly. "But her mother is. A wizard, I mean, not a wench. She was at the College of Stars."

"Indeed?" One of Curmagh's eyebrows twitched. "A magistatrix, blown out and burnished at the starry College itself? How grand!"

"Yes, very grand," Alauda said. She realized that she wasn't going to be able to drag Toni away. *In for an argie* – "How does this work?"

"Three arrows for a groat," he said at once. "Knock a pitcher from a post; that'll earn you five. Break one, you win ten. Break all three – that's a golden crown! The flossy glint of the mighty western Empire!" He produced the coin in question, spun it into the air, caught it again, made it dance across his knuckles, and dropped it back into his purse.

Quick hands, Alauda thought. No surprise there. "Right," she said. She banged a pair of groats down onto the table, then turned to Tonlees. "You first."

Alauda had watched her friend in the lists. All high elven children were taught bow and blade; even the common folk plied the longbow and knew the small-sword. It was as much an element of upbringing throughout the Realm as the intricacies of grammar, the deeds of ancient heroes, and a solid grounding in the gossip of the noble houses. Tonlees was good; Alauda had seen her friend put five shafts out of five into a hay-bale at a fifty paces. The clay jugs were smaller, but they were closer, too.

The bow might have been long for a Halfling; in Toni's hands it looked like a toy. The elf-girl drew and loosed three times. All three arrows went wide – or at least, given the lack of any noise of impact and the stunned look on her friend's face, she assumed that they had. Curmagh, for his part, crowed words of praise for Toni's form, her strength and grace, and bemoaned the hints of wind or the ill luck that must have caused so fine an archer to miss her target.

Alauda offered neither praise nor remonstration. She hadn't been watching the targets; she'd been watching Tonlees' hands. She was fairly certain that she had the measure of the halpies and their games. "Right," she said evenly. "*My* turn."

She hefted the bow. It was considerably lighter than those upon which she'd trained; her old arms-mistress, Aire Peregrin, would've called it a 'three-quarter bow'. She twisted it in her grip, getting a feel for the weight of the limbs, then selected one of the three arrows that the stall-keeper set out for her. She checked the nock and fletching, verified that the iron bodkin-point had been hammered flat, sighted along the shaft...and smiled.

Without a word, she nocked the arrow, drew, and released, all in one swift motion. The string sang, and the arrow hissed. It passed a full hand-span to the left of the centremost jug, missing it cleanly.

She turned to stare at the stall-keeper, her eyes narrow and thoughtful.

"A shame," Curmagh murmured, staring into the distance. "You've a good eye, and a steady hand."

Alauda was about to say something caustic about the irrelevance of her eye and hand when a girl stepped out from behind the curtains, just to Curmagh's left. Alauda recognized her at once; she was the pretty, braided thing from the gaming stall they'd visited earlier. Up close, the girl wasn't merely pretty – she was beautiful. Her hair had streaks of red and orange in it, and her braids were fixed in place with tiny rings of hammered gold. She was the same height as the stall-keeper, which put the top of her head, very roughly, at about the level of Alauda's nose.

As Alauda watched, the girl whispered something into the Curmagh's ear. <Ah, indeed?> he murmured – speaking, Alauda noticed, the travelling tongue. She tried not to react.

Curmagh turned back to the elf-girls. "Apologies, ladies. And you, my darling," he added, putting a hand on Alauda's forearm, "might I suggest that you aim just a hair – just a hair, mind! – to the right? Do that and you'll split it like Chuadwaith split the great wolf's skull, doubt me not!"

A hair, indeed, Alauda growled to herself. She aimed a full half-pace to the right of the jug...and the arrow, snapping from the bow, sailed off to the left again. This time, though, it struck the jug squarely with a hollow *clonk*. The clay pitcher tottered back and forth, left and right...but it didn't fall.

"Wondrous!" the stall-keeper exclaimed. "Flush and fair, my dear! A grand hit, and the worst of luck that it didn't fall!"

"I did hit it flush," Alauda noted coolly, "and from a full draw – and it didn't break. Just what are those pitchers made of, Sirrah?"

"Clay, my dove, clean river-clay," he said soothingly. "A little longer on the draw, mayhap, if yon arc be not too stiff for a lovely lady's slender arms." He smiled. "One arrow left."

"Would you like to replace the middle jug?" Alauda asked, pointing. "It's half off the edge already. A stiff breeze would knock it over, sure as springtime. Hardly just, wouldn't you say?"

"No need," Curmagh said, still smiling. "Call it my gift to you, young miss."

Alauda met his gaze directly. She smiled the same smile – cool, and empty. "Fair's fair," she said, "and we're not pressed for time. Put it back." She let her smile stiffen just a little. "I insist."

"Why are you pushing this?" Tonlees whispered.

Alauda didn't answer. In truth, she had no idea why; something about the night had lit her ire. Perhaps it was the amount of apple ale she'd consumed – or the pastry that was even now burning its evil way through her entrails. Mostly she was irked at having been tricked, time and time again. That made the bile rise in her throat.

Curmagh gave her an odd look. Then he shrugged and ambled down to the fence. He repositioned the jug, then turned and smiled again. "Better?"

His easy smile faltered. Alauda had the third arrow nocked and aimed at his face. "Much better," she grated. "Thank you." She squinted along the shaft.

Tonlees turned to stare at her. "What are you –"

Twaaang.

The braided girl and Tonlees squealed in unison as the arrow sped toward the Halfling. Alauda had aimed for his right eye. Just as she expected, the arrow twisted to the left, striking the newly replaced jug a glancing blow before whining off into the darkness. The jug teetered again...and once again, it neither broke nor fell.

Throughout it all, Curmagh didn't move. The expression on his face didn't even change.

Alauda tossed the bow onto the table with a clatter. Turning to Tonlees, she said, "The grip's been carved off-centre. That bow's not worth kindling; Anja Antaíssin herself couldn't have shot a straight shaft with it."

The stall-keeper walked back to the table. "My dear," he said firmly, "I don't take kindly to any suggestion that my game might be –"

"Spare me!" Alauda snapped. She leaned over the table and pulled another arrow from the enormous stand-quiver. She slapped it into Tonlees' hand, tightening the girl's fingers about the shaft. "Give it a rub," she commanded.

Tonlees felt the arrow-shaft, running her fingers up and down the wood. Her eyes widened after a moment. "It's thinner in the middle!" she exclaimed.

"Exactly," Alauda nodded. "Shaved to bend nearly double when you loose them." She stared at Curmagh. "And I suppose those 'pitchers' are a solid block of fired porcelain? With a lead slug in the base for balance?"

Tonlees gaped.

Curmagh drew himself up to his full height, bristling like a waist-coated hedgehog. "Madam!"

"I hit the damned thing flush," Alauda rasped, "and it neither fractured nor fell. If *I* were running this...this swindle, that's how I'd do it."

"Swindle?! My good lady, deceiving folk is dishonest! I'll never be accused of such!" He reached into his pouch and extracted Alauda's coins, sliding them across the table. "Consider that an apology. I'm shattered, simply shattered, that you might not have enjoyed yourselves, or that you would see fit to question my integrity!"

"You shatter a lot more easily than your wine-jugs, then," Alauda snorted. "And you can keep the coppers, Sirrah, with my compliments. Teachers deserve their coin, and it was a small enough price to pay for such a valuable lesson in larceny." She took Tonlees by the elbow and marched the girl away.

"That was rude!" Tonlees gasped as she stumbled after her friend.

"So is cheating," Alauda snarled. "Rettik was right! Scurrilous race of fuzzy-footed ditch-rats. A lesson it was, and a good one too – about my own damned cupidity. Once burned, though, and never again. Am I right?"

"I don't even know what you're talking about," Toni grumbled. "I *never* know!"

Behind them, Curmagh pursed his lips, thinking. Then he turned to the braided Halfling chit, caught her eye, and jerked his head in the direction that the two elf-girls had taken. She bent and kissed the stall-keeper's cheek, then hurried off into the bustle of the market.

◆

Seven

The pair continued on their spree, but Alauda's heart was no longer in it; she was still fuming over how long it had taken her to detect the stall-keeper's legerdemain. As a consequence she set a blistering pace, so that as they reached the far southern end of the market, both girls were panting and perspiring.

"Are we...in a hurry?" Tonlees asked, when she managed to catch up to the younger girl.

Alauda ran her fingers through her hair. "Not especially," she sighed. "I'm just...I'm a little...*akh*." She spat, then leaned against a convenient fence-post.

That was the problem; she didn't know *how* she felt. Annoyed, yes; but mostly embarrassed.

Tonlees joined her, breathing heavily. The southern end of the hayfields abutted the Great Road, and the track that separated them became the path that led to the bridge, which in turn provided access to the smelly chaos of Buckhill. The bridge over the Whyle – Alauda knew the name, but had no notion of its origin – was all but invisible beneath the tramping feet of scores of miners and other townsfolk venturing out into the Halflings' market. Most of the men she could see – they were almost *all* men – were human. Some appeared to have taken the time to wash and don different clothing. There were few dwarves among the throng.

"That's a rough-looking lot," Tonlees remarked, staring. "I hope they don't cause too much trouble."

"I wouldn't mind if they did," Alauda grumped. "With luck, they'll start with *Sieur* Curmagh and his crooked archery range."

The older girl struggled to stifle a grin. "You really don't like to lose, do you?"

"Not especially. But I really don't like liars and cheats."

"Hypocrite!" Toni scoffed. "You lie all the time! You just don't like being beaten at it."

Alauda told her friend precisely what she thought of that notion, using an Orkan phrase that would have earned her a whipping had she uttered it in earshot of her mother. Tonlees burst into laughter. "You're actually angry!" she cried. "You're angry, because you very nearly got played!"

"What if I am?" Alauda growled.

"It was only two groats!"

"What's your point?"

"My point is, who cares about two groats?"

Alauda shot her a poisonous glance more eloquent than any

expostulation. "Let's go back in," she huffed.

"I'm not going back to that archery range," Tonlees averred.

"Are you afraid I'll make a scene?"

"Yes!"

"Fine," Alauda sighed. "But I'm thirsty, and my mouth is still burning. Isn't yours?"

"Not just my mouth," her friend said with a meaningful glance. "And I'm not looking forward to tomorrow morning, if you catch my meaning. I'm nearly out of coin, though."

"I'm not," the younger girl shrugged. "We just have to find a place that isn't quite so dear."

That, as it turned out, was not an especially difficult task. The girls managed to locate a vendor – an elf, of all things – who offered watered wine at a far less usurious price than the ciderer.

That, unfortunately, was where the evening's course once again jogged askew. As Alauda was turning away from the taps, looking for the water-jug, another reveller cannoned into her. The cup went end-over-end, and the bulk of its contents ended up on her face, in her hair, and soaking into the front of her gown.

"Oh, no!" her assailant exclaimed. "Powers above, I'm so sorry!"

Alauda wasn't moving; she'd frozen stiff in shock, one hand extended, with droplets of wine stinging in her eyes and dripping from the end of her nose. The blanket over her shoulder – the one that she'd bought for her mother – was drenched.

Beside her, Tonlees, true friend that she was, made an odd *snrk*ing noise, then exploded into gales of laughter.

The fellow who'd run into her, still babbling apologies, produced a small cloth, and began dabbing at her forehead and cheeks. Alauda, half-blind and too flabbergasted to speak, snatched the thing from his hands and went to work herself.

Somebody passed her assailant another cloth, and he dabbed helpfully at her shoulders, neck, and bosom. Alauda, shocked out of her stupor at this liberty, seized his wrist in one hand. She was about to proclaim her rage, when she found herself blinking dumbly, caught by a pair of bright, golden eyes. "It's you," she said weakly.

The boy – *Gods, he's so beautiful!* she thought, cursing herself for an imbecile – stared back at her. "And, uh...it's...it's you," he replied, his shame-faced rictus easing slowly into something less terrified. After the briefest of pauses, he began dabbing at her bodice again, sponging scarlet droplets from the slight swell of her breasts before moving on to the front of her dress.

Alauda scarcely noticed what he was doing; it was all she could do to articulate words. "You bumped into me." Somewhere in the back of her mind, her pride was raging at the seeming paralysis of her brain.

Her brain paid her pride no heed; it was, apparently, thoroughly hostage to the leaden tingling in her belly. She didn't think it was the pastry; or at least, she *hoped* it wasn't.

"I did!" the boy said at once. "I'm sorry! About your dress, too. If you take it off, I'll have it washed for you."

"Take it off?" Alauda blinked several times more. "Right here?" She wasn't certain what broke her out of her daze: her clumsy attacker's inappropriate suggestion; the fact that Tonlees, standing a little to her left, sounded as though she were having a seizure; or the realization that there was nothing she wanted more at that very moment than to take her dress off for the lad, and find out exactly where that might lead.

"Well, no," the boy replied, his face purpling. "No, of...of course not. You could come back to my wagon and take it off for me there, and...and, no. No." He ground once more to a halt. "No, not that either, I guess. Ah..."

Alauda, coming out of her bemused daze, was half-way to asking him where his wagon was – he was *very* pretty, and his red-faced babbling was charming, in a way – when he stuck out his hand. "A-Alainn," he stammered. "Alain Fionan. O'Dell."

She glanced at the boy's fingers. They were long and strong-looking. The backs of his hands were older than his face. Hesitantly, she reached out and touched them with her own. A sudden spark of skyfire shivered up her arm, burning through her belly to the earth beneath her boot-heels. The problem was that she didn't know whether she really felt it – or felt it because she'd *expected* to feel it. Maybe it was the pastry after all. "Alauda," she managed.

The boy nodded. "Beautiful."

Alauda blinked. "My name? Or me?"

It was an easy toss, and as she expected, he caught it. "Both."

She felt a girlish giggle bubble up in her throat, and strangled it before it could escape to mortify her further. The urge to titter died, however, when he held up a stitched leather purse that looked remarkably familiar. "That's mine!" she exclaimed.

"I thought so." Alainn looked pained. "I saw one of the youngsters jostle you, and..." he shrugged. "Well, you know what these places can be like."

Alauda scowled. She thought she'd tucked it back inside her chemise. "That was in my bodice," she growled, wondering how one of the scores of Halfling urchins had managed to find it in there.

"Would you like me to put it back for you?" he asked.

She blinked. "You don't talk to women a lot, do you?"

"Not a lot," he confessed. "Why?"

Despite her better judgement and the odd whimsy of the circumstances – or perhaps because of them – Alauda found herself smiling. "I think I'll just take it," she said, holding out her hand. "With my thanks."

He passed it over at once, and she tucked it into a pocket without a glance. It felt light. No surprise there.

"Look, I'm...I'm truly sorry about your gown," he was saying. He took a fleeting look over his shoulder. "I'd like to stay, and talk with you some more – Mistress Alauda," he said, "but I'm late for a...for another engagement. Will you be in Buckhill long?"

She shook her head. "We're leaving the day after tomorrow," she replied. "We're just here for Second Spring. The festival, tomorrow night."

"Oh," he exclaimed, "Oh! That's wonderful! I'm going as well. Maybe I'll see you there?"

Alauda's dimples – again, despite her better judgement – made an appearance. "I hope so – Alainn."

He looked uncertain, like a diver about to hazard a deep plunge. "I don't suppose..." he essayed, "that you might consent to – to enter on my arm?"

Alauda actually felt her heart skip a beat. "I'd be –" *Delighted? Honoured? Overjoyed?*

The boy waited, his cheek twitching erratically. She swallowed hard. *Aroused?* That was probably more accurate, given the feeling in her stomach and elsewhere. "Enchanted," she managed at last. Yes, that was it. "I'd be enchanted."

His grin changed from painfully shy to painfully eager with such rapidity that she almost didn't notice. "Wonderful," he breathed. "Well. Until then – my lady?" He was still holding her hand; when he raised it to his lips, he did so slowly enough to give her plenty of time to withdraw it.

She didn't. The tingle was even stronger the second time. When he bowed before departing, she actually sighed.

Tonlees was staring at her. Alauda caught a glimpse of her friend's appalled regard. "What?" she asked. "Did I grow a second head?"

"A second head?" the older girl exclaimed. "Hardly! I just thought I ought to maybe stand back. It looked like you were going to trip him and straddle him right here in the street!"

"Don't be vulgar," Alauda sniffed. "He was a perfect gentleman, wasn't he?"

"Yes, he was," Tonlees exclaimed. "He was indeed. A perfect *halpie* gentleman!"

Alauda scowled. "That's ridiculous, Toni; he's my height. No Halfling's that tall!" *Or that delectable*, she thought, biting her tongue to keep the words behind her teeth.

"Really?" Tonlees drawled. "Did you happen to notice his feet?"

The younger girl blinked. "Er – no," she confessed. She'd actually been wondering about other parts of his anatomy, but she had no intention of admitting that to Toni. "It's...not the first thing that came to mind, frankly. Why?"

"They were bare!" Tonlees exclaimed. "And big! And hairy!"

Alauda blinked again – several times. How had she failed to notice *that*? "If you say so. I'll have to take your word for it." She glanced around. "Did'ye see where he went?"

"I did not."

"That's a shame." Alauda looked around, her face blank. "I wonder who his parents are? D'ye suppose they're Third House?"

"No," Tonlees cried, "I suppose they're *halpies*! Because he's a *halpie*, you mad thing!"

Alauda gave her friend a stern look. "I told you, he's too tall. And far too pretty!"

"Pretty? Save us!" the older girl exclaimed. "D'ye even remember his name?"

"Alainn," Alauda said at once. A small smile touched her lips. "Alainn Fionan O'Dell."

"Hara be praised! I was certain you'd been enchanted." She cocked an eyebrow. "Especially after you *said* you were!"

Alauda opened her mouth to say something caustic...and closed it again. "I did say that, didn't I? Well, it's just a figure of speech."

Wasn't it? Come to think of it, her wits did feel a little fuzzy, something she'd put down to the cider. She struggled to apply her brain to the problem. It was an uphill battle; her head felt as though it were stuffed with wool.

She *did* feel drawn to the boy; that much was clear. *Drawn* might not have been a strong enough word, in fact. That thought alone brought her up short. Had he been 'pulling' her – the same way that she pulled others, with her subtle winks and secret whispers? Alauda's own mother hadn't been able to enchant her. Could the boy be a mage, and a more powerful one to boot? He didn't seem old enough.

"If I'd been enchanted," she said thoughtfully, "would I even know?"

"No idea," Tonlees huffed. "Here's a thought, though: why not ask your mother? You know, the College-trained wizard?"

"Maybe I will." Alauda bit at her thumbnail, suddenly discomfited. "Why are you so worked up about this, anyway?"

"Oh, I don't know!" Tonlees expostulated. "Maybe because now you – *we* – are going to the festival both with Alacer, and with this halpie rake!" She crossed her arms, scowling. "Can you wait until I'm watching to introduce them? I wouldn't want to miss *that*!"

Alauda's gaze narrowed briefly...and then her eyes bulged, nearly protruding from their sockets. "Oh, hells!" she whispered faintly.

"And there it is at last," Tonlees sighed, shaking her head. "Let it never be said that Alauda Volo can't take a hint, when it's applied with the butt-end of a mattock!"

The mists enveloping Alauda's mind were slow in clearing, but panic helped them along. She held her head in her hands, aghast. "Hara's blood, Toni – what am I going to *do*?"

"Tell the truth," Tonlees shrugged. "That's what I'd do." There was something a trifle sharp in her tone. "But you'll probably lie. You're much better at that."

"Don't be that way!" Alauda's mind was racing. "Let's find him."

"Blast me!" the older girl exclaimed. "What's gotten into you?"

Alauda couldn't have offered an explanation if her life had been hanging in the balance; she just knew that she had to follow, to find him. It seemed like the right thing to do at the moment – and that was how she lived her life. *It'll probably be on my gravestone*, she thought.

All she knew was that she wanted to see him again; he was so very, *very* pretty. "Come on!" She threaded her way back into the crowd.

Tonlees followed her, fuming like an overfull cauldron.

♦

Eight

It took some time to locate their golden-eyed quarry; the boy, as Tonlees put it acidly, had vanished 'like a furry-footed fart on the breeze'.

Alauda, determined to track the lad down, didn't allow herself to become frustrated; she knew what she was looking for. Sieur O'Dell was sufficiently distinctive by way of appearance that he would stick out in a crowd, especially a crowd of Halflings. The fact that he was only as tall as Alauda herself was an added enticement; she was short and slight even by elven standards, even taking into account her age. She would not, for example have to crane her neck to – to -

She blinked furiously, struggling to banish the image from her mind. She rarely let that fact of her limited stature bother her. Height, after all, was no indicator of potential; Princess Ælyndarka, the king's sister, was herself only a gnat's whisker over five feet, and she was admired – and feared – by every woman in the Realm. All the same, it was galling that whenever she and Tonlees encountered men of their own race they tended to dismiss Alauda as a child, while paying heed and fulsome compliments to her taller, prettier, and much better-endowed friend.

The fact that she had to go up on her toes to kiss Alacer was the reason that she'd contrived to spend as much of their time together as possible in the prone position. Well – *one* of the reasons. And not so much time lately as in the mountains, but...

Thoughts of Alacer drifted through her mind like wisps of fog, vanishing the moment she tried to concentrate on them. She was looking for someone else. She swept the throng like a sharp-shooter, looking for the boy's build, his distinctive mop of hair, and his peculiar, entrancing eyes. She had nothing more to go on; in fact, several moments passed before she realized that she couldn't even recollect what he had been wearing. That in itself was alarming; clothing was usually one of the first things she noticed about a person.

What's wrong with me?

At length they found him. It wasn't difficult; as Alauda had more or less expected, he'd retreated to the gaming stalls run by the folk of the carnival, at the very spot at which she'd first noticed him. He was standing near a trestle-table talking to a pretty Halfling girl with long brown braids. It was the same girl she'd noticed before, at Master Curmagh's crooked archery game. The crown of her head, Alauda noticed, came only up to the level of his nose.

Curiosity warred with a spark of tension in her breast as they approached the stall. The brown-haired girl was pretty, very pretty, at least for a halpie – though nowhere near as pretty as Alainn, of course. She was dressed in a gown of green wool that left her shoulders bare, and that was pinched in at the waist by a broad belt, emphasizing her shape both above and below. That shape was sufficiently buxom that it made Alauda feel a little like a twig. She had no idea how swiftly halpie folk matured, but the girl was clearly further along that particular path than Alauda was.

While she was staring, the braided beauty put a hand on Alainn's forearm, then looked directly at her and smiled – and Alauda felt a stabbing pain in her midriff. It was either the pastry...or a sudden, inexplicable, piercing dart of jealousy. She felt a brief, irrational urge to strangle the girl with her own braids.

The table was narrow and occupied by a trio of chipped tea-cups, inverted. Another Halfling – a boy this time, even shorter than the girl, clad in a green tunic and cloak, with short homespun trousers and a broad, lumpy hat atop dirty blonde hair, was idly sliding the cups about. Alauda remembered him, and his cups to boot. Then she heard a thick, heavy snort, and felt a sudden blast of moist air on her ankles. She stooped; beneath the table lay an enormous hound with sad eyes, heavy jowls, and long, worn fangs. Alauda waggled her fingers at the creature, and in response it panted happily, its tongue lolling out. Thick, gooey runnels of saliva spilled to the dirt, where there was already a substantial puddle.

Tonlees, to Alauda's dismay, marched straight up to the table. Halpie-sized, it barely came up to her waist. "*Heya*, lover-lad!" she exclaimed. "How many girls do you intend to proposition tonight?"

"Toni!" Alauda squealed, mortified.

The older girl made a placatory gesture. "Well?"

Before anyone else could speak, the smallest of the group – the boy with the hat and the teacups – burst out laughing. <Powers below, Al! you didn't chat them *both* up, did you?>

He was speaking the travelling tongue. His accent was a little odd – to Alauda, he sounded like a merchant who'd once visited her parents from Skywaters and points east – but it was perfectly understandable. Dunholm, the Halflings' homeland (to the extent that such inveterate wanderers had one), lay well to the east of Skywaters, in a sheltered river valley north of Zare, and east of the dwarves' subterranean realm of *Dwéorgaheim*.

Alainn evidently saw her watching the smaller boy's lips. "I certainly did not!" he exclaimed, keeping to *elvii*. To Alauda, he sketched a bow. "My lady."

"My lord," Alauda said coolly. "I believe introductions are in order." She put her hand on her sword's hilt, wondering whether it was impolitic to do so, but not really caring. No lady meeting a romantic rival in Starmeadow would have done any different.

"Of course." He nodded at the braided girl. "This is my foster-sister, Breaghan. Bree, may I present..." His voice trailed off, and his cheeks reddened. "Er...Alauda."

Alauda hear only one word: *Sister*. She breathed a silent sigh of relief. She had no idea why she ought to feel relieved, of course.

The braided girl – Breaghan – rolled her eyes. "You didn't bother to ask her family's name?" She reached up and, to Alauda's shock, slapped the back of her brother's head sharply.

"Ow!" he exclaimed, rubbing the injured spot. "I was distracted!"

"That means he thinks you're pretty," Breaghan sighed, gave Alauda a cursory once-over look – and, to the elf-girl's bemused annoyance, nodded approvingly. "I suppose you are." She pointed at the front of Alauda's gown. "I'll wager that was Al's fault."

"How'd you know?" She unclenched her fingers from the hilt of her sword.

"Because the sight of a pretty girl – especially a pretty *elfy* girl –" she elbowed her sibling, who flinched "– turns his brains to porridge." She held out a hand. "Breaghan Curmagh." She pronounced it 'BREE-ghin', aspirating the 'gh' slightly at the back of her throat. "I saw you at father's booth; I liked your fire. Not many folk spot the scam, and even fewer bother to give him any trouble about it."

Alauda blinked. "You're pleased that I faced your father down?"

"He'll survive it, I'm sure," Breaghan grinned. "And everyone's the better for a slap in the face now and then. Teaches humility. Too much deference makes you sloppy. Honestly, missy, I'm delighted to meet you. We all are. Most of your kind wouldn't give a 'thieving halpie' the time o'day."

That's because most of you don't look like Alainn O'Dell, Alauda thought. Bewildered, she took the girl's hand. Breaghan's grip was considerably stronger than her own. "And your Alainn's...did you say foster-sister?" she asked.

Breaghan nodded. "Al's an orphan. He didn't tell you?"

Alauda shook her head. "We didn't really...talk. Not as such."

The Halfling girl snorted a laugh. "That's Al's style. The ladies flock to him for his looks, so there's no never any need for badinage." She elbowed the boy again. "What'd I tell you, you clot? Chit-chat! Con-*verse*!"

"Stop it, Bree!" he complained.

Alauda observed their interplay with a bemused scowl. "Orphan?" she prodded.

"Aye. Well, it's hardly a secret," the Halfling girl shrugged. "There're a lot of'em our age. Can I ask, though," she interrupted herself, "what was your name? All of it, I mean. Since my dear brother was too baffled by your beauty to bother asking." She shot Alainn a wry glance. His cheeks were the colour of an apple.

"Volo," Alauda replied. "Alauda Alyssa Antaíssin Volo. Of Corymbus, in the Realm."

Alainn's jaw dropped. Even the short fellow at the table looked up at her, frowning.

Breaghan's eyes narrowed. "Indeed," she murmured. "Indeed. Your mother is a wizard, is she not? A credentialed mage, from the College of Stars?"

"How'd you know that?" Alauda exclaimed. Beside her, Toni crossed her arms. There was a dark, pinched look on the older girl's face.

"My father mentioned her by name," Breaghan explained. There was a calculating look in her eyes. "He'd had word of you – your family, I mean – from a business partner in Vitrafoss, and was hoping to meet her. He's been looking for an elfy scholar to answer some questions for him. He's been looking for months, in fact." She was staring at Alauda with an intensity that was vaguely unnerving.

Alainn leaned toward his sister. "Bree, are you –"

"*Tá*," she snapped. "Mistress Volo," she continued more gently, "have you ever tried the game of cups?" She nodded at the table.

The elf-girl cocked an eyebrow. "Call me Alauda. And no, I haven't. Why?"

One corner of Breaghan's mouth lifted. "Why not give it a go?"

Alauda was about to scoff – she'd sooner have invited any three of the little folk in the crowd to paw at her pockets for a stick or two – when she caught sight of Alainn. He was staring at her hopefully.

She sighed and tugged her coin-pouch from her bodice. Like her gown and chemise, it was dotted with purple spots. When she loosed the ties and upended it, however, only a single shilling fell out. "Hmm," she frowned.

Alainn leaned down to Breaghan again. "Somebody plucked her purse," he explained.

"*Cé a bhí sé?*" the girl asked. Alauda didn't recognize the language.

"*Glyn Cionnan*," he replied.

"*Buille dó ina dhiaidh sin*," Breaghan snapped. "I know who did it. We'll see if we can't get your gilt back. Later, though." She smiled at Alauda, and nodded at the table once more.

Alauda stood before the board. The short fellow glanced up at her from under his hat's brim. "Fearghan Corruch O'Dell," he said gruffly, holding out his hand. "*Condelector, domina.*" *Delighted, lady.*

"A pleasure, Sirrah," Alauda nodded. "You'd best explain this to me, I think." She tossed the single shilling in her palm, stuffing the stained, empty purse into her pocket. There wasn't much point in safeguarding it anymore.

"Naught to explain, love," Fearghan shrugged. He tipped each of the cups up in turn. "It's your eyes against my hands. I stick an acorn under one of these –" he showed her the acorn in his palm, then slowly tucked it under the middle of the three cups "– move them around a little, and you put your coin before the one that holds the nut. If you choose the right cup, I put another coin atop yours. If you don't..." He pointed at himself, then spread his hands. "Simplicity, no?"

"It sounds easy enough," Alauda said. "I'm in your hands, then, master O'Dell."

He slid the cups gently around the board, weaving them back and forth in a simple, slightly hypnotic pattern. Alauda glanced up at Alainn and Breaghan, cocking a skeptical eyebrow. "That's it?" she asked.

"That's it," the braided girl shrugged.

Fearghan took his hands off the cups and crossed his arms. "Well?"

Alauda put her coin on the table beside the left-hand cup. Fearghan tipped it up – and there was the acorn. Fishing in his pockets, he produced another shilling and laid it carefully atop hers. "Nicely done, missus."

"That was slow enough for a blind man to follow," Alauda said pointedly. She picked up both shillings. "Again. And faster this time."

Fearghan shrugged. He moved the cups across the board. She realized that he must have polished the wood; they slid smoothly, quickly. After a dozen swift passes he stopped, and Alauda, without hesitation, laid both shillings alongside the centre cup.

Once again, she'd found the acorn. Fearghan nodded and produced two more shillings, placing them gently atop the coins already there. "You've a good eye. Again?"

Alauda cast a questioning glance at Tonlees. Her friend nodded breathlessly. Alauda shrugged. "Again."

This time, the cups moved like greased skyfire. Alauda didn't dare look away. When they stopped, she was...*almost* certain where the acorn was. Biting her lip, she put a single shilling down by the right-hand cup.

Before Fearghan could lift the vessel, Tonlees piped up. "Can I play, too?" she exclaimed.

Fearghan glanced at Breaghan. The girl shrugged. "Why not?"

Tonlees dumped her own purse into her palm, hesitated, then slapped five shillings down on the board, next to Alauda's single coin. "That's it," she exclaimed. "I'm tapped."

"Toni!" Alauda hissed. "I'm just guessing!"

"Good guess," Fearghan growled. He tipped up the right-hand cup – and there was the acorn. He swept up the coins, dug about in his pockets, and began counting their winnings out carefully. "Two more for you, missus, and full ten for the flame-haired beauty."

Breaghan sighed, rolling her eyes. Alainn actually clapped.

Tonlees grabbed the coins, squealing in delight. "Good job, Ala!"

"Yes," Breaghan murmured. "Very good."

Alauda smiled. It wasn't a particularly pleasant smile. "I've always had good eyes," she said. "But it's not eyes that matter here, is it?" Before anyone else could react, she reached out, and tipped up the other two cups.

Two more acorns sat on the board. Alauda tapped one of the cups on the table, looking between the Halflings. "Well?"

Fearghan glanced at Breaghan again. *"An bhfuil mé in iúl di?"*

The braided girl bit her lip. *"Fós."*

Tonlees was staring at the cups. "What just happened?" she said blankly. "I don't understand."

"What's there to understand?" Alauda said, still staring at Breaghan. "They controlled the game. They wanted us to win."

"But *why*?"

Alauda's eyes narrowed. "That's always the question, isn't it?" She was rubbing one of the shillings between her thumb and forefinger. Suddenly she smiled – and again, it wasn't an especially friendly smile. She held up the coin. "Look at this."

Tonlees took the shilling. "Look at what?" she asked.

"Anything odd about it?"

Her friend looked puzzled. "Odd? It's a coin, Ala!"

Alauda sighed. "What does the coin *say*, Toni?"

The older girl tilted the coin until it caught the light of one of the lanterns. *"Cudorum Imperialus Ekhanium,"* she read. "Imperial Mint of Ekhan. So?"

Alauda closed her eyes briefly. "How d'ye spell *'imperialis'*, Toni?"

"Oh," Tonlees frowned. "Gods, a faulty die! Somebody's going to hang in Norkhan! Humans are entirely too serious about their money." She glanced at Alauda. "Don't tell me you could feel that with your fingers?!"

"No," Alauda chuckled. "I saw it. The question is, what was it that made me look for it in the first place?" She spun the other shilling through the air…and instead of catching it, let it fall to the table. It struck the wood and bounced – not with the telltale ring of silver, but with a low-pitched *clank*.

Fearghan glanced at the braided girl a third time. This time, Breaghan was beaming. So, Alauda noticed, was Alainn.

Unlike his sister's, Alainn's smile sent a shiver through her. Her belly knotted almost painfully, and her knees felt weak. She'd felt those symptoms before, and they had nothing to do with the pastry. The thought panicked her a little.

Oh, no. No, no, no –

She resolved to do her best to ignore the beaming boy. When she looked back at Tonlees, though, her friend was still staring at her handful of coins in confusion. With a sigh Alauda retrieved one of them, drew Elspeth's dagger, and scraped the edge of the blade along the stamped face.

Tiny flakes of silver peeled off, revealing bright, yellowish metal. "They're brass," she explained. "Only a little lighter than silver – and a lot less costly." She tossed the slug to the table, where it rattled and rolled. "They're fake. They're all fake."

Fearghan scooped it up and tucked it into his pocket. "Keep your voice down," he hissed.

Tonlees was blinking like an owl. "I thought counterfeiters used lead?"

Alauda glanced at Breaghan; the Halfling girl half-bowed, and gestured for her to continue. "Lead's too soft," Alauda said slowly, without taking her eyes from the braided girl. "A lead coin that thin you could bend between your fingers, or dent by biting it. Brass is more like silver. Harder than gold. Lighter, too."

"*Bene!*" Breaghan glanced at Alainn, rubbing her hands together in glee. "Well done, brother. She's *perfect!*"

"So are you," Alauda growled. "Perfect gaol-bait, that is. I'm calling the guards!"

"What guards?" the Halfling girl laughed. "Where d'ye think you are, *domina*, Starmeadow? This is a mining camp! The only guards here are a half-dozen thugs with pick handles who stand watch over the factotum's vault."

"My mother, then!" the elf-girl barked. "She'll have a word with your parents! All of them!"

Breaghan chuckled. "Fear' and Al are orphans, and my father's the Bridle-bearer. You've already met him, at a certain archery range. D'ye think he'd mind me running an innocent little swindle such as this? Besides, as I've already told you, he's looking to chat with your mother anyway. He'll be calling on her in the morning, right after fast-breaking. You could have her ask him to beat us all, if you like. He might do it, too – if he could catch us."

"You could all of you do with a good caning!" Alauda exclaimed hotly. She turned to go. It was a wrench to tear her eyes away from Alainn's face, but her anger helped. "Come on, Toni."

Breaghan glanced at her brother. "Alainn? I think an apology might be in order. And a gift."

Alauda felt a burst of relief; she hadn't really wanted to storm off, and so was glad of any excuse to stay. Alainn reached into his tunic. "I've something I'd like you to wear tomorrow, my lady," he said hurriedly. "If you'll still consent to accompany me to Second Spring, that is."

There was something odd about the whole tableau. Beneath her bemusement (and arousal), Alauda's well-honed skepticism screamed at her to run, *run!* The smile on the boy's face, however, muffled her inner voice. Instead of running, she said, "Indeed? And what might that be, Sirrah?"

Alainn produced a tiny porcelain decanter sealed with a stopper of cut glass. The flask was no bigger than Alauda's thumb. "A rare scent," he explained. "A perfumer from Windhaven – that's the capital of the Isles of the Accord, as far to the west as the winds go – lost to Fear' at the game of cups last month. He lost a lot, actually. He gave us this to redeem a debt of four hundred 'orries. None of us had any idea what to do with it." He dimpled. "Until now."

"Some of us still don't," Fearghan growled. "That's coming out of your shares, you ninny."

Alauda took the tiny bottle. The porcelain was painted blood red and covered with a fine intaglio of silver enamel. Curious, she wriggled the stopper loose and sniffed it. In an instant she was reeling; goose-flesh stippled her skin, and the knot in her stomach seemed to have intensified a thousand-fold.

It was a lady's scent; she knew that at once. But it was like no perfume that she had ever encountered. It was, as far as she was concerned, the most wondrous thing she'd ever smelled: fresh bread and candy, rose and Morbannen and wine and cassia –

– grass and wind and snow and stamping horses and steel and starlight –

Toni was staring at her. "Ala, are you all right?"

Alauda swallowed, not trusting herself to speak. The hand holding the tiny flask was shaking. There was more than perfume in it; she could smell Elspeth's scent, and Jantun's – and Alacer's.

Her eyes momentarily lost their focus. Scowling, Toni tugged the stopper from the younger girl's frozen fingers and waved it under her own nose.

She made a face. "*Gah.*"

Alauda's eyes bugged out. "W-what d'ye mean by that? It's wonderful!"

"Wonderfully horrid." Tonlees made a face. "There's too much musk in it by far. It stinks." She passed the stopper back.

"You're insane," Alauda hissed. She turned to Alainn, her brows raised. "What do *you* think of it – Alainn?"

"If I didn't know it would smell marvelous on you," the golden-eyed lad replied, beaming, "I'd never have offered it to you."

Alauda felt her cheeks grow warm. She took the stopper from

Tonlees and jammed it back into the bottle. "Thank you. It's a princely gift."

"If he calls you his princess next," Tonlees grated, "I'm going to vomit."

"Me too," Breaghan chuckled. "Oh, this is perfect! Too perfect! Tell me, ladies – are you still planning on turning us in?"

Alauda waggled the flask. "Why? Did you think you'd just bought me off?"

"Not at all. I was just wondering if you might consider an alternative."

The elf-girl frowned. "What did you have in mind?"

"You could come along on a little adventure we've got planned," Breaghan said, her eyes alight. "You just passed the audition."

Alauda froze. "Excuse me? Audition?"

"The cups," Alainn explained, red-faced. "And the coins. Alauda, you're clever, and you speak and read your tongue better than any of us. I'm sorry, but this was a test."

"*What?*" The knot in her stomach became a fist.

"All of this was to find someone like you," Breaghan laughed, waving a hand at Fearghan's table and cups. "I'm – *we're* – going after a treasure, and I needed to know if you had a head on your shoulders, as well as elfy blood in your veins. Seems you do."

Alauda put her hands on her hips. "A treasure?" she sighed. "Please, Alainn, tell me you're not planning on robbing the miners!"

"Gods, no," the golden-eyed fellow chuckled. "What would we do with cartloads of ore?"

"Their payroll, then?"

"Didn't you hear me mention the big boys with the pick handles?" Breaghan said. "No, the treasure we're after isn't guarded. Not anymore, anyway. At least, not by the living."

Tonlees stiffened. "Ala…"

"Quiet," Alauda commanded. "You're going to have to give me more than that."

"I will, if you're willing to tolerate one more test," the braided girl grinned.

Alauda's brow knotted. "Which is…?"

Breaghan fished about in one of her pockets, extracting what looked like a rolled-up bit of cloth. She passed it to Alauda. "Can you read this?"

The 'cloth' was actually rag paper, old but of reasonably good quality. One side was blank; the other was covered in streaks of black soot. Alauda touched it with a finger. "Charcoal?"

"It's a rubbing," Breaghan said impatiently. "I made it myself. Can you read it?"

Alauda laid the roll of paper on the table, pressing it flat with her palms. Fearghan helpfully brought the lantern over.

She glanced up at Breaghan. "It's in *lingua curium*!" she exclaimed. "The court dialect! High Speech. The nobles use it in Starmeadow, for ritual, religious observances, gossip, and fornication." *And mother uses it to criticize me, and make me feel twenty years old.* "But nobody, not even poets, actually writes in it anymore. Not since the Darkness."

She flipped the paper over again. "Where did you make this?"

"If you can read it, I'll show you," the Halfling girl promised. "None of us ever learned your court-speech. It's not taught outside your blasted Realm. What does it say?"

Alauda frowned. She'd learned the court dialect in schola. It used the *elvii* alphabet, but the words were ancient, archaic. It wasn't so much a different tongue from *elvii* as it was a different mode of speaking it. Breaghan was correct; *lingua curium* was almost unknown outside of the Realm. It was considered a violation of historical precedent and a breach of national pride to teach it to any who were not of the Third House.

She traced the lines with her finger, speaking the words out loud; it was the easiest means of working her way through the convoluted syntax. "*Tum Imperator ... seditionis et posuit milites ...*" she began.

> *... the General ... mutiny, and placed ... soldiers in charge of Kulkisari's well. And then he prepared ... and bow in hand. But before departing... his ancestors... beloved Anja's dowry – the fruit of his life's work – into the ... friend... upon their return ... their love, and be wed. Thus was General Fineleor's second greatest treasure ... primus of House Orkarel, and she, the ... of House Antaíssin, might be joined ... escutcheon of their mingled Houses, making one House out ... and out of two hearts, one.*

Alauda translated as she read, speaking the words in the elven tongue. She faltered several times, particularly as she read the final shaky, ill-copied words.

When she was finished she looked up, her eyes wide and red-rimmed. "Is this a joke?" she whispered.

Breaghan shook her head. "I'm afraid not. So...now you know what this is all about."

"It's about Fineleor!" Alauda hissed, sounding as if she were being strangled. "Fineleor Orkarel, and his lifemate Anja Antaíssin! The martyrs of Bardan's war – the war that put an end to the Realm, and ushered in the darkness!" She flipped the page over again; there was still nothing on the obverse. "Where did you get this?" she repeated.

"I'll show you," Breaghan said softly, putting a finger over Alauda's lips. "I will – I promise. Now hush, I beg you!"

"Show me later," the elf-girl hissed, "but for Hara's love, tell me now! Where did you get this?!" She was holding the paper with shaking hands.

"I copied it from an urn," Breaghan whispered. "For the love all the gods, not just Hara, lower your bloody voice! There's more to it than just this; it was the best I could do on the fly." She rolled up the cloth and tucked it away again. "Mhaister Cloughsen – he's our lore-speaker – keeps the thing in his wagon. We need to get you in, so you can take a closer look at it, and I can make a better copy."

She beckoned to the elf-girls, leading them away from the table, past a tent, to the remains of a campfire. A half-dozen chairs and stools stood around it. Breaghan gestured to everyone to sit.

When they were seated – Toni frowning like a thunderhead, Alauda leaning forward, her hands on her knees, trembling with anticipation – Breaghan explained. "We've been rotting here for months!" she began. "I couldn't figure out why. None of us could. We'd never stayed this long anywhere. Nobody explained the delay – not my father, not the Lore-speaker; no one. And then, one day, I found – this."

She fumbled in her blouse, producing another small scrap of paper. She passed it to Alauda, who fingered it thoughtfully. The writing was thin, fine, and distinctly masculine. More to the point, the paper was rag vellum, one of the more costly writing materials available. "It's a stock count," she said. "Sheep and rams, ewes and kids." She frowned suddenly. "Who'd write that on such expensive paper? Is that what you were thinking?"

Breaghan smiled sourly. "Actually, that was my second thought. My first thought was, why was the lore-speaker reporting to my father on the herds? That's hardly his responsibility." She waggled her eyebrows suggestively. "My third thought was this: why did the paper smell sour?"

Alauda lifted the scrap to her nose. It *did* smell sour. "Why?"

"Turn it over."

The obverse of the paper was blank...except for thin, light brown writing. She squinted, but could just barely make it out. It was in the travelling tongue, and it said: *It's genuine; the treasure's real.* C.

She raised her eyes, frowning.

"Hidden writing," the braided girl grinned. "The Mhaister penned the lines in milk. Once the letters dry, they can't be seen. Heat them up, though, with lamp or torch, and they turn brown like that." She flicked the paper with a fingernail. "This is why I started following my father. It didn't take long to uncover what was going on. I overheard him whisper to the lore-speaker one night about 'the urn' and 'the treasure'. The treasure hidden beyond Arx Cervus." She patted the pocket containing the paper roll. "Fineleor's second-greatest treasure: the dowry of his betrothed, Anja Antaíssin."

"Ha!" Tonlees squealed. She punched Alauda in the shoulder. "I *told* you there was a treasure!"

"You said it was in the castle," Alauda reminded her stonily. "The writing that Breaghan copied says it's in 'Kulkisari's Well'."

"Kulkisari's Well *is* Arx Cervus," Tonlees said triumphantly. "They're the same; it's the old name for the place. Honestly, what *were* you doing in history class?"

Alauda shot her a poisonous look.

"Fineleor renamed it 'Arx Cervus' when he took it over," Tonlees went on, "because the sigil of his house was a –"

"Stag's head," Alauda interrupted. "Obviously." She scratched at her chin, ignoring her jubilant friend. "Fineleor and Anja have been dead for more than four thousand years. What makes you think any treasure he hid is still there?"

"Why are our wagons still sitting here after four months, with no one to fleece but the dirt-stinking dullards of this gods-forsaken mining town?" Breaghan countered. "Why are my father and the Lore-speaker talking in whispers and passing secret notes about two ancient elven heroes?

"And why," she whispered, glancing around, "is the urn I got that rubbing from full of *these*?"

As the two elves watched, Breaghan produced a small bundle of cloth no bigger than her palm. Unwrapping it, she revealed a tiny, blackened disk-shape. Without touching the metal, she held it up for inspection.

Alauda squinted. It was another coin – an old one, this time. *Very* old. The silver was black with age. It wasn't an Ekhani coin, but one from the Realm. At least, she *thought* it was; it looked...odd. "That's the royal seal, isn't it?" she muttered. "But the crown looks...wrong."

"Look at the legend," Breaghan urged.

The raised lettering was almost illegible. After a moment, though, Alauda was able to puzzle it out. "*Yarchian Deos Gratia V-v-victor*," she gasped, stumbling a little over the last word.

Tonlees clapped her hands over her mouth in shock. "It's a victory coin!" she gasped. "They were minted by Yarchian when he took the throne, after the fall of Mærglyn Kin-Slayer at the hands of Holy Bræa and the *Sarvaloka*!" The older girl's hands were shaking. "Those things are worth a fortune today! People will pay hundreds of orries for just one of them!"

"I know," Breaghan said soberly. "And the urn I took the rubbing from...it's full of them. Scores of them. It's from a trove, ladies."

" 'Fineleor's second-greatest treasure'," Fearghan said. His accent in the elven tongue was lilting, soft.

Alauda couldn't bring herself to touch the tarnished silver. "Turn it over!" she commanded. Breaghan flipped the coin upon the cloth. On the obverse was a stylized dragon's head. "*Jawartan Argentum*," the elf-girl breathed. It was an homage to Jawartan, the great silver dragon who'd been King Yarchian's closest companion for centuries. After the King had fallen at the Field of Oldarran, the battle that had ended the elves' domination of the ancient world, Jawartan had borne his friend's body to *Dracosedes* – Dragonhome – in the outer realms. There he had curled his immense coils about the king's corpse, closed his silvery eyes – and embraced the Twilight. Yarchian the Renewer was *still* the only mortal ever to be accorded the honour of burial at the Field of Skulls, the vast and ancient grave-cairn of the First-Born.

"Hara's love!" Tonlees swore. "That'd be worth a fortune!"

"Our thought precisely," Breaghan said. "The only thing that worried me was...what if this is it? The urn, I mean. What if that's Anja's dowry?"

"Don't be ridiculous," Alauda scoffed, afire with excitement. "Fineleor was *primus* of House Orkarel, and Anja was the founder of House Antaíssin; even if you didn't know that before, I just read it out for you. House Orkarel died out centuries ago, but the Drýva – House Drývanteum, I mean – are one of its cadet branches. And House Antaíssin still exists. Both are wealthy beyond imagining. And the dowry, remember, is supposed to be the fruit of Fineleor's life's work'." She hesitated, then tapped the coin with a fingernail. "I can't imagine how big the treasure might be – but it certainly has to be more than a single urn full of dull silver."

"That's what we thought, too," Breaghan nodded. "More importantly, it's what my father and Mhaister Cloughsen think. They're looking for an elven scholar to read the urn, and tell them where to look – and they've found your mother. But I out-thought them; I found *you*."

Alainn put a hand on Alauda's knee. Her tightly focussed concentration immediately went to pieces. "They're going to speak with her tomorrow morning," he murmured. "Do you think she'll help them?"

"Are you joking?" Alauda snorted. "Help a bunch of hal...Halflings?" She gave her new acquaintances an apologetic glance. "Halflings who want to put their hands on an ancient treasure of incalculable value and historical importance to our people?!" She snorted a laugh. "They'll be lucky if she doesn't blow them out of their shoes!"

"Halflings don't *wear* shoes," Tonlees said helpfully.

Alauda glared at her friend. She massaged her temples, still marvelling at the cupidity of her hosts.

"Well, that's good!" Breaghan grunted. "Isn't it? If your mother says them nay, then that gives us our chance."

Alauda blinked. "Chance? What d'ye mean, chance?"

The Halfling girl tapped her finger in her palm. "Tomorrow morning, when father and the lore-speaker are off trying to talk your mother into helping them, you and I will take a look in Mhaister Cloughsen's wagon. You'll read everything on the urn, so we'll know where we have to look, and what we need to expect. Then tomorrow night, we'll all make an appearance at the festival. You, my lady, will have a drink, and dance a few dances. Later, as is usual, everyone will drift off in pairs for the, ah...the customary mischief. You'll go with Alainn, of course."

Alauda couldn't stop herself; she glanced at Alainn. He was smiling at her. The shiver struck her anew; she hoped Tonlees hadn't noticed. "If I must," she said weakly. There was nothing, nothing in all the wide world, that she wanted more at that moment then to slither off into the darkness for a little mischief with Alainn O'Dell.

"There won't be much time for naughtiness, unfortunately," Breaghan grinned, "because as soon as you can tear yourselves away from the party, we'll all meet up at the west end of the camp field. And then we'll go and break into Arx Cervus, find Kulkisari's Well – and steal Anja's dowry. Even splits all 'round, *heya*?"

Tonlees sat bolt upright. "What?!" she squealed.

Alauda didn't squeal; she merely nodded. "Done."

Alainn, to her delight, was beaming at her. Her feigned composure melted, and she smiled back. His hand was warm on her knee. She put her own atop it, shivering a little, and not with the chill of the night air.

♦

Nine

Afterwards, Alauda wasn't certain exactly how Alainn had convinced her to leave Tonlees and walk about the Halflings' market with him. Her memory told her that he'd asked, and she'd giggled and agreed, ignoring Toni's outraged sputtering; but surely it had to have been more than just that. Hadn't it?

She found that it was easier to think when she wasn't looking at him. If she kept her eyes to the front, with one hand on the hilt of her sword, and concentrated resolutely on putting her feet before her, then she was able to think clearly. In those brief moments of lucidity, she went over in her mind everything that she'd seen – everything that Breaghan and Alainn and Fearghan had shown her – and did her best to poke holes in their story. Try as she might, she could not. There was no question that the language in the rubbing was the court dialect; and despite the missing text, its content was clear. And the victory coins minted at High King Yarchian's bidding; those were real, too. She'd seen one before. One of her mother's colleagues, a wandering mage who'd taught from time to time at the schola in Corymbus, had possessed one, and had worn it as a pendant on a chain about his neck. It had been an heirloom, passed down through generations from parent to child within his family, immensely valuable. And now these halpies were telling her that there were more of them – hundreds – right here in their camp, and thousands more stick's ride away?

It was unbelievable – except that everything they'd shown her thus far was *entirely* believable. Since leaving Corymbus, her personal threshold for pooh-poohing a seemingly incredible notion had risen considerably.

The idea of storming a castle – especially one newly fortified by a visiting Ekhani warlord – made her only a little nervous. They weren't going to storm it as such, after all; it wasn't as if they'd be hauling ladders and siege towers up to the walls. And it wasn't that she doubted her abilities, such as they were; she'd spent a good deal of her childhood sneaking about, and apart from the somewhat different penalties for getting caught, this wouldn't really be all that different. Nor was she overly concerned about the lord's mage-trained lifemate – although the fact that she was evidently an alumnus of the College of the Eye was some cause for concern. Alauda knew a little bit about the differences in curricula between the Gasparri school and its high elven parent in Starmeadow. The magisters of the Eye laid far greater emphasis, it was said, on the arts of divination, of magical defence – and of mage-to-mage combat. Its graduates were reputed to be skilled, ruthless, and without pity, if somewhat lacking in the theory and history of the Art Magic.

Or, she sighed to herself, that might have been nothing more than her mother's snooty dismissal of a rival academy. No, the real concern was how little they knew about the place. Arx Cervus – *Fons Kulkisario*, or Kulkisari's Well, the moniker it had borne for an eon, before Fineleor had taken it over – was truly ancient, dating from an age when some of the greatest war-chiefs and masters of the Art Magic had walked the earth. When it was built, the High King had been none other than Tior Magnus, and his brother, the War Chief Dior Fell-Handed, had been charged with the security of the Realm. Dior might very well have walked the crumbling ramparts – except that they wouldn't have been crumbling then. And Fineleor would only have added to the defences – particularly if he had chosen them to conceal his 'second-greatest treasure'.

Alauda ascribed no importance to the confidence the Halflings displayed, because none of them had much idea what to expect. Behind the high walls the place could be a ruin...or it could be an ancient labyrinth purposefully designed to ensnare or even obliterate the unwary. Fineleor, she recalled, her memory sparked by her conversation with Captain Rettik the previous day, had had a dwarf as a battle-companion. Dwarves were passed masters at turning fortresses and underground facilities into death traps, were they not? The thought made her shiver. She wasn't fond of enclosed spaces; she certainly didn't feel like stumbling about a crumbling ruin that was liberally salted with booby-traps.

They didn't know *anything*. If the Halflings did know more, they hadn't told her. She was loathe to embark upon so dicey an operation with so little in the way of information, even if the prize was so potentially immense – and for that matter, of such immense historical importance. Besides, she mused, their party – three halpies; herself, an undersized girl with no skills to speak of; and Toni, slightly taller, and equally unskilled – wasn't exactly the stuff of which epics were written. She hadn't –

"I like your name," Alainn said suddenly.

Alauda glanced over at him, startled out of her reverie. He was smiling at her, his eyes luminous in the darkness. All of her careful analysis came clattering to a halt, washed away by the golden light in his eyes. All at once she was warm again; too warm, in fact, to even think of anything to say.

"Where does it come from?" he went on, when she didn't reply.

Alauda had to clear her throat before she could speak; she was damned if she would allow herself to squeak like a mouse in his presence. " 'Volo' is a cadet line of Domus Solostyriannis," she began.

Alainn halted in his tracks, staring at her, mouth agape. "You're noble? You didn't tell us that!"

"No, we're not – we're not noble," she clarified. "We're related, through father's line, but distantly. Very distantly. It's been centuries since we were...since we were close enough for blood to matter. Long before the Shadow King."

"Ah." He took her hand, and held it up to admire the ring on her left index finger. "So this isn't a hidden signet?"

"It's a tourmaline," she laughed. "From my mother's side. Her mother found the stone the day she came of age, and had it made into a jewel." A sudden thought jolted her. Her mother had always told her that grand-mama had found the stone 'on the day she came into her right'. Alauda had taken that to mean the day her grandmother had passed without the walls of her father's house – but maybe that wasn't the case. Perhaps she had seen the stone while kneeling naked on a flat rock, while her own mother, the formidable Elspina, held an obsidian blade to her throat. The chill returned, and she shivered anew.

"Is something wrong?" Alainn asked.

Alauda shook her head. "No. Why?"

"Your hand is trembling." He touched the back of it with gentle fingers.

The girl smiled. "It would probably stop," she hinted, "if you held onto it."

"As my lady commands," Alainn chuckled. He did as she suggested.

After a few steps she interlaced her fingers with his. It was comfortable as well as mildly stimulating, the more so because they were the same height. Whenever Alauda tried to hold hands with Alacer her arm was bent, and when he kissed her, the tall, silver-haired lad had to stoop. There would be no craning her neck kissing Alainn, that was –

She bit her lip, hard. There would be no kissing Alainn *at all.*

The thought of Alacer had momentarily upset her sense of contentment. He'd been distant lately, even standoffish; still, she was looking forward to winkling her way back into his good books. The following evening's festivities, she reasoned, ought to provide plenty of opportunity for her to make amends.

"What's her name?" Alainn asked suddenly.

"Who?"

"Your grandmother."

"Oh." Alauda nodded. "Thuvinia Letira; she went to wind more than twenty years ago. And *her* mother was Elspina Elus Ventior. She's the one who began the..."

She paused. Did she *really* want to tell him about all of the Horned God nonsense? "She's the one who began our family's...tradition of service. To the Green," she finished awkwardly.

The lad dimpled. "Are you planning on becoming a woods-walker?"

Alauda had a brief vision of riding about the mountain glades on the back of a giant wolf, bare-breasted, her spear high, and her braids flying in the wind. "Gods, no," she laughed weakly. "I'm rubbish with a bow. Toni would probably take to it like a duck to water, though, save that she's a little too delicate for sleeping out-of-doors."

He shot her a querulous glance. "Who's Toni?"

"Tonlees," Alauda repeated, puzzled. "The girl I arrived with? She just left us a few moments ago."

"The brunette?"

"Her hair is auburn," the elf-girl said, eyeing her escort strangely. "She's my best friend. And a lot prettier than I am."

"Truly?" Alainn shrugged. "I don't seem to remember her."

"You only had eyes for me, is that it?" she teased.

"In a word – yes," he said. "Alauda, when you say that your family serves the green – what exactly does that mean?

Alauda chuckled weakly. "I don't really know, Alainn. I'm new to it myself. I've had a few adventures, if you can call them that, in the last month or so, but nothing that might cause me to run off an make a career of being a guardian of the forests. Perhaps I'm too fond of my comforts." She wrinkled her nose. "Or the sort of comforts I used to enjoy, before my home became a glorified ox-cart.

"At the same time, there's...I don't know, something exciting about it, I guess. I've spent some time in the forest, with the *elvii*, and I didn't mind it." *Liar – you* loved *it*. Alauda gnawed briefly on her lip. Was she lying even to herself? Is that what she really wanted – to be back with the clansmen of the Raven? "It's...difficult to explain, I guess."

"I think you're doing a fine job of explaining it." He squeezed her hand. "It's the thrill, isn't it? Of discovering new places, learning new things. Of challenging yourself, meeting standards that you yourself have set – not that have been imposed upon you by someone or something else. The danger, too – that can become an end in itself."

"What makes you think I know anything about danger?" Alauda smiled.

He held up their interlaced fingers. "What happened to your hand?"

She shot him a more considering glance. "You *do* understand."

"Of course I do," he said. "I've met a few elves from the Realm – some like you, brought up in the hinterland between the nobility and the peasantry, who are neither one nor the other. Let me guess: you had the misfortune to be born into a very traditional family. For budding ladies like yourself, there's nothing but the paths that others have trod a thousand times before you: marriage, maybe a trade, children – unless you're willing to take on something unusual but still respectable, like service to the Powers, or a military career.

"And you'll pardon me," he continued with a slow wink, "if I very respectfully suggest that you're too pretty to be a priestess, and too wonderfully petite to be a soldier."

"Another compliment, *heya*," Alauda glowered. "You'd best ration them, my buck, lest you run out." *'Wonderfully petite'* – *ass*!

Alainn laughed. "Should I ever fail to compliment a pretty lady, I'd have to hang up my harp."

She started. "You play the harp?"

"No, regrettably," Alainn chuckled. "Figure of speech. Other instruments, yes, but not the harp."

"That's a shame. I like the harp." She gave him a frankly appraising look. "Don't take this the wrong way, Alainn, but you're not exactly army material yourself. Unless you'd consider the Halfling army; there, you'd probably be a giant."

"Thanks, I already stick out enough." He raised his free arm, curling it so as to comically admire his musculature. There wasn't anything particularly impressive about it. "Perhaps I could convince them that I'm an avatar of Almighty Esu himself."

"Almighty Nosa, maybe," Alauda chuckled. Nosa was the fourth of Holy Bræa's brothers, and was generally depicted as being slight, dextrous – and not overburdened by a sense of honour or honesty. He was, naturally, the patron deity of the Halflings.

"I choose to take that as a compliment," the boy said loftily. He glanced at her sidelong again. "You speak like someone who enjoys music?"

"That's like asking me if I enjoy food," Alauda smiled. "Or breathing. There's simply nothing better. Why do you – oh!"

They were passing a stall where an artisan had a number of instruments on display. Alainn sought permission from the shop-keeper with a glance and a nod, then selected one of them, a small, pear-shaped stringed device, and checked the tune with flicks of his thumb across the strings.

"Know what this is?" he asked.

"It looks like a viol," Alauda frowned. "Except that it has five strings instead of four."

"Close enough," the boy grinned. He borrowed a short, deep-bellied bow from the merchant, tucked the body of the instrument under his chin, and sawed across the strings. The tune he drew from them was harsh and rasping, almost metallic in character – worlds away from the sweet and dulcet tones that she expected from a bowed instrument.

It was interesting, to be sure, but not what Alauda would have called pleasant. She made a face, and Alainn moderated his movements. The pitch and volume both dropped, and an entirely new tone issued from the fist-sized sound-hole, a deep and mellow melody that made her eyebrows climb in appreciation. "I've never heard one of these before!" she exclaimed. "What do you call it?"

"It's a *rebekken*," he explained. "That's in *dwéorgaspræc*, of course. The thing comes from the Deeprealm. In the traveling tongue, it's called a rebec."

"What makes it sound so...so odd?" she marvelled. "That tinny warbling, I mean?"

He paused and tilted the instrument's body up to allow her to look through the sound-hole. "Metal tines. Combs fixed to the inside of the face," he explained. He shouldered the instrument again and began a new tune. "They vibrate when you play. It can be a little off-putting when you're soloing, but even I have to admit that it's quite complimentary when you're in company with a couple of tambours. And it goes especially well with that odd instrument the dwarves use; the one that sounds like a box of hammers falling down a flight of stairs. I don't know the name."

"It's called a *stingursteinn*," Alauda said. "And it's supposed to sound like picks, not hammers."

Alainn grinned and bowed. "A scholar of music, too," he chuckled. "That surprises me not at all."

"I should hope not. And I'm not much of a scholar, since I've never heard of a rebec before. Well? Are you going to play something for me or not?"

"As my lady commands. What sort of music does my lady prefer?"

Alauda pursed her lips, wondering. "Oh, anything by Ceorlinus would do," she said casually. Her tone belied the state of her nerves; in point of fact, her heart was tripping in her breast, wondering whether he knew anything more than skaldic doggerel. The thought that he might make a hash of her favourite composer was too painful to bear.

In the end, she was not disappointed. Alainn proved to be a competent musician, on the rebec at least, with a good memory, decent rhythm, and an acceptable voice. And the song he chose made her shiver with delight.

Alainn sang:

Ah, fishing for a pretty little wife
Takes rod, and line, and bait;
And I've been fishing all my life,
To find the perfect little mate.

Alauda beamed. When he repeated the last line, as required, she sang it with him, harmonizing automatically in counterpoint. They repeated it again. Alainn laughed, and launched into a complicated pizzicato trill, holding the bow away from the strings and plucking at them with the nails of his thumb and middle finger.

She was grinning like an idiot, and tried to stop, but she couldn't; she just couldn't. Her heart was soaring. *He could play!*

The tune – of course – was from Ceorlinus' masterpiece, the 'Meddlesome Coachman', and it was the introductory aria for the opera's eponymous hero. The play's first act opens on Trebax, the count's coachman, sitting on a stump beside a pond, rod and line in hand, trying to catch his supper. The vocal range of the song was designed to allow the singer to display his virtuosity, while the lyrics gave the audience an introduction into Trebax's character, and thus a solid foundation for accepting the serpentine plot of the remainder of the piece.

Alainn continued:

The mate for me has hair as black as night,
And eyes of brilliant green;
She'll keep her love for me alight,
And be my happy little queen.

He winked at her as he sang the lines. Alauda's dimples deepened into pits. Then he ran into a transitional phrase that led to a new melody. She knew it well; in the play it presaged the arrival of three birds – a canary, a nightingale, and a jay – who sing to Trebax about love. The birds, of course, are costumed ladies of the chorus. In stage productions, depending upon the quality (and the amount of coin available to the company), the women wore feathered hats, or might be draped in gowns constructed entirely of coloured plumes.

Alauda sang the canary's part; it suited her lofty soprano:

Ah coachman, why sit ye here pining?
Thy comrades are drinking and dining;
A beauteous mate can be thine,
And true love is better than wine!
<an arpeggio> *...yes, better than wine!*
<another arpeggio> *...much better than wine!*

Alainn laughed aloud, nearly missing a chord as he played.

Together, one after the other, they sang the remainder of the verses. As Trebax, Alainn lamented the paucity of eligible girls; as the nightingale, Alauda, struggling to reach the lowest notes, counselled him to expand his search by the light of the moons and stars, instead of merely looking for love under the light of the Lantern. As Trebax, Alainn complained that ladies simply didn't seem to notice him; and as the jay, Alauda suggested that he sing all the louder.

She nearly stumbled over the final phrase; she made the error of glancing at Alainn, only to see that he had crossed his eyes and was sticking his tongue out at her. Avoiding a sudden fit of the giggles and hewing to her lines took a titanic effort.

By the time they finished they were both laughing uncontrollably. They had also accumulated something of an audience; a dozen halpies and a roughly similar number of folk from Buckhill had thronged about the booth. When the rebec fell silent at last, the applause was uproarious. Alainn and Alauda bowed simultaneously.

The crowd cried for more. Shouts of *Denuo, denuo*! brought a flush to her cheeks. *Bugger true love*, she thought, her eyes shining; if anything was better than wine, it had to be the stage.

Alainn dropped her a sly wink. "How about a solo?" he murmured. "I think they deserve to hear the lark's true voice, untainted by my meager efforts."

"I don't think they were meager at all," Alauda replied *sotto voce*. "And I didn't come here to warble on command for a passel of pick-swingers! If anything, I should be getting home."

He nodded soberly, plucking at the strings; they gave a mournful twang. "If not for them," he said, staring down at the instrument and not meeting her eyes, "then sing for me?"

Later, after everything had gone awry, Alauda recalled that precise moment, and ruefully identified it as the last chance she'd had to walk away from Alainn O'Dell with her heart, her maidenhead, and the skin of her backside intact. She didn't realize it at the time, of course; such is the nature of last chances: they are obvious only in hindsight. All that she knew was that when he raised his eyes and grinned at her, she felt a knot tighten exquisitely in her vitals, and unthinkingly smiled her acquiescence in return. From that moment of blissful surrender onward she was lost, and events both fair and foul unfolded accordingly.

But that all happened later. In the moment at hand, when Alainn asked her what she wanted him to play, Alauda simply shook her head. Clasping her fists at her side, she took several deep breaths, closing her eyes so as to better see the words before them.

In the third act of the Coachman there was an anomaly that had attracted the ire of critics for centuries. In the midst of a scene of unparalleled ridiculousness, Fidelia, the sister of the countess' seamstress, and the object of the count's unrequited lust, is found walking alone in the garden at night; and, inspired by the moons Chuadan and Lodan, and their storied, ancient love, launches into an aria of such surpassing beauty that it seems completely out of place in the context of the comical action going on all around her.

Alauda often felt that way – completely out of place – and so she had no difficulty identifying with Fidelia, whose artfully idealistic notion of the true nature of love she'd always subscribed to, no matter how often events proved it a chimera. Both cynic and romantic, she had long since decided that just because something was ridiculously implausible, that was no reason to spurn it.

Fidelia's song demanded not only a coloratura soprano, but one that could reach the highest part of the register with power to spare. It took poise, skill, and a good deal of vocal clout. Alauda had all three, and she knew it. And she loved proving it.

Spurred on by the challenge of Alainn's smile, she sang:

> *O Lantern bright, who through the night*
> *Reclines in silent leisure*
> *While gold and silver moons above*
> *Conspire thus in pleasure;*
> *Their gleaming glow, to we below*
> *Bequeaths an sky resplendent*
> *And thus we know as, to and fro,*
> *They rise in fire ascendant.*

As she began the chorus, Alainn matched her with a slow, simple rhythm on the lower register of his instrument. He had a good ear, and struck the proper chords without error. His plucking of the strings served as a perfect counterpoint to her soaring soprano.

> *O show us, lamp of day, where hide the moons*
> *Who light our loving night with star-shine strewn;*
> *O show us, lamp of day, where hide the moons*
> *Who light our loving night with star-shine strewn!*

> *O silver moon, grant us this boon,*
> *Who far below observe thee*
> *We see thy love so far above,*
> *And only wish to serve thee*
> *The hour is late, and so thy mate*
> *Arises swift to claim thee*
> *With ardour hot, and so has got*
> *No reason for to shame thee!*

She caught his eye, and saw that he was staring at her, enraptured.
His whole heart was in his golden eyes. Alauda felt a sudden ache in her
breast, and a wash of warmth. The crowd faded into shadow; she was
singing for *him* now, for her love, and her love alone.

O show us, lamp above, where silver shines
Thus followed by thy love, who for thee pines;
O show us, lamp above, where silver shines
Thus followed by thy love, who for thee pines!

O golden moon, we raise this tune
Unto thy gilt-edged glory
We know thy name, and blush for shame
To hear thee tell thy story
Thy silv'ry mate thy rich estate
Desires not to plunder
She rides above on wings of love
And fills the world with wonder

O tell us, lamp of gold, the reason why
Thou dost pursue thy love across the sky
O tell us, lamp of gold, the reason why
Thou dost pursue thy love across the sky

Her audience was frozen in place, locked in attitudes of rapture.
Alauda decided, figuratively speaking, to blow the rust off of the pipes.
Alainn was still watching her, and she wanted to do him proud. She
stepped up the power for the final verse until her high, clear voice echoed
throughout the halpies' camp.

O heed my tunes, thou loving moons,
Who ply the sky above me
Perchance thy light, this darkling night
Shall find me one to love me
My aching heart must play its part,
For 'tis alone and tender
And waxing bright, in thy fair light,
Shall rise to nightly splendour!

O prithee tell me true, ye moons above –
Shall I have naught but thee to be my love?
O prithee tell me true, ye moons above;
Shall I have naught but thee to be my love?

She held the last note while Alainn slowly drew a solemn descending scale from the rebec's strings. The crowd surrounding them, which had grown to about four- or five-score in the course of her song, was utterly silent for the space of a half-dozen heartbeats. Then they exploded into howls of praise, and a flurry of furious applause.

Alauda turned to thank Alainn for the quality of his accompaniment; but when she opened her mouth to speak, the shouts and cries from their listeners drowned her out. She satisfied herself with a shrug and a smile; her golden-eyed companion returned her grin, and saluted her with two fingers. He too was clapping madly, his rebec and bow tucked under one arm.

The cries of *denuo, denuo!* arose once more. Alauda was exhausted, her throat raw from the effort of singing. But none of that mattered; she was afire with the passion of the music that bled through her veins.

Alain was mouthing words at her. She caught one of them – *Another?* – and nodded wearily. She was fatigued, to be sure; but she was also fire-hot with the glorious joy of performance. She qualified her response by pointing a stiff finger at him, indicating that she expected him to sing a part in the next piece. He responded with an eager nod, and set to playing at once.

As his fingers warmed to the instrument the bow flew across the strings, and a new melody emerged. It was slower, more regal; a gentler, kinder piece. But it was still Ceorlinus (*Of course*, Alauda thought, blessing the boy for his consideration).

This time, though, it was a duet.

Alauda stiffened as the notes told her which tune he'd picked. It was the penultimate song of the Coachman – a duet sung by Trebax, the eponymous protagonist of the piece, and Fidelia, the perpetual victim of his innumerable schemes. Having succeeded, by dint of convoluted and mind-boggling plots, in tying up the matrimonial bonds of every other couple in the play, Trebax and Fidelia find themselves at loose ends, with no more tricks to play. The meddlesome coachman has spent his best efforts to make love blossom between his compatriots, but has found no lover for himself; and Fidelia, once the Count's objet d'amour, has been set aside, now that the Count has rediscovered his passion for his long-suffering wife. Together, they sing a song lamenting their respective losses – and in doing so, discover that, as co-conspirators, they are eminently suited for each other.

It was one of the most touching and heartfelt pieces in the great master's oeuvre. Alauda wasn't certain that she was ready to sing it with Alainn – and yet she had no choice. His fingers were already there, so she took a deep breath, and sang:

<table>
<tr><td>Fidelia:</td><td>My heart is empty, my heart is aching
To know that love which life fulfills;</td></tr>
</table>

Alainn knew his limits. He didn't try for the same complex warbling that a practised baritone would have attempted; he contented himself with filling in the masculine part in a manner that left the field clear for Alauda's flawless soprano.

<table>
<tr><td>Trebax:</td><td>My heart is broken, my heart is longing
For aught to mend its endless ills!</td></tr>
<tr><td>Both:</td><td>I live for love, that gift divine;
True love is sweet, as sweet as wine;
True love is sweet as the sweetest wine!</td></tr>
</table>

Alauda's heart nearly burst with pride; Alainn, for all his lack of experience, had excellent pitch, and his counterpoint to her melody was flawless. He didn't reach for the notes, or try to overpower them. If there hadn't been another verse coming up, she might very well have kissed him then and there.

Instead, she sang:

<table>
<tr><td>Fidelia:</td><td>The Lantern has set on my ambition,
No more do I long for a golden crown;</td></tr>
<tr><td>Trebax:</td><td>My master now hates me; my mistress berates me
I've no more use for a nuptial gown –</td></tr>
<tr><td>Both:</td><td>There's naught as sad as a love-lorn life;
And naught as noble as man and wife;
Nothing as noble as man and wife!</td></tr>
</table>

Alauda stepped behind her accompanist and laid her hands on his shoulders; it was as close as she could come to a display of affection without interrupting the sawing of his bow. When Alainn, feeling her touch, laid his head back against her bosom, smiling beatifically, she gave his right cheek a gentle slap. The audience laughed.

She gathered her wits for the final verse:

<table>
<tr><td>Fidelia:</td><td>And so in sorrow, I hasten whither
My love-lost heart may heal for true;</td></tr>
<tr><td>Trebax:</td><td>While I, patient maiden, with heart heavy laden
Must seek my blunders to undo.</td></tr>
</table>

Both: *With hopes of love blighted, and all uninvited*
                 I'll make amends, and begin anew;
                 I'll make amends, and begin anew!

As applause exploded around them, Alauda bent, put her lips to the boy's ear, and mouthed one word: "Beautiful."

"My thoughts exactly," he replied, glancing up at her.

A half-stick later saw the moons of which she'd sung riding high above the wagon-choked hayfields, illuminating the distant snow-capped peaks with a rippling blend of gold and silver light. Alauda and her self-appointed escort – Alainn had promised to see her back to her parents' conveyance – were walking slowly along the broad track that separated the caravan from the halpie laager. It was late, and most of the merchants' booths had been taken down and their goods stowed away – until, Alauda assumed, the following morning, when they would doubtless be trotted out again.

"I've never heard anyone sing like you," Alainn was saying.

He'd expostulated about the beauty of her rendition until, red-faced, she'd had to beg him to stop. "Then you need to go to the theatre more," Alauda muttered. "I'm nothing special."

"That's *kak*," the boy said fervently. "Begging your pardon, my lady, but you're extraordinary."

She cocked a skeptical eyebrow.

"An extraordinary singer," he amended rapidly. "And extraordinary in other ways too, of course."

Alauda laughed gently at his red-faced backing and filling. She was flattered – and more than that. There was something of reverence in his words, and not a hint of deception. That quiet, awed sincerity was the nicest compliment he could have paid her. "Thank you," she replied, not looking at him. "You've a fine ear yourself."

"I'm just a plodder on the strings," the boy insisted. "But you – you should be on the stage."

"I've *been* on the stage," she replied with a shiver, thinking of the theatre at Vitrafoss, and her impromptu duet with Elspeth. "It's harder than it looks."

"You make it look easy," Alainn smiled. "I'm serious, Alauda. You've a magnificent talent."

"I'm sure the fine folk of Buckhill would get sick of my highly varied repertoire of Ceorlinus, Ceorlinus, and yet more Ceorlinus, in pretty short order," she smiled. "And for an encore – well, maybe some Ceorlinus?"

He laughed.

"I'm not jesting, Alainn. I don't know any...any mining songs, or sea shanties, or whatever it is folk hereabouts like to listen to."

"What they listened to tonight was *you*," he said softly. "And I don't know if you noticed, but no one looked bored." He reached out and took her hand. When she didn't pull away, he raised it and pressed her fingers to his lips. "Least of all me."

Alauda's stomach rolled; something within her gurgled alarmingly. A terrible sense of foreboding was building up in her bosom. "Alainn –" she began.

He cut her off with a gentle squeeze. "I won't sully what for me was a perfect night by suggesting anything too forward," he smiled. "But I will say this: if you were sincere in what you asked the moons during your song, then you may rest assured that they've answered you, fairly and in full measure."

"That wasn't forward at all," Alauda replied, chuckling, tugging on his hand until he stopped walking and turned to face her. "In fact, it was so urbane as to be downright cryptic. Are you trying to tell me that tonight, the moons are not my only love?"

"Well, to put it bluntly," Alainn laughed, "yes. Yes. And not only for toni–"

That was as far as he got. Alauda put her hand on the back of his neck, pulled him forward, and kissed him.

It was everything she'd imagined it would be, and more; so much more. Her eyes closed, and time vanished into a warm, sensual blur. The moons could have risen and descended thrice for all she knew; all she was conscious of was the press of his lips against hers, the feel of his hands upon her hips, and the pressure of his coat-buttons against her breasts.

Alainn evidently felt it, too; he stumbled back a pace, dropping down into one of the furrows. Alauda stepped forward to compensate, rising up onto one of the ridge-rows. This changed their respective heights by close to a foot, with the result that she was now above and bending over him. Their altered postures proved eminently satisfactory, and she slid her free hand into his hair, grasping the roots between her fingers to keep him pinioned in place.

This of course left Alainn's hands free. It didn't take long before he found something interesting to do with them.

By the time they separated, it was as if an age of the world had passed in silent thunder and fire. Both were gasping. Golden eyes met green, and neither could look away.

Alainn was the first to recover his wits. He reached for her, his eyes wide with surprise. "My...my lady – "

Walk away! The voice that barked in Alauda's mind wasn't her mother's, but it might as well have been; it had her mother's commanding tone. *Walk away, girl; walk away now, or walk away never.* "No!" she gasped, holding up a hand, "no. No more, I beg you. I c-can't..."

"What's wrong?"

She shook her head, struggling to clear it. "Tomorrow, Alainn. Tomorrow."

He reached for her hand, and she stepped back, shaking; she couldn't trust herself, and she knew it. Every nerve in her body was screaming at her, demanding fulfilment. If once she allowed him to touch her, there would be only one way that the evening could end.

He nodded as if he understood. "Tomorrow, then," he said, sounding a little hoarse himself. "My love, I shall count the moments."

Alauda turned and stumbled away without answering him; there was nothing that she could have said that would not have been a heartfelt confession. Rather than betray herself, she fled.

By a supreme act of will she forced herself to put one foot in front of the other until she had made her escape. This left little scope for navigation, and it was not until a dog growled at her – Alauda and her parents did not own a dog – that she realized that she was ascending the steps of the wrong wagon.

She found the right wagon after a brief search, and treated herself to a good rinse of her face, neck, and ears at the rain barrel before slipping in through the half-opened door. Her parents were sound asleep. She undressed in the darkness, and climbed into her bunk.

She was exhausted, but that didn't help; not a jot. She spent the next stick staring at the wagon's ceiling and thinking about Alainn O'Dell – the taste of his lips, the touch of his hands – and how badly she'd wanted to trip him, force him back into the furrows, and show him in exquisite detail and at great length precisely what sort of trouble he'd gotten himself into.

Even Elspeth's pendant, once she remembered it, did not help her to sleep; if anything, the visions that it imparted only inflamed her further, until she was nearly frantic with need. And yet, with her parents snoring only a few feet from her left hand, there was nothing, nothing at all, that she could do about it.

She lay awake until the first gray fingers of morning clutched at night's blankets and began to draw them back. Only then did she drop into brief and fitful slumber.

♦

Ten

When she awoke her head was pounding with a combination of fatigue and, she suspected, too much drink. Alauda had overindulged in wine on occasion, so she knew what to do. Slipping noiselessly from her blankets so as not to wake her sleeping parents, she padded out of the wagon into the pre-dawn shadows, returned to the rain-barrel, and plunged her head into it down to the shoulders.

It was not a warm morning, and the combination of a wet head and a damp night-gown brought about an instant shiver. Back in the wagon she found a bathing-sheet and a block of rough soap. On reflection, she fumbled about in the darkness, trying to be silent, until she located her mother's herb-bag. She knew where the willow bark was kept. A short time later she was walking carefully between the wagon lines, dodging lowing oxen and sleepy horses, chewing a strip of bark against her headache.

She had decided that she needed to talk to Alacer. Night is for reflection, her mother always sais, while morning's light brings remorse. Alauda was deeply chagrined at her behaviour of the previous night. She needed to explain it, mostly to herself; and she needed, desperately needed, forgiveness.

She seemed to have two separate and parallel memories of her long walk with Alainn. In one stream, she recalled speaking with him at length about all manner of inconsequential things, none of which had anything to do with the mystery that the adolescent halpies had laid out for her. She'd *had* questions – she remembered that much – but she couldn't recall ever asking them. There was something about his easy manner, his quick wit, his turn of phrase, that completely disarmed her native caution.

In the other stream of memory, she recalled almost nothing at all – nothing, that is, but what the touch of his hand had felt like, and his lips, and how rapidly her heart had been beating beneath her chemise. She remembered singing with him – and, more importantly, *for* him, pouring every ounce of her love for music into the song she'd sung at his behest; a song which, in the whole enormous pantheon of her idol Ceorlinus' masterworks, was considered to be one of his most achingly perfect evocations of unrequited passion. She'd warbled like a demented thrush for a lad that scarcely knew – and the performance had left her as flushed and durvy as a mare in heat. She'd been the first to leap, not him – a fact that embarrassed her no end, and resulted in her muttering *Audax, audax!* under her breath as she dunked her head in the rain-barrel.

Torn between arousal and dismay, she'd scarcely slept a wink – and as a result of lack of sleep, her fevered brain had begun to entertain fantastical theories about what had happened to her. Had her mother not gone to great lengths to demonstrate her resistance to arcane enticements, Alauda might have begun to wonder whether Alainn had used magic to entrance her. In the cold light of morning, the notion was ludicrous; whatever else he might be, her new suitor was no wizard.

She had no choice but to face an unpalatable truth: that, contrary to all right and reason, she had fallen in love with Alainn O'Dell. Or at least in lust; she was sufficiently self-aware to acknowledge the fact of her yearning, even if she had no idea what to do about it.

Well – that wasn't entirely true, was it? There was *one* thing that she could do about it – the tried and tested, ages-old remedy for desire. Except that she couldn't do that. Absolutely not.

The mere thought of that delightful expedient brought the colour back to her cheeks, and she dunked her head again.

Hence, she decided as she flicked water from her dripping locks, the importance of baring her soul to Alacer. She wanted – no, she *needed* to apologize. She needed to be absolved. She'd allowed a golden-eyed stranger to seduce and man-handle her, and had only just stopped short of throwing herself to the grassy riverbank and pulling him atop her. There was something about Alainn, she now understood, that suited her like a hand suits a glove. His glance set her afire, his voice was like a caress, and his touch was simple ecstasy. She didn't understand it at all. It hadn't been anything like her usual wink-and-whisper; he hadn't winked even once at her, and after leaving Tonlees, they'd spoken of nothing but inconsequentialities. He'd entranced her with nothing more than his attentions, his smile, and his words. She wished that she could remember how he'd done it.

She shook her head vigorously, struggling to banish what few memories remained. That proved to be a mistake; it only made the throbbing worse.

To her vexation, Alacer's wagon, when she reached it, was empty. His parents were already abroad, and the boy himself was nowhere to be found. Alauda cast briefly about, hoping that he might merely have stepped away for a moment, but there was no sign of him. Frustrated, she carried on down to the river.

She mounted the bank between the river and the road only to find Alacer and Tonlees climbing it from the opposite direction. The two were chaffering and laughing. Both were freshly scrubbed; Tonlees' auburn hair was still so wet that it was nearly black. "There you are!" Alauda exclaimed. She trotted down the hill to meet them.

The pair halted. Alacer's mouth hung open; Tonlees looked blank at first, then smiled and waved. "We came by to fetch you a half-stick ago," she called, "but you were still snoring, drunken wretch you are. Alacer thought it might be dangerous to wake you."

"He was probably right." Alauda, without any preamble, put her arms about the silver-haired boy's waist and squeezed. "Good morrow, good lover."

Alacer hesitated, then grinned. "Good lover, good morrow!" he replied. It was a line from a play – one of Ceorlinus', naturally – that they'd recited together upon occasion.

"If you two break into song," Tonlees said, "then I'm leaving."

"I was going to tell you to scamper off anyway," Alauda chuckled, "so that I might have my lord here all to myself. But there's no point; I smell like a midden."

"Worse than that," Toni sniffed. "You still reek of that wretched perfume."

Alacer frowned. "Eh? What perfume?"

"She tried it last night," Tonlees shuddered. "*Ugh.* Some sort of halpie toilet-water, emphasis on 'toilet'. It made me want to vomit then, and I can still smell it on her."

"I don't smell anything," the boy frowned.

"That's a gallant lie," Alauda said, forcing a chuckle; she could still smell Alainn's gift on her wrists, though she thought it was wonderful. "I need no added scent to reek like a civet; that's the sad truth. I'm off to bathe." She gave his hand a squeeze. "Would you care to scrub my back, my love?"

"I can't. I'm helping with the scaffold and staging for the festival." He nodded at the brightening horizon. "And I'm already very late." He glanced briefly at Tonlees. "So we're all going together?"

"That's the plan," Alauda nodded. "Why not meet us at my wagon tonight, after sundown?"

"Done," Alacer said, relieved. "I'll take my leave of you – my lady."

Alauda turned went up on her tiptoes; Alacer gave her a brief peck on the cheek. Alauda was having none of that; she seized his ears and kissed his mouth with enough force and passion to knock him back a step.

A part of her mind wondered – briefly – how much of her desire was genuine, and how much of it feigned, a consequence of chagrin or regret at having kissed Alainn much the same way only a few sticks earlier. Another part told the first part to hold its wagging tongue, and mind its own *bekakt* business. She decided to listen to the second part, and allowed her misguided misgivings to be bowled over by the delicious heat of the moment.

When at last she broke their embrace and Alacer could breathe again, he said, "What was that about?"

"That, my lord," she replied, whispering into his ear, "was about a week of unsatisfied longing. I ache for tonight!"

Alacer smiled again, prying her arms gently away from his neck. "So do I. But I've very late, Ala."

As he walked away, Toni muttered, "You 'ache'?"

"I was being poetic," Alauda protested.

"He *must* love you, then," the older girl said, "because that was dreadful. And your breath smells worse than the rest of you."

Alauda stuck out her tongue.

Tonlees, having nothing better to do for the moment, accompanied Alauda to the river. She perched on a convenient stone, listening to Alauda's chatter and tossing the block of soap when the younger girl called out for it.

There was no need for Toni to contribute to the conversation; Alauda, keyed up and giggling after finally being able to see her beloved, furnished more than enough banter for the both of them. She decided not to mention her various indiscretions with Alainn; the sight of Alacer's cloud-grey eyes had driven the memory of them entirely from her mind. The feel of his lips, his hands, were like a tonic, banishing unmentionable might-have-beens into the depths of what now seemed like a fog-filled dream.

They returned to the wagons together, Tonlees – as usual – tagging along in Alauda's wake. Alauda had brought a bundle of clothing, and dressed at the water's edge, as simply as she could get away with, in chemise, skirt, and cote. As they approached Alauda's rolling home, however, they slowed. A pair of Halflings was waiting just at the wagon's tail.

Two men – short ones. Halflings. Alauda's eyes narrowed; she recognized one of them. His long coat, neck-cloth, and elaborate side-whiskers were burned into her memory.

He evidently recognized her as well. "The archer!" he exclaimed, grinning happily.

"The charlatan," Alauda replied without expression. "What can I do for you, *Sieur* Curmagh?"

"I – we – have come to meet your mother," the fellow replied, grinning all the more broadly at her insult. "Word has gone 'round; a wizard of the College has come to Buckhill. Mhaister Cloughsen and I were hoping for a word with her."

Alauda nodded. To the second of the two men, she executed a deep curtsey. "Mhaister Cloughsen, a pleasure," she said. "You would be the lo…th-th-the lore…"

Her voice trailed off. She was staring at his feet.

Cloughsen, the Lore-speaker, was a Halfling of middling height, which meant that the top of his head lay somewhere near Alauda's lips. While her co-conspirators had described him as a scholar, he didn't look especially old; his face was only a little lined, and his hair was still mostly brown, with only the slightest hints of grey at the temples. He was dressed far more simply than his comrade, in a loose shirt and snug trews with a simple leather coat thrown over all. Like the rest of the Halflings Alauda had met, he was barefoot.

Which was where Alauda's difficulty lay. Cloughsen's feet were...*not*. Not feet – or at least not the sort of feet she'd come to expect from Halflings. Or mortals in general. Protruding from the cuffs of the Mhaister's trousers were warty, pale bird's feet, complete with talons – three long, flesh-coloured, wrinkly toes facing to the front, and one to the rear, each tipped with a curving scimitar claw as long as Alauda's index finger.

Cloughsen must have been used to the scrutiny. "The answers to your questions, dear girl," the Lore-speaker chuckled, his *elvii* all but unaccented, "are 'no', 'yes', 'I was cursed', and once more 'no'."

Tonlees was standing stock still, her hands over her mouth. Alauda blinked. "My questions, I take it," she said slowly, "are 'Are you part bird', 'Is this magic', 'How did it happen', and...er, 'Have you tried to break the spell'?"

"Capital!" Cloughsen exclaimed. "Capital! Oh, I hope your mother's as clever as you."

"No one," Alyssa said drily from the wagon's door, "is as clever as my daughter. Or as clever as she thinks she is, at any rate."

Alauda felt her cheeks redden. She clamped her mouth shut, mostly to avoid saying anything she might later regret.

"Ah!" Curmagh cried. "Magistatrix Volo!" He swept his arms wide, and bowed so deeply that Alauda thought his nose might touch his knees. Cloughsen followed suit, though Alauda noted that he seemed to be staring at her, rather than her mother, as he bowed.

" 'Madam Volo' will suffice," Alyssa said, scowling in bemusement at the spectacle of the two miniature gentlemen bobbing on her threshold. "You sent the note, I take it?"

"I did," the Bridle-bearer nodded. "Madam – *Domina* Volo, we stand in sore need of a scholar's wisdom."

"You can keep your '*domina*' too, Sirrah," the wizard said coolly. "And if it's wisdom you seek, you'd do better to pester a scholar. I'm a housewife."

"A housewife who attended the College of Stars," Cloughsen said smoothly. "We beg you, lady – a moment of your time? A moment only!"

Alyssa rolled her eyes, but nodded. She disappeared into the wagon, beckoning the pair to follow her.

Curmagh ascended the steps at once. Before Cloughsen could follow, Alauda seized him by the elbow. When he glanced up at her, surprised, she said tersely, "Why wouldn't you try to break the curse?"

The Lore-speaker grinned. "My dear girl," he said softly, "have you any idea how useful a hawk's feet can be?"

Alauda thought about that. "Er..."

"Besides, my wife is fond of eggs," Cloughsen added with a wink. He trotted up the steps, talons clacking on the wood, and ducked into the wagon.

Tonlees stared after him, her eyes bugging out. "Eggs?" she squeaked.

Alauda was too busy snickering to reply.

"*Hsst!*"

She glanced to the left. To her surprise – and delight – Alainn was waving at her from behind a neighbouring wagon. Alauda's breath caught in her throat. Lifting her skirts, she ran over to him, seizing his hands in her own. "Good morrow, good lover," she whispered, putting her lips to his cheek. All thoughts of Alacer had vanished from her head.

Alainn missed the musical cue. "Hullo, my lady Lark," he replied, giving her fingers a gentle squeeze. "Are you ready for some mischief?"

Alauda leaned back, raising a playful eyebrow. "Just what did you have in mind, Sirrah?"

"We're paying a visit to the Lore-speaker's wagon while he's occupied with your lady mother. Remember?"

"Ah." *Right – that.* "Fine," she sighed, "lead the way."

He did, taking her hand into the bargain. That almost made up for the disappointment. Alauda felt the colour rising in her cheeks, and did her best to fight it back down. What *was* it about him?

As they crossed the dirt track to the Halfling side of the field, he gave her a sidelong glance. "I found something for you. May I give it to you?"

His fingers were stiff in hers; she could tell that he was nervous. It was charming. "If you like," Alauda nodded.

Alainn fumbled in his pocket, then pressed something into her hand. Alauda stared, puzzled. When she realized what it was, she twitched violently, and very nearly dropped it.

It was a roll of ribbon; scarlet ribbon, about as wide as her thumb. "Where did you get this?" she gasped.

"Mistress Peony," he said, perturbed. "She's a seamstress, and knows your customs. She told me all high elven ladies receive one as a gift from – well, from gentlemen who want to court them." His brows drew together. "Why? Don't you like it?"

Alauda was having difficulty breathing; it was a moment before she could speak. When she could manage to get words past the knot in her larynx, her voice was a bare squeak. "It's a *virga!*"she squealed. "You can't give me *this!*"

Alainn frowned. "What? Why not?"

"Don't you know what a *virga* is?!" She glanced around – then, for lack of any better ideas, she stuffed the roll of ribbon into her crumena.

"Well, no," he frowned. "I mean, I've seen elven ladies wearing them; everyone has. You tie them around your waist, and to the shoulder, too." He tapped her right shoulder with a finger.

"That's because they're affianced!" Alauda hissed. "You…you ninny! The *virga lætitia* is a betrothal gift! Women wear it to show all comers that they've been invited to a life-mating, and have said *yes!*" Her hands were shaking again. *Damn* the boy!

Alain frowned. "Oh. Sorry, I didn't know." He blinked several times…then his face went white. "Oh! Oh, Powers below!"

"Well said, sir," Alauda muttered, staring at him – and vaguely amused by his sudden and obvious discomfiture. "That's what *every* girl likes to hear from her fiancée; 'Powers below!'"

"I'm not – we're not –" he stammered. "I – I wasn't asking!"

"Good, because I certainly wasn't saying 'yes'!"

His consternation was so obvious that Alauda couldn't even keep up a pretense of anger. "Of course," she said with a coy smile, tweaking his nose gently, "I wasn't saying 'no', either."

"Oh," he said. "Oh, well…well, that's good, then."

She patted her pocket. "You won't see me wearing this tonight, though," she chuckled. "That's for sure and certain. After all, we've only known each other a day! What manner of loose-kneed strumpet falls in love so quickly, *heya?*"

Yes, her traitor mind asked. *That's the question, isn't it?*

Alauda strangled her carping conscience. They held hands all the way to the opposing wagon lines. Tonlees followed in their wake, watching the oddly matched couple with a peculiar look on her face.

Breaghan, Fearghan, and another girl were waiting in the Halfling's camp. The third Halfling – fourth, including Alainn – was taller than the other two, though still a good hand-span shorter than Alauda or Alainn. She came up to the bridge of Alauda's nose.

"My lady," Alainn said with a bow, "may I introduce Sîol – our captain."

The taller girl stuck out a hand. "Sîol falt-Ruadh," she said. Her accent was thick; she pronounced her given name 'Shoal'.

"That means 'true-redhead', doesn't it?" Alauda chuckled. "I believe it."

The girl was as pale as Breaghan was swarthy, with a spray of freckles across each cheek and a mass of tangled, knotted locks pushed back behind her ears. Her hair was what the dwarves called 'forge-dim', a deep red shade that was closer in hue to Tonlees' auburn tresses than to the mass of near-orange curls that Renvig, Lady Elspeth's junior disciple, had proudly displayed. Sîol wore tight leather trousers, a thin chemise of gray linen, and a brown coat with a collar of sheep's wool. Her feet were also bare – and they were only twice the size of Alauda's own. For a Halfling, the elf-girl mused, that was practically dainty.

"Aye," Sîol nodded. "And you'd be Alauda the Lark. The woodsy-witch, *heya*?"

Alauda turned to stare at Alainn. " 'Woodsy-witch'? What in the World Made have you been telling people about me?"

"Nothing, my lady, nothing!" the boy swore.

"Bollocks," the elf-girl sniffed. "You told her about the singing, didn't you?"

"He didn't have to tell anybody about that," Fearghan growled. "You've got a penetrating voice, 'my lady'. They probably heard you in Skywaters." He reached up and punched Alainn sharply in the arm. "Well done, Al."

Sîol took Alauda's hand. "Dinna worry. Our Alainn is dumb with lust for ye, and no mistake." She winked solemnly. "Just don't wander you too far from the crowds on his arm, me girl, lest ye'd have yer legs in the air, an' yer bare arse in the dirt."

Alauda blinked. She'd been enjoying Sîol's idiomatic performance when the import of her words sank in. "Thank you. For the advice."

"Free advice be worth what ye pay fer it," the redhead shrugged. "Ye ought to have figured yer pretty Alainn out for yerself. Now…how do ye be with the arts o'magic?"

"I've no skill with magic at all," the elf-girl said stiffly. "I presume pretty Alainn told you that much. And for the love of all the Powers," she added with some asperity, "would you leave off nattering like a *kak*-heeled country bumpkin? No one in all the wide world really talks like that. Not off the stage, anyway."

"Spoken like a true scion of the Duodeci," Sîol said with a grin, her accent suddenly as clear and her diction as cultured as Alauda's own. "Thou'rt a veritable daughter of the Third House, Fell-Handed Dior's true-born get: 'fierce ire, proud eye, heart o'fire, head high'! No?"

Ceorlinus again. "That's better," Alauda snorted, amused despite herself. They could turn the flood of meaningless banter on and off at will, it seemed; all of them. *All of them but Alainn,* she amended hastily. "And yes, I am; Third House, I mean."

"Come on along, then, and follow me," Sîol said with an evil grin. "Magic or no, me darlin', mayhap we'll find some use for'ee."

"If she doesn't give over with that ridiculous brogue," Alauda murmured to Alainn, "you're going to need a new captain."

"She's just doing it to annoy you," the boy whispered, winking. "She wants to know how much of a prig you are. Ignore it and she'll stop – eventually."

She shot him a dubious glance. " 'Eventually'?"

"It might take a while," he confessed. "Sîol really likes annoying people. Especially your people. Elves."

"Wonderful," Alauda sighed. "If I happened to stab her by accident, would you miss her?"

Alainn grinned and squeezed her hand. Then, glancing around to ensure that no-one was watching, he leaned over and kissed her ear. Alauda forgot about the redhead's irritating affectation almost at once.

The Lore-speaker's wagon differed only in decoration from those of the rest of the Halfling camp. It was wrought of some dark wood – walnut, Alauda thought, stroking the polished planks appreciatively – and had been scored with a hot iron in all manner of weird, cabalistic symbols: moons and stars, hooves and antlers, strange runes and whorls, and twisted, toothy smiles. The very sight of them gave her pause; they made the small hairs stand up on the back of her neck. Some of the symbols, she realized, were eerily similar to those she'd seen on the standing stones.

Sîol didn't seem to mind the wagon's adornments; she trotted gamely up the steps and threw open the door as though she owned the vehicle. "You first, Lady Lark," she grinned. "Here we make trial of your storied wisdom."

"My name is Alauda," the elf-girl snapped.

Sîol bowed her apology, motioning to Alauda to precede her into the vehicle's interior.

Cloughsen's wagon was a horrid mess; Alauda's first impression was that even her order-obsessed mother would have needed a month or more to set things to rights. All manner of oddments lay scattered about. She saw cups and bowls, charts and scrolls, bits of bone and metal, a bent sword, a score of odd, silvery quills; books and blankets, lamps and candles and a lantern that burnt brightly, but that had no reservoir for oil, and was not even warm.

The strangest thing that Alauda remarked, though, was the architecture that held up the oiled canvas roof. The wooden beams were well-made, polished – and scratched. Badly scratched. She wondered whether Cloughsen owned a large bird of some sort – and then she remembered his feet.

"He sleeps upside-down now," Sîol explained in response to her questioning glance. "Hanging from the rafters, like a bloody bat."

"It's a little unnerving," Alainn added, "when you have to bring him a message, or his dinner."

"Yes, I imagine it would bother his mate," Alauda allowed. She swallowed convulsively. *Eggs indeed!*

"He's got no mate," Sîol sighed. "His wife's gone to wind, seventeen summers since. Like all of them; all in the same strike. The same day the Mhaister got his funny feet, that was."

Alauda turned to stare at the redhead. "What are you talking about?"

"Didn't Alainn tell you?"

"Tell me what?"

Sîol scrubbed her face with one hand. "We dinna have time for this," she said harshly. The accent, Alauda noticed, was back; maybe that was how the girl truly spoke. "Briefly: seventeen summers ago, we were all north and east of Porta' – you know, the city in the plains? East of here?"

"Portacaminus," Alauda nodded. "I know it. Go on."

"There's not all that much to go on about," Sîol shrugged. "We must've broken some law o'hern, b'cause the Midnight Shadow fell on us, and ruined us. Burnt the wagons, and killed one in three, woman, man, and child. Only one to stand against'er was Cloughsen." She shuddered. "She could've et'im, I suppose; instead, she cursed him. Made'im like what you see. Gave'm 'is birdy-feet."

The elf-girl frowned. "The 'Midnight Shadow'? What in the World Made is a…a…" She clapped her hands to her mouth. "*Aiyah!* Do you mean *Umbranoctis*?" she gaped. "The dragon, Shadow-of-Midnight?!"

"Say *heya*," Sîol nodded soberly. "The azure wyrm. Call'er what you like; her true name's Tychsyrreth."

"I know her name!" Alauda shrieked. "Nobody told me you were attacked by a *dragon!*"

"It was a long time ago. These days there's not much to say about it, other than that it happened." Sîol looked bleak. "There's not a family among us what wasn't death-struck. Fearghan's mum and da' perished that day, and the same fate befell poor, lovely Alainn. An' Breaghan's brother." She looked at her feet for a moment. "And my sister, Looly. My ma', too."

"Powers above!" Alauda said faintly.

"No Powers stood above us *that* day," Sîol said, suddenly solemn. Her accent had disappeared again. She whistled, and Alauda heard boots on the wagon's steps. "We all learned an important rule, my lady: when a dragon is angry it doesn't matter why; all that matters is being somewhere else."

Sound advice, Alauda thought. The pair waited while Fearghan, Breaghan, Alainn, and finally Tonlees crowded into the wagon bed. Toni had to stoop to get through the door.

When everyone was watching, Sîol threw back a heap of skins and blankets, revealing a chest. "He keeps it in there," she said. "The urn, I mean. I only saw it the once."

Alauda squatted before the wooden crate. The thing was finely made, polished…and locked. Not a padlock; an internal mechanism. "Who has a *scalpo*?" she asked, squinting at the tiny keyhole.

When no one said anything, the elf-girl looked up. "Are you telling me," she said softly, "that in this covey of confidence artists, pick-pockets, and outright thieves, not a one amongst you has a set of lock-picks, and knows how to use it?"

At once, Sîol, Breaghan, and Fearghan dug in their pockets – in Sîol's case, it was the top of her boot – and produced small packets of metal implements.

Alauda turned her iron gaze on Alainn. He looked uncomfortable. "Not I, my lady," he murmured at last. "I'm – er, not very good at this sort of thing."

The elf-girl's scowl broke, and she smiled. "I knew there was something I liked about you."

She turned back to the others. "Right. I've no doubt that most of you are better at this than me. Get it open." She shuffled out of the way, leaving the front of the chest clear.

"We've tried," Sîol protested. "We got the lock, but it still won't open. Cloughsen's bewitched it. That's why we need *you*. Somebody who knows magic!"

"Who told you that?" Alauda snarled. "Bardan's ball-sack! How many times do I have to say it? Just because I'm *elvii*, it doesn't mean I'm a bloody wizard!"

"But we can't even *touch* it!" Fearghan growled. "I've tried! It feels…it's like being bitten!"

"And you want *me* to touch it?" Alauda shook her head. "That's the stupidest thing I've ever…*gah*! All right; all right. I don't know what you're all on about, but…all right." She clenched her fingers several times, then laid a hand upon the chest.

The wood felt smooth, smooth and cool beneath her fingers. It had been sanded and buffed, and beautifully polished. Still, there was something elemental about it – something ancient and pure. Alauda stretched out with her senses, trying to smell the wood, to taste it, to...to –

– the heat of the flames seared her as she leapt through them, soaring high above the burning logs, feeling the sand crunch between her toes as she landed on the far side of the bonfire. She pivoted at once, laughing, and flung herself into the flames once more, glorying in the kiss of destruction against her bare flesh, shrieking the words of the songs along with her clan-mates. When one of them passed her a wooden bowl she drank deep, feeling the familiar sting of the kesko *in her throat. And when she stumbled, and one of the warriors caught her, she threw her arms about his neck and kissed him; and together they stumbled off into the shadows, and there in the darkness she lay back and welcomed him – his heat the fire's heat, her pounding heart the heart of the doe, as her stag mounted her, and thrust and thrust and thrust –*

The heat, the fire, built within her until a white shriek of lust and fury exploded from her heart. Flame, verdant and sweet, burst from her fingers, blowing back the lid of the chest with a sibilant *crack*.

At the same instant, Tonlees shrieked – and Alauda came back to herself, hauled from the depths of gut-clenching fantasy by sheer force of will. *A spell*, she thought, her hands shaking; *a glamer, nothing more.* Something to frighten off an incautious burglar, perhaps.

Her lifebeat was racing, and her belly felt hot and tight; clearly her instincts disagreed with her intellect. Had it truly been fantasy? She wondered about that. The sensations, the traditions, had been so similar to those of the *Suku Gagak* that they might easily have seen her own adopted people in the eye of her mind. And it had felt real, so very real; she could still feel the fire's heat upon her flesh, the taste of the *kesko* upon her tongue, the stiffness in her thighs...and the deep, pleasurable ache in her loins.

"*Cad é sin?*" Breaghan gasped.

"*Ciúin!*" Sîol barked. "Lady Lark – are ye in there?" She put a hand on Alauda's shoulder.

The elf-girl took a deep, shuddering breath. "My name is...is Alauda," she said unsteadily.

"What'd ye do?"

"What do you mean?"

Sîol was pointing at the chest. The lid had flown open...and looked different. So did the chest itself. So, for that matter, did a good deal of the surrounding papers, books, instruments, carpets, wine-skins...

They were, all of them, covered with some sort of dark, thick shadow. Alauda reached out and touched it. It was cool, fuzzy...and full of life.

Moss?

More than just the chest had been touched. Splashes and blots of lichen coated the carpets, and tiny, blind mushrooms sprouted from the wood of the wagon floor. Tiny tendrils waved amid the flora – shoots of vines. The sight of them growing, quickly and eagerly, made her shiver.

"Ala, what did you *do*?" Tonlees murmured, drawing back a little.

Alauda had no answer to offer. She stared at her hands, but saw nothing unusual about them. She shook her head. "It's just moss," she muttered. "It comes from the Green. There's nothing – nothing dangerous about it."

Tell that to the lions you killed, her conscience prodded. Her hands began to shake, and she clenched them together to still them. She could feel the Green pressing in upon her, seeking an outlet for its irresistible might. Try as she might to forget the Horned God, he was always there.

"Nothing dangerous, maybe, but it's a right mess," Sîol growled. She dove into the chest, emerging a moment later with an armload of blankets. She placed these on the floor and unwrapped them, revealing a beautiful porcelain urn. The thing was white and shapely, with bright blue highlights, and gold scroll-work around the mouth and base. And it was old; a fine, web-like intaglio of cracks scored the glaze.

The moment she saw it, Alauda stiffened. So did Tonlees.

"What is it?" Sîol demanded.

The elf-girls pointed simultaneously. "Look at the ornaments!" Tonlees exclaimed. "A stag's head on one side, and a bent bow on the other? It's a funerary urn! *Their* funerary urn!"

"What do the markings have to do with it?" the Halfling frowned.

Alauda ran her fingers over the enamel. "Arx Cervus, remember? 'The Fortress of the Stag'? The stag's head is Fineleor's sigil – and the bent bow is the mark of House Antaíssin. It's simple heraldry."

The Halflings stared at her blankly.

She sighed. "You didn't study heraldry in schola?"

"What's 'skola'?" Alainn asked, puzzled.

"That's about what I thought." Alauda bit her lip. "Right. What's in it?"

"Not ash," Sîol said. She plucked the lid from the costly thing and up-ended it. A trickle of black dust mixed with corroded silver coins poured into her palm.

Alauda plucked one of the coins from the mess and inspected it. It was identical to the victory coin she'd been shown before. On a whim she tucked it into the pocket of her dress. "No wonder it's empty. Fineleor and Anja died a long way from here, in the pass west of Arx Vespertinus. Their bodies were brought back to Starmeadow, and they were sent to wind together in the Eternal Grove."

The Halfling's brow furrowed. "Hang on," she said. "I thought they stayed behind, so their army could escape, and fell together? Isn't that the legend?"

"Yes." Alauda nodded. "So?"

"So, who brought their bodies back?"

The elf-girl's nose wrinkled. "A dwarf. History remembers him as Folgest. 'The Deed of Anja and Fineleor', a song about their fall, says, 'Folgest the dwarf, their staunchest friend / stood at their side at their journey's end / and rather than lay them in foreign loam / he gathered them up, and he brought them home'."

"Folgest, eh?" Sîol mused. She flicked the urn with a finger; it rang softly, like a muted bell. "Never heard that part."

"It wasn't his real name," Alauda said. "Just ignorance on the part of my countrymen, I'm afraid. It's a contraction of *folcgestealla*, a dwarven word that means 'war-companion'."

"What was his true name, then?" Alainn asked.

He was watching her closely. Alauda felt his eyes, and shivered with delight. "Nobody knows," she replied. "There's no record of it." She touched the urn again. "Unless...maybe we'll find something out at the castle. Arc Cervus was the last place that Fineleor visited before he made the journey to the east, to meet his beloved, and face Gryshgranax, and perish."

She nodded at the urn. "Where are the markings you traced?"

"You have to feel for them," Sîol replied. She took Alauda's hand and ran her fingers over the cool porcelain.

There were raised characters beneath the glaze. They were all but invisible, but the ridges in the porcelain could be felt easily enough.

Alauda's heart began to hammer with anticipation. The court dialect was complicated, but it was still only a dialect of the *elvii* tongue; she could puzzle it out without difficulty. The letters beneath Alauda's fingers became words, and she spoke them aloud for the benefit of her comrades.

> *In the sixth year of the war, Count Fineleor of House Orkarel, the wise, the master of Arx Cervus, the general, put down the mutiny, and placed loyal soldiers in charge of Kulkisari's Well. And then he prepared himself for war, taking sword and bow in hand. But before departing, having made his vows unto his ancestors, he gave his beloved Anja's dowry – the fruit of his life's work – into the care of his loyal friend, concealing it with great and mighty magicks, so that upon their return they might celebrate their love, and be wed.*

Alauda sat back on her haunches, thinking. "It's real," she breathed. "I don't believe it! This urn, and the coins within it…they'd fetch a prince's ransom! King Callaýian would shower you with your own weight in gold if you were to return them to him in Starmeadow. Even more, if you brought news of where to find old Fineleor's trove." She glanced at Sîol, and grinned slightly. "You're pretty small, the lot of you. He'd probably pay you your whole family's weight in gold."

"Maybe," the Halfling said, dubious. "But wouldn't he be happier still if we brought him the whole of Anja's dowry?"

"I don't doubt it," Alauda shrugged. "But I still can't see how you're – we're – going to get our hands on it in the first place. What part of 'concealed by great and mighty magicks' didn't you understand?"

"That's why we're bringing you," Sîol winked.

"The you're bringing the wrong Volo," the elf-girl exclaimed. "I don't know any magic, mighty or otherwise!"

"I beg to differ," the Halfling snickered. "None of us was able to open that chest, but you got it open in less time than it took to say 'duck your head'."

Alauda glanced at the moss-covered wood. She wouldn't be trying that sort of thing again; not any time soon. "I don't know what happened," she muttered. "I have no idea what that spell-trap was supposed to do. If it was supposed to stop an interloper, then why didn't it…I don't know, put me to sleep, or stiffen my limbs, or even freeze my heart?" There were too many questions; too many. "Why don't you just go to the Lore-speaker?" she demanded at last.

"Because he's had that urn for the better part of a year," Sîol said contemptuously, "and he and Bree's da' are no nearer the treasure today than we were when we got here! Someone has to take this thing seriously!"

"Hmm," Alauda grunted. "And what about the new lord of the manor? Sieur Plowbrace, wasn't it? Why not approach him with your problem?"

"Because he's a stinking human!" Fearghan snarled. "A human from the Empire! They hate us. Anything he found would end up in Norkhan – like as not to buy arrows to be shot back at us!" He stabbed a finger in Alauda's direction. "And at you! They're no fonder of elves, you know."

"It's not just Lord Alfaric," Sîol said, making a calming gesture in the agitated lad's direction. "It's his mate. You know why he was exiled, don't you?"

"Because he married a Gasparri mage, no?" Alauda frowned. "What's that got to do with it?"

"She's not just a mage," the redhead said. "She was one of the Magisters of the College of the Eye."

"Magistatrix," Alauda corrected.

"Whatever. They're all fiend-worshippers, evil through and through. If we went to her, she'd hang us by the heels so she could flay the hides from us, for no reason other than entertainment with her afternoon tea."

"That's nonsense!"

"Spoken like a true child of privilege," Sîol snorted. "Magi hate our kind."

"Cut-purses and pick-pockets? I can't imagine why," Alauda snorted. "You have no idea what you're talking about. My mother's worked with magi from the College of the Eye before. They're a little...oh, I don't know – grim, I suppose. But they're not a bunch of blood-thirsty, whip-wielding lunatics. And they're certainly not evil." She shuddered. "I'd liefer put myself in their hands than those of the ghouls at the College of Bone, in Eldarcanum. And they're elves, mostly."

"You're fooling yourself," Sîol said darkly. "Lady Nidlo drinks the blood of the righteous. At all costs, we need to steer clear of her."

"You *could* steer clear of her, and easily," Alauda reminded them, "by giving up this idiotic plan."

"Never!" Sîol snapped. "And we can't do it without you!"

Alainn leaned forward and put a hand on her wrist. His touch was electric, and Alauda jumped. "Please, my lady," he breathed. "We *need* you."

That was not what Alauda heard; she heard '*I* need you'. Her stag stood before her in the clearing, beautiful and strong, calling to her with his eyes – waiting for her to run for him, that he might take her in the chase, their hearts pounding together.

She missed the next several sentences, lost in a rose-coloured haze.

"And," Breaghan was saying when Alauda regained her equanimity, "don't forget who you are. Fineleor locked away his treasure until he could be with his one true love – and you bear her name."

"That's just a coincidence!" Alauda objected. "That was my mother's idea, a homage because before our link to the Solostyriannii, House Volo used to be a –"

"– a cadet line of House Antaíssin," Sîol finished. "You're not the only folk who study history, you know. Hells, Larkie, you're practically Anja's heir! She never lived to receive her dowry. I'd say that treasure's yours as much as anybody's!"

"How do you figure? I'm certainly not marrying Fineleor! If a treasure of such historical import is going to go to anyone," Alauda said, deeply furious, "then it's going to Starmeadow, to the care of the king!"

"Fine," Sîol shrugged. "If that's the price for your aid – we accept."

Alauda stared at the smaller girl from beneath lowered brows. "Are you trying to tell me," she sputtered, "that you – a crowd of halpie pick-pockets, thieves and confidence men if ever I saw one! – are planning to loot Arx Cervus of a treasure guarded by 'an ancient sorrow', and by life and death, too, whatever that means…and then, after going through all of that, you're actually going to turn any plunder you find over to the Elvenking?!" She gave an amused snort. "Pull the other one!"

"Why wouldn't we?" Sîol shrugged. "You really don't understand us at all, do you? It's not about the money; it's never about the money! It's a rite of passage." She glanced down at her jacket front. "I may not look like much to you, but I'm on the cusp of coming of age. If I can pull this off now, before I'm legal in years, my name'll be legend. And so will all of theirs." She nodded at her cohort. "And so, Lady Lark, will yours."

Alauda glanced at the others. Fearghan looked sullen, Breaghan hopeful. And Alainn…

She jerked her eyes away from his smiling face. If she wanted to be able to think rationally, she had to…to not…

…*kak*. She swallowed heavily, crossing her arms. "The last thing I want," she said firmly, "is anyone knowing that I, or anyone of my name, was associated with you lot. If I agree to help you, you forget me. And you swear – on your lives! – that the treasure goes back to the Realm. I'll have your word on that, before I agree to one more breath of this…this lunacy!"

Sîol held up her right hand. "I swear, before Cham's own face, that every scrap of treasure we find will be returned to the Realm." She glanced over her shoulder at her comrades. "This binds you lot too, by the way. So says your captain. Accord?"

The other three nodded in unison. "Accord," they echoed.

Alauda sighed, shaking her head. "Fine," she sighed. "And may Hara *Sophus* forgive me."

"I'm not sure the god of wisdom is the right one to be praying to at the moment," Toni murmured, looking aghast.

"Nor am I," Alauda replied in a whisper. "But as there's no patron deity for suicidally reckless imbeciles…"

Her voice trailed off; Alainn was smiling at her again. She shivered, and returned his grateful wink with one of her own.

"Excellent!" Sîol rubbed her hands together briskly. "Right, here's how it'll go. We'll all attend the festival tonight, and drink and dance with our betters. Go easy on the wine, by the way; Arx Cervus is no lark. There'll be a spot of climbin'.

"When the time's right – say, just at moons'-set – we'll all meet at the westernmost wagon, with whatever we need, and we'll make for the fortress. An hour to walk there, and we'll still have most of the night to find Kulkisari's well, whatever that might be, and pinch old Fineleor's bundle." She held out her hand. "Agreed?"

Alauda took it and gave it a firm shake. "Agreed." After a sharp glance, Tonlees did the same, followed by the other three Halflings.

"*Aontaithe*," Sîol said, when all had sworn. "Equal partners, equal shares of glory – and all of Fineleor's treasure, every last groat of it, to the Elvenking. So it is promised; so shall it be done." She broke out into a broad smile. "And now, ladies and gentlemen – we've only a few sticks left to make us ready for the night's revels. I don't know about you, but it'll take me most of that to do something with this rat's- nest." She put a hand to her tangled braids.

The new-forged conspiracy piled out of the Lore-speaker's wagon. Before they left, Sîol and Alauda did their best to set everything to rights – or at least to return the mess to its original state. "What about the moss?" the elf-girl asked, deeply worried.

Sîol shrugged. "Nothing to do about it now. Not enough time to try to scrape it away, and we'd never get it all." She smiled wickedly. "Do you think we should fire the wagon."

"No!" Alauda exclaimed, appalled.

"Then I'm all out of ideas," the Halfling shrugged. "Look at it this way: he's a Lore-speaker, odd things must happen in there all the time. We didn't take anything, and we put everything back where we found it. I'm sure he'll hardly even notice."

"You're very confident about that," Alauda grumped.

Sîol shrugged again. "No sense worrying yourself into the grave; you'll get there soon enough. Well…maybe not you and your elfy friend, but the rest of us, surely."

"Surely," Alauda said drily. *Probably at the end of a rope.* She glanced at the rising Lantern, estimating the time. "We have to go."

"Remember the plan," Sîol cautioned. "And have fun tonight. Remember – it's a party." Then she too turned and walked off.

Alauda and Tonlees walked back to their own wagons together. "Remember *our* plan, too," the younger girl said. "Alacer's coming to fetch me at my wagon, so you should meet us there. That way, we'll all be able to arrive together."

"If you say so," Tonlees said, looking dubious. "Ala – are you sure about this? The castle, and this Well thing?"

Alauda made a face. "Of course not. There's something damned odd about it. What sort of spell was on that chest anyway?"

"You said you didn't know," Toni reminded her. "Why, what happened?"

Alauda didn't quite know what to say. "Er...what did *you* see?"

"Not much," the older girl said. "You touched it, and your eyes closed. Then you started breathing heavily, gasping almost – and then, bang! The chest was open, and that...that mossy stuff was everywhere."

Alauda blinked. "That's it? That's all that happened?"

Toni nodded. "Why, what did you see?"

"It's not important," the younger girl averred. "But that's sort of my point. If that was supposed to be a magical trap...well, I've read all about them, in mother's book. It should have burned me, or blinded me, or something like that. Not...not show me things."

"What did it –"

"Not important!" Alauda exclaimed. "It just...it doesn't make any sense."

Tonlees uttered an exasperated sputter, not unlike a boiling kettle. "None of this makes any sense!" she exclaimed. "The whole thing's insane! Ancient urns, ancient-er coins, a hidden treasure from before the Eon of Darkness..." She shook her head. "I think you should tell your mother."

"No," Alauda said flatly.

"Why not?"

"Just – just no." The younger girl cast her friend a pleading look. "Please, Toni – don't say anything." All that she could think of was her mother putting a stop to the plan – and that she, Alauda, would be responsible for letting down her comrades. More importantly, for breaking her promise to Alainn.

Tonlees stared at her. "Fine!" she said at last. "Fine! But if you die on me again, I'm going to...to...I'm going to sing off-key at your funeral!"

"Some threat," Alauda sniffed. "Like you've ever sung *on*-key. Look, if I die, you can have Alacer. All right?"

To her surprise, Toni didn't laugh. The older girl was staring at the ground. "What's wrong?" Alauda demanded.

"Don't joke about that," Toni whispered. "Please – don't ever –"

Alauda's laughter tinkled brightly. "Gods, show some spirit!" she exclaimed, linking her arm through her friend's. "It's Second Spring, the morbannens are blooming, and we're a pair of beautiful virgins, all ready to be worshipped by legions of adoring men."

"If you say so," Tonlees said dourly.

"I *do* say so," Alauda said happily. "Oh, Toni – this is going to be a night like no other!" Her spirits were still bubbling over. Were it not for the likelihood of yanking her friend off her feet, she would have been skipping.

"That's what I'm afraid of," the older girl said, looking a little grey.

◆

Eleven

The afternoon passed in a blur as Alauda, normally not the most fastidious of girls, indulged frantically in every conceivable form of preparation for the evening's festivities. Her mother, recognizing the symptoms, did her best to keep out of the path of what was in essence a small, black-haired whirlwind. By the time the Lantern was dipping toward the eastern horizon, Alauda was feeling faint with worry – until she realized that it wasn't worry at all, but rather the fact that she hadn't eaten anything since the night before. Alacer was due in less than half a stick, however, so when her mother wordlessly offered her a slab of honey-covered bread, she downed it like a wolf bitch with an oversized litter – and then spent precious moments scrubbing her teeth again, reapplying her lip paint, and checking her gown for stains and crumbs.

The gown still bothered her, thought not nearly as much as when she'd first laid eyes upon it. In the evening light, the aging fabric looked ivory-hued, rather than faded and drab. As galling as it was to admit, her mother had worked wonders with needle and thread, and the once-bulky thing now fit her diminutive form to perfection. The corset left her neck and shoulders bare, and hugged her ribs without choking her; and when her mother snugged the laces at the rear, it did a creditable job of enhancing her otherwise underwhelming assets. The skirts flared out from her hips, and would have brushed the floor-boards of the wagon, save that she had once again borrowed her mother's better pair of boots; the heels, which she was finally accustomed to, provided the necessary clearance.

When her mother's back was turned, Alauda fished about in her crumena, found the perfume flask that Alainn had given her, and dabbed the glass stopper in the usual places. She had the tiny bottle sealed and tucked away again before Alyssa turned back, sniffing suspiciously at the air, her nose wrinkling as if some foul odour had wafted past the wagon. Alauda sighed internally; clearly her mother didn't like the scent either. She still thought it wonderful, though she was sufficiently self-aware to realize that its source was a large part of its attraction.

Most surprising had been the fact that, when she was otherwise ready, her mother had wordlessly offered her the sword that Lord Trivinako had given her. There was a different baldric and belt attached to the scabbard: black leather polished to a high gloss, and picked out here and there with bits of silver. "Where did you find that?" Alauda exclaimed, delighted.

"In the bottom of one of my chests," her mother said drily. "It's mine. Tonight it's yours, if you want to go suitably attired, like a lady of a noble house."

"I'm not, though, am I?" Alauda sighed. "Wouldn't that be too much like...well, lying?"

Her mother stared at her, incredulous. *"Now* you develop a conscience? And over something as trivial as formal accoutrements?"

"It's different, though, isn't it?" the girl mused. "I mean, pretending to be someone you're not – that's all right if it's for a good purpose. But if it's only for show, or self-importance, then it's just...well, vanity." She wrinkled her nose. "I'm not making much sense, am I?"

Alyssa crossed her arms, watching and listening carefully. "On the contrary," she said with a puzzled smile. "You've managed to work your way around to the first principles of the Art. We've spoken of them before; do nothing that is unnecessary –"

"– 'and that which is necessary is never wrong'," Alauda finished. She snorted a laugh. "So you're saying that deception is all right, in order to achieve something important?"

"No, *you* were saying it," her mother chuckled. "I was merely pointing out how closely your notion accords with what I was taught by the magisters of the College."

"But do you agree with it?" the girl pressed.

The wizard glanced away. "If I did," she said after a moment's reflection, "then perhaps I would still be there. I'd far rather be here, helping my daughter dress for her Second Spring."

She reached out as if to pat Alauda's cheek, thought better of disturbing her cosmetics, and tweaked the girl's ear instead. Alauda flinched – and giggled. It was a reflex; once upon a time, when she'd been much younger, her mother had flicked her ear-tips at every opportunity.

Alauda the child had retaliated by throwing her arms about her mother's neck and sputtering wetly into the nearest ear. Alauda the young lady was much more conscious of her dignity. She stuck out her tongue instead.

When the two women stopped laughing, Alauda considered her mother's offer. "I do love it," she said, hesitant, "and the baldric won't clash too badly with my gown. But won't it get in the way of dancing?"

"Absolutely," Alyssa said. "And of other things, too. But bearing arms is your birthright. And it was a gift from a mighty friend, O citizen of the Empire."

Alauda flushed. "Let me try it on."

Her mother offered the sword across her palms. "It comes with a word of caution, though."

Alauda took hold of the scabbard. *Heavy.* She hadn't recalled it being that heavy. "You're going to warn me about duelling, aren't you?"

"No!" Alyssa laughed. "Though perhaps I should; schola may have covered the bow, but I don't believe you ever studied the small-sword, did you?"

Alauda shook her head. She hadn't.

"*Bene*; I thought not. No," her mother said, "I was simply going to point out that that dress isn't cut for a baldric. It'll fall right about here." She tapped the centre of Alauda's corset. "Just something to think about."

Alauda did think about it, for about as much time as it took to draw a breath. "Maybe just the knife," she murmured. She threaded her cincture through the eyes of the scabbard, and tucked Lady Elspeth's gift to the rear, just to the right of her crumena. "Do I still need the lecture?"

"Swords aren't what I'm worried about," her mother said drily. "Thou'rt old enough, now, to show a little wisdom child. Thou hast...ah, *ut nihil!*" She rolled her eyes. "This isn't a time for the court speech, is it?"

Alauda frowned, perplexed. She wasn't accustomed to seeing her dam flustered; it was a novel experience, like seeing water catch fire and burn. "What is it, mother?"

"Time for a little truth, perchance," Alyssa scowled. "You've had your mark set upon young Alacer for months now. I was a girl once, believe it or not, and I know what that means." She leaned forward. "And even if I did not – I have eyes. And so does the everyone else about the wagons."

Alauda flushed. She remembered being surprised by her mother at the standing stones; the shock of that moment was going to stay with her for a long, long time.

"Too many children think of Second Spring as a rite of passage," the wizard went on carefully, "but in truth 'tis just another night. Have a drink, dance and flirt, and ply your wiles as you will. Kiss him all you like – but nothing more. Keep your wits about you. And remember who you are. Think upon what you owe your family's name."

She patted Alauda's hand. "I'll say no more than that."

"Really?" Alauda was flabbergasted; she'd expected a far more extensive talking-to. "That's it?"

"What more need I say?" Alyssa shrugged. "You're growing up, girl. Anyone can see it, but I...I can *feel* it. There's strength in you, and power too. The magisters were wrong there. They didn't see it, mayhap because it's not their kind of power; but even a blind man ought to be able to feel a fire's heat upon his face. I know what burns within you, little lark, for it burns within me, too." She put a hand on her bosom. "Your strength is different, but it comes from the same dark place as mine."

Alauda swallowed, unwilling to speak. This was far, far more of an unburdening than she had expected.

"So, my duck," Alyssa went on, "I shall tell you the same thing told me by my masters, and by my mother too. Power can be a useful tool, but it can also be a grim and forbidding tyrant. The flux is like the sea: we bend it to our will, with great effort and great skill; but take a single ill-chosen step, and it will drown you."

She took Alauda's hand. "I can *feel* it; it's right here, ready to burst forth. But it's stronger here –" she touched Alauda's lips, and then her temple "– and even more potent here." She laid her hand on the girl's bosom. "You're like a heap of tinder-dry wood. It would take but a spark to set you alight."

"You're talking like I *am* a mage!" Alauda murmured, confused. "What –"

"You're not," Alyssa interrupted with a wan smile. "I don't know what you are, in truth. Something more than I was, at least until I learned something of the Art Magic. Maybe you, my dear, are what a true servant of the Horned God looks like."

That thought – the memory of kneeling, naked and terrified, among the standing stones, an icy line of stone against her throat – chilled her to her marrow. "I'm a servant of the Forest Mother, too," she said, banishing the terrifying image, and struggling to recall the shrine in the mountains, and the gentle touch of the old singer of the Raven. "Akaryah shed my blood for Her, just as you did for Cernunnor."

"I know, and I bless him for it," the older woman nodded. "Perhaps that will be what saves you."

"Why should I have to be saved at all?!"

"Because all power has a price. Another lesson we of the Art are taught."

"I thought Elspina paid that price. For all of us."

"If that were true," Alyssa said, "then why did my mother shed my blood? And why did I shed yours?"

Alauda's shoulders slumped. "I don't understand any of this."

"Nor do I. Not entirely." The older woman looked pensive. "The Art Magic as practiced by the magi of the book – as I learned it – has rules. For magi of the blood, there seem to be fewer rules. There are some who think that the Green has no rules at all – that the power of those who feel *kesatuan* in their bones face fewer limits than the rest of us."

"Do you believe that?"

"I don't know." She leaned forward and plucked a speck of thread from her daughter's shoulder. "The problem, dear, is that I don't know enough to know *what* to believe."

"Will I be…I don't even know how to ask this," Alauda shuddered. "Will I be stronger than you are?"

"I don't know that either," her mother shrugged. "Time will tell, I suppose. Just remember, though, it's not really about strength, unless you mean the strength of your heart. The weakest warrior can still lie, cheat, steal, betray a friend, murder an ally. We can all do terrible things; it's just that magi, who have access to powers that normal folk can only dream of, are able to do truly terrible things." She patted Alauda's breast again. "*This* is the only strength that matters, dear. That's the one lesson that you must remember above all others: to do nothing that is unnecessary. To hold your hand, unless there truly is a need to act."

"But who decides what's necessary?"

"Whoever has the power to act."

"So...magi answer to no one?" Alauda exclaimed. "That's insane! What's to stop one of you from trying to take over the world?"

"The rest of us, I would hope," Alyssa replied soberly. "Hence the importance of our fellowships, our associations, and our vows. And," she glanced at the floor between her feet, "hence the dread with which the world regards a mage who refuses to heed the voices of his peers – who believes that he has none."

Alauda frowned initially; then she nodded. "The Shadow King."

"Just so," the wizard said. "*Rex Ombris*, whom no mage or cabal of mages could hope to challenge, came nigh to destroying the earth. He is a cautionary tale. The fall of Yl and the sundering of the world show what can happen when a mage's power runs deep, and he allows himself to drown in it." She took her daughter's hand and squeezed it. "Thus the importance of keeping your head above the waters, of paying heed to the strength of your heart. Magic is our servant; it must never become our master."

Alauda nodded soberly. There was something gratifying in being treated like an adult instead of an errant child. "I'll remember, mother." She struggled into the short, open jacket of stitched midnight satin that went with the gown. She was grateful for the extra layer; the night promised to be chill, and the thing would serve to conceal the lamentable deficiencies of her décolletage.

"Good," Alyssa said briskly. "It's nearly dark. Two matters more, and then I'll leave ye be."

"Yes?"

Her mother held up two fingers. "First: stay with the white wine; red will stain thy teeth, while ale and cider will have thee pissing the night away, when thou should'st be dancing. And second..." she grinned. "Kiss him here –" she tapped the hollow of Alauda's throat "and behind the ear. His knees will unlock like a marionette's."

Alauda flushed. "Mother!"

Alyssa shrugged. "It's my duty to instruct thee in all manner of magic, dear. Mundane women's wiles will be more useful to thee than all the fluxy fire in the world." She winked, and tweaked the girl's nose. "Ask thy father whether I speak the truth. Were it not for mine own judicious use of the oldest arts, thou would'st not be here to scowl at me so."

"Mother, for the sake of all the gods – *must* you?"

Her mother gave her a perfunctory hug. Alauda returned it.

When they separated, Alyssa was frowning. Alauda froze. "What is it?"

"What's that smell?" Alyssa demanded. "It's dreadful. Did you step in something?"

"No idea," the girl said hurriedly. "Could you pass me the hairbrush?"

Alacer arrived as the Lantern touched the eastern hills, just as she'd known he would. The sky was thick with clouds, and the suns' waning light lent a luscious red and orange cast to everything. It looked as if rain might be in the offing, but she refused to let that possibility dampen her excitement. There were tents, after all.

To Alauda's relief, Tonlees was with Alacer. Alauda was afraid that her friend had fallen behind in her preparations, and would miss their rendezvous.

The three met at the bottom of the steps to Alauda's wagon. Alacer, she saw, was dressed with simple elegance, in snug breeches, high boots, and a new shirt of white linen beneath a long, elaborately-frogged vest. There was a carefully starched and folded neck-cloth beneath his chin. To her delight, he'd evidently taken some time with his hair; instead of the usual magpie's nest of tangled grey it was brushed behind his ears, and fell to his shoulders in gentle waves. There mere sight of him set her knees a-shiver.

Tonlees was an entirely different affair. Her friend's auburn tresses were caught up in a coronet of braids held in place with silver pins and a gossamer veil. Her gown was stunning – a slender sheathe of emerald satin that enclosed her from throat to ankles, but that followed her shape so closely that she might as well have been wearing nothing at all. A long shawl of fine wool covered her shoulders. "You look wonderful!" Alauda blurted out, simultaneously delighted and depressed by her own comparatively drab appearance.

Tonlees grinned. "Which one of us?"

"Both of you!" She walked carefully over to Alacer, took his hands, and kissed him carefully. It was novel to be able to reach his lips just by going up on her tip-toes; he didn't have to stoop at all. "Good e'en, good lover!" she giggled. "Have you naught to say?"

"You're beautiful."

Alauda shot Tonlees a playful grin. "Don't you just hate how he prattles on all the time? Nothing but talk, talk, talk!"

"Yes, it's terrible," the older girl murmured. "Ala, before we go over, do you mind if – if we..."

Alauda wasn't listening to her; she was staring at Alacer's eyes.

The grey irises were positively luminous in the flaming light of the sunset. On a whim, she hugged him…and kissed him behind the ear.

Alacer started, but that was his only reaction. Alauda was vaguely disappointed when his knees didn't immediately buckle. So much for mother's advice; she'd gotten a more electric reaction out of him on any number of prior occasions, albeit under rather more intimate circumstances.

Well, maybe later. Seeing as how her lips were already next to his ear, she whispered, "I've missed you terribly."

"And I, you." He gave her an abbreviated squeeze.

"What d'ye think of Toni?" she stage-whispered. "Isn't she positively delectable?"

He glanced sidelong at the auburn-haired beauty. "Yes."

"'Yes'!" Alauda mocked, her eyes twinkling. "'Yes', forsooth – a ringing endorsement if ever I heard one. She's lovely, as always, and she makes me look like a cow pat, as always." She flashed her friend a toothy grin. "If ever I wanted to know what a breaking heart sounds like, I'd just have to follow you around tonight!"

Tonlees looked uncertain. "I don't want to break any hearts."

"Tosh," Alauda sniffed. "It's what we Third House ladies do, isn't it? Lead would-be suitors hither and yon by their dangling tongues, then shatter their hopes and dreams, and leave them broken and weeping in our life's wake?"

Toni's brows knotted. "Have you been drinking?"

"Only from the cup of life," the younger girl gushed. "My mother actually said something encouraging to me! It was so unexpected that I figured I was dreaming. I'd like to get to the party before I wake up."

"What did she say?" Toni asked.

"We should go," Alacer interjected before Alauda could continue with her effervescent babbling. "I could hear the skalds tuning up while I was getting ready."

"Excellent." She took Alacer's hand – then with a flourish, extended the other to Tonlees. "Let's be off! I want to dance and dance, and then dance some more – until one of us cries for mercy, and throws down his arms, and quits the field!"

The three set off for the fair-grounds, Alacer and Tonlees exchanging worried glances over her head. Alauda, transported by excitement, didn't notice.

♦

Twelve

'Fair-grounds' was a grandiose name for an empty spot in the centre of the as yet unsown hayfields. The fields – mercifully dry, an oddity given the season, though the lowering rain-clouds suggested that they wouldn't be dry for long – straddled the road where it emerged from the bridge across the river. Alauda had seen similar festival grounds in Corymbus and Astramicor. There, of course, they were somewhat more established; in the heart of the Realm, Second Spring had been observed annually for the better part of three thousand years, and the earth of the grounds was paved with close-set stones, and strewn with dry evergreen needles and new ferns. These served to symbolize the transition between old life and new, and did double duty by absorbing the litter of what generally proved to be a raucous celebration.

Buckhill wasn't even a tenth as old as Corymbus, and the extemporized party site had been thrown together with the same slap-dash energy and disregard for refinement that, in Alauda's experience to date, seemed to characterize the majority of human settlements. There was a roofed-over dining hall, the temporary kitchens were at least equipped with walls and doors, and there were several large tents with the side-walls rolled up and tied in case of rain; but the dancing-stage, usually the focus of the festival, was little more than a flattened section of field covered over with freshly sawn and sanded planks. Some effort had gone into evening out the ridges between the boards, but Alauda, looking askance at the platform, wondered whether she was destined to catch a heel and break an ankle. She would liefer have danced barefoot amid the furrows.

The evening's oddness escalated at the entrance to the grounds. When the trio, laughing and nearly running, arrived at the break in the rail fence that encircled the riverside lot, fumbling in their pockets for the shillings that their parents had provided for entry, Alainn stepped from the shadows between two tents. He bowed without preamble. "My lady."

His unexpected appearance brought Alauda up short – not least because, as a consequence of their arrangement (to say nothing of the previous night's shenanigans), she ought to have been expecting him. Where had her mind gone? "Ahh…" she temporized, fumbling for the right words. "Hello." It was the best she could do.

Alacer turned to stare at her. Tonlees clenched her teeth and looked away.

Steady on, girl, she cursed herself. "*Sieur* O'Dell," she said, taking refuge in knee-jerk formality, "I believe you've already met my friend, Tonlees Leat Havintalla."

"Of course," Alainn replied, bowing again. "Madam."

"*Sieur* O'Dell," Tonlees said, dropping a minimal curtsey.

Alauda turned to her left, gritting her teeth. "This is –"

"Alacer Tiivus," Alacer said, extending a hand. "A pleasure."

Alain took it. "Alainn Fionan O'Dell. Your servant." Before anyone else could speak, he stepped to Alauda's side, insinuating himself smoothly between the two girls, and holding out an arm. "My lady, your beauty outshines the stars. Shall we proceed?"

Alauda shot a frantic glance at Alacer, who was looking at her with no expression whatsoever; and then at Tonlees, who merely shrugged. Bereft of options – oddly, even at this late stage it never occurred to her to decline – Alauda took Alainn's arm, and allowed him to lead her through the gate.

As they entered, he dropped a pair of shillings into the palm of the attendant at the gate. After they had passed the man, he leaned over and whispered, "Washed brass. D'ye suppose he'll notice as quickly as you did?"

Alauda gaped, then emitted something between a cough and a snort. Her friends were momentarily forgotten.

Behind them, Tonlees and Alacer looked at each other. The grey-haired boy held out his arm. Toni took it with downcast eyes.

Alauda followed her escort's lead, weaving her way between circling groups of all sizes and compositions. Alainn chatted quietly as they progressed, dropping hints and jests and anecdotes that fell unheeded upon her ears. She was too distracted by the press of the crowd to listen. She was absurdly gratified to catch the eye of more than a few of the male attendees – though a little less than flattered when she realized that most of them were miners fresh from the pit, with their well-washed hair slicked back and their clothing stinking of earth no matter how hard they'd scrubbed. And the rest, she noticed belatedly, seemed to be less appreciative of her appearance than they were astonished at the fact that she, an obvious child of the third house of the elves, was on the arm of a light-fingered, curly-haired, bare-footed –

Wait. She looked down – and gaped again. Alainn was wearing boots – brown leather boots, with big, brassy buckles. They were larger than anything an elf might wear, nearly human-sized in fact, but they were definitely boots.

No Halfling ever wore – ever *could* wear – boots. "Alainn, what *are* you?" she demanded.

"Ah-hah!" he chuckled. "So much for idle banter, I see. Never fear!" he held up his hands as her brow furrowed, "I'll answer! But it's easier to talk while dancing."

"I don't think that's true."

"Perhaps not. But it's certainly more fun than standing around." He bowed low, and extended his hand.

"Fine," she sighed. She took his hand, casting a brief glance over her shoulder. Tonlees and Alacer were nowhere to be seen.

The planks of the platform turned out to be smoother than she had anticipated. Alainn, not surprisingly, was both dextrous and light on his feet. He also appeared to know something of the terpsichorean art, at least as it applied to country dancing. When the band, a heterogeneous mishmash of strings, pipes, tambours, and at least one set of orchestral bells, struck up a lively reel, he guided her through the steps with hardly a stumble.

Halfling folk dances were more strenuous than she realized, involving enough spins and turns that she nearly succumbed to vertigo. It wasn't as taxing an exercise as, say, riding a horse at a gallop, but Alauda did not find the paces at all conducive to conversation. "I thought...we were going...to talk!" she gasped as he gathered her in with one arm, spun her like a spindle, then tossed her away again. A burly human – a cattleman, by the smell of his tunic – caught her and flung her back.

"Later!" Alainn laughed. "Save your breath, my lady!"

This continued for some time. Eventually Alauda began to perspire. That worried her; she wasn't all that heavily made-up, but she didn't need rivulets of sweat cutting gullies through the carefully-applied powder. With a raised finger she signalled for a halt. Alainn dutifully took her arm and led her from the stage.

"You dance very well," he said, beckoning to an attendant at the kegs. The fellow slid two wine-cups toward them, receiving another shilling in return. "Better than me. Though I don't suppose I should be surprised at a lady of the Third House being light on her feet.

"And forgive my boldness," he added with a waggling of his eyebrows, "but you smell as good as you look. Are you wearing my perfume?"

"I am," she confirmed with a self-conscious flush. "Mother hated it, but I don't. I think it's delightful." *Like you.* "But I don't recognize the scent. What flowers are in it?"

"No idea," he grinned. "I know nothing about perfume, or about flowers for that matter. I just know that you smell...er...what is it?"

Alauda had been staring at the coins he'd dropped on the board, hoping that the brass wasn't showing through the thin layer of silvering. She emptied half the cup at a draught – then, remembering her mother's advice, topped it up with water from a handy pitcher. "Nothing. Nothing at all. You dance well too, even in those boots," she observed. "How old are you, Alainn?"

"I've seen twenty-nine summers," he replied. "I know I don't look it. Fearghan's ten years my junior. Breaghan's twenty years old, and Sîol's twenty-one."

"I'd've put you at seventy or so," Alauda smiled. "Assuming you were an elf. But you're not. Or – well, are you? Forgive me, but you look much more like one of my people than like a...like your friends."

His grin widened. "You were going to say 'like a halpie', weren't you?"

She lowered her eyes. "I'm sorry. It's just...everybody uses the term. It's impolite, I know."

"I don't mind," he replied. He emptied his goblet and set it aside; Alauda was relieved to see that he was perspiring as well. "D'ye know what it means? In our tongue?" he asked.

"*Halpinya*?" Alauda frowned. "Actually, I don't."

"It's a jest. Most folk think it comes from the *nordmannir* speech, where *hal-* means half, and *inya* means growth. Half-grown. But that's not it.

"According to legends," he said portentously, softening the gravity of his tone by crossing his eyes until Alauda tittered, "– if you believe the priests of Cham – when Holy Bræa tried to destroy her children, Ana took them from her care and gave them to her younger brothers. Hara got your folk, Mighty Esu ended up with humans, and Lagu eventually agreed to adopt the dwarves. When she tried to find a patron for the Halflings, though, her fourth brother, Nosa, was nowhere to be found."

"Off pinching Vara's jewellery, probably," Alauda commented. She knew a little bit about the Halflings' mercurial god.

"Likely enough. Anyway, to hear the priests tell it, the only beings with the patience to tolerate the mischief of the most mischievous of Bræa's offspring were the First-Born – the dragons."

"Indeed?" Alauda smiled. "I don't believe I've ever heard this tale in temple, Alainn."

"It's probably not part of Wise Hara's catechism," Alainn allowed. "Any road, it's said that no lies can ever be spoken in the wyrm-speech, and that that rule holds true for sobriquets as well. Dragons use nicknames, just as we do – but their names can only reflect the wearer's true nature. According to legend, therefore, the dragons spent an age watching over my forebears – and when Nosa finally consented to claim them, they'd already been named. The dragons named them for their curiosity." The boy winked. "In the dragons' speech, *halpi-* means holders, or bearers, or seekers; while *-nya* means 'the new'."

Alauda nodded, smiling. "That's a good tale, Alainn. But it only piques my curiosity further." She toyed with her cup. "You said, '*my forebears*' – but you look like no Halfling I've ever seen. You're also so – so

_"

He cocked his head. "So-so?"

Alauda was stymied. She couldn't very well say *beautiful*. "So tall," she extemporized. After all, it was true. "So I'll ask you again: what are you?"

He put a hand over his heart: "I'm your adoring admirer, my lady; your very slave."

"Stop stalling!" she exclaimed, stamping her foot – in time with the music, of course. "Answer me!"

"It's an easier answer than you think," he said. "No gods or dragons or other mysteries. As simple as this: my mother was from your lands, a servant of the Forest Gods – of Shanyreet the Forest Mother, in fact, or *Hutanibu* as the fey folk call her. She spent her life walking abroad on this side of the mountains. Not one for cities, though she was Third House, like you.

"And as for my father – he was a wagon-skald: a disreputable, thieving ne'er-do-well who sang for his supper, picked pockets, schemed, stole, and likely never earned an honest coin in his life." He winked at her. "Exactly what you'd expect of a 'filthy halpie', *heya*?"

She didn't rise to the bait – but she did smile in bemusement. "A wagon-skald. Indeed. And of Nosa's folk. I suppose that would make you...what? A half-Halfling?" She blinked, then grinned. "A quarterling?"

"It makes me Alainn Fionan O'Dell," he replied. "A bit of a mongrel, perhaps. But is not the mongrel said to be the most loyal and lovable of all hounds?"

He had the 'hound' part aright, Alauda thought. "Right. Well, tell me this, then: how in the World Made did that sort of scruff scoundrel ever convince a lady of the elves to take him to mate?"

"You have it wrong. She asked *him*." He took her cup, set it aside, drew her in close, and bent to whisper his next words into her ear. "The way she told it," he murmured, "it was because he made her laugh."

Alauda drew back and stared at him. There was no artifice in his smile; not a jot. She felt a sudden lump in her throat.

The night air was teetering on the precipice between too hot and too cold, and the stars above were full of promise. When Alainn nodded at the dance floor she smiled her assent; and he led her back into the maelstrom of legs, laughter, and wild, skirling song.

♦

Thirteen

They danced long and long. The platform was lit by a dozen lamps, by scores of torches. The lamps ran dry and were refilled, the torches burned down and were replaced; and still the company danced.

When the troupe of musicians retired they were succeeded by a simple trio consisting of harp, horn and shalm. The music slowed at last, to something simple and throbbing. Alainn held her close, belly to belly and breast to breast. Her cheek was against his, her heart hammering in her bosom; his breath was upon her neck, making her shiver with delight. In the lamp-light she could see a slight fuzz of whiskers upon his cheeks, something no pure-blooded elf in history had ever known. Rather than repulsing her, she found herself rubbing her own cheek against them, and shivering when they tickled her skin.

She enjoyed the touch of his hand upon her waist, the gentleness with which he intertwined his fingers with hers. She also found herself responding to the subtle pressure of their interlocked thighs as they slowly spun in place. She was conscious of an ache deep within her, a heavy, familiar weight, like a fist in her vitals, clenching and unclenching. It was urgent, and yet not so; a sort of niggling, throbbing compulsion that was nearly as delightful to deny as it would be to satisfy.

Alainn felt it, too; she could tell. Not just by the more obvious symptoms of his arousal, though at least one of those was present and unmistakeable; she could feel his lifebeat galloping in time with her own. He hadn't entirely given in to desire, though. At one point he pulled his head back, staring fixedly into her eyes, and she felt as though twin golden lances had speared her through the loins; she raised her face, and let her lips fall open – and he winked, then slapped her gently on the backside. She responded by giving one of his ears a vicious flick with a fingernail. They laughed together – and he held her more tightly, to Alauda's inexpressible delight.

His laughter reminded her of his tale, about his woods-crafty *elvii* mother and her comical Halfling mate. Small wonder, Alauda realized with a slight start, that she found herself longing for his touch; if as he claimed his dam had indeed been a servant of the Forest Mother, then he was practically a kindred spirit: a true child of the Green, like Alauda herself. It made her all the more concerned about dallying with him. She was more than half-way to loving him already, and she knew that it wouldn't take much to push her off the narrow precipice of indecision upon which she'd taken up her precarious and uncomfortable perch.

After all, there was Alacer. What of him? To distract herself from that prickly question, she talked. "What happened to them? Your parents, I mean," she asked after a few more songs had come and gone. She was half wondering whether he would tell her the same tale as she'd heard from Sîol. Alauda's mother had always said that a halpie would lie as long as his mouth was open. She couldn't – or didn't want to – bring herself to think of Alainn in that way, but it was difficult to stifle her native caution. After all, Alainn's father had been –

"They died," he said matter-of-factly, interrupting her train of thought. "It was Shadow-of-Midnight, the dragon of Mons Lacrimosa. She struck our caravan one day, and killed half of the adults. Some of the children, too. We never knew why."

"Oh, Alainn." She was ashamed – mortified – that she had ever doubted him. "I'm so sorry!"

"It was a long time ago," he shrugged. "I remember it well enough; I was twelve. The others don't, not really; they were still babes in arms. Fearghan claims he remembers the crack of skyfire, and the lowering clouds, and the shadow as she overflew the wagons – but I think he just remembers the tales he's been told. He couldn't even walk yet when it happened." He smiled wanly. "I think he just *wants* to remember. It'd be something to share with the rest of us. Those who lost everything."

"Well, he already shares a name with you." She paused, and nearly stumbled. "Just a moment. You're both O'Dells. You didn't say you were brothers!"

Alainn laughed. "We are, in a way. In our tradition a 'child o'the dell' is an orphan; the whole camp is responsible for him. Fearghan's parents were both killed in the attack, just like mine. It does make us brothers, more or less."

His hands tightened momentarily on her waist. "I have more brothers and sisters of that sort than I care to count." He held her close, and she was glad; his matter-of-fact tone brought tears to her eyes.

"Fearghan's sworn a vow of vengeance against her, you know," he added after a few more slow, stately spins.

"Shadow-of-Midnight?" Alauda started. "That's ambitious. And what about you?"

"Me?" he chuckled. "I'm no warrior, my lady. I figure the further I stay away from dragons, the longer I'll live."

"A sensible sentiment," she teased, touching her nose to his, "if hardly a courageous one."

His regard turned serious. "Dying is easy, Alauda; anyone can do it. People do it all the time, for good reasons and bad. It takes courage, to be sure – but it can take more courage to live."

"I didn't mean to offend you."

"You can't offend me," he chuckled. "But you can crush my heart, all too easily. That grey-haired fellow – Alacer, yes? – would he be your light'o'love?"

Alauda stiffened in his grasp. She had to force herself to relax. "It's that obvious, is it?"

"Hmm," he murmured. "What's obvious is the way you feel about him. I can see it in your eyes. He doesn't look at you the same way, though. I'm sure you've noticed that."

Alauda swallowed thickly. The hell of it was, she had. Now that the dreaded words had been spoken aloud, she couldn't deny them. She nodded, not trusting herself to speak.

"You're too young to take a mate," he mused. "You and he *can't* be promised. You aren't, are you?"

She shook her head. "Not yet."

" 'Not yet'," he echoed knowingly. "But you – you were hoping that maybe, just maybe, someday he might –"

"He *asked*!" she cried. Fortunately, the music was at a crescendo, and her outburst went unnoticed by the other dancers. "He asked me! A m-month ago! He said we could go to P-Portacaminus, or Skywaters and…and b-be wed under Imperial law!"

She had to clench her teeth to keep from blubbering like an infant. In a sudden torrent, she explained how it had all come about: the journey from Astramicor into the mountains; the interlude at the standing stones; how Alacer had greeted her after she'd survived the snowstorm. And more recently, how her passion for him had waxed, while his for her had just…seemed to fade. How it had withered and died, like an unwatered flower.

Her hands were shaking; Alainn patted the one that rested on his shoulder. "Hearts are changeable things," he said. "I can't imagine anyone not loving you. Give him time. You've plenty of it, after all," he added with a wink, "seeing as how you're *real* elves, not silvered-over brazen counterfeits like me."

"Maybe you're a little brazen," Alauda said, "But I don't think you're counterfeit at all." She put her head on his shoulder, absurdly gratified that their similarity of stature made it possible.

Alainn laughed. It wasn't the reaction she'd expected. "It's novel, you know," he remarked. "Being trusted. You make me feel – well, noble. Nearly as noble as you, my good lady. As if I were more than what I am."

"I'm glad," she replied. "I don't give a fiddler's damn for nobility, and I don't really know you at all. But – I think I want to. I like you a great deal, Alainn O'Dell."

"And I like you a great deal, Lady Lark." He chuckled mirthlessly. "So much so, I think, that if I were you, I'd go and find my gray-haired friend, drag him off to a quiet spot between the wagons, and give him a chance to make you forget about me."

Alauda's throat hurt. She pulled her head back. "Really?" Her glower was less effective due to the tears in her eyes. "Aren't *you* supposed to be trying to seduce *me*?" She wasn't sure whether her outrage was feigned or genuine. "It's Second Spring! Why're you trying to push me back into Alacer's arms?"

"Because I don't want to be your second choice," Alainn said, all seriousness. "As for the other...do you *want* me to seduce you?"

He was looking into her eyes as he said it. This time, she didn't look away. In a small voice, she said, "I'd like you to at least try."

Alainn grinned. "Well, I won't." He released her hip, spun her out like a top, and tugged her back in again.

She nearly stumbled, and signalled her ire by swatting his shoulder with her free hand. "Why not?" she demanded.

"Because it's not a one-way street. It's supposed to be mutual."

"You mean that I'm supposed to seduce you, too?"

"You did that the first time you smiled at me," Alainn said. "And then you thought it was enough, and let it go. Your timing is terrible, my lady.

"That was your problem with Alacer, you know," he went on, sounding for all the world like a *coricularius* – a counsellor of the heart. It was a profession almost unique to the Realm, where bonds between lovers could last as long as centuries. "It's as clear as lantern-glass. He wanted you, when you were still unsure; and then, by the time you'd made up your mind about him, his heart had already moved on." He nodded over her shoulder. "To your fire-haired friend, it would seem."

Alauda's head whipped around; the tendons in her neck creaked alarmingly. Behind her, a dozen paces away, Alacer and Tonlees were dancing. They appeared to be gazing raptly into each others' eyes.

Alauda wasn't a complete dullard; the evidence of the past few weeks, especially Alacer's deliberate absences, hadn't been lost on her. But to see the proof of her loss portrayed so blatantly –

A stab of pain caught in her throat; her eyes welled up. She crushed Alainn's fingers in her fist – he winced – and said huskily, "I – I need to, to –"

"Of course," the boy nodded. He took her hand and led her through the throng. She followed in his wake, swiping angrily at her eyes, caring not a whit who might see her weeping, her heels hammering into the boards.

They dodged dancers, drinkers, chatterers and miscellaneous revellers, winding their way between folk of all age and race. The babble of the throng, the thrum of the music, gradually faded. Alauda didn't look up until Alainn paused. They were standing between long rows of silent wagons – small ones. He'd brought her to the Halflings' camp. "It's a little quieter here," he explained, when she looked a question at him. "Would you like to walk for a while?"

She brushed the last droplets from her eyes with her thumb. "What I would like," she said softly, "is for you to kiss me."

Dimples appeared in his cheeks. "As my lady commands."

There followed a long, long period when not a word was spoken. Alauda, careless now, let her passion mount, until every last vestige of rage, jealousy, and contempt at her own feckless cupidity was consumed in the white-hot fire of her need. He held her, pressing her back up against one of the wagons, the hard wood digging into her shoulder blades, and she didn't care. His lips were soft and sweet, the teeth beneath them clean and even. The hands on her body were at once both strong, and surprisingly gentle. When, after a time, he dropped to his knees before her, she felt a momentary qualm; was he going to propose, right then and there?! But that wasn't his intent. Before she could protest his hands were beneath her gown, his fingers tracing lines of fire around her boot-tops, and then up the backs of her thighs.

All conscious thought vanished from her mind, swept away by the maelstrom of her desire. She helped him, gathering fistfuls of fabric and hiking her skirts higher and higher. Hands touched her, and lips – and then stars were bursting in the skies above, shrieking through the night trailing fire in their wake, echoing the thundering of her heart. Alauda breathed deep, allowing her lover's gentle insistence to wash over and drown her, throwing her head back and scrabbling for purchase at the wagon's wall with her nails, transported by ecstasy. She caught a fistful of canvas, and let her thighs fall open, hooking one over his shoulder, digging her boot-heel into his spine; drawing him in, her opposite knee trembling as she struggled to hold herself upright, supported and tormented by him in equal measure.

The moment came; the skies and stars were within her grasp, and she had to bite her tongue to keep from squealing aloud. The canvas caught in her fist tore with a whisper. She knotted the fingers of her free hand in his hair, holding him there, forcing his lips against her aching flesh as she trembled on the very brink of ecstasy, wanting more from him, wanting *everything* – praying, begging all of the Powers both above and below that that single, luminous fragment of time might endure forever.

It did not; it could not. But it did last long enough to leave her limp and shaking, leaning on Alainn's shoulder as he stood and helped her adjust her skirts. She released her grip on the wagon's cover and fell against him, her arms about his neck.

He held her easily, laughing into her hair. "Does my lady need a moment?"

Alauda had just enough strength left to close her teeth gently on the lobe of his ear. "Yes, your lady does," she gasped, willing her breathing to ease. "Your lady needs many more moments. Exactly like that one!" She knotted her fingers in his hair again, and gave his head a gentle shake. "And after that, still more!"

He put his lips to her ear. "As my lady commands," he repeated with a chuckle. And knelt again.

Alauda gasped, her eyes rolling back as she clutched anew at the torn canvas. Almost at once that familiar, star-filled moment came again. This time she did cry out; but her shriek vanished into the night sky like birdsong, swallowed up and overwhelmed by the distant roar of the dancers, the thunder of the drums, and the skirl of the pipes.

By the time they returned to the dancing-stage nearly a stick had passed. Golden Chuadan was high in the sky; his spring-time pursuer, silvery Lodan, lay just above the western horizon. Alauda was walking carefully on legs that felt as limp as wilted flower-stems; leaning on Alainn's arm, but doing her best not to look it. Her hair was slightly awry, and there were smudges on her skirts. At one point in the evening's festivities they'd lost their balance simultaneously, tumbling to the ground. They'd both been too far gone in mutual pleasure to notice, let alone to disengage and find a more convenient position.

Alainn had helped her adjust her raiment, and had brushed away the worst of the dirt and old straw, but she was still going to have to explain the state of her attire to her mother. Her only hope for survival lay in the likelihood that her parents would have retired by the time she returned to the wagon – if indeed they'd decided to come to the party at all.

She was holding Alainn's hand, nearly beside herself with exhausted delight. She was also calm; ecstatically so. Alainn's caresses had been almost magical; she'd lost count of the number of times she'd managed to reach beyond the clouds to touch the stars. It had taken every last vestige of her volition not to throw her golden-eyed lover to his back, mount him, and ride him like a stolen stallion. That she'd managed to throttle the temptation to do so was down not only to her mother's hectoring, but to her own burgeoning sense of guilt. She'd forced Alacer to stay his hand so many times that it simply wouldn't be just to spread her legs and offer that ultimate benison to a virtual stranger – no matter how pretty or enticing that stranger might be. Not even now, after her silver-haired playmate had evidently turned his attention to her best friend's auburn hair and radiant smile.

I'll just have to win him back, she thought, her resolve strengthened by sated desire. Alainn's touch, and the pleasures that they'd shared, had somewhat irrationally reawoken her resolve. Her 'half-halpie' had been a delight, but a momentary delight at best; they would part on the morrow, never to see one another again. Alacer was her first and only love. Time and a true heart, as Ceorlinus had written, would tell. Tonlees, Alauda was certain, would understand.

And if she didn't – well, did that matter?

When they reached the platform, the musicians, fatigued as well, were playing something slow and melodic. Without an invitation she stepped into Alainn's arms, pulling him into a solemn and simple series of measures, a children's country dance. He responded with a happy grin. On an impulse she kissed him – and when she did, another wave of heat flooded through her; another tingling knot tightened betwixt her thighs.

That thought brought with it another, one that made her stiffen. He noticed the sudden tension in her arms and back. "What is it?" he murmured.

"You've got my frillies!" Alauda whispered, blushing furiously. The silken wisps had necessarily come off in the course of the evening's entertainment, and Alainn had thoughtfully pocketed them.

"Oh, of course!" he nodded. "Would you like them back?"

"No!" she squeaked, glancing around at the mob of dancers. "Not here! Later." She swallowed, and essayed a smile. "Unless you'd like to keep them. As a reminder of a marvellous night."

"The marvelous night is not over yet," he winked.

Alauda's heart skipped a beat. Then she realized that the anticipation in his eyes was less about her than about their plan to pillage Arx Cervus. Her face fell.

He took her hand again. "Of course," he added, "I'm not certain I should be seen with you. Only a bawd would traipse about in public without her underthings."

Without taking her eyes from his, Alauda slid her thigh between his legs, and twitched her knee menacingly. "*Concedo!*" he gasped.

"That's better," she murmured. *Bawd, indeed!*

At that moment the music changed, becoming even slower and more mournful – and Alauda's ears pricked up. " 'O my love'," she said reflectively, " 'won't you come lie with me?'"

Alainn drew his head back and stared at her, baffled. "I'd like nothing better," he exclaimed softly. "But you're still a maid, and I thought you meant to remain one."

"I do," she snickered. "Don't be horrid! It's the song. Do you not know it?"

Alainn listened for a moment. He shook his head. "I don't. Ceorlinus?"

"Older. It's from the Shadow War, I think." Alauda waited for the right moment, and then took up the words, murmuring them directly into his ear. They'd originally been written for a male singer, so she modified them on the fly:

> *In the dark night, 'neath the moons' light*
> *We were dancing and singing*
> *To the songs of our home far away*
> *I was lying with my true love*
> *With my heart nearly breaking*
> *As he told me that he could not stay.*
>
> *(Chorus) I remember that night, and the stars in his eyes*
> *How they glimmered and glistened for me*
> *He was gone upon the morrow*
> *And my heart filled with sorrow*
> *For the home that he'd never more see.*
> *(O my love, won't you come lie with me?)*
>
> *In the dark day, at the gateway*
> *Of the wall where we waited*
> *For some word of our comrades to hear*
> *I was waiting for my true love*
> *To return from his sortie*
> *But no word came to gladden my ear.*
>
> *(Chorus) I remember that day, and the bright clash of steel*
> *What a terrible sight, you'll agree;*
> *And I brought my fallen love in*
> *With a green shroud above him*
> *To the home that he'd never more see.*
> *(Wait, my love, and I'll come lie with thee!)*

That was all she could remember. The musicians continued for several more verses out of deference to the dwindling number of dancers, and Alauda let her partner lead her through another set.

"That was wonderful," he said solemnly as the music ended. "I could listen to you forever."

"I could listen to your compliments forever," she said with grateful smile. "Though it's really down to my teachers; they made the most of my meager talents. I've been in training since before you were born."

"It shows. Your mother?"

"My father, actually," she snorted. "Mother could probably turn a whole orchestra into hedgehogs if she felt like it. But she couldn't carry a tune even if it had handles."

He laughed. "You know, that song is even more romantic in the travelling tongue."

"How so?"

He pointed out how, in the elven tongue, *dormi mecum* had only one possible meaning, while the travelling tongue equivalent, 'lie with me', could mean two different things. "It could mean the first, obviously; that the singer was longing for her mate. But it could also mean that she wanted to…you know, *lie* with him. To tell untruths."

Alauda made a face. "How is that romantic?"

He kissed her cheek. "What could possibly be more romantic than getting in trouble together?"

"You're a strange people," she complained.

He didn't reply; he just moved his lips around until they met hers.

She responded eagerly…at first. He was holding her closely enough that Alauda could feel him stiffening once more. His hand, she also noticed, had slid down to cup her backside. A sudden flash of appalled intuition struck her. "Which is it? Are you thinking about bedding me?" she demanded. "Or are you thinking about pillaging the castle?"

He drew back his head, gave her a mischievous wink – and squeezed her bottom. "Can't it be both?"

The elf-girl's eyes bulged dangerously. "Is this some sort of halpie thing? Or are you just insane?"

Alainn's eyes gleamed. "Can't it be both?" he repeated.

"You talk too much," she scowled. "Isn't there something else you could be doing with that mouth?"

"There certainly is," he allowed, glancing about them. "But this doesn't seem like the right place. Perhaps if we went back to the wag –"

Alauda shut him up with her lips.

A long, blissful interlude stretched out thereafter. The music changed, and changed again. As it changed, so too did Alauda's sense of tranquil glee. She was subsumed by a transport of panic, and had a sudden, impulsive desire to kick her escort in the shins and run for home.

A few deep, even breaths restored her equanimity – and helped her to realize what a wretched hypocrite she was. Didn't she have a talent for trouble, after all –indeed, a liking for it? Would she have been half as pleased with puzzling out the origin of the victory coins if she hadn't had to break into the Lore-speaker's wagon to do so? Would she have agreed to go along on Sîol's insane expedition if it hadn't been utterly mad to even contemplate it?

Who was she, of all people, to condemn Alainn for being aroused by the prospect of risk? And for that matter – she bit her lip, horrified – would she have shivered so violently at the touch of Alainn's lips if their tryst hadn't been illicit?

Maybe I'm *the one who's insane,* she thought with a self-conscious shiver.

The boy mistook her misgivings for a chill, and held her more closely. She didn't mind that at all, her megrims notwithstanding. "Can I ask another question?" he murmured over the music. "About *your* customs?"

Alauda frowned. "I suppose. What question?"

The boy sucked wind through his teeth. "You told me that you couldn't wear the sash I gave you. The scarlet ribbon, I mean. That it would mean that we were betrothed."

Alauda's face drained. "You saw it."

"Difficult not to," he said with a strained smile. "You had it wrapped around your waist, under your chemise. The, uh – the ends were hanging down."

"Hara's blood," she grated. She took a deep breath. "Wearing the *virga* in public – yes, that means a maiden is betrothed. But if she wears it beneath her clothing, against her skin..."

Her pale cheeks reddened anew. "Ah, that means that she accepts her petitioner as a...well, as a paramour. A love-mate. Even if she isn't yet ready to take him as her life-mate."

"Oh." He pursed his lips, suddenly pensive. "Well. I hope I didn't disappoint you on that score, my lady."

Alauda smiled weakly. "My lord, you most certainly did not."

He pulled her back to his breast. "Perhaps I might not disappoint you again, a little later?"

"I'm counting on it," Alauda smile, refusing to meet his eyes. "All we need is some privacy, and maybe a blanket, and you can not disappoint me to your heart's content." She paused, then asked. "What's Sîol doing?"

Alainn pulled his head back, his eyes wide. "Eh? You – you weren't thinking of inviting her along, were you? Because I don't think she –"

Alauda seized his chin and turned his head forcefully. Sîol was standing nearby, at the edge of the dancing-stage.

"Ah," Alainn said faintly, clearly relieved. "She's waving. At us."

The elf-girl sighed. "Is it time already?"

"No, it's too early." He frowned. "I wonder what she wants?"

"I guess we'd better go and see." She kept a tight grip on his hand as they left the boards.

♦

Fourteen

"They're *here*!" Sîol hissed.

Alauda and Alainn had followed the red-haired girl's beckoning finger behind the stage. Alauda was unsurprised to see that Breaghan and Fearghan, along with the latter's immense dog, were waiting as well. Fearghan was still wearing his shapeless hat; and the dog, she noticed with a shiver of amused revulsion, was still drooling. A glistening puddle lay beneath the creature's generous jowl.

"Who's here?" Alainn frowned.

"Lord Alfaric, and Lady Nidlo! They've come to the festival!"

"Really?" Alauda goggled. "You're joking!" It was unthinkable; in Astramicor, no noble would ever be caught showing their face at a commoners' revel. It just wasn't done. There were rare exceptions, but...

Sîol's thoughts mirrored the elf-girl's. "This isn't the Realm, princess," she said pointedly. "Lord Alfaric's from Ekhan. They have a better grasp than you lot of why it's important to keep the classes from drifting apart."

" 'My lot'?" Alauda snapped. "I'm not noble. And I don't need a civics lesson, thank you very much." She glanced around. "Where're Alacer and Tonlees?" She was morbidly afraid that she knew the answer to that question. She just didn't want to think about it.

"Who cares?" Sîol snapped. "We don't need'em."

Breaghan looked alarmed. "That wasn't the plan!" she exclaimed. "The boy – the gray-hair – he needs to come, too!"

"We can do without him," Alainn shrugged. "Can't we?"

"No!"

Alauda stared at the pretty Halfling, puzzled. "Why is Alacer so important?"

Breaghan spun to face her, eyes wide. "He's tall!" she exclaimed. "And there are w-walls to climb!"

Alauda rolled her eyes. Breaghan was clearly love-struck. She briefly considered teasing the girl about it, but with Sîol fuming with impatience, she decided to hold her peace.

"Alfaric brought his guards with him;" Sîol was saying. "The castle will be almost empty. There'll never be a better time to go, so I say we go now. Agreed?"

"Agreed!" Fearghan growled. Alainn nodded.

Breaghan turned to Alauda, her eyes pleading. The elf-girl sighed. "Not agreed." When Alainn turned to remonstrate with her, she whirled on him. "Breaghan's right. Alacer's taller, and he's stronger than any of us. If we're house-breaking, we will need him."

"Fine!" Sîol sighed. "But we *don't* need the girl!"

Alauda leaned against the back of the stage, crossing her arms. "Her name is Tonlees," she said calmly, "and if you need me, then you need her. Because I won't go without her."

"*Scrios dé*!" the redhead snarled. "Bree, go find'em, wherever they are, and drag'em back here! With their knickers or without, I really don't care!"

Breaghan nodded and ran for the dancing platform.

The quartet waited, Sîol tapping her toe impatiently. Alauda occupied the time by scratching the dog's thick, matted ruff. He wasn't quite as tall at the shoulder as Shambir, and nowhere near as lean and menacing, but he was probably twice as heavy as the immense wolf. His barrel was so broad that she couldn't get her arms even half-way around it.

It was while she was attempting this that she noticed that buried amid the brown and white fur was a saddle. Heavy leather satchels, along with a quiver and a coil of tightly-braided rope, hung from the animal's tack.

She turned to Fearghan. "You ride him?"

"Why not?" the diminutive fellow bristled. "He's deadly in the charge!"

If he was charging down a line of chipmunks, maybe, Alauda thought, struggling to contain a titter. "I don't doubt it," she said, as solemnly as she could.

"I don't think I like your tone."

"Well, Smuggy does," she crooned, worrying the dog's pendulous jowls, and getting smeared with gobbets of gooey saliva for her trouble. "Doesn't he?" 'Smuggy' rumbled contentedly.

"It's 'Smugaid'!" Fearghan protested.

"I don't think so," Alauda chuckled. "He looks more like a 'Smuggy' to me. Isn't that so, precious?"

The dog's jaw fell open, and his immense tongue lashed out. She managed to dodge it just in time. He woofed happily, his furry tail thumping the earth.

Fearghan crossed his arms, visibly annoyed.

Alauda leaned against Alainn's shoulder. "You're quite taken with me, aren't you?" she whispered.

He threw her a perplexed glance. "Very much so. Why?"

"You'd forgive me nearly anything, I suppose?"

"Certainly. But what could I possibly have to –"

"This." Alauda bent and scrubbed her palms against his thighs, leaving long trails of glistening dog spittle behind. "Sorry."

Alainn watched her with a tolerant scowl. He said nothing, but his expression spoke volumes.

Breaghan returned moments later with Alacer and Tonlees in tow. Both were red-faced and puffing, as if they'd come at a run – or, Alauda thought, feeling mildly nauseated, as if they'd been engaged in some other physically demanding activity.

She shoved her misgivings – and her sense of guilt at her own indiscretions with Alainn – into a corner of her thoughts, and explained the situation. Sîol added details, and closed with the makeshift cabal's proposal: adventure, silence, and fair shares all 'round.

Both of the elves agreed to come along without hesitation: Tonlees with a delighted grin, and Alacer with a tolerant, worried smile. Her friends' readiness to accompany her was absurdly gratifying. Alauda took their hands on an impulse, and tried not to squeeze too hard when Alacer and Toni exchanged a fleeting but profoundly expressive look.

Sîol gathered them all with a glance. "Follow me," she said tersely. "No talking, unless you need to warn me of something. And keep to the elven tongue, everyone; most of our people only speak a smattering of it, and the folk at Arx Cervus are all humans, every last one of them. Accord?"

Breaghan, Fearghan, Alainn, and Tonlees all said, "Accord." Alauda and Alacer merely nodded.

"Good," the redhead winked. "We're off. And may Cham's luck be with us all."

The oddly balanced troupe – three-and-a-half elves, and three-and-a-half Halflings, Alauda thought with a bemused grin – departed the campsite under cover of darkness. Both moons were high now. Sîol, with admirable foresight, had left a pile of blankets near a fence-post. None were new, and all were of dark, patterned wool which, once thrown about the shoulders, made the wearer as good as invisible to any casual observer.

Unless, Alauda clucked to herself, the observers happened to be elves. The light of Chuadan and Lodan together was more than sufficient for her and her friends to see just as well as if they had been abroad at high noon. Sîol was obviously aware of this; the redhead steered a course away from the caravan's wagon lines, keeping to the low ground near the river, where the bracken and new ferns provided at least some concealment.

The course she chose wasn't easy, meandering between trees and across boulder-strewn meadows. It quickly became obvious that Halfling eyes were at least as sharp as those of the elves. That was a revelation to Alauda; she'd had no idea that halpies could see so well in the dark. It explained, at least in part, their storied prowess as burglars and second-story men. It also made her wonder what *else* they might be able to do.

The river also offered a simple and relatively direct path to their destination. Alauda had forgotten precisely how far Arx Cervus was from Buckhill, but she had a rough idea. From their ride she recalled that it was too far to be seen from Buckhill, but still somewhat less than two leagues. Two leagues to the stick, she knew, was a reasonable rule of thumb for a group attempting to move unseen and unheard. As it was still at least a stick before midnight, she reasoned, they ought to have plenty of time to reach the castle, work their way in, and locate their objective before sunrise.

Her only concern was her attire. Her boots were built for strutting in ladylike fashion, not for long marches over broken terrain. The exaggerated heels threatened to turn an ankle at every step. The gown was worse; it was heavy, the corset constrained her breathing, and the over-jacket made it difficult to move her arms. She couldn't take the jacket off, however, because her shoulders were bare beneath it, and night's chill was settling in. Too, more than a month of being a passenger in an ox-cart had done her conditioning no favours; the forced march found her out, and in no time at all she was sweating and gasping despite the cold.

The others were doing only a little better. Alacer seemed fine, but Tonlees was having even a worse time of it. Her dress was snug about her thighs, making it difficult to walk, while her heeled shoes were even more impractical for cross-country strolls than Alauda's boots. None of the Halflings, she noticed, looked as uncomfortable as the three elves; even their finery, such as it was, seemed practical in cut and craft. They clambered easily over the uneven ground, moving with such confidence that when Alainn offered her his hand to help her out of a ditch, she accepted with a sweaty-faced smile.

Tonlees gave up before long, removing her shoes and carrying them in one hand, and wincing whenever she stubbed a toe on a stone or fallen log, or trod on an unseen thorn-bush. Alauda watched her carefully, and was relieved rather than wounded when Alacer stepped up to lend her his arm. It helped to alleviate some of the guilt she was feeling. This was the worst-planned enterprise upon which she'd ever embarked, and she'd allowed her friends to be drawn into it. If she hadn't spent so much time day-dreaming about Alainn or pining after Alacer, she might've thought to hide a cache of more pragmatic clothing somewhere along their path.

All they needed now, she thought dourly, was to be caught in a sudden spring snowstorm.

They marched in silence, and were not disturbed. Nothing, no one, was abroad so late at night. Alauda could hear animal sounds in the distance – birds, bats, the thud of hooves, the rustling crackle of leaves beneath talons, the distant cries of wolves, and the nearer yipping of coyotes. She could smell things, too: the moss, the new grass, the stones – even the water. It was...*peculiar*. It reminded her of the nights she'd spent with the Raven Clan. With Akaryah, and Mua...and especially Jantun. It was as if her time with them had awakened something new in her; something wild and feral, that refused to go back to sleep. She began to feel better – less winded, and more at ease, as if the exertion and the night's wind had tapped some essential reservoir of strength within her.

The howls and yips, she noted, remained distant. Whether because of the size of their group or the bellows-like snuffling of Fearghan's enormous canine companion, they were not challenged by any of the night's denizens. That at least was a comfort.

They heard Arx Cervus long before they saw it. The river they were following – the Whyle – grew narrower and more ferocious as they approached its headwaters. The roar of the waterfall loomed out of the night while they were still a mile or more from the hillocks of stone where the mountain's knees jutted out into the Wastes. It reminded Alauda incongruously of Vitrafoss – and, inevitably, of her plunge over the frothy near Ringcastle in the course of escaping from the well-manicured clutches of Lady Kalanna and her paramour, Bale Laws. And now here she was, haring off upon another ill-thought-out adventure without any idea of what might lie ahead.

She vowed to herself that, come what may, she was *not* going over any more waterfalls.

Her vow unfortunately did not entirely preclude bathing under other circumstances. Shortly before reaching the outermost point of the jutting spit of rock, Sîol turned suddenly to the left, leading the party down the river-bank and toward the water. "Where are we going?" Alauda hissed.

"We need to cross the river," the redhead replied, nearly shouting so as to be heard over the roar of the water. "This is the best place. Unless you feel like trying to talk your way past the guards at the gate!"

"That's better that than *swimming*!" Alauda hissed. "Especially in this dress!"

"She could, you know," Toni said, gratifyingly defensive. "Talk her way past them, I mean."

"Not a chance," Sîol snarled. "You could talk yourself blue in the face; nobody lets *halpinya* in after dark."

"And with good reason. After all, you are here to rob the place. Aren't you?"

"Aren't *you*?" the Halfling girl asked pointedly.

Alauda bridled at the Sîol's tone; but then Alainn laughed, and she had to laugh along with him. Their erstwhile leader had a point.

Her fears were allayed a moment later. The river was at its narrowest – and hence, deepest and fastest – point. At its very edge stood an enormous, straight-limbed fir. A significant wedge had been cut from the side facing the river – and, standing amidst the mound of white woodchips, there was an axe.

Sîol turned at Alacer. "Alainn got it started this morning. You, my handsome buck, can finish it."

To Alauda's surprise, Alacer threw her a querulous glance before complying. When she nodded her approval he stepped forward, picked up the axe – and smiled.

"What is it?" Sîol asked.

Alacer held up the 'axe'. The haft was no longer than his forearm. "It's so small!"

"We don't have your ape-arms!" the Fearghan growled.

Alacer shook his head and went to work on the tree's undamaged flank.

Each axe-stroke echoed through the night, making Alauda twitch. She worried that the castle's guards might hear the din – but then realized that they were so much closer to the waterfall that they probably couldn't hear anything at all. That was just as well.

Alacer paused to doff his coat, then took up the axe and went back to work. Alauda watched, a slight smile on her face. Though tall and slender, he was as strong as several months of demanding physical labour could make him, and the play of muscles beneath his shirt was mesmerizing. It was some time before she realized that Tonlees was watching him as well. So, to her mounting amusement, were Sîol and Breaghan. *Especially* Breaghan.

Alauda rolled her eyes. A sudden stab of anger soured her mouth. Tonlees was one thing – but a *Halpie*?

A moment later she was castigating herself for her hypocrisy. She'd only just come from doing a lot more with Alainn than exchange calf-eyed looks.

Alacer paused only once for breath. He'd made good progress; the wood was already creaking and crackling. She leaned over to Alainn. "How long did that take you?" she asked.

"Most of the morning," he replied, his eyes wide. "Though in my defence, your friend's arms *are* a lot longer than mine."

"Hmm," Alauda murmured. That was something that she knew from first-hand experience. It would, however, have been impolitic to mention it.

After a few more moments' work, the tree teetered. Alacer dropped the axe and stepped back, watching the stump carefully. The remaining wood snapped and groaned – and tree fell, right across the river, its upper branches just catching on the stones of the farther shore.

"Go!" Sîol commanded. "Bring the axe, pretty boy; we might need it."

Fearghan started across the tree's trunk at once, his mount close upon his heels. Smugaid, despite his immense size, was surprisingly light on his feet.

Breaghan went next.

When Sîol stepped up, Alauda seized her arm. "His name's 'Alacer'," she glowered. "Not 'pretty boy'."

It was a novelty to be looking down at someone. Sîol, however, returned her glower without expression. After a moment, she nodded. "Fine. *Sieur* Alacer, my apologies."

"Accepted," the grey-haired boy laughed. "But as a rule, pretty girls can call me whatever they like." He tossed the axe over his shoulder, beckoned to Tonlees, and started across the makeshift bridge, leaving Alauda feeling like an idiot.

She didn't feel any better when Sîol smiled triumphantly, made some sort of obscure, possibly obscene, gesture at her, and danced off in Alacer's wake.

Alauda and Alainn crossed last, the golden-eyed boy staying close behind. As it happened, she needed the help. She stepped up onto the broad trunk without difficulty, trotting along the smooth bark – but the instant she put out a hand, grasping a branch to steady herself, everything changed.

A bolt of slivery agony shot through her fingers, up her arm and into her heart, settling like a coiled serpent in her belly. She snatched her hand back at once, but the feeling didn't go away; it stung her fingers as though she'd grasped the blade of a sword. She jerked to a halt and studied her palm, expecting to see a sudden flood of scarlet, but saw nothing. Her flesh was not especially clean, but it was unmarked.

Behind her, Alainn hissed, "Keep up, my lady!"

Alauda didn't move. She could feel the stinging through her boots now; a sharp, burning sensation that spread up her legs, as if she were walking in a pool of vitriol. Her knees trembled, and her hands flailed for balance – but she didn't dare touch any of the branches.

"What's wrong?" the boy asked, worried now.

"Help me!" she grated. "I need to get off! Quickly, please!"

Alainn, to his credit, didn't badger her with any more queries; he sidled past her, holding her by the waist, then took her hands and placed them on his shoulders. Walking slowly, he led her forward.

Alauda followed as swiftly as she could, placing her booted toes gingerly on the bark. Every step stung a little, though nowhere nearly as badly as when she had grasped the branch. Walking this way, they managed to negotiate the fifteen-pace length of the log without further incident.

At the far end, Alainn leapt to the sand, and then helped Alauda down. "What happened?" he murmured.

She was staring at the leaves and branches, swaying in the gentle breeze. She could smell the sap, as fresh and biting as blood. "I don't know." She looked at her hands again; they were still pristine.

Sîol's voice echoed back from ahead. "Come on!"

The river-bank was steeper on the southern side. They stumbled through impenetrable brush for several hundred paces, scrambling up the slope on their hands and knees. Alauda stopped worrying about her gown; after only moments it was filthy, and well on its way to being a total loss. "You had the foresight," she gasped at Sîol during one of their infrequent pauses, "to come all the way out here, and cut a tree half-way through to serve as a bridge; but it didn't occur to you to hide more practical clothing for us?!"

"Did it occur to *you*?"

"How could it?" Alauda hissed. "This was *your plan*!"

"I told you we were going to penetrate a fortress," the redhead shrugged. "Weren't you listening?"

"Of course I was! But –"

"How am *I* responsible for your failure to properly prepare?" Sîol asked reasonably.

All Alauda could do in response was sputter incoherently.

"Well, live and learn, princess," the redhead shrugged. "If you do manage to live, that is. It'll be something to remember for the next time."

"The next time?" Alauda exclaimed, her eyes bulging dangerously. "The *next* time?!"

Sîol glanced at Alainn. "You do know how to pick'em. She's so loud we might as well have come in a farrier's cart."

Alauda whirled on her escort. "*Alainn!*"

"Quiet, my lady, please!" Alainn pleaded. "We're getting close."

She managed to choke back her mounting irritation – but only just.

They were closer than she'd realized. When they emerged from the trees, Alauda could see the castle's outer curtain wall just above them. There was neither light nor movement atop it. Another hundred paces, crouched over and stepping softly through the low bracken, put them against the lichen-speckled buttresses that jutted from the ancient stone.

Alacer was rubbing his hand over the weathered, pebbled surface. "Bedrock," he whispered. "This wasn't built up; the foundations were cut from the mountain. Gods, can you imagine the work involved? No wonder it's lasted so long." He glanced up. "Where are we?"

Alauda followed his gaze. The wall wasn't as high as those she'd seen from the road. They'd reached part of the lower fortifications, a rectangular outwork topped by a projecting parapet. There were no bastions, and only a single slender tower in one corner. Then the night breeze wafted past them, bringing the answer to Alacer's question. Her

nostrils flared; she smelled a profusion of herbs just beginning to sprout –
chara, comfrey, ferula, mint, sage – as well as the more common and
comforting odours of old garlic and leek, onion and cabbage.

And of rot. The stink of decomposing vegetation was
overwhelming. "It's a kitchen-garden," she murmured. "And compost."

"Yes," Sîol replied, barely moving her lips. "I hope you don't mind
getting a little dirty."

"I think that ship has sailed," Alauda growled, brushing
ineffectually at the most and brambles clinging to her dress.

The redhead led them around the corner of the structure, right to
the centre of the stench: a garbage heap. Old soil mingled with rotting
vegetable scraps lay in a fan that spread out downhill across the slope. The
hillside was more precipitous here, dropping away from the garden wall
to a steep cliff that led down to the river's edge; most of the detritus,
Alauda realized, would be rinsed away into the river by any significant
amount of rainfall.

They were right below the Old Keep now, Sîol told them; the
black, sombre mass of it loomed above them like a vulture. Keeping their
left shoulders to the wall, they clambered up the spray of rubbish, digging
their toes into the moist, clinging ordure to keep from slipping over the
cliff's edge. When Fearghan lost his balance, sliding a little and spitting a
vile oath in momentary panic until Smugaid slobberingly seized the back
of his collar and halted him, Sîol didn't remonstrate; she simply put her
fingers to her lips, and pointed up. Alauda knew what she was getting at;
there were lights in the windows of the keep. The Lord and Lady might be
at the party, but the rest of their retinue was almost certainly at home.

Any sentinels, at the very least, would be awake. Very much so,
Alauda suspected; she'd seen how Imperial commanders dealt with
common soldiers who failed in their duty. It still gave her nightmares. The
current custodian of Arx Cervus wasn't a mage like Lord Trivinako, but
one didn't have to be able to command the arcane arts to order an
execution. There was always a rope nearby.

For that matter, there was also the commander's wife, the
mysterious Lady Nidlo. A mage trained at the College of the Eye might
very well command the same sort of power that Alauda had seen Lord
Trivinako wield. She hoped fervently that the couple would remain at the
party.

Alauda recognized their destination as soon as she saw it. Right
above the steepest part of the cliff-face tell bastion changed from bedrock
to close-fitted stone – and here there was a gap. It stood as high as her
head, and was as wide as she could spread her arms. Behind it was a solid
wooden door.

Sîol beckoned to Alauda, and the two of them hunkered down

near the filth-encrusted planks. "Can you see all right?" the Halfling whispered.

Better than you, Alauda thought. "Of course."

"Got a knife?"

"Yes."

The redhead pointed. "There're latches on both sides, just inside the wall." She drew her own blade, a long dirk with a heavy pommel and a leather-wrapped hilt. "Slide your hand twixt wood and stone. You ought to be able to feel it."

Alauda drew Elspeth's dagger and did as she was told. She heard a tiny *clink* as the point touched something made of metal. "Got it."

Sîol glanced back at Alacer. "We two'll push the latches back," she hissed. "When we do, you raise the gate."

The boy stared at the massive wooden wall. "I can't lift that!" he said, appalled.

Alauda touched his shoulder. "Nobody could. Don't worry, there'll be counter-weights. Right, Sîol?"

"There are," Sîol replied. "It took all four of us last time, but pretty boy here ought to be able to do it one-handed."

"Alacer!" Alauda hissed.

Sîol rolled her eyes. "Fine! Come on, do it!"

Alauda pressed her knife home, and felt the metal blockage give. At Sîol's nod, Alacer dug his fingers into the muck, got them under the wooden barrier, and heaved. The gate came up so swiftly that Alainn had to leap over Alauda and grab the lower bar to prevent the thing from knocking into the overhead stops, and causing a racket.

At Sîol's gesture, the party piled silently through. Alacer lowered the gate behind them, and the paired latches clicked home. Alauda glanced at them; they could be opened readily enough from the inside. That was reassuring; there seemed to be every likelihood that they would have to make a hasty retreat.

As she had expected, they were standing in the rectangular outwork. It was about twenty paces in width by sixty paces long. To her left, the parapet-topped wall stood only three paces above her head; the small corner tower she'd seen was nothing more than a stairway to reach the top of the wall. To her right, though, the body of the castle proper looked immeasurably larger. The wall was once again made of solid, seamless granite. Carved from the rock of the promontory itself, it rose more than thirty paces from the garden furrows to the parapets far overhead. It was pierced by the odd dark, narrow window; an eerie sight. Behind the wall, the Old Keep loomed even higher.

Her nose wrinkled again. Beyond the stink of the muck that stained her clothes and the more welcoming odour of the newly turned soil, there was a darker, more disturbing scent. She would have known it before her time with the Suku Gagak, but here in the moon-lit darkness it was more pressing, more terrifying. "Death," she whispered.

"What?" Alainn said, scarcely moving his lips.

"I smell *death*!"

"So do I," Alainn said. "It's old, though. Isn't it?"

The elf-girl frowned. He was right; the reek of clay was ancient. She began to unbend – just a little.

Sîol scowled at her and pointed overhead. *Bone-yard*! she mouthed, then put a finger angrily to her lips. She turned her back and trotted off, her fingers trailing along the castle wall. Alauda, feeling like a ninny for giving voice to her megrims, followed, her face red.

At the far end of the furrows the garden wall rejoined the castle at an odd angle. Within that angle was a door. Alauda spotted it at once, even though its makers had evidently gone to some pains to conceal it. The thick, iron-bound wood had been carefully finished and stippled to resemble the surface of the granite, and had even been painted a similar shade. Time and weather, however, had done their work, and the sally port stood out plainly even by moonlight.

She frowned. "There're no hinges."

"Maybe it opens inwards," Tonlees remarked.

Alauda shook her head. "No sally port opens inwards. It'd be too easy to force."

"This one *is* easy to force," Sîol announced, keeping her voice low. "But you're right, it opens this way. Pretty boy – Alacer, I mean," she amended, "I'd like your head between my thighs, if you'd be so kind."

"I *beg* your pardon?" Alauda gasped.

Behind her, Alainn whistled tunelessly and put a surreptitious hand on her backside. She stepped on his toe – hard – and was rewarded with a wheezing grunt.

Alacer blinked. "Excuse me?" he said hoarsely.

"You people have no sense of humour, do you?" the redhead sighed. "Bend down, my darling. I need to get up on your shoulders."

Alacer knelt, and Sîol ran up his back, steadying herself with the hand he raised to assist. He stood again easily.

"Not too heavy, I hope," the redhead whispered in his ear.

"I spend my days carrying half-hundredweight grain sacks," Alacer grunted. "I'd much rather carry you."

"That'd be my first choice too," Sîol tittered, knotting her fingers in his hair for purchase. "Wups! It's like having my own walking ladder. Over to the door, slobkins!"

Three steps put the pair in front of the sally port. This put Sîol's face on the same level as the door's upper edge. Drawing her knife once more, she slid the blade between the peeling planks and the stone lintel, feeling her way. After a moment she grimaced and pushed, nearly shoving her makeshift pedestal backwards.

The door's top popped out from between the stone jambs. Sîol caught it, then directed Alacer to back away slowly. He took over from her, lowering the thick portal to the ground.

Alauda glanced at Alainn. "How in the World Made did you manage it the last time?"

"We climbed each other. I was on the bottom, as usual. This was a lot easier." He dropped a wink. "Every burglar should bring an elf along."

"You're enjoying this too much."

"What's life without a little danger?" He patted her backside again. Alauda cuffed his ear, and not gently.

Behind the portal, a narrow cavity had been cut into the stone: a short passageway – and then a stair. The risers led up to the left, and down to the right.

Sîol disengaged her legs and slid down Alacer's back as though he were a tree – and, to Alauda's exasperation, kissed him lightly on the cheek as she did so. "My thanks, my lover," she said briskly. "You're not the biggest thing I've ever ridden, but you're definitely the prettiest!"

"Happy to help," Alacer said, flushing a little.

She pointed at the steps. "Down to the cistern and the crypts; up to the cemetery, and the castle proper." She stepped into the dark hollow, and led off up the stairs.

Kiss him again, Alauda thought, *and I'll leave you in crypts!* She held her peace, smouldering in silence.

"Are you all right?" Alainn asked, concern etched into his expression

"I'm fine," the elf-girl grated. "But I don't think I like your friend very much "

He took her hand. "Jealous?"

His touch was surprisingly soothing. Alauda sighed. "Yes," she said truthfully, "and...well, no." She didn't know *what* to feel. What right had she to be jealous anymore? Alacer hadn't been dancing with *her,* after all.

"Well," Alainn grinned, as they waited for the rest of the troupe to mount the steps, "at least she's not pawing at me anymore."

Alauda stiffened. "You and Sîol? Did – did you –"

"Cham's cleft, no!" he expostulated in a fierce whisper. "D'ye think I'm mad?"

"Why would you have to be mad?" she said sullenly. "She's pretty enough."

"She's also terrifying," the boy said chuckled. "I'd follow her anywhere as my captain, but it'd be safer to mate with a marten. Besides, my heart's set on a certain elfy lady."

"Oh? Have I met her?"

He raised her fingers and pressed them to his lips. "Only in your looking-glass, my love."

She regarded him with a lopsided smile. "I've been crawling through garbage, Alainn."

Alainn touched his tongue to his lips, his smile slipping slightly. "Yes, I…uh, I just remembered that." He turned his head and spat.

Breaghan brushed past them – and to Alauda's surprise, gave Alainn a shove. "*An urrainn dhut nach cùm do làmhan dhith?*" Her tone was an angry hiss.

Alainn glanced at Alauda. "*Feumaidh sinn i,*" he replied.

"*Tha feum agam ort!*" The girl stormed up the stairs, her eyes full. He watched her go, an unhappy look on his face.

Alauda crossed her arms. "So," she said without expression, "Not Sìol, but Breaghan."

"I thought you didn't speak our tongue?"

"I don't have to," she sniffed. "I speak 'angry woman' just fine."

"It's not what you think," he said quietly. "Her father, the Bridle-Bearer…he took me in after my parents died. Breaghan was just a wee thing. I helped raise her. She's my sister, Alauda, in everything but blood. But –"

"But she doesn't see it that way," Alauda finished. It wasn't an unfamiliar story.

Alainn sighed. "No, she does not. Unfortunately."

The elf-girl clucked. "Well, I'm certainly not going to be angry with her for falling in love with you." She gave him a quick kiss on the ear and clambered up the stairs, cursing her luck at having managed to insert herself into a family drama. While the last thing she wanted to do at the moment was leave Alainn O'Dell in her life's wake, there was certainly some consolation in the fact that the caravan would soon be moving on.

Alainn followed behind her in gloomy silence, bringing up the rear.

The steps were steep, almost ladder-like; descending them would be tricky, particularly in her mother's boots. As they climbed, Alauda recalled suddenly that Alainn was below her. As far as she knew, he still had her smallclothes in his pocket; if he troubled himself to raise his eyes, he would have a clear view 'right up the serpentine to the barbican', as she'd once heard her mother put it. She blessed the comforting fact that Halflings couldn't see quite as well in the dark as elves.

On the other hand, she reasoned a moment later, what did it matter if he did see something? He'd already done a thorough reconnaissance of her barbican. Were it not for her better judgement, she might – in other circumstances – have considered raising the portcullis for him. Fortunately, her better judgement retained a firm grip on her passions. For the time being, anyway.

They emerged, as Sîol had promised, in the base of one of the tower bastions. Narrow stairs led up to the top of the wall; a small door led out into the cemetery. As Alauda's nose had suggested, it was truly ancient. The marker stones had mostly fallen over, and were weather-worn to the point of illegibility. Several of the graves had fallen in – and that, she realized, was proof positive that men had fought alongside elves at the darkest time in the history of the ancient world. The elves sent their fallen comrades to wind; only men committed the dead to soil.

The outer curtain formed two of its walls, while the third, to the south, was part of the Old Keep; the field consequently had a crooked, trapezoidal shape. Up close the ancient fortress was even more impressive. Alauda was under no illusion as to who had built the original structure; it was grim and solidly forbidding, with none of the airy beauty of elven fortifications. It might have fallen to Fineleor's family in ages long past, but the original keep and its outworks had all too obviously been built by humans. The yellow-lit windows, high up, stared down upon them like the eyes of a bloodthirsty kite. She found herself wanting to slink away and hide between the unkempt tombs.

The fourth wall of the cemetery was formed by a different structure, smaller but more elaborate. "That looks like a chapel," she whispered.

"It is," Sîol replied. "That's our path. Don't worry, it ought to be empty; I think the lord's men are still cleaning it out."

It was, and by all appearances they were. The redhead led them through an unlocked door and into the nave of the church. It was so old and clotted with debris that Alauda couldn't even hazard a guess as to which Power it might once have been dedicated. If humans had built the place, it was likely Vara the Merciful or Almighty Esu. Then she realized that House Orkarel would hardly have continued either tradition. *Maybe Fineleor hadn't used the place at all*, she thought. He'd been a devotee of the Forest Gods, after all, and so probably worshipped at a sacred grove somewhere, complete with standing stones and towering Morbannens. But a human-built castle wouldn't've been that likely a place to find a *lucum*, and if there were Morbannen trees here, she ought to have seen them by now.

It was a puzzler. Perhaps Fineleor hadn't lived here long enough to establish a place of worship.

They didn't linger. Sîol led them out the opposite side of the church and into another courtyard. From the layout of the furrows and planting boxes, Alauda guessed that it had been another garden, perhaps for herbs. There was also a well in the centre of the yard – a big one, with the remnants of a complicated hoisting mechanism rotted and rusting beside the stone berm. A newer bucket and rope lay next to the detritus of yesteryear. "How long have Lord Alfaric and his lady been here?" she asked.

"They arrived last autumn, I think," Alainn replied. "Not long before we got here ourselves." He glanced around. "From the look of things, they're still trying to make the place livable."

"They've got walls and a well," Alauda shrugged. "They're halfway there. All they need now are food and arms, and they'll be ready to stand a siege."

The boy chuckled. "Who's going to besiege them all the way out here?"

Alauda shot him an apologetic glance. "Forgive me, Alainn," she said quietly, "but who killed your parents?"

Alainn winced. "Oh." He shuddered visibly. "D'ye really think this place could stand up to a dragon?"

"It did, once upon a time," she murmured. "In mighty Fineleor's day."

There was a small alcove at the eastern end of the garden. Sîol gathered her troupe briefly. "The kitchens come next, followed by the servants' quarters. They're all likely to be occupied, so we can't go through them; we'll have to go around. That means we'll be in the open until we get to the old gatehouse." She bit her lip. "This is the most dangerous part. There could be a lot of people about."

"How did you manage it last time?" Alauda asked.

Sîol wrinkled her nose. "That was months ago, before Alfaric moved his whole bloody staff here. It was a lot easier when it was only the lord and lady, and a few grooms and guards."

"Of course," Alauda sighed. "But why are we going to the old gatehouse anyway? I thought we were looking for the well. Isn't it right there?" She pointed at the pit in the courtyard.

The four Halflings turned to stare at her. Breaghan barked a laugh; Fearghan put a hand over his eyes.

"Alauda," Alainn said, taking her gently by the elbow, "That's not Kulkisari's Well."

"It's not?" Alauda blinked. "Well, then…where the hells is it?"

Sîol stepped out of the alcove, beckoning to Alauda. She followed, her friends trailing after her. The redhead led them through an arched gateway, to the castle's inner ward. Behind the jumble of masonry, the mountain loomed like a brooding titan.

There was a covered gallery running around the interior of the fortress, elevated a few paces above the flag-stoned square. Sîol named the castle's features. "There's the Old Keep," she whispered, pointing to the right. Sweeping her hand to the left, she said, "the new gatehouse...the Knight's Hall...apartments for guests...and the White Tower. That's where the mint is – where they're making all those new silver shillings, I mean."

"So where's the blasted Well?" Alauda demanded.

The redhead pointed over the roofs of the apartments, just to the left of the imposing bulk of the Knight's Hall. "Look at the mountainside," she said quietly. "Can you see the black line?"

"Better than you can," Alauda growled. "So?"

"And the tower to the right, with the broken bridge – with all the mist from the waterfall?"

Alauda nodded again.

"Right," Sîol said briskly. "We need to get to the old gatehouse, because that's the only path to the mountain road. We take the mountain road until it peters out near that bridge, then we take a rope to the bridge. The Tower is a tomb for some ancient lord or other. From there, there's a bridge through the waterfall, to an old statue. Kulkisari's Well is beyond it."

Alauda blinked. "Up there?" she squeaked, appalled. "Half-way up the mountainside?!"

"That's what we hope," the Halfling shrugged. "We never got any further than the statue. There's some sort of spell on the place, that stops anyone who isn't an elf. *Your* sort of elf, I mean. Third House."

"And how d'ye know *that*?" the elf-girl demanded.

"Because we've tried it," Fearghan grunted. "All of us, and we all got a nasty shock for our trouble. It's like a wall; a wall made of skyfire. Alainn did better than the rest of us; he managed to get an arm through sparks before they kicked him back."

Alauda glanced at her escort. He gave her a sheepish smile and spread his hands. "Half a Halfling, right? But also – half an elf."

"You got further than the others," Alauda said faintly. "And that's why you wanted *me*?"

"Actually, it's why my father wanted your mother," Breaghan interjected with an embarrassed smile. "He and Mhaister Cloughsen were the first to investigate the place; I only found out about it from reading his journals, and I told Alainn. Together we told Sîol, and we four came to take a look.

"You see," she said, looking indecently pleased with herself, "Mhaister Cloughsen knows something about magic, and he thought the spell was too dangerous to attempt without professional aid. He and my father decided they needed a wizard's help to break it. Your mother is only the second mage to happen along in the last few months, and she was the first to even agree to hear them out. Asking you instead was my idea; I thought, why try to break the spell, when all we really need to do is meet its conditions?"

"By finding a high elf," Alauda muttered, appalled. "One idiotic enough to agree to serve as your – your prodding-stick! Me."

"Just so," Sîol nodded. "You."

It was as if someone had lit a lantern in the stuffy recesses of her reason. "So all of that nonsense with the cups, and so on – that was to test me? Why bother, if all you needed was an elf?"

Sîol screwed up her face. "We needed to know whether you were really as clever as you thought you were. Whether you were any good you are at seeing through puzzles. According to Mhaister Cloughsen's research, there's something like that up there; a riddle of sorts. It's supposed to be nigh impossible to untangle."

"And your father *approved* this – this lunacy?" Alauda hissed. "Sending children – his children! – into some ancient arcane death-trap? What kind of maniac is he?"

"Well, of *course* he didn't 'approve' it!" Sîol scoffed. "Don't be silly! We didn't tell him; this is our plan, not his. If he knew what we were up to, we could never hope to beat him and Cloughsen to the treasure."

"Wh – " Alauda nearly screamed, but checked herself at the last possible instant. "Why?" she hissed, sounding as if she were being strangled. "Why do you have to beat him to *anything*?!"

Alainn took her hand again. When Alauda, quivering with indignation, snatched it back, he looked a little sad. "It's tradition," he explained. "Children have to outwit their parents before they can be counted among their number."

"That's insane!" Alauda protested.

He shrugged. "It's a rite of passage. You understand that, don't you?"

Alauda goggled at him for a long, painful moment. Then she put her head in her hands. At that moment, she would have given anything for the luxury of being able to scream her frustration at the night.

♦

Fifteen

"Right," Alauda said thickly. She'd taken a moment to gather her wits, ignoring the impatient glares of her diminutive cohorts, and had indulged in a dozen deep, even breaths. "If we're going to go through with this...this suicidal idiocy, then we're going to do it intelligently. Why not just go across the parapets?" She pointed at the bastion from which they'd emerged, and the curtain wall.

The redhead stared at her. "Where do you think the guards are?"

"Are there no guards out there?" the elf-girl asked, waving at the inner ward.

"She has a point," Fearghan observed sourly. "Doesn't matter where we are if we run into Lord Alfaric's troops; we're cooked either way."

"When did this company become a debating society?" Sîol said crossly.

Alauda crossed her arms. "When you failed to tell me that we were infiltrating an ancient stronghold," she hissed, "that's half-way up a mountainside, and defended by lethal magicks to boot!"

"I don't recall saying anything about 'lethal'," Sîol objected.

"The Mhaister's notes did," Alainn interjected helpfully. "Bree's father's, too."

The redhead looked daggers at him.

"This is exactly my point," Alauda snapped. "You don't keep information like this from your comrades!"

Sîol's eyes bulged. "Lessons in leadership, now!" she exclaimed, executing a mocking half-bow. "Harken all to the words of the great general, descendent of Anja herself!"

Alauda's teeth grated together; it took all of her self-restraint not to snap back at the girl. "Look," she said calmly, "if you can prove to me that going through a barracks full of bored soldiers is safer than going over it, then I'm in. But speaking from personal experience, that's a sure and certain way for Toni and I, at the very least, to end up spending the rest of the night on our backs." Her cheek twitched. "Since we have the most at stake, I say we do it my way. I'd rather try to handle a guard or two who're alert and on duty than a couple of dozen who're taking their ease and deep in their cups."

Sîol was too obviously making the same sort of effort to curb her rising ire. "You're certain you can do that? Silently?"

"I've done it before." If she could ensnare someone as intimidating as Tanju Berat – or for that matter, a hungry mountain lion – then a couple of round-eared pike-pushers oughtn't to pose too much of a challenge.

"Fine," the redhead sighed. "You and me then, up front. I – what now?"

"Not 'you and me'," Alauda corrected. "Me and Tonlees, with Alacer in tow. If any of the guards sees a halpie, they'll know something shifty's afoot. No one in their right mind would let one of you into a castle except in chains." She cocked her head and smiled thinly. "No offence."

"None taken," Sîol snarled. She nodded at Alacer. "Take the dog with you, pretty boy; he's battle-trained. Just in case things get titchy." She tugged on his sleeve; when he bent down, she put her ears to his lips, and said, "*Ionsai* means 'attack'."

Alacer frowned. "Yun-sei?"

"Close enough." She turned back to Alauda. "Right, madam general – lead on, if you please."

"What should *I* do?" Tonlees hissed, nervous, as the pair of them climbed the stairs to the parapet.

"You're already doing it," Alauda murmured. She bent and attempted to brush some of the filth of the midden heap from the skirts of her gown. "Look beautiful. If we see anyone, just take my arm and laugh, as if you'd said something funny. In fact, take my arm right now."

The two girls locked elbows. Tonlees' arm was stiff and trembling; Alauda, choking back another unexpected burst of rage at the thought of her auburn-haired friend kissing her beloved Alacer, patted the older girl's hand to calm her. "If we see a guardsman, wet your lips, wink at him, and wiggle your hips. Try to look as if you're thinking about pulling him into a stairwell and making *basz-basz* with him until he passes out."

Tonlees stared at her. "What in the World Made does 'bash-bash' mean?"

Alauda cocked an eyebrow at her.

"Oh. Oh! Powers below, Ala, you're *awful*!" She blushed scarlet.

"Perfect," Alauda chuckled. "Just like that." She ordered the Halflings to remain within the walls of the bastion, and to come out and dash across the intervening distance only after the three elves had cleared the path to the gatehouse. Sîol was the last to nod her agreement.

Once atop the wall Alauda set a slow, leisurely pace, reasoning that the only logical excuse for two well-dressed if somewhat dishevelled young ladies of high elven birth to be walking the parapets at such a time of night was to take the air, and look at the stars. She played the part to the hilt, as if her life depended upon the quality of her performance. She smiled and whispered – brief, nonsensical phrases intended to provoke giggles from her stiff and unresponsive friend – pointing at nothing in particular, and turning to giggle brainlessly at Alacer.

Her gestures weren't entirely feigned. Alauda was surprised to observed that from the vantage of the north-facing wall she was able to see over the wooded promontory to the solid moons-lit clot of Buckhill in the distance, and the much brighter, glimmering lights of the Second Spring festival. The party appeared to still be a-boil.

"I guess nobody missed us," Tonlees whispered.

"Why would they?" Alauda whispered back. "It's Second Spring. Our parents will be expecting us to return long after dawn." Her mother probably thought she was off in the dark somewhere with Alacer – which, she reflected with an internal snort, was the gods' own truth.

"I just hope the guards miss us, too," Tonlees replied. Her helpful flush had faded; her face was white.

They carried on, taking their time. From the bastion to the old gatehouse and the White Tower (as Sîol called it) was a little less than a hundred paces. Alauda glanced over her shoulder as they neared the gatehouse, and was relieved to see Alacer and Smugaid trailing behind in their wake.

As they walked, her nostrils flared. Two new scents perturbed her senses. The first, and by far the most obvious, was the thick, stinging stench of hot metal, underscored by charcoal and brimstone. The source of the reek was clear; an enormous stone chimney protruded from the White Tower's outer wall, and it was belching thick clouds of smoke. Alauda had never seen a smelter, much less smelled one, but she had no difficulty identifying the process by the odours it produced.

The second scent, however, was far more subtle; beneath the overwhelming assault of the coal fire's billowing exhalations, it tickled the back of her throat, making her eyes itch, and the tiny hairs behind her ears stand erect. She shook her head swiftly, as if attempting to dislodge a bothersome insect. "Can you smell that?" she whispered.

Tonlees glanced at her sidelong. "Are you joking?" she replied. "It's all I can do not to cough!"

"Not the smoke. The…the other thing." Try as she might, she couldn't place the odour. It reminded her of Akaryah, though, and Mua Licik; and, too, of Elspeth. And Jantun. A shudder of old desire rippled through her.

"All I can smell is *that*," Tonlees gagged, pointing at the chimney.

Behind them, Smugaid snuffled and spat, clearly in agreement with the two girls.

The gatehouse parapet hung out over the old bridge, which stretched across a cavernous ravine to connect to the barbican that straddled the mountain road. The three elves, accompanied by the enormous dog, made the crossing without incident. They were looking between the merlons, trying to adjudge how to affix Fearghan's rope (which still hung from Smugaid's saddle) in a fashion that would allow them to recover it after they'd used it to slither down the outer wall to the surface of the bridge. Alauda, satisfied that they'd made their approach without being observed, waved her arm in the general direction of the far-off bastion – and cursed herself for failing to leave Alacer or Tonlees behind. She didn't know whether any of the Halflings had the visual acuity to spot her gesture in the darkness, from so great a distance.

Tonlees watched her gesticulate, a grave look on her face. "This is dangerous," she muttered. "Why did I let you talk me into this?"

"I didn't talk *you* into anything," Alauda grumped. "I wanted Alacer along. I only insisted that the halpies keep a place for you because I didn't want you to feel left out!"

"It's no great hardship to be left out of a suicide pact!"

In the distance she saw shadows slip past the bastion's iron door and begin moving toward her. The four kept low, hugging the machicolations. "If that's how you feel," Alauda growled, "then maybe you should've mentioned it before we got to this point. Unless you feel like falling out now, and heading back alone."

Toni bit her lip. "No. No, I'll stay. It's just that – Ala, I'm scared!"

Alacer took the older girl's hand. Alauda rolled her eyes.

They followed the tip-toeing Halflings as they followed the parapet in the darkness. So intent were the three on their observations that they didn't notice the trio of guardsmen that emerged from a door in the flank of the White Tower. The hinges had been oiled, so that the portal made no noise as it swung open; but when it clanged into the stone wall, the three elves jumped.

And Smugaid barked.

That attracted the attention of the guardsmen. <You, there!> one of them cried, drawing his sword. <Don't move!> The two men behind him drew as well.

Alauda's mind went white with panic. Her heart raced, her bowels clenched – but none of it affected her wits. The same chill that froze her limbs seemed to liberate her reason. Turning to her friends, she snapped, "Stand still, stay silent, smile, and laugh. You're surprised and amused, but not frightened."

Tonlees and Alacer managed the first two, but not the last two. "Laugh!" Alauda hissed.

Alacer chuckled mechanically – "Ha-ha-ha! –" while Tonlees burst into as brainless a high-pitched titter as Alauda had ever heard. She sighed, wondering what she'd done to warrant being saddled with such a pair of dullards.

The three soldiers ran across the breadth of the gatehouse roof, their gear rattling and clattering, and surrounded the trio, sword-points levelled. One of the men brought a torch along – and Alauda blessed him for it. She didn't know whether her 'wink and whisper' would work if her subject was unable to see her winking.

<Who are you?> one of the men barked.

It was the same man that had spoken before, and he was clearly the leader of the trio. Alauda turned the full focus of her attention on him. He was a big fellow, tall and broad across the shoulders, though not quite as large as Knight Serikar, Lord Trivinako's shield-bearer, had been. His hair was as black as that of any Third-House elf – but he was also bearded, and clad in some semblance of a uniform, with an earth-coloured cloak and tunic over dark, woven trews and high boots.

He wasn't wearing armour, but she could see tiny semi-circles of rust here and there on his tunic, the tell-tale marks of a mailshirt. <Good evening, Captain,> she said, tilting her head in a polite nod, and deliberately pitching her voice a little high. <A lovely night, is it not?>

Her casual reply left the man nonplussed. <It is,> he said slowly. He squinted at her, obviously puzzled at her lack of trepidation. <Who are you, little girl?>

<Alauda Volo,> she replied, smiling and holding out her hand. <And you, Captain?>

<Ove Killing,> the soldier said. He stared at her outstretched hand for a long moment...and then he lowered his sword-point and took it. To Alauda's relief, he bowed over it.

<And it's not 'captain',> the fellow added with an amused smile. <I'm a corporal.>

Alauda didn't care whether it was 'colonel'; all that mattered was that the other men were following their senior's lead and lowering their swords. The fellow's surname had momentarily shaken her; in the travelling tongue, its connotations were unpleasant. She furrowed her brow prettily to mask her discomfiture. <What's a 'corporal'?>

<It means that I command ten men.>

<A *decarius*!> she exclaimed, using the elven word. <And these are two of your knights? Charmed, gentlemen.> She nodded regally.

Killing glanced at the other two swordsmen, both of whom were grinning despite themselves. <We're not knights,> he said drily. <Nor gentlemen either. And we're getting ahead of ourselves, little miss. What are you three –> he spotted Smugaid, who was sitting comfortably, panting, and drooling on the stones <– and that beast, doing up here?>

<We came to watch the stars,> Alauda replied. She allowed a wistful note to creep into her voice. She was doing her best not to look past the soldier's shoulder to see whether the Halflings were still crouching against the parapet. She gestured away from them, at Buckhill and the distant glow of the lanterns. <And the party. Our parents sent us away early.>

Killing scowled. <Your parents?>

<Sorry, I thought you knew,> Alauda said happily, weaving lies into truth – a far more effective technique, she'd learned through bitter experience, than crafting nonsense out of nothingness. Half-truths were easier to remember. <Our mother is Lady Alyssa Volo, chief mage to the leader of our caravan. She was Lord Alfaric's guest at the festival tonight, and he invited us to stay here, at his lovely fortress. We got here a little while ago, as I said.> She pointed at the oldest part of the keep. <Did you know that most of this was built by old Fineleor?>

<Who told you that,> the swordsman chuckled.

Alauda tossed her hair. The gesture felt stupid, but she knew that it worked. <Everyone knows! Why, who do you think built it?>

<Men, of course,> the corporal said laconically. <Your Fineleor may have added a garden or two, and his dwarfy friends added on to the place, particularly this very gatehouse, and higher up in the mountains; but the old keep was built by my people, girly. Not yours.>

<Well, 'your people' did well then,> Alauda smiled. <The view is lovely, don't you think?>

The man didn't look away from her. <It's all right. So, little miss. You've all the same mother, you say? You three don't look much alike.>

<Just me and my sister Tonlees here,> Alauda amended swiftly. <Alacer – Alacer Tiivus – is a friend.>

As if to support her mendacity, Tonlees reached out and took Alacer's hand. At the same time, she licked her lips, winked at the soldiers – and, to Alauda's horror, waggled her backside. *She looks like a duck*, the elf-girl thought, despairing.

<Right,> Killing frowned, looking oddly at the older girl. <Who let you lot in?>

Alauda pointed at the gatehouse next to the Old Keep. <The guards at the gate, of course.>

<And you arrived a little while ago,> the soldier repeated. <Odd, I didn't hear the bell.>

Alauda didn't say anything. Her mind was racing, wondering what she'd missed.

<You know,> Killing said softly, his sword coming up again. <The bell the gate-guards ring, to warn everyone that the portcullis is open while the bridge is down?>

Damn it! Alauda thought, frantic now. Taking a deep breath, she stepped forward until the sword's point was pressed against her bodice. Killing reflexively withdrew it a hand-span.

<I'm certain it was just an oversight, corporal,> she said softly. She waited until he was looking at her eyes before she went on. <You won't speak too harshly too them, will you? I'd hate to think that anything might prevent us from being friends.>

Killing blinked at her at least half a dozen times, his eyes remote. At last, to her infinite relief, he smiled.

♦

Sixteen

Alauda waited, waving happily at the three soldiers until the tower door had closed behind them. Then she slumped to the flagstones of the gatehouse roof, struggling not to vomit. Her mouth tasted like sour wine, and she was acutely conscious, and exceptionally grateful, that she'd eaten almost nothing all day.

She scarcely noticed that neither Alacer nor Tonlees had leapt to help her. It was Breaghan, surprisingly, who rushed to her side. "Are you all right?" the girl gasped.

Alauda nodded feebly. "I don't suppose...anyone thought to bring...any water?" she gulped. The taste of bile stung her tongue.

The Halflings shook their head in unison.

"You'll have all the water you can drink before long," Sîol warned. "And then some. Fearghan, your rope. Get us off this roof before something else goes wrong."

The rope that Fearghan had brought was thin, tough, and nearly thirty paces long. It was only ten paces from the parapets to the surface of the old bridge. They hung a loop over one of the merlons, and one by one the troupe lowered themselves carefully to the stone ledge outside the ancient gatehouse door.

Alauda found herself looking through the loophole with considerable trepidation. She'd never climbed a rope before, and the bridge, though not at all narrow, looked like a thread strung across the forbidding depth of the chasm. Her reason told her that she wasn't likely to miss her target – but she no longer trusted her reason. She'd made an absolute hash of her attempt to lie her way past the guards they'd encountered; had it not been for her ability to 'wink and whisper' her way out of trouble, she had no doubt that she and her companions (she couldn't bring herself to think of Sîol as a 'friend') would already have been shown to some noisome dungeon, there to await the arrival of a quartet of irate parents.

The thought made her shiver. She hadn't been lying when she'd told Tonlees the previous day that it had been years since her mother had last seen fit to take the cane to her, and that had been the truth; but the other side of that bitter coin was that she had no doubt whatsoever that, were the appropriate circumstances to arise, she would once again find herself bent over a convenient chest or chair for a vigorous birching. That prospect worried her more than the (for the moment, at least) far greater threat of being chained to the wall of a rat-infested oubliette dating from Mighty Tior's day. If nothing else, she reflected with a shiver, the fact that she feared one more than the other spoke volumes about the nature of her relationship with her mother.

"I wish I knew how you did that," Tonlees murmured as they huddled near the merlons.

"What, the winking and whispering? God, so do I!" Alauda replied, gulping back saliva. It was one thing to use her wiles to entice Alacer into a friendly wrestle in the long grass; it was quite another to try to do the same to a glowering human while staring cross-eyed at the wrong end of his sword. She didn't like relying on a phenomenon she scarcely understood to save her skin.

Alainn came up behind her; he and Fearghan had not yet made the climb. "The longer you think about it," he said softly, "the worse it'll be. Just go hand over hand, and clamp the rope between your thighs, and between your boots as well. I'll be below to catch you if you fall." He clambered up into the gap between the stones, gripping the rope in one hand.

"If I fall on you from this height," Alauda said nervously, "I'll flatten you."

"Then I shall die a happy man," the boy chuckled. "Courage, my lady!" And with that, he was gone.

Alauda leaned out, watching him descend the rope hand over hand. He'd obviously done it before. When he reached the bottom, he stared up at her, beckoning her to follow.

"Night's waning, 'my lady'," Fearghan growled.

Alauda whirled on the boy. "You're not helping," she snapped. Then she frowned. "Wait, how're you going to get Smuggy down?"

"His name," Fearghan grated, "is Smugaid! And that's my worry, not yours." He made a shooing gesture.

Irritation overwhelmed trepidation. Alauda climbed up into the loophole, knotted her fists about the rope, sat on the stone, and slid off.

Everything went well, for a little while at least. She kept her arms bent, locking her fists over the rough cord, and managed to lower herself a few paces. Her gown, however, was too wide; she couldn't squeeze the rope between her knees, or even find it with her feet. And without the support of her legs, her arms tired quickly.

One hand slipped, and then the other. She gripped the rope more tightly, and cried out in pain as the running hemp flayed the skin from her left palm. She fell the better part of twenty feet, landing in a crumpled heap atop Alainn – who, true to his word, had been waiting to catch her.

She didn't quite hammer him flat; she hadn't fallen far enough for that. But she did manage to knock the wind out of him. She also managed to wrench her ankle.

It took a few moments, but eventually Alainn was able to breathe again. Alauda helped him to his feet, balancing awkwardly on one foot. "I warned you," she said.

"You did," he chuckled. "Of course, this means you have to marry me."

She put her hands on her hips, hissing as her damaged palm contacted the fabric. "Indeed? How so?"

"Halfling law," the boy said solemnly. "When one of us saves another during a burglary, they have to wed."

Alauda glanced at Breaghan, her eyebrows raised. The girl shook her head, waggling her braids. "It's more a custom than a law, really."

"An *ancient* custom!" Alainn exclaimed. "What say you, my lady? You wouldn't flout an ancient custom, would you?"

Alauda shrugged. "As I see it, you're only half a Halfling, so the custom should only apply to one of us. You'll have to marry yourself." She patted his cheek. "I'm sure you'll be very happy together."

The others began probing the surface bridge, Sîol directing them to the path they'd already proved. Alauda, to her surprise, felt a droplet strike her cheek. At first she thought it was raining; but when she touched the spot, her fingers came away coated in drool.

She looked up. Above her, Smugaid was spiralling slowly down out of the sky, hanging from a loop of rope that ran under his forelimbs. He was whining plaintively. As he neared the flagstones she stepped aside, dodging a particularly vile gobbet of spittle.

A moment later he was on his feet. The Halflings disentangled the dog, comforting him, and Fearghan drew the loop back up to the parapets. A moment later he lowered himself, sitting easily in the loop, and paying out the rest of the rope. He reached the flagstones without incident, tugged the rope from the stones overhead, coiled it, and hung it on the dog's back. "Ready."

Sîol led them across the bridge, warning them all to keep to the left edge, as part of the arched buttresses had fallen away on the right. That knowledge comforted Alauda not at all. Had she been in charge of the expedition, she would have used the rope to tie all of them together – particularly, she realized with a gulp as she set foot on the bridge, as the ancient stones were both moss-covered and slick with evening dew.

"I'm right behind you," Alainn said soothingly. "Take my hand, if you like."

Alauda seized the proffered fingers in a grip that drew a hiss of discomfort from her escort – and an accompanying squeal of pain from her own throat. She had clutched at his hand with her lacerated palm. The stinging made her eyes tear up.

Her misgivings notwithstanding, the party made it across the narrow bridge without incident. Alauda had all but closed her eyes as they reached the centre of the span; the drop beneath the stone arches was nearer a hundred paces than fifty, and the bottom of the chasm was strewn with boulders fallen from the mountain over the course of ages. Her recent tumble made her hesitant. She froze up briefly, lurching into motion only when Alainn spoke softly to her; and when she reached the antediluvian barbican at the far end of the span, she all but threw herself at its reassuring bulk.

The barbican was the ancient entrance to Arx Cervus, and dated from a time when the Old Keep had been known only as 'Kulkisari's Well'. It was crumbling in disrepair. The gates had rusted and rotted away, and the old archway lay open to the mountainside. Alauda stared at the missing barriers, then glanced back over her shoulder at the still intact bridge. "Why is this unwatched?" she demanded. "Someone could easily assault the castle by this road. They'd be up to the old gatehouse before the defenders could string their bows!"

"Nobody but the birds could assault anything from here," Sîol replied. "The mountain road dates from Tior's day. What you can see here is all that's left of it. Downhill it's completely fallen away; a sheer cliff. If there'd been anything left of it, anything at all, I'd've brought us up that way, and avoided the bloody castle entirely.

"And uphill..." she nodded to the right. "That's our path tonight. Nothing's coming from that direction to trouble Lord Alfaric, I can promise you that. You'll see why soon enough."

"I'll go first," Fearghan muttered. "I'm lightest."

"*Tá,*" Sîol nodded. "And your drooling destrier can bring up the rear. We can't get him past the chasm in any case."

Chasm? Alauda didn't like the sound of that. But she said nothing, allowing Fearghan, followed by Sîol, Breaghan, Tonlees and Alacer, to lead off. When Alainn gestured to her to precede him, she shook her head. "You go first," she murmured. "I'll keep Smuggy company."

"*Snaugaid!*" Fearghan growled from the head of the column.

It soon became obvious why the old mountain road had been abandoned. By all appearances it had been a natural track, opened up here and there with judicious use of pick and maul until it was wide enough for a horse to pass with ease. That, however, had been thousands of years in the past, and time had taken its toll. The roadway was cluttered with the debris of eons – and where it wasn't, it had almost entirely crumbled away. Moreover, the path was steep, climbing like a stair as it followed the curve of the mountainside. By the time they had rounded the first bend, circling the White Tower at a distance of a few hundred paces, they were well above its parapets – and still the path climbed on.

Alauda hugged the mountain wall, the chill of the stone soothing her damaged hand even as its rough texture abraded the slowly clotting wound. The surface of the rock was wet here; they were approaching the waterfall, and the mist that hung in the air dampened everything. Moss and lichen were more prevalent, making for a slick surface; more than once her mother's damnable boots skittered on an errant boulder, making her lurch for the safety of the stone. And more than once, Alainn's hand shot out to steady her. He seemed to be just as nimble as she, and considerably more sure-footed into the bargain. Of course, Alauda reflected, he wasn't wearing heels. Or a damnably voluminous ball gown.

Tonlees, she could see, was in similar straits; she was still walking barefoot, and she was limping slightly. The rock was cold, but replacing her shoes would have been fatal. Alacer walked close behind the older girl, ready to catch her. Far from making her jealous, the sight of her lover's solicitude for her best friend was an enormous relief. She was still regretting having insisted that Toni accompany them. If anything happened to either of them –

Thankfully, the ancient architects that had built the road had done more to make it passable than merely smoothing the road-bed. Once, when she slid, her flailing hand struck metal, and she seized it with a gasp of relief. Upon closer inspection – the moons were high enough now to provide real light; as far as Alauda and her two friends were concerned, it might as well have been noon – she discovered that someone in the far-distant past had hammered iron pitons into stone wall along the path, probably to serve as anchors for some sort of railing or rope. There were in uniformly poor condition, rusted and even crumbling in places, but some vestiges of their original form remained. Every now and then, she touched one that was still reasonably intact, with an open eye of iron at the outermost end. She wished that the hand-holds they'd originally supported had still been in place.

They were far above the castle now, looking down upon the eastern wing of apartments. She could see movement on the parapets – guards striding about in desultory fashion; searching, sensibly, for any hint of movement upon the wooded hills below the walls. From their new vantage, they could see something else: a third bridge, projecting from a bastion near the Knights' Hall, slender and finely-made, that climbed toward the mountain in the form of a narrow stair. The bridge was the first bit of architecture she'd seen that reminded her of her homeland; a light, curving structure supported by soaring, gracefully arched plinths.

Like the mountain path, it hadn't stood the test of time; only a score of paces of the stone structure remained. The rest had crumbled away. There was something to be said for building heavy and strong. Maybe the dwarves had it right after all; she reflected, her teeth chattering; their stonework *never* seemed to fail.

To her dismay, the path they were following began to mimic the bridge. As they approached the southern hook of the mountain's face, the stone roadbed grew increasingly narrow and fragile. The rock was running with water now, and they were stumbling through a billowing cloud of mist. The roar of the waterfall hammered an echoing din into her ears; they had to shout to be heard, and even a scream (*As, for example, of someone falling to her death*, she thought, grinding her teeth) would in all probability go unnoticed at the castle. She clutched at Alainn's hand again, reassured by his damp but steady grip as they felt their way along the wall.

At what proved to be the last wide point in the path Fearghan spoke sternly to his lumbering mount in the sibilant halpie tongue – presumably, insofar as Alauda could guess, to order the drooling beast to stay put. The hound whined but complied, and the adventurers eased their way past him. Fearghan, Alauda noticed, took the rope from Smugaid's saddle-hook before leading them onwards.

They walked even more carefully from then on. Beyond that spot, the roadway was all but gone, and the drop below them was sheer. Alauda took a single glance over the edge, and threw herself back against the stone, her knees a-quiver. The chasm below them was hundreds of paces deep, and thanks to the brilliant moons-light, she could see that it ended abruptly in a boulder-choked, tree-girt river bed. A single slip would be as good as a death sentence. *What the hells am I doing here?* she groaned under her breath.

She might as well have shouted the words; no one would have heard her over the din.

On the heels of that thought came another: Why in the names of all the Powers had she talked her *friends* into this lunacy? Alacer and Tonlees, their respective ages notwithstanding, were no more house-breakers or mountaineers than she was. Anything that happened to them would be *her* fault. While that grim thought strengthened her resolve, it did nothing for her knees or ankles; they shook even worse at the prospect of one – or both – of her companions lying bloody and broken at the bottom of the ravine.

When they at last rounded the mountain's hook, the scene that greeted them was one of silver-gilt magnificence. They were facing a deep cleft in the mountainside, a narrow gash that looked as if it might have been made by the stroke of a giant's axe. From a gap high to the left, the thundering cascade poured in an unbroken blast, fuelled by the spring-melted snows higher up the mountainside. The waters soared out into the air in a sparkling argent arc. Now that they were out of the mountain's lee, they might as well have been standing in the rain; they were all soaked in an instant. The water was ice-cold, leaving all of them shivering violently.

Sîol gathered them with a gesture. The seven stood as closely together as the narrow path allowed. "It gets a little chancy here!" the redhead shouted. "Not much of the road left. Use the spikes, and lean into the wall!" She demonstrated, gripping the rusted vestiges of one of the pitons, and pressing her left shoulder to the stone.

Alauda looked down. It gets *worse?* She groaned, aghast. But Toni and Alacer were watching her, and so she went on.

Sîol hadn't exaggerated the danger. The roadbed was almost entirely gone; nothing was left of it but the merest scraps of a ledge, hardly wider than the length of Alauda's boots. Cursing the blithe ease with which she'd accepted the Halflings' ridiculous offer, she put her back to the wall, leaning against it, and hissing in annoyance as icy water ran down her spine. She was shivering constantly now, the cold beginning to seep into her limbs. Such was the chill that when Alainn took her hand, steadying her again, it felt as if she'd thrust her fingers into a fire. She shot the boy a grateful smile, wondering briefly what she must have looked like: drenched and bedraggled, her hair plastered to her forehead and cheeks, her carefully applied cosmetics a splotchy ruin. *I'll certainly make a wretched-looking corpse,* she thought.

At that moment, a stark and grimly humorous realization struck her: if she fell and perished, the first question her mother would ask about her daughter's sad remains wouldn't be why Alauda had been crawling about a mountainside in the middle of the night; it would be why her dead daughter wasn't wearing her underclothes. The thought of her mother indulging in exasperated eye-rolling over her broken body steeled her nerves in a way that not even the threat of imminent death had done. Alauda straightened her back, sliding her heels along the rock ledge, feeling for the next iron spike with numb fingers. She would be eternally damned before she would give her mother some final excuse to heave theatrical sighs of disappointment about her departed daughter's questionable virtue for the rest of her long life.

Their progress was slower now; agonizingly slow. But progress was made. The hook of the mountain endured only about a hundred paces before easing northwards again. As they neared this final curve, Alauda was able to make out, amid the mists of the waterfall, an enormous, artificial structure. It was, she realized, the continuation of the elf-wrought bridge that had projected from the castle wall. The broken end was a little below them, surprisingly near; she could have hit it with a thrown rock. The stretch of buttressed stairs climbed higher and higher, following the curve of the mountain wall until they reached the side of a squarish tower that had been built a little out from the mountainside.

She realized at once that the tower was no defensive work; it was too slender, only about five paces on a side, despite being better than thirty paces tall. And it was top-heavy; the superstructure to which the stairs were connected was thicker than the base. The thing was topped with a battlement; but even at a distance, the machicolations looked slender and decorative rather than functional. She tapped Alainn's arm and pointed.

"What's that?" she shouted.

"You'll see!" he yelled.

She squeezed his wrist. "Alainn, my hand hurts, I'm chilled to the bone, and I'm bloody terrified!" she cried. "I'm not in a mood for games!"

"That's good! Because what comes next isn't a lot of fun!"

What came next very nearly made Alauda turn around and make for the comparative security of Arx Cervus and its no doubt dry and comfortable dungeons. As the rest of them watched, Fearghan sidled past Sîol, easing his way along the mountainside, feeling with his fingers until he located one of the iron spikes set into the wall. He uncoiled his rope carefully, knotting one end to the eye of the piton, and the other about his waist. Gripping the rope near the spike, he slid out a ways…and stepped off the path.

Tonlees shrieked. Alauda averted a squeak of her own only by the simple expedient of clapping her hands over her mouth. Fearghan, however, appeared to know what he was doing. He ran along the mountain's steep slope to the very end of the length of cord he had let out, then spun on the line like a spider and ran back. At each arc, he let a little more line run through his fingers. Alauda noticed that he was wearing gloves now, and wished that she'd done the same; her flayed palm ached abominably.

By the time his rope was expended, Fearghan was all but flying back and forth along the mountainside. The cord scraped and tugged over the stone, and Alauda wondered briefly whether the continued rubbing was abrading the fibers. Before she could voice her concerns, however, Fearghan reached the end of one of his swings – and kicked off from the mountainside.

Her breath caught in her throat. The Halfling soared through the night air, through the plummeting wash of water from the distant fall, toward the broken end of the bridge. To her amazement the boy swung past it – until the rope intersected one of the steps, snapping him into a new trajectory. He slammed into the stone – despite the roar of the fall, Alauda could hear the grunt as the breath whooshed from his lungs – and to her immense relief hung there, waving to show that he was unhurt.

She turned to Alainn, her face white. "I am not doing *that*!" she exclaimed.

"You won't have to," he reassured her. "Fearghan did it for us. All we have to do now is slide down the rope."

Alauda stared at the gap between the mountain wall and the lower end of the broken stair. "That's twelve…maybe fifteen paces," she said faintly.

"Just so. Not so far."

"Over a hundred-foot drop!"

"Don't think about the drop," Alainn suggested.

"Don't – you're insane!" Alauda shrieked. "All of you, insane!"

"It's the only way in," he shrugged. "Unless you can fly."

The elf-girl felt like strangling her placid paramour. "Not even my mother can fly," she grated, "and she's a mage!"

"There's no other way." He pointed. "Watch Bree. It's easier than it looks."

Alauda watched. The Halfling girl had removed her belt, rebuckling it over the rope. Leaping a little, she threw her arms and legs over the line and began shimmying along it, aided by the downward slope.

She turned to gaze at the end of the stairs. To her horror, Fearghan hadn't climbed up, and he wasn't moving; he was simply hanging off the far edge of the stone platform, dangling more than a hundred feet above a lethal drop. "Isn't he going to tie it off?" she gasped.

"There's nothing to tie it off to," Alainn said soberly. "Compose yourself, my lady; it's why the lightest go first. By the time your friend Alacer has to cross, there'll be more than enough of us down there to serve as a counterweight."

She shook her head. *Insane.*

Sîol followed Breaghan, and was followed in turn by Alainn. Alauda was next. Tonlees – who didn't look anywhere near as terrified as Alauda felt – gave her a cheerful pat on the shoulder, and helped her loosen and reattach her cincture. The belt, Alauda knew, was decorative rather than functional; she had no illusions about its ability to support her weight if she should happen to lose her grip on the rope. *Best to hold on tight, then*, she told herself grimly. As a precaution, she tugged Elspeth's dagger from its sheathe and transferred it to a boot-top.

To her surprise, it was over almost before it had begun. She clenched her eyes and moved her arms and legs. When she passed under the blast from the waterfall she was drenched anew, and so chilled that she could scarcely feel the rope under her hands. She shifted her grip a little, locking her elbows about the cable, and keeping her legs moving. Before long she felt hands at her hips and shoulders, and Alainn and Breaghan were pulling her onto the platform of the stair.

While she sat out of the way, panting and shivering, Alainn slid down the opposite side of the pillar, sitting on Fearghan's shoulders; Breaghan followed. Alauda heard the rope creak audibly as it tightened under their weight. Tonlees started down from the mountainside, reaching the platform – Alauda counted – in only a score of breaths.

She sat up, refastening her cincture. "That was fun!

Alauda merely shook her head. She wasn't suited either by physique or by temperament for this sort of nonsense.

Alacer came last. When the rope started to bow under his weight, lifting the three Halflings visibly, Tonlees slid to the edge of the platform. She hooked her knees over the stone lip and threw her arms around Breaghan, locking the four of them into a solid anchor. Alacer made the balance of the trip in a trice. He the hauled the others back up onto the platform, and helped Fearghan untie the rope from about his waist.

That made Alauda sit upright. "How do we get back?" she cried. She pointed at the rope. "You don't seriously expect us to climb up that, do you?"

Sîol shook her head. "There's an easier way down," she explained. "You just can't get up that way. When the time comes, I'll show you."

Alauda blew out a relieved breath, thanking the Powers for that small mercy.

After the crumbling mountain path, the stairs were almost a joy. They were slick with water and not at all wide – about a pace or so at most – and they sloped steeply upwards to the tower that lay ahead; but they were flat, level, and firm. Best of all, there was no sign of deterioration. Alauda wondered why so long a span had crumbled, and then realized that in the course of more than four thousand years, virtually anything could have happened to knock them over: tumbling boulders, an earth tremor, even a falling sky-star. She didn't let speculation preoccupy her; she was content with the comforting stability of the remaining steps.

There was no door where the steps reached the tower; only an arch that led into its depths. The arch was decorated with elaborate scrollwork that looked achingly familiar. She'd seen similar motifs carved into the doors of temples and old, magnificent manors in Corymbus and Astramicor. It lent credence to her judgement that the tower had been built for some purpose other than defence. So did the fact that the façade was clad in smooth, age-worn marble. The tiny crystals in the stone, dampened by the omnipresent spray, glimmered like diamonds in the moons'-light.

She followed the Halflings into the tower, blinking a little at the absence of illumination. Elf-sight was powerful, but as she had observed in the warm, sweaty depths of Jantun's snow-lodge, it needed some source of light, however feeble, to work upon.

She paused, waiting until her eyes had adjusted…and then discovered that there was no need. A warm yellow glow sprang up. Near the far wall, at the base of a narrow stair, there stood a small, angular pillar. Atop the pillar was an irregular, river-smooth stone. Sîol was rubbing it gently with her fingers. The light, to Alauda's astonishment, emanated from the rock, shining redly through the Halfling's flesh.

Alauda stiffened instantly. The chamber in which they stood was small, only about four paces on a side, and windowless. The ceiling overhead was low, barely a hand-span above Alacer's skull.

In the centre of the room lay a massive black of stone. She'd seen them before, in books, and knew what it for what it was: a sarcophagus. "What's this?" she breathed, appalled.

Alacer's face was equally bleak. "It's a tomb, I think."

"I know it's a tomb!" she exclaimed. "But what's it doing here? I thought *elves* built this place!" Her hands were shaking with disgust.

Alainn was at her shoulder at once. "What's the matter?" he murmured.

"We don't *do* this!" Alauda cried. "We don't…store our dead! We don't bury them in earth or stone. We send them to wind, to be one with Wise Hara and the Forest Gods!"

"Not this fellow," Tonlees shivered. " *'Varinyr Orkarel, Dux et Imperator'*," she read, her fingers trailing along characters cut into the stone. " *'Anno Dea-Mater 181 – 507'*."

Duke and General. "A war-lord?" Alauda guessed. "One of Fineleor's ancestors, maybe. He must be!"

"We didn't understand the dates," Breaghan said softly. "Do you know what they mean?"

"Of course," Alauda nodded. " 'Year of the Mother-Goddess'. It's how the first children of the Third House – the descendents of the two Powers, Bræa and Hara, I mean – measured the years from her marriage to King Cîarloth. Today it's called the Age of Wisdom. It ended fifteen hundred years later, with the battle of the Field of Oldarran, and the Gloaming of the Wyrms, and…and the coming of the Darkness." She swallowed heavily. "Duke Varinyr was born more than five thousand years ago. He…Gods, he was alive at the time of Tior. Tior *Magnus*!"

"Oh, that Tior?" Sîol murmured.

Alauda ignored the sarcasm. "He must have died in Biardath's rebellion," she went on, trying to recollect the lessons that had been pounded into her head at schola. "Or thereabouts. 507 was the year the Sorcerer-King murdered his father Xiardath and seized control of the Realm."

"There's more here," Tonlees said, frowning. "It's not elven script; it's something else. Like…lines, with scratches across them."

Alauda's eyebrows rose. She stood next to her friend, leaning over the low stone bier. She ran her fingers over the sharp, rectilinear lines in the stone. "It's feyspeech!" she said, astonished.

"I thought the fey folk didn't write," Alainn frowned.

"They don't," Alauda replied. "The nymphs and the pixies and the sprites don't, I mean. But the wilders do. The runner tribes, and – and the hunter clans." Like the *Suku Gagak*. She swallowed hard, remembering. She'd seen similar marks, carved into peeled sticks in Akaryah's pavillion.

"Can you read it?" Tonlees pressed.

Alauda shook her head. "I only learned a few words of their

tongue; I never learned their script. What I can't imagine is why a noble's tomb would be marked like this." She shuddered. "Or why he's even in a tomb in the first place. The very notion is…ghastly."

"Halflings bury their dead," Breaghan said, somewhat defensively.

"The old *elvii* did, too," Alacer said unexpectedly. "Before Bræa came. At Starmeadow, in the catacombs beneath the palace, there are…bodies. Or what's left of them, anyway. Sealed in stone, just like this." He made a face. "That was a long time ago, of course. Even before the first dawn, when there was nothing in the sky but the stars."

Alauda grimaced. "Different times." She leaned a little closer, struggling to puzzle out the lines and scratches, gripping the edge of the bier for purchase. "Today we don't…we would never –"

It came from nowhere, without warning. The scents, the sounds, the images exploded from nothingness, and overwhelmed her.

All about her, the towering trees loomed like sentinels against the shadow, their intertwined branches proof against the rain of arrows that snapped and whickered through the leaves. Dark faces lined the lip of the dell, eyes bright, maws gaping; fangs and claws glistening with bile, with venom, and with drops of scarlet – the blood of her comrades. Her own blood pooled at her feet, seeping from a dozen wounds, staining the gambeson beneath her shattered mail and gore-spattered surcoat.

She was weary, and sore hurt. The Lantern lay hid behind lowering war-clouds, concealed by the fume and smoke of battle and death, banked by the colossal, hideous reek of the pretender's hordes. There had been no succour in the day, and now night was coming on, when the foe's strength would be multiplied tenfold by darkness. They were enough in their number to bury the remaining defenders alive in mounds of rippling, quivering, reeking flesh.

Warriors fought and fell; the beasts that aided them suffered and bled, and breathed no more. And yet the trees still stood; they still resisted. They fought on, when most of his kin had already given in and laid down their arms, bending to kiss the pretender's black hand. They fought on because of what was at stake: the ending of all, the sundering of the balance; the extinction of Life throughout the Realm – Mighty Tior's Realm. The end of the Unity, and the banishing of the Green. The trees fought on, she knew, because they had no choice. There could be no retreat; not for them. In the absence of victory, there was only fire and darkness. There was only death.

And so she too would fight on. Her sword was still in her hand, still hard, still keen, and stained black with the blood of the fell foe. The last rays of evening, warm and life-giving, pierced the clouds and foliage to glisten upon its notched edge, to fall upon her face, kindling a spark of hope. Not for victory; that hope was long past. But hope that some word of their deeds – hers, and those of her last companions – would live on, to inspire and encourage all who might come after her. Those whose task it would be to one day rise up against the Ill-Born, rout his

*minions, and take back the Realm. To once more taste clean air and sweet water; to
hear the rustling of autumn leaves upon the hillside.*

*As the hordes of red eyes and scarred, shrieking faces closed in, slavering
and howling for death, she raised her sword one final time, and she smiled. She
swung, and saw the bright steel bite into flesh, again and again and again; until
one of them lunged at her, snarling, and the blade of the spear slipped past her
guard –*

Alauda screamed, staggering back from the bier, her hands
clasped to her breast, fingers clenching at the agony of the spear-stroke,
struggling to hold back the tide of scarlet bursting from her torn flesh. A
flash of hot, verdant skyfire momentarily blinded her, all but extinguishing
the yellow glow of the light-stone. When Tonlees reached for her she
lashed out with a fist, striking hard enough to send her friend spinning
into a wall.

It wasn't until she'd managed to draw a few harsh, steadying
breaths that her hands stopped twitching and her eyes cleared. "Sorry,"
she said thickly. "Toni, I'm…I'm sorry."

The girl was staring at her, her face white with fear. "You did it
again," she whispered.

Alauda blinked. "Did what?"

Tonlees pointed at the bier.

Alauda looked. One corner of the sarcophagus had been chipped
and shattered away. The stone around the damaged spot was thick with
verdure: clumpy, clotted patches of moss and lichen that steamed a little in
the chill air of the crypt. Beyond the bier, more lush, emerald life lay
spattered against the floor, the walls. In the yellow light, it looked as if it
were moving; perhaps even growing. Tiny shoots and tendrils writhed in
the lamplight.

Alainn put a hand on her shoulder. "What frightened you?" he
murmured. "What did you see?"

Alauda was panting heavily, her mind afire with astonishment.
Her heart was thudding in her breast; she could feel the blood throbbing in
her fingers and toes. Her injured palm stung horribly, and there was a
bloody handprint atop the weathered stone of the bier. "*Centeng'rimba*,"
she husked. "That's what it says; the wilder script. *Centeng'rimba*. The
Watchman. The Warden of the Woodlands."

Tonlees clapped her hands to her mouth. "You're not serious!" she
breathed.

"He was…he was the heir," Alauda nodded, her head throbbing.
"Heir to Arngrim. Arngrim the Elflord, mightiest of the wardens. Heir to
Eldukaris, the first man, and the first warden. Eldu of the songs: born of
the sea, who bested the King of Winter, and won the hand of Csæleyan the
Wood-Maid, and upon her sired all the beautiful folk of the forest. Ten

thousand years ago." She laid her hand upon the bier again, where she'd left the blood-stain. It felt warmer now.

Sîol cocked a skeptical eyebrow. "This place is old, princess, but it's not *that* old!"

Alauda waved a deprecating hand. "I didn't say Duke Varinyr *was* Eldukaris; I said he was heir to Eldu's mantle. The mantle of the Watchman."

Her head was spinning, and she leaned against Alainn's shoulder for support. "There's always been a Watchman," she said distantly, "though most folk never know who it was until after he's already passed his mantle on. The Watchman – in *elvii*, we call him *Custos Sylvanus*, the Warden of the Green – can to speak to the animals, and command their service. He can send his thought through the waters, and awaken the trees. He is the embodiment of the life of the woodlands, at once both their nursemaid and their general. He can touch every *sielu* that's bound to Kesatuan, the Unity – every last one. Not just the living, but the dead as well."

Sîol crossed her arms. "Sounds like he ought to be one of your Forest Gods," she said, wrinkling her nose. "And you're saying that this Varinyr fellow…that he was this Warden, once upon a time?"

"At the time of Biardath's rebellion," Alauda murmured, still a little dazed. Her knees were trembling with the force of recollection. She fumbled for Alainn's hand, for the warmth and reassurance that it offered. The touch of his fingers was electric; it sent a shock through her, buttressing her against the pervasive chill of her wet clothing and the damp and misty wind. The heat that his touch had kindled within her returned threefold, throbbing in her belly. This place was rife not only with memory, but with the fecund glory of the Green. The vision of the duke's death in defence of his homeland had awakened something deep within her; a like spirit calling unto like, perhaps.

Something primal was blossoming in the fertile garden of her *sielu*; something green, and strong, and hungry.

She *had* to go on. "That's what I saw," she gasped. "I saw Duke Varinyr make his final stand against the hordes of Biardath the Sorcerer-King. He called to the trees to aid him, and…and they did. They slew thousands of the Ender's minions; tore them to pieces. They bathed their roots in polluted blood, poisoning themselves in their victory." She stretched a hand – her bleeding hand – toward the bier, but couldn't bring herself to touch it again. "It still wasn't enough."

Sîol frowned. She put her fingers on the damp and dusty stone. "I don't see anything," she said stiffly.

"You're not a daughter of the Horned God," Alacer said, staring at Alauda sidelong with an odd look in his eyes. "Ala is. She's bound to the

Green, and the Unity, and – and you're not."

"Thanks for the lesson in elfy faith," the redhead growled. "It's not relevant to our task, though. Is it?"

Alauda shook her head. It wasn't a negation; it was a confession that she was exhausted, drained. And yet, somewhere at the core, the very kernel of her being, something verdant and bright had been ignited. She could feel its warmth spreading through her, counteracting the chill. The weight in her belly reminded her forcefully of Akaryah, and Mua, and Jantun – of the shrine of the Forest Mother, and her bleeding hand (the same hand, she realized with a start, that was bleeding now). It reminded her – painfully, and yet with an ache of longing that all but choked her – of the trembling, exalted terror she'd felt when she'd knelt in sanguinary homage to Cernunnor at the standing stones.

Light-headed, she levered herself to her feet. In response to a sudden, fanciful whim, she pulled Alainn close, kissed his cheek, and fought down an irrational urge to go further. She released him, standing unsteadily on her own. "I'm ready," she said, blinking rapidly, willing her eyes to focus.

The throbbing in her extremities, the heat in her belly – they wouldn't go away. She resolved to ignore them and carry on.

"Good," Sîol snapped. "One last leg and we're there. Then we'll need all of our wits. Follow me." She set off up the narrow stair toward the parapets of the tower. Fearghan, her two friends, and Breaghan followed.

Alainn didn't; he waited for Alauda to move.

She held out a hand to the bier, wanting to touch it again, to feel the strength and fury of the Warden coursing through her veins once more; but she didn't dare. She was afraid that she would fall into the depths of the dream once more, and not waken from it. Instead she clenched her fist, and let a few drops of blood fall to the mildewed, mist-slicked stone.

"A sacrifice?" her golden-eyed lover asked gently.

"He gave his life to the Green, to defend what he cherished," she whispered. Just like his descendent Fineleor had done; and Anja, Fineleor's promised mate, who'd perished at his side. She'd felt a hint, the merest sliver, of the ancient warden's faith and dedication while writhing in the throes of her vision, and it had all but overwhelmed her. Alauda, in a rare moment of honest introspection, didn't think that she would ever be able to make the same sort of sacrifice: to see past her own selfish wants and desires, and find within her the strength to make an offering of her life in the service of something grander and more glorious than she.

That brief moment of self-awareness galled her. She didn't have it in her heart to be that person; she knew that much, and was honest enough to admit it. At the same time, she admired that quality in others; and she knew, with iron-clad surety, that she could love someone like that. "I wish I'd known him," she sighed. "Duke Varinyr. The Warden of the Green."

"Maybe you'll meet someone like him some day," Alainn said gently, taking her uninjured hand. "But it won't be today. Alauda – my lady – we *have* to go."

Alauda nodded. They mounted the steps together, leaving the bier of Varinyr the Watchman in their wake – a cold and silent block of worked stone.

Ccld and silent...but not dead. Nourished by the spray and the light of the moons, the new life that Alauda had painted across the ancient stone took hold; and, driven by the inexorable, indomitable might of the Green, began to grow.

♦

Seventeen

Alauda stared up at the statue, dumbstruck. "Yes, it's her. It's Anja."

Of course it was. Though amazed almost beyond words, she spoke without inflection. The evening's events had all but exhausted her capacity for extremes of emotion.

The passage from the parapets of Duke Varinyr's tower-crypt had been the oddest and most nerve-wracking yet. Alauda had no idea what she was looking for until Breaghan pointed it out to her.

The seven companions stood atop the spire of stone, staring into the thundering roar of the waterfall. It poured from high above, the water jetting from a deep cleft in the mountainside to plunge in a shimmering moonlit sheet to the depths of the crevasse below, forming the headwaters of the Whyle so that it could run sluggishly past the tin-pits of Buckhill a few miles downstream.

Beyond the thundering mass of water, Alauda could see, just barely, a deep gorge in the cliff face – a cleft, an alcove in the pinnacle of black stone that clawed at the sky. Something bright shone within the gap. Assuming her sense of perspective hadn't been knocked too badly askew, it was something big.

She didn't want to puzzle it out; she didn't, in fact, want to go any further at all. She was tired, weary in her bones. Every last vestige of strength had been sapped by the chill. The exhilaration imparted by the scent of the Morbannen trees was fading, drained away by the night's chill. It penetrated her damp clothing like a spike.

Her hands, both the wounded one and the whole one, wouldn't stop shaking. Even when Alainn held them between his own, trying to warm them, they trembled uncontrollably.

When Sîol pointed out their path, Alauda didn't know whether to weep or laugh. "That's it." The Halfling pointed at the glimmering alcove. It was at least a score of paces away – through the worst of the waterfall itself. There was no path that Alauda could see.

"How do we get there?" Alacer asked, frowning. "We don't have any more rope."

"Don't need rope," the redhead replied. "There's a bridge."

Tonlees squinted. "I don't see any bridge."

"You're not meant to," Breaghan spoke up. She walked to the northernmost corner of the parapets – and then, to Alauda's shock, clambered up onto the merlons. "Look here," she said, pointing directly toward the alcove.

The three elves bent and followed her pointing finger. Alauda saw it first: a strange splashing pattern in the midst of the waterfall. The glinting droplets painted a long, straight line right at the level of the parapets. It was as if the water was crashing into something, something that no one could see, and pouring off to the sides. "What *is* that?" she murmured.

"The bridge," Breaghan grinned. "It's invisible."

"Invisible?" Of course; the answer was evident at once. *Magic.*

Tentatively, Alauda reached over the parapet. There was no plummeting water here, nothing to mark the outlines of their path. She ran her fingers lightly along the outermost edge of the merlons – and jumped when they ran into something solid. Something she couldn't see.

Stone. Cold, wet stone. And...something else.

A slow smile bent her icy lips.

"A spell?" Toni gaped. "I thought this place was thousands of years old! How could any spell last so long?"

Alauda was chuckling under her breath. "A relic. You lot think there's a relic here, don't you?"

The Halflings exchanged alarmed glances.

"You do!" She laughed aloud. "You do! That's why you're here. You think that because this – this glamer has lasted as long as it has, it must be anchored to something mighty. That's what you're here to find, isn't it? You think Fineleor's 'second-greatest treasure' is some ancient, powerful...what, a weapon, or something! Don't you?"

Alacer touched her shoulder. "Ala – what are you talking about?"

"This is what I get for messing about with mother's book," the elf-girl sighed. "First principles. Nothing is eternal; not even the Art. Magic is always powered by something. Generally, it's the strength and spirit of the caster – her life-force, if you will. Most spells last only an instant, or a few moments at best. But spells can also be anchored to a source of power – like a relic. An object imbued with immense power can furnish the force to sustain a lesser enchantment for years. Decades, even."

She pointed at the Halflings. "That's why they're here. Someone cast a spell to keep this last bridge unseen. They think it was Fineleor, or someone from his time. That means the spell's lasted four thousand years. So they think it's been anchored to some sort of...of ancient source of power."

"It's not just the bridge," Sîol growled. "There's more of the Art beyond. Great spells, things you can't even imagine. Including the one that searches for Third House blood, and allows no one else to pass. And it wasn't our idea; Cloughsen discovered the link. He knows magic, he does! He said the spells are all anchored to something ancient, and incomparably mighty!"

"Fineleor's treasure?" Alauda grinned.

"What's so funny?" the redhead demanded.

"You are. All of you." She ran her fingers out over the stone again, then laid her palm against the surface of the span, and let out her breath with a slow sigh. "Cloughsen was right – but he was wrong, too. The magic is anchored to something strong...but not to the Art Magic. Not to some ancient relic."

"How do you know that?"

Alauda lifted her hand. Beneath it, seemingly hovering in the empty air, was a splash of green: a clot of verdure the exact size and shape of her palm.

The Halflings stared. Even Toni and Alacer took a step back. Alauda saw the identical looks on their faces, and her heart missed a beat. "It's the Green," she said hurriedly. "That's all. The magic that conceals the bridge is tied to *kesatuan*. Akaryah showed me, when I was with the clan."

For good measure, she ran a finger swiftly across the invisible stone, leaving a line of moss behind. She was warm again, and couldn't help but laugh.

Sîol stepped forward. "Could you do that again?"

"It's hard not to," Alauda replied. "The power that's here...if you dropped an acorn on the stone, it would probably sprout an oak."

"Could you do the whole bridge?"

"Probably. But I don't."

"Why not?" the Halfling cried. "It'll be easier to cross this time if we can see it!"

"Will it be easier to cross if it's covered with wet lichen, moss, and mildew?" Alauda asked. "I don't think so." She bit her lip, rubbing her palms briskly together. "In fact, I should probably go last. I'll try to hold back, but even touching that thing makes me feel as if I'm about to take fire."

"Fine," their leader growled. "The bridge is about two hand-spans in width. Walk it if you like, but when you get to the water, it's best to crawl. Stay on your hands and knees until you're out from beneath the water's force." She clambered up beside Alauda, shoving the elf-girl aside – and, to Alauda's trembling astonishment, began to sidle out onto nothingness. It looked for all the world as if she were crawling on empty air.

"Hara's love!" Tonlees swore faintly. "Do we have to do that, too?"

"It's the only way across," Breaghan shrugged. Just as Sîol reached the outermost edge of the cascade, she climbed up beside Alauda, and made her way out into the air as well.

When Fearghan had gone, Alainn held out his hand. "Come with me," he urged gently.

Alauda shook her head. "Last." She glanced down – and her exhilaration vanished. The plummeting water took her breath away. *Too far; too far!*

Tonlees and Alacer exchanged glances; Alacer shrugged, and started out onto the invisible bridge. Tonlees hesitated a moment longer, an anguished look on her face, before following the grey-haired boy out into the air.

Alauda slid off the parapet, sitting on the damp stone, her knees clutched tremblingly to her chest. "I can't," she muttered again and again, "I can't, I can't!"

"We can't do this without you," Alainn urged, kneading her shoulder with tender fingers.

"It's too high."

"I know." The boy pursed his lips. "Do you trust me?"

"What?" Her head came up. "Yes. Yes."

"Good." He lifted his jacket, tugged his shirt from within his trousers, and proceeded to tear a long strip from the bottom edge. When he was finished, his midriff was bare, and he had a strip of wet, ragged cloth in his hand. He folded it thrice lengthwise, until it was no more than three fingers in width. "Stand up."

Alauda stood. Alainn spun her about – and then, to her alarm, laid the bandage across her eyes. "What're you doing?" she cried, seizing his wrist.

"You'll do better if you can't see the drop." He spoke in her ear. "It's how sailors get horses on and off ships, you know."

Alauda blinked; she *did* know that. Slowly, she nodded. "All right."

With swift, economical gestures, he tied the blindfold over her eyes, snugging the knot at the back of her head, and tucking the dangling cloth-ends out of the way. Then he took her hand and led her to the edge of the parapet. "Just feel your way with your hands," he said softly. "I'll be right behind you. I'll touch your foot every now and then, so you'll know I'm there."

"All right," she repeated. "All right." It was like a mantra. Her knees were trembling again.

Somehow she did it; somehow, she summoned up the strength, the force of will, to slide out into nothingness. The blindfold did help; with her sight blocked, the invisible bridge beneath her hands and knees felt like the top of a narrow wall. Its two feet of width, a mere thread against the vast depth of the crevasse, felt like a highway. And when, every few moments, Alainn seized her ankle and gave it a gentle squeeze, she was overcome with gratitude.

In a way, her terror served a useful purpose; it forced the

overwhelming pressure of the Green back from the surface of her mind. She'd been worried about accidentally surrendering to its force, and slicking the bridge with oozing life, but the fear of falling to her death resolved that difficulty.

The force of the waterfall crashing into her back nearly panicked her. The freezing deluge drained the life from her limbs, deadening her senses anew. But she held on, gripping the stone until her fingers ached, and kept moving. Alainn, she knew, was close behind her, and the longer she delayed, the greater the risk that he too might be washed away. For his sake, she forced herself to move.

She crawled and crawled, and did not stop crawling until her fingers touched a broader expanse of stone. Hands helped her to her feet. Before she could mouth a word of thanks, strong arms encircled her shoulders, drawing her into a warm embrace; lips touched hers. Without thinking, she gave herself over entirely to passion, revelling in the fact that she had once more come through alive.

At the same moment, the Green surged back. Sudden heat burned through her, reigniting the slumbering fire in her loins, warming her limbs, her fingers and toes, even the tips of her ears. She smelled the forest anew; the tree-scent of pine and spruce and fir, the clammy reek of moss, the clean, chill odour of the waterfall.

And the Morbannens; they were stronger than ever here. Second Spring had come. She put her lips to her lover's ear and whispered, "Thank you."

"My pleasure, my lady," Alainn replied. She could hear his smile in the tone of his voice.

And then she was tugging the blindfold from her eyes, and staring in dazzled wonderment at the bright, towering statue before them. "It's Anja!"

"I didn't think you'd recognize her," Sîol said clinically. "It's not how she's usually depicted, is it?"

"It's her." Alauda pointed at the plinth upon which the effigy stood. The letters that had been carved into the ancient marble were faded and half obscured by moss, but still legible nonetheless: ANYA ANTAYYSSIN.

"That's an odd spelling, isn't it?" Alacer frowned.

"Scripts change," Alauda shrugged. "The texts from the Age of Wisdom are all like that. Students of language say that the *elvii* didn't adopt the 'j' until the Eon of Darkness; it came over from the feyspeech, I think."

Like Jantun, her heart whispered; in those ancient days, the Raven huntress' name would have been 'Yantun'. She shook her head; she couldn't afford to be thinking of her Wilder rescuer at a time like this.

"And the double-Y is now rendered as an accented 'I'," she added.

"My lady is a scholar," Alainn chuckled. "Are you certain, then, that it's the right Anja?"

"Who else could it be?" Alauda snorted. "This was Fineleor's keep! How many Anja's do you think he knew? Besides, the bent bow is the sigil of House Antaíssin; that at least hasn't changed in five thousand years." She crossed her arms, shivering. "But...you're right," she added, frowning. "It's the depiction that's odd. It's not how she's normally..."

Her voice trailed off. The statue wasn't one of the classical works that one saw about cities and palaces; it was rawer, more elemental. It depicted the ancient heroine crouched on one knee, a long bow in her hand. The upper limb of the bow was broken off. There was a quiver at her hip, and she was depicted with little more than bits and scraps of leather as clothing. Her off-hand held a sword – a sword with no guard to speak of, and a hilt was nearly as long as its blade.

There was a very similar sword stashed in the bottom of her parents' wagon. A chill of recognition rippled the length of Alauda's spine. What if...

She shook herself. There were other clues, too. The walls of the alcove provided a colourful counterpoint to the statue's grim lines; they were a study in verdant life. Long vines, with new leaves bursting from their buds, criss-crossed the stone, covering almost all of it like a tapestry woven by the Forest Mother herself. Alauda stepped closer, running her fingers over the finely polished marble, and felt it at once; the Green. If anything, it was stronger here than it had been on the bridge. She jerked her hand back, lest it overwhelm her.

The stonework was ancient, and it had been exposed to the elements for more than forty centuries; it was neither clean nor in good condition. But it was still largely intact. She rubbed her thumb over the effigy's thigh, and nodded in approval. The artist had been a genuine craftsman; the mottled skin-tones were clearly visible, depicted with great subtlety and skill. "She was *elvii*," Alauda breathed. "Not Third House. Not Third House at all!"

"A Wilder?" Alacer breathed. "I don't believe it!"

"I can't see that there's any other explanation," Alauda shrugged. "She wasn't *Suku Gagak*; the patterning...her coloration isn't right. She must have been from one of the other hunter clans."

"But that's...that's not..."

"No, it's not," Alauda agreed. "It's not what history teaches us. We remember her as Third House, like Fineleor. Like us. But it certainly explains a lot." She smiled lopsidedly. "Amongst other things, it explains...well, me."

"A Wilder?" Tonlees said, baffled. "Then how could she have

come from a Duodeci family?"

"She may have been adopted," Alauda reasoned. "Raised in the city, perhaps, as a true daughter of the *Antaíssinni*. But when war came, she returned to the forests, to her home. To fight alongside her people."

"How can you possibly know that?" Sîol scoffed.

"Because it's what I would've done." Maybe not before, when she'd known no more of the natural world than what lay within the walls of their garden at Corymbus. But now, now that the eyes of her *sielu* had been opened to the Green; now that her blood had been promised to the Forest Mother, and to the Horned God, mighty guardians of the woodlands –

Alauda ran her fingers over the marble, feeling the throbbing heat of life breaking upon her, like storm waves upon a rocky shore. She half expected to be struck by another vision, but all that she felt was cool, damp stone. Stone, and...something. Something else. Something that echoed within her, behind the racket of the waterfall.

She turned back to the Halflings, shaking her head, her ears ringing slightly. "This might explain why the Antaíssin line descends from her younger sister. History tells that it was because Anja died before she could take Fineleor to mate; she never bore children of her own. But maybe it was because her sister was the true daughter of her House – the legal heir."

Sîol scowled. "This is all very interesting. Or it might be, if we were elfy scholars of genealogy. But it's not getting us any closer to old Fineleor's hoard."

"Shut up," Alauda said softly. "Shut your barking mouth, and let me think."

The four Halflings turned to stare at her. Alauda ignored them. She put both hands on the statue's knees, leaning forward, feeling for the tenuous threads of the Unity – seeking them this time, instead of allowing them to come upon her unawares. She could feel it; there was *something*, something there, something old and hoary...but also something new, very new. Something bright and steely, with the hot, hissing strength that she had felt emanating from her mother during a working.

It was the flux; she knew it at once. "There's magic here," she said, taking her hands off the marble and stepping back, suddenly apprehensive. "Both kinds. Old magic, anchored to the Green; and new magic, too. The Art. Someone's put a spell on this place. I can feel it."

"How?" Tonlees cried. "I thought you didn't...you couldn't –"

"It sticks out," Alauda interrupted, shivering. "It feels wrong. This place belongs to *kesatuan*. Book-magic, the kind my mother works...it doesn't belong here." She actually felt a sense of outrage building within her. It vied with her deep immersion in the sensations flowing from the stone all around them. She felt as if she were being pulled between two worlds.

"We know about it," Sîol said, still looking a little nettled. "Calm yourself. We found it when we were here before. It's a trap, and a potent one. It was almost certainly set by Lady Nidlo, Lord Alfaric's mate. She was at the College of the Eye, remember, before she resigned to join him here."

"What does it do?" Alauda asked, eyeing the statue warily.

"Nothing dangerous," the redhead shrugged. "At least, we don't think so. As near as we can tell it creates a barrier to keep out the curious." She nodded at Breaghan. "Bree spotted it the last time we were here, and I managed to figure a way around it. It's simple; you just need sharp eyes.

"When we got past it, we found the *next* obstacle – the one that truly balked us." She poked Alauda in the belly. "The one we need you for, princess."

"Show me," the elf-girl commanded.

Alainn, looking worried, swept aside a portion of the hanging vines on the wall to the left of the effigy. Behind the vines lay a cave – a tunnel. A passageway chiselled into the side of the mountain.

Alauda brushed past him – or tried to; the boy flung out an arm, holding her back. "We need light in here," he cautioned. "All of us."

Sîol rummaged about in her pouch and produced a firestick and a number of small balls, each about the size of an egg. Igniting the stick, she touched the flame to each of the balls in turn and rolled them one by one into the passageway. Alauda caught the pungent odour of burning pitch, and made a mental note not to step on one of the fireballs by accident; it would cling like honey.

"That stinks," Tonlees complained. "Why not use torches? Or a lantern?"

"Don't tell me you have a lantern in that bodice," Breaghan said with a smile. "We need these. They cast a special light; it reveals magic."

"Let me guess," Alauda muttered. "You stole them? From Mhaister Cloughsen, I suppose?"

The braided beauty's response was an eloquent shrug – and a telling grin.

The balls cast eerie, flickering shadows, and produced a distinctly unpleasant odour that masked every other scent, even that of the trees. She found herself longing for Akaryah's mystical dancing lights; they were far prettier, and didn't stink. The pitch-balls did, however, produce enough light for her to easily make out what Alainn was pointing at.

The floor of the passage was filthy with dirt, old litter, dead leaves and bits of branches, and even the skeleton of a rat. A line had been cleared in the mulch. It was about the breadth of her hand, and stretched from wall to wall. In the midst of this relatively clean expanse, someone had laid a sprinkling of bright, reflective powder. It glittered like gemstones in the flaring light of the pitch-balls.

"Don't touch that line," Sîol warned, pointing it out. "You can step over it, but give it a wide berth."

Alauda dropped to her haunches. "What is it?"

Tonlees crouched beside her. "*Argentum pulvii*," she murmured. "Powdered silver." She glanced at the walls, and then the ceiling. "It's a shield. Break the line, and a force-wall will spring up."

Fearghan glowered at her. "I thought you weren't a wizard?"

"I went to *schola*," Tonlees sniffed. "And unlike Ala, here, I paid attention."

Alauda rolled her eyes. "We learn this sort of thing, Fearghan," she explained. "Or at least, our masters try to teach it to us. Some are quicker to pick it up than others."

"Especially if the 'others' spend all their time daydreaming," Toni chuckled.

Alainn put a hand on Alauda's shoulder. "We've been across it before, and nothing happened. Don't worry; just don't step on it."

"I'm not worried," Alauda scoffed. She knew about forcewalls; despite having paid little attention in her formal classes, her mother had attempted to explain them often enough. She'd managed to grasp the basics, and reading her mother's book had filled in the blanks.

She glanced at Tonlees. "Where do you suppose it came from? Lady Nidlo?"

"Probably," her friend muttered. "That silver dust isn't even tarnished. It can't have been here long." She tugged an ear, clearly nervous. "It's a potent spell, Ala; we don't know anyone who could cast it. Your mother certainly couldn't."

"No. Nidlo must be fairly powerful."

"As powerful as Lord Trivinako, d'ye think?" Alacer murmured.

"Let's hope not." A brief image of the aftermath of the battle at the church of the White Hand in Vitrafoss flashed through Alauda's memory, bringing with it the stench of burning flesh. Her gorge rose briefly.

Toni glanced at her, worried. "Are you sure we want to annoy a wizard?"

"Why not?" Alauda snorted. Feigned bravery was as good as the real thing. "I do that just by waking up in the morning."

They stepped carefully over the line. The corridor continued, gloomy and dark. "So where's this obstacle?" Alauda asked. "The impassable one, that you want me to somehow break." Her nerves were humming with barely contained excitement; whatever was in the air (*apart from the fumes from the burning pitch-balls*, she thought, gagging) was more potent up ahead. She could feel it work upon her senses. It was like wine, subtle and intoxicating. She was doing her best to take shallow breaths, out of fear that taking deep ones would cause the gathering urgency to build and build, until she burst apart.

"Right here," Sîol glowered. She paused about five paces past the line of silver dust. "Same sort of thing, but...well, different." She pointed at the floor of the passage.

Alauda knelt again. She saw another bead of silver – but this one was solid, set into a mortise cut into the very stone. It was fine work, and ancient, too; the silver inlay, wide as her index finger, was chased with spirals and whorls, like some unfamiliar alphabet. And it wasn't tarnished either. Given how long ago it had to have been set in place, to had to be a potent spell. Another magical anchor, perhaps?

"Is it another force-wall?" Toni frowned, echoing Alauda's thoughts.

"Sort of," Sîol said. She tapped Alauda's shoulder, and when the elf-girl glanced up, the Halfling pointed up the wall, and across the ceiling.

Alauda followed the gesture, and saw at once that the silvery bead encircled the entire hallway. "*Aiyah*," she sighed. "This isn't good. This is original, isn't it? From the old days."

"Who knows?" Sîol shrugged. "It's definitely been here longer than the dust back there."

As long as the passageway itself, probably, Alauda mused silently. She glanced at Tonlees. "Any idea what this one does?"

Her friend spread her hands. "Same thing, probably," she guessed. "But it's permanent. It's been here for a very long time."

"I told you, we already know what it does," Sîol said. "We found out the hard way. Bree?"

Before Alauda could say anything, Breaghan walked forward, and stepped over the silver bead.

Or at least she tried to. A plane of air following the glimmering rails coalesced out of the dark of the passageway, solidifying into a solid block of light. Breaghan bounced off of that light like a gum-rubber ball bouncing off a stone wall.

The force of the rebound sent her staggering back, stumbling. Alacer caught her, and she gave him a grateful glance.

"*Aiyah!*" Alauda said again, this time with feeling. She turned to Sîol with an incredulous stare. "And you want *me* to do something about *that*?!"

"Ask me again in a moment," the redhead grinned. "Al, you're next."

Alainn winked down at Alauda. He turned to face her, extended an arm...and leaned nonchalantly on the glimmering force-wall.

His hand sank into the white air up to the shoulder – but no further.

Alauda's jaw dropped.

Alainn pushed. The light surrounding his arm brightened perceptibly; tiny sparks of skyfire burst along his flank where it pressed against the arcane wall. He grimaced at her, struggling to grin. The sparks obviously stung.

"Stop, stop!" Alauda cried. "I see it!"

The golden-eyed boy stepped back, flexing his fingers. The instant his arm was withdrawn, the light-wall vanished.

Tonlees stared, baffled. "What kind of protective spell is *that*?" she objected. "It stops some people entirely, and lets others half through?"

Alauda already knew. "A very finely crafted one," she said coldly. "And given what you've told us, we know how it works." Standing, she brushed the grime from her knees. It was a pointless gesture; her gown was already a lost cause, and even her shift would be good for nothing but a washing-cloth once the evening's revels were done. She dropped a casual wink at the grinning Alainn – and stepped through the wall.

A flash of light exploded out of nothingness, crawling over her, tickling and pricking like a regiment of ants. She was through it in less time than it took to draw a breath, and yet it still left the small hairs standing up on the back of her neck. Her entire body tingled as if she had been scrubbed from head to toe with a horsehair brush.

The light didn't go away; it continued to burn, bright and chill, as if the air itself were afire. She turned, and despite the glow she could clearly see her companions standing amazed on the other side of the luminous veil wall. "Toni, Alacer – come on!" she cried, waving to them, and beckoning with a finger. "You should be able to pass too!"

Confident that they would follow her, she inspected her surroundings. The corridor continued for another few paces before breaking into steps leading down. The first thing she noticed was that it was clean; there was none of the muck and detritus she'd seen outside, none of the wind-blown leaves or rat skeletons. Apart from a little dust, the corridor was dry and pristine – ancient, to be sure, but showing none of its age.

The second thing Alauda noticed was the savour of the air. She'd felt the brief change in pressure when she passed through the force-wall, and had expected it to be stale with disuse – and so she was shocked almost into insensibility at how fresh and clean the passage smelled. The stink of burning pitch was gone; the air was as crisp with promise as any forest glade. More so!

She breathed deep, and felt the same electric, tingling sensation at the back of her throat that she had tasted outside. Here, though it was multiplied a hundred-fold. Her shoulders shook with anticipation, her fingers trembling, but not from exhaustion or fear; every breath she took seemed to wipe away her fatigue, restoring strength to her weary limbs, rebuilding the awareness dulled by weariness and the bone-chilling torrent through which they'd passed. She felt as if she were walking a hand-span off the ground.

The intoxicating purity seeped into her through every pore, bringing with it an eldritch awareness that she'd experienced only once before: in the high col where Akaryah had introduced her to the Forest Mother's bloody sacrament. She'd felt the same sensory assault then, when the visions of revels past had overwhelmed her, leaving her trembling on the very pinnacle of urgent, cramping need. She could feel some of the same symptoms now, and was beginning to understand what they meant. It was Akaryah himself who'd spoken of it, albeit at a different time, and in response to different questions: of how the wild elves celebrated the rites of spring with the first flowering of the Morbannens, giving themselves over to the intoxicating hunger spawned by Hutanibu's great gifts, often forging the bonds of life-mating with that first union. *That* was what she smelled: the scent of the golden flowers, lofted upon the wind. Spring flowers, bursting with life and promise. Her body was responding to the forest's pressing, overwhelming need to bring forth new life

But there was no forest here. Where was it coming from?

The air of the cavern was too much for her; she was suffocating now, drowning in luxuriant, overwhelming fecundity. She felt constrained, confined; she couldn't breathe deeply enough to sate her desire for the life that floated upon the inexplicable breeze. Drawing Elspeth's dagger from her boot, she set the edge against the laces that snugged her gown under her arms, sawing through them one at a time, heedless of the number of times the needle-sharp point pricked her through the thick layers. When the laces were cut, she wriggled out of the sodden mass of satin, sighing with relief as she kicked the crumpled fabric into a heap. In the warm, enticing atmosphere of the passageway, her linen shift was more than she needed. It left her shoulders bare and fell to mid-thigh, clinging damply to her meagre curves. She kept her boots – one never knew, after all, what sort of horrors one might tread on underground – and rebuckled her cincture, scabbard and crumena about her waist.

Thus freed of the damp, clinging weight of her dress, she shivered and breathed deep. The savour of the Green filled her, lifted her up. She heard a furtive step behind her, and then a second and a third. Tonlees and Alacer had followed in her wake, as she'd known they would. They walked through the shimmering arcane barrier, identical looks of wonder on their faces. The looks changed to surprise when they noticed Alauda's state of undress. "Too heavy, and too hot," she explained; her cheeks, flushed and sweating, might've told the tale for her.

"What's wrong with the air?" Alacer gasped, tugging at his neck-cloth.

"Nothing!" Alauda laughed – a mad, high-pitched titter that bounced and echoed down the hall. "Nothing at all. It's Second Spring!"

She started down the stairs, her friends hurrying to follow. "Why could we get through," Tonlees asked, "but the others couldn't?"

"Can't you guess?" Alauda replied. "I understood it as soon as I saw Alainn try. Whoever wove that spell keyed the barrier to elven blood. He could almost make it – almost, but not quite. The other half of his heritage stopped him." She shook her head. "*This* is why the halpies needed us, Toni. They never got this far; they couldn't pass the wall of light. They may know what's down here, or at least they say they do – but only from their research, or Cloughsen's. They've never seen it themselves. No one has."

"What d'ye mean, 'no one'?" Tonlees demanded, panting.

Alauda shot her a grin. "Calm yourselves. Breathe. Can't you feel it?" It was like coming home. She breathed deep, again and again; the air of the cavern was intoxicating.

Her friends imitated her warily. Neither seemed any more comfortable.

Alauda shook her head, pitying them. She noticed everything; she understood everything. "Look at the floor," she murmured, pointing at the deep prints their booted feet left in the fine dust laid down by the ages. "No one's been in here for centuries. Eons, maybe."

"That's not very comforting," Tonlees said nervously. "We're none of us...well, house-breakers, Ala. Burglars. What if we come upon another trap? A real one?"

"We won't," the younger girl assured her. "It's not that sort of place. It's not a...a treasure-vault. The halpies had that wrong. Don't you see? This is something else."

She was buoyant with self-assurance; the air that filled her lungs, that penetrated every fibre of her being, had ignited a fire that would not be easy to beat back, let alone extinguish. Alauda had no desire even to try. She was suddenly, breathlessly aware of Alacer – of the breadth of his shoulders, the strong muscles of his thighs, the calluses on his hands, the angle of his jaw, and the curve of his lips. Of the *smell* of him; of hair, his clothing, his breath and sweat – his essential masculinity. A single glance in his direction awakened a thrumming deep within her, one that she'd felt before. It took all of her swiftly deteriorating resolve not to hurl herself at him.

The stairs – there were three dozen; Alauda, by force of habit, had counted them – emptied into a broad chamber with a high, vaulted roof.

Its walls were easily ten paces on a side, the ceiling more than that in height. Careful chisel-work had left soaring buttresses, polished to a low sheen, supporting the vast dome overhead. The work was rectilinear, gloriously perfect – and at the same time as solid as the gutrock of the mountain from which it had been hewn.

But it was not finished; it was not dead. Not that there was anything left undone; even in the dim light that came from...from somewhere, Alauda could see not a hint of uncut rock. The chamber was perfect, and perfectly complete. And yet the stone of the room seemed...vital; yes, that was the word. It waited, crouched with anticipation, as if it held the secrets of life locked within the sparkling crystals that shone like stars set into the polished walls. As she descended the last stair and turned she could see that the walls were otherwise devoid of decoration, save only for...

Alauda stopped on the final step and stood stock-still, rapt with wonder. Here it was at last: the thing they'd sought; the ancient vault beyond whose doors Fineleor had secreted his second-greatest treasure.

And what doors! Three times her height and wider than she was tall, they were wrought of polished marble the shade of midnight – and like the night sky, they were shot through with sparkling pinpricks and deep veins of glimmering gold. They fit so perfectly together that she could scarcely make out the seam that separated them. And they were carved; the doors' surface had been cut with a shallow, almost invisible representation of two sigils in relief. The right door held a stag's head; and the left, a bent bow, with an arrow nocked.

Alauda recognized both symbols at once, but her attention was drawn immediately away from them. The doors were flawless, magnificent – and yet their majesty was utterly obscured by the wonder of the work that enclosed them. Flanking the doors, framing them, was a pair of columns carved from some white stone – alabaster, perhaps, or dolomite – into two pillars of climbing vines. From roots like those of the greatest Morbannen, the vine-columns stretched the height of the doors, woven and intertwined, exquisitely detailed. Some of the strands were as thick through as Alauda's body; others, thinner than her smallest finger. Up, up they reached, arching over the doors and forming a lintel roofed over with leaves, carved in such exquisite detail that Alauda could almost smell them.

And among the vines...what? She couldn't resist; she had to see. Trotting to the doors, she ignored Toni's squeal of alarm and ran her fingers over the stone-cutter's masterpiece. She looked more closely – and she saw them: figures amid the vines, carved with unthinkable delicacy. Tiny figures, each no more than a hand-span in height, leaping and cavorting amid the polished branches. They were so small that little detail was visible – and yet she knew what they were: their form, their indistinct features, the tiniest hint of pointed ears, gave them away.

They were elves. And from their attitudes and postures, their bent bows and short spears; from their bearing in the hunt, tracking tiny carved replicas of boar, bear, and elk, she knew what sort of elves they were. True *elvii*; the Wilders, her ancient forebears. The people from whom the so-called 'high elves' of the Third House had been bred by intermingling their blood with that of the Powers; the sole remnant of the elven folk as Holy Bræa had made them.

Folk like Akaryah, and Mua, and Tanju Berat; folk like Jantun, her snow-bound saviour, her beloved huntress of the singing heart. They were the source of the light; the tiny figures gamboling among the vines of stone. They did not shine, or even glow; they glinted in the darkness, each spark among the hundreds – thousands! – of effigies contributing to a soft emanation that made the whole a wonder to behold.

With trembling fingers she reached out and touched the tiny figures, and felt the throbbing power of the life locked within the stone. The doors, the columns, even the whole room...it was a contradiction. A deliberate one. No elf built in rectilinear buttresses, or constructed doors of polished marble tall enough to allow a giant to pass with ease. At the same time, *only* an elf could conceive such a piece of art as the carved vines that enveloped those doors. How...

A drop of water fell upon her head. She looked up – and she saw it.

The architect was looking down at her.

Despite her exalted state, or perhaps because of it, she jumped. It was a face; an ancient, brooding face, staring at her from the centre of the lintel. The face, of all things, of a dwarf. He was bald, big-nosed, and bewhiskered, and appeared to be glowering – but appearances weren't everything. His beard seemed over-thick, and she understood at last: amid the delicate tracery of the stone-work, real moss had sprung up over time, intertwining itself with the carvings and hanging down to form an extension of the dwarf's beard.

That was the source of the water. "Folgest?" she murmured. It was more a question than a statement.

Tonlees glanced at her. "What?" she whispered.

"Folgest the dwarf," Alauda said dreamily. "From the poem: who gathered them up, and brought them home. We don't even know his real name; just his title. *Folcgestealla*; battle companion. I'll bet this is him. I'll bet he built this place for Fineleor, his friend."

"Alauda, are you all right?"

Alacer was looking at her strangely. She didn't answer. She glanced down, and saw that she was standing upon damp stone...and metal.

Metal?

She turned, staring at the floor.

"What's that?" Alacer muttered. He too was looking at the floor.

Centred among the flagstones was a…Alauda didn't know *what* it was. Some sort of carving, like a shallow bas-relief. She squatted, running her fingers over what looked like an oddly interlocking pattern of tiles, which taken altogether formed a gigantic circle. Several circles, actually; circles within circles.

When she touched them, her suspicion was confirmed; they were made not of stone, but of metal. It was dull yellow, in places tending towards brown. "Brass?" she asked.

"Bronze," Alacer replied. He bent as well, flicking the plaques with a fingernail. "Harder, though not as ready-wearing." He pointed. "Look here; letters."

"Not letters," Tonlees interjected, walking around the outer ring, careful not to step onto or across it. "Words. Ala, those are words."

Alauda followed her, circumnavigating the outer part of the ring. She was finding it difficult to concentrate; the scent penetrating her nostrils, and the vibrations deep within her belly, were a hazardous combination. Combined they made her skin tingle, blurred her vision. She felt as if the figures carved into the living rock were watching her; judging her. She stumbled more than once, her toes catching on the uneven flagstones.

"Are you all right?" Alacer asked.

Alauda shook her head to clear it. "I'm – I'm a little on edge. Aren't you?"

Toni sensed it too. "What's wrong with the air?" she whispered. "Why do I...I feel..."

"Sssh!" Alauda commanded, following the arc of words in the floor, striving to focus her thoughts. "Nothing's wrong. Concentrate!"

They were gibberish; nonsense. "Just random," she muttered, circling the ring. "*Blandior, Reservare, Convomo, Induro, Colatus, Indireptum, Turpiter*...it doesn't make any sense!"

"There are three rings," Alacer noted, standing back a little, and frowning in confusion. "Three, each within the other. What d'ye suppose that means?"

Alauda shuddered to a halt. It meant something; something. She cursed her feeble, scent-sodden brain, struggling to tamp down her rising passion. Her lifebeat throbbed hotly in her neck, echoing in her ears like a war-drum.

The figures amid the stone vines watched her, waiting.

Three rings; meaningless words. Three – "Turn them!" she snapped.

Tonlees and Alacer stared at her.

"Turn the rings!" Alauda repeated. When neither of her friends moved, she fell to her knees. There was just enough depth to the letters to offer purchase – and when she pushed, the outermost ring turned easily. Well, she thought after a moment, not easily; not without some grunting and at least one broken fingernail. There was a great deal of grinding, and the odd, nerve-shattering squeal of recalcitrant metal, but at last the ring turned.

She realized that it had to have been carefully balanced, and was obviously set upon some sort of rollers; otherwise she'd never have been able to budge it. The fact that it moved at all after so long was, she reflected, a miracle of engineering in itself.

Tonlees knelt next to her. "What are we doing?" she hissed.

Alauda shook her head. "I know how it works," she panted. "We turn the rings until a phrase lines up. A three-word phrase. We just need to figure out what it is."

"Start with the inner ring," Alacer said thoughtfully. "It has the fewest words. Pick the last word, and work backwards from that."

Alauda shot him a grateful smile. At the same instant, a stab of desire shot through her, nearly doubling her over; she'd never wanted him more than in that moment. She bit her tongue until the paroxysm passed.

The trio stood and stared at the innermost of the three rings. Alauda's finger shot out almost at once. "*Viridi*!" she exclaimed. It meant 'green'; or, more precisely, 'The Green'. "It has to be that!"

"Right," Tonlees shrugged. She knelt, and spun the ring. "Er…which way should it point? To line up, I mean?"

Alauda thought about that. "With the doors," she said at last. "What else could it be? That's the only point of reference down here."

Tonlees turned the innermost bronze ring until the word was parallel to the vast expanse of midnight marble. "Now what?"

Alauda was gasping now, the power of the air bleeding into her, making her head spin like strong wine. *Viridi.* The word shuddered through her, echoing against the bulwarks of her *sielu*. She'd heard it, used it herself, not long ago – and in a phrase of three words. A sacred phrase.

She blinked. Actually, it had been six. Six words. She'd spoken them to a darker power, kneeling bare and defenceless upon a sacrificial stone with her mother's blade at her throat. "*Veniam ad te,*" she breathed, "*colatus in viridi!*"

I come to you, purified by the Green.

"Sorry?" Tonlees asked, frowning.

Alauda pointed a shaking finger at the bronze circles. "Are the words there?" she gasped. "All of them? *Colatus in viridi?*"

Her friends scanned the metal rings. Alacer was the first to look up. "How did you know?" he exclaimed, stunned.

Alauda had no intention of regaling either of them with the nauseating details of how her mother had devoted her daughter's lifeblood to the service of the Horned God. The very thought that this place – this enticing, eldritch place! – was somehow connected to the grim rites that she had endured at the standing stones was enough to make her tremble.

Tonlees too was staring at her, clearly troubled. "Do we do it?"

"Yes," Alauda said decisively, before Alacer could offer an opinion. "It's why we came, isn't it?" She knelt, rotating the second ring until "*In*" was aligned just above "*Viridi*"; and then, scrambling to the outer ring on hands and knees, spun it slowly until "*Colatus*" appeared above the other two words.

Nothing happened.

"Maybe it's the wrong phrase," Alacer said hopefully. "There are hundreds of possible combinations, after all."

"Four-and-twenty thousand," Alauda growled. There were forty words on the outer ring, twenty on the inner, and thirty on the ring that lay between them. "It's more likely that there's a trigger somewhere."

Tonlees wrinkled her nose. "It's probably here," she said, stepping to the circular flagstone that lay at the centre of the rings.

The instant her foot touched it, a deep, grinding noise echoed through the cavern. Alauda looked up, the colour draining from her face.

"Oh, good!" Tonlees cried. "I think I found –"

A thunderous deluge burst from hidden vents in the walls, blasting into them with the force of a tsunami – hurling them from their feet, and spilling the three elves head-over-heels. The chamber filled in an instant.

Alauda caught a momentary flash of Alacer's grey hair as it whirled past her. She flung out a hand, trying to grasp a limb, but touched nothing but water. She'd managed to seize a breath before the water had risen above her head, and hoped that her friends had done the same. Still, she was afraid that they'd –

WELCOME, CHILD OF THE GREEN!

The voice echoed in her mind, clamouring like trumpets. She gasped – and, consequently, inhaled a lungful of water. To her astonishment, it didn't burn, suffocate or sting; it filled her chest, feeding her life instead of snuffing it out.

Strength poured into her limbs; the strength of giants, of titans. She floated within the whorl of the deluge, breathing the eldritch water as easily as she might have breathed air – and the water was a thousand times more potent, more nourishing, than even the air of the cavern had been. It burned through her vitals, cleansing her flesh of bruises, easing her weariness. She felt rather than saw new flesh spurt from her injured hand, the skin growing together, healing itself. Even her scars – the scars of her encounter with the mountain lion, and the knot that still stood above her left ear, the legacy of her trip over the Vitrafoss waterfall, with an unconscious Renvig tucked under one arm – were all effaced, washed away by the irresistible healing glory of the waters.

The deluge drained slowly away, the waters fleeing the cavern of the bronze rings by a hundred tiny outlets. One instant she was swimming easily, glorying in her newfound freedom, marvelling at the sensation of breathing liquid without care; the next, she was lying on wet stone, spitting out the last of the water, and inhaling the warm, invigorating air of the cavern, gasping at the sudden infusion of strength, of magnificent, matchless power. Her bones gleamed with it. Her lifebeat thundered in her ears, echoing like distant drums. She wasn't cold; far from it. Her flesh was afire.

Gasping, she looked down at the rings, and saw that they had reconfigured themselves, spinning of their own accord, so that a new phrase lay revealed, lined up facing the great doors: *Coniunxit in Æternum*.

Forever joined. Even the central flagstone, the circular escutcheon that lay at the centre of the rings, had changed. It now showed the same sigil as the stone doors: the bent bow and the stag's head, brought together by the intertwining branches of the great tree.

"Forever joined," she breathed.

Two houses, forever joined. Joined by the Green.

She glanced up at the doors. They were still closed and motionless – but the columns were not. The stone vines thrummed with life, the carven figures sliding between them, writhing and dancing with abandon. She saw it, knew what it meant: the Wild elves, her people, were alive this night, drunk on the scent of the trees, and they were celebrating Second Spring: the renewal of life, and the glorious bounty of the living world.

It came to her in a flash of intuition, of inspiration; she knew what had to come next. Anja's bow; Fineleor's stag; the glory of the Green. The heroes, the promised but yet unmated martyrs, had ridden away to war. Betrothed in blood, they had never lived to wed, to be made one in flesh, as they already were in spirit. They had fought together, perished together, and were venerated for their sacrifice by all the generations that followed; but who mourned the loss of the lives they might have lived? Who mourned their wasted vows? Who gave a thought for the children, the mighty children, they might have borne together, enriching the magnificent bounty of the Green?

She staggered to her feet, her heart aching with the weight of ages, with sorrow at the death of two lovers. To her they were no longer legends or heroes – they were people, just *people*, who had been robbed of their chance at happiness by the vicissitudes of war. She spun slowly, blinking, her mind whirling with visions – trees and stones, running, the lion's roar, its heart's-blood staining her lips, the softness of Shambir's fur against her back, the slick warmth of Jantun's body in her arms, the chill press of the stones beneath her knees, the keen kiss of the blade at her throat, the tight, urgent need at her centre, the chilling churn of the waterfall, the eyes of the moons, all silver and golden, Alacer's hard, white body beneath the standing stones, his smile, his scent –

– oh the scent the scent of the trees –

Her eyes sought him out; but when she spotted him he was already engaged, huddled with Tonlees against one of the walls. The pair were already half-clad, locked in a passionate embrace, hands and lips and hearts searching, searching.

A brief snarl of outrage twisted her lip, and she tasted blood and fury. She wanted to tear them apart, to set her teeth in her auburn-haired friend's throat for poaching her mate; but it was too late. She'd known; somehow, she'd known what had been going on. She'd seen the furtive glances, heard the brief hesitations in their speech, sensed the evidence that her over-active mind had been too obtuse to recognize. She'd seen the signs, and had chosen to ignore them. She'd smelled her rival on his flesh – on her mate! – and had been too locked into her own fantasy to realize that Alacer's heart had moved on.

A knot rose in her throat, but she choked it back. Despair was nothing new; she had turned away from her heart's desire once before: at Jantun's tent, when the huntress, locked in the embrace of Kambali the clan-chief, had beckoned to her, inviting the Courageous Lark into their shared bower, to join with her and her mate. She'd moved on then. She knew what it was to move on, to always move on.

At the same time, her need was real and otherwise unanswerable; and it was a need that they all shared. She understood at last how magic had been bound to stone; she knew how the doors must be opened.

She staggered to the steps, splashing through puddles, and all but ran up them. The gleaming force-wall was still there, with the Halflings huddled together on the opposite side, staring into the darkness with wide eyes. Without an instant's hesitation she lunged at the wall, hurling herself through the crawling kiss of magic with scarcely a blink, and seized Alainn by the collar of his jacket.

His jaw dropped at the sight of her: clad only in shift and boots, drenched to the skin, her hair a ragged, dripping mess, her eyes wild and glowing like sunlit emeralds. "We heard the water!" he gaped. "What hap–"

Alauda threw herself at him, seizing him by the shoulders and stopping the flow of his words with her lips. The force of the impact knocked him back a step. When he pulled away from her in surprise she snatched at his lapels – and with a sudden access of strength, spun and hurled him against the glowing barrier.

He yelled in shock; she ignored him, seizing and kissing him again, clawing at his garments, stripping the jacket from his back.

When Breaghan, her pretty face twisted with jealous outrage, pulled at her shoulder, Alauda whirled snarling and swung her fist, backhanding the girl into the vines. Alainn barked a cry of protest at that, but she ignored him. She pulled him into a tight embrace and, setting her feet, pushed with all her strength against the gleaming, hissing veil, focussing her thoughts into a single stream: of paying just and long overdue homage to the wasted vows of Fineleor and his lost bride.

Alainn screamed briefly as talons of arcane force clawed at his flesh; but Alauda didn't care. She wasn't listening; her eyes were screwed shut. She was afire with lust, adamant and pure. She was a daughter of the Forest Mother, a blood-promised servant of the Horned God, and *this* was her chosen mate. She shoved him through the barrier, forcing the snarling crackle of the ancient magic to bend to her will and acknowledge Alainn's dilute elven blood.

Before he could draw breath for a second cry, they were through.

She allowed him no respite, taking his wrist and pulling him stumbling down the stairs. He was distracted briefly by the sight of Alacer and Tonlees, moaning together in a fervent, struggling clinch; Alauda was not. She knew, with crystalline surety amid the crumbling shipwreck of her reason, that while their instincts were correct, their deed would not suffice. New life, they had; but new blood...

Don't think of them. Tugging Alainn in her wake, she strode to the centre of the rings, turned, and embraced him again. He seized her shoulders, forcing their lips apart. "Alauda, what is this?!" he cried.

She regarded him hotly, panting. "It's what you wanted," she gasped, "and it's what I need." She cast a glance at the stone doors, feeling the rising heat of the green in her thighs, her loins, her breasts, and her fingertips. She had to fight it, had to choke it back to keep it from bursting into a frenzy of wild, verdant fire. "And it's...it's what *they* needed, but – but never..."

She could bear it no longer. She grasped his ears and kissed him, kissed him until he was choking for breath. Her fingers tore at his belt, at the buttons of his breeches. When at last she had found what she sought, hot and hard and surprisingly weighty, she pulled him to the floor, yanking her shift up about her hips, spreading her legs, and welcoming him into her soft, inviting depths.

Amid the carven vines, the writhing figures halted in their frenzy and turned to watch. The very stone seemed to hold its breath.

The flagstones – *water and rock, silver and brass, bow and stag and tree*

- were cold and hard against her backside, her shoulders, but she didn't care; their cool caress, the warmth of the air and its intoxicating scent, and the deep fire of the Green all worked their magic, breathing new life into her, filling her as her lover filled her, with peerless, panting glory.

A vision of sylvan perfection descended upon them, and the cavern was gone, replaced by an autumn glade in sunlight, trees swaying in the uplifting airs. Two lovers walked hand-in-hand through falls of orange leaves. *She went to muster her fighters,* Alauda thought, her hips rocking slowly, *and they parted thus, never to meet again, save on the field of battle, and in glorious death.* She put her hand on the back of Alainn's neck, drawing his face down to hers, and kissed his lips as he thrust into her. She'd expected pain – her mother had warned her that there might be pain the first time, and perhaps even blood – but she felt nothing apart from the hard, insistent length of him, and his warm breath upon her cheek, and a gentle, delicious friction.

Gentle, yes; too gentle. Fineleor and Anja had been warriors, and had denied their own passions for too long. In the end, they had perished before being able to give vent to them. Alauda's heart cried out for their loss. *Too gentle.* She seized Alainn's shoulder and, none too tenderly bore him to the stone, rolling him atop the paired escutcheon and straddling his hips. She resumed her seat, sinking slowly down, down, until they were one, joined and moving together; rocking, rocking and pitching like a fury until her breath came in short, hitching gasps and her thighs knotted with the extravagance of effort. She grasped his hands, pressing them to her breasts; crushing his fingers in her fists as together they reached for the skies and the stars, touching them as one, both in the same instant; crying out in unison as a thunderous wave of shimmering culmination enveloped them, sealing them together into a single panting, ecstatic whole.

Beneath them, the floor trembled. A deep, crackling rumble echoed through the cavern.

She collapsed atop him, spent and struggling for breath. Her fingers touched his face, and it was as if she were touching the face of a stranger. He moved a little, shifting his hips; and at that brief, delicious friction she burst once more into flame, shuddering and crying out again and again, bucking involuntarily as seemingly endless, rapturous waves billowed through her, racking her frail and evanescent flesh.

When the second chain of wrenching spasms had run its course, Alainn put his arms about her, holding her to his chest. Alauda lay there, enjoying the warmth about and within her. Somehow she found breath to speak. "Now *that,*" she gasped into his ear, "was a rite of passage. In the most literal sense." She giggled suddenly, struck by the humorous incongruity of her circumstances.

Alainn, evidently, saw nothing funny in it. He took her face in his hands and looked directly into her eyes. "Wonderful," he breathed, "wonderful! Oh my lady, thou'rt aye and truly a marvel!"

Alauda froze. Without a word she put her palms on the stone, levering herself off of him. She stood, tugging her shift back into place, her face a blank and expressionless mask. She raked her fingers through her tousled mane, shoving her lank and filthy hair back behind her ears.

"Bree?" the boy shouted.

An instant later, bare feet slapped on the steps as Breaghan, Sîol, and Fearghan ran down into the chamber. Alauda had been expecting that. Alacer and Tonlees, who were still entwined in one corner of the room and struggling to adjust their garments, had not.

Fearghan, who held a makeshift torch in one hand, was the only one to smile. "I wondered why this was taking so long," he snorted.

To Alauda's oblivious amusement, Breaghan strode directly to Alainn and, as he struggled with his trousers, began slapping him about the head and ears, snarling and cursing in the lisping halpie tongue. Alauda didn't catch a word of it. The girl was red-faced with rage – and, Alauda noted with bland amusement, she was weeping at the same time. She nodded to herself, mildly annoyed at having missed the signs of something which, in retrospect, ought to have been obvious; as blindingly obvious, she thought ruefully, as Toni's infatuation with Alacer, and the extent to which he'd reciprocated her sentiment.

No matter; the antics of others were inconsequential. She'd already heard what she'd been waiting for. She strode to the stone doors, feeling the polished marble under her fingers, cool and inviting, and running her nails over the shallow reliefs. They were no longer tightly shut; something had come loose within the mechanism that kept them locked, and they had opened a bit, showing a gap a hand-span in width between their tight-fitting edges.

She had to steady herself briefly, one hand flat against the rock, as another pleasurable aftershock rippled through her, knotting her belly and lingering in her loins. The scented air was even more potent now, and it was doing her no favours; every fiber of her being was shrieking at her to throw herself upon Alainn once again – or even better, upon Alacer. The brief release, however, had helped, as did knowing what had provoked her into momentary madness. Consequently, she was just able to lock her rampaging lust in the talons of her will, and wrestle it back under control.

She glanced at the carved vine-columns...and shivered in recognition. The tiny figures were motionless once more – but were they? They seemed to be nodding in satisfaction. She saw more than one with a hand seemingly raised in acknowledgement or salute. Had those hands been raised before? She couldn't recall.

When she had regained her composure, she pushed on the left-hand door. It moved, but only fractionally; once again, her muscles simply weren't up to the task. She turned back to her companions…

…and sighed. The other six were standing in a loose semi-circle. The Halflings were watching her with wary eyes. Sîol's gaze was cold and appraising, Fearghan's amused. Alainn's heart was in his eyes – and Breaghan's were full of rage.

She glanced at her friends. Alacer was watching her carefully, his face unreadable. *Amazing*, she thought bitterly, *he's finally learned to hide his feelings*. Tonlees clearly had not; she was staring at her shifting feet, refusing to meet Alauda's gaze.

She decided to seize the ram by the horns. "There was no other way," she said softly – but not apologetically. She would *never* apologize for doing what was necessary. That was the first principle, after all; Lord Trivinako had taught her that, and her mother had agreed. What was necessary was never wrong.

Still, she felt a need to explain; not to justify herself, but to help them understand. "Fineleor built this place to protect the treasure he'd left for his love. He and Anja had been promised for years – but they were both obedient to the Codex, and had never joined in body. The doors couldn't be opened until they were together again, in every sense. *Every* sense. Bound as one in the flesh, just as they were bound in spirit by the Green.

"That's what the message of the rings meant." She pointed at the floor. "*Coniunxit in æternum, colatus in viridi*. 'Joined forever, purified by the Green'." She shook her head in sympathy. "He was Third House, and she was wilder, from one of the hunter clans. I don't think history remembers that. I certainly never knew it, not until I saw her effigy outside. Which means that Fineleor was a lord of the Duodeci, a peer and general of the Realm, and wanted to take to mate a woods-walker of a hunter clan. It would never have been allowed. The law – Dior's law – divided them.

"This…" she waved a hand, indicating the watery cavern, "this was the only way they could…could be one. The Green brought them together, and sanctified their love. The magic – Fineleor's last act of magic, maybe, before he marched to meet his love, and go together to their doom – his magic protected this place, sealing the locks that had been built by his comrade, the dwarf." She pointed up at the lintel. "Him, I assume. Of course, it was only supposed to remain sealed until they could finally be together, but they didn't live to fulfill their vows. Someone…someone had to do it for them."

"If it was meant to keep this place locked until Fineleor and Anja could 'unlock' it – if that's the right word," Sîol said with a sardonic grin, "then how could you two open it with nothing more than a quick shag?"

"Sîol!" Alainn looked stricken.

"Shut it, lover boy. I want answers."

"I don't have any for you," Alauda said levelly. "I'm not a mage. But I can tell you this much: this wasn't the sort of magic you're used to. This was the power of the Green. Those who work its might aren't following a set of instructions, like a book-mage; *kesatuan*, the Unity, is alive, and very much aware. Somehow, we met Fineleor's conditions. Would you prefer we hadn't?"

"I was just asking," the red-head growled.

"And I was giving you the best answer that I can." Alauda glanced at her late lover. "Alainn – I'm not sorry for what I did. But I'm sorry for how I did it. I should've explained –"

"Don't apologize to *him*!" Breaghan screamed suddenly, tears streaming down her face. "I'm sure *he* didn't mind! Apologize to *me*!"

"I won't," Alauda said flatly. "He courted me, remember? I didn't know how you felt about him; you hid it too well. People call me a good liar, but you lot are far, far better at it than me."

"Why didn't you pick *him*?!" the braided girl raged, pointing at Alacer. "Why d'ye think we brought *all* of you?"

"Bree!" Sîol hissed.

Alauda blinked. Then she nodded. "I see. At least, I think I do. You knew about the magic, then?"

"Of course!" Breaghan cried. "We thought *he* was your lover!"

Alauda looked at her friends. Her face was as unreadable as Alacer's had been. "So did I."

Toni put her face in her hands. Her shoulders shook – and, as Alauda had expected, Alacer put his arm about them. He looked sad – but not apologetic.

And that's that, she sighed.

Breaghan was still livid. "But –"

"*Tacete!*" Alauda spat angrily. "It's over; it's done. What kind of burglars are you, anyway? Aren't you here to sack a castle? Bree, you're acting like I cut someone's throat, when all I did was make *basz-basz* with your man!"

Sîol and Fearghan exchanged looks. "Bash-bash?" Fearghan frowned.

"Never mind!" She jabbed a finger at the doors. "I'm going on. The rest of you can join me if you like, or stay here and piss about like play-acting children. It's your choice." She crossed her arms, tapping the toe of her boot impatiently. "Now, somebody help me open the damned door!"

Alacer stepped forward at once. As he grasped the edge of the door, he murmured, "Thank you. For…for not –"

"Shut up," she growled. She put her hand on his forearm and

squeezed gently. "And don't for an instant think I've given up on you, because I haven't," she added in a terse whisper. "If you so much as *smile* at me, I swear by Hara's stiff shaft that I'll trip you, mount you, and ride you 'till you can't see straight!"

He stared at her, his eyes bulging. "*Me'scuso?*"

"I'm in earnest," she hissed. She reached up, grasped a fistful of his wet, stringy hair, and yanked his head down until their noses were almost touching. "Toni's my friend, and I'd rather die than hurt her – but you were mine first! If there's an honourable way to have you back, I'll find it."

And maybe even if there isn't, she didn't say.

He stared at her, flabbergasted by her fiery promise. "Fair enough," he said after a moment. He was too obviously struggling to come to grips with the prospect of being pursued by two girls at once.

Alauda cuffed his ear, and not gently. "And remember, she's the only person in all the wide world that I love as much as you. So be good to her, or once I've gotten what I want from you, I'll have your bollocks off."

Alacer's eyes widened. "Er…fair enough," he repeated weakly.

Contrite, he put a foot on the left-hand door, and with a convulsive heave, managed to open it a pace or so. Though exquisitely made and balanced, the doors were enormous, heavy, and old. A grinding squeal pierced the air of the cavern, making Alauda wince.

Beyond the door was darkness, the beginnings of a flight of stairs…and in the distance, the merest glimmer of light. Bright, white light.

"Come on," she said, stepping past Alacer, and beckoning Fearghan to come forward with his brand.

♦

Eighteen

Alauda's knees were trembling so badly as she mounted the stairs that she had to put a hand on the wall to reassure herself that it was her legs that were shaking, and not the stone itself. It wasn't fatigue; the flood of Green-laden water had washed that out of her, leaving her better rested than if she had slept the night through instead of spending it clambering over the side of a mountain. Her unsteadiness was the consequence of the growing potency of the air. What had previously been enriching, enlightening, was now so rife with shuddering, fecund power that with every breath she feared that she might burst into incandescence.

She glanced over her shoulder. The others, following close on her heels, didn't appear to be as deeply affected by the potency of the atmosphere as she was, but even the Halflings looked as though they were feeling its effects. It was worse for the elves, apparently; Alacer and Tonlees were gasping in unison, flushed and red-faced – even more so than could be explained by their recent exertions.

Alauda understood their preoccupation, but did not share it. Rather than exhaustion, she was flush with exaltation. Apart from that, she didn't know *what* to feel. There had been nothing of love in what she'd done with Alainn; there had been need, of course, and desire – but she'd been driven to the deed by the overwhelming expectation of the place: of the potency of the magic that Fineleor had left behind, which seemed to have been intensified rather than diluted by the passage of eons; the throbbing lifebeat of the Green; and the blind, breathless regard of the tiny figures of stone that had watched the pair of them as they consummated an ancient, unfulfilled promise.

All those things had driven her to complete the riddle in the only possible way. She had no regrets. She liked Alainn, and had risen with gasping urgency to his touch at the festival, and in time things might, just *might*, have gone further; but the power of the Well had had different ideas. She had responded to the scent of the trees, and the unsubtle demands of Second Spring. It had been nothing more than obedience to the irresistible summons of the Green.

It was similar, she realized with a wry smile, to being washed downriver and thrust over a waterfall. Then, her last choice had been to dive into the welcoming waters; thereafter, nature itself had taken control. So had it been with Alainn and the Well. And so too, she knew, had it been with Tonlees and Alacer.

When resistance was impossible, could there be shame in acquiescing to the inevitable – particularly when the inevitable was something that the heart so clearly desired? She wished she could have asked someone. But when she turned to speak to Tonlees, her friend turned away at once. Alauda ground her teeth. *I'm going to have to do something about that,* she sighed, *and before too long.* Toni was too good a friend to lose over something so...so very trivial.

Unlike the first passage and the chamber of the doors, the staircase they followed was in large part natural, a winding, irregular shaft that twisted and turned within the gut of the mountain. The stairs were straight and even, evidence that someone at least had seen fit to ply the chisel to make the tunnel easier to negotiate, but there was no other evidence of artifice. What intrigued Alauda the most, however, was the light. The glimmers ahead of them were growing steadily stronger, reflected along the passageway by the multitude of crystals in the rock.

She didn't understand what she was seeing until Fearghan spoke up. "Fire-glass," he grunted, tapping the wall with a finger. "That's what's passing the light along. This is a flowstone tube." He glanced up. "We're standing in a fire-mount."

"A what?" Toni asked.

"*Mons igneus.*" He used the elven term.

"*Aiyah!* What if it erupts?"

"It won't," Alauda said. "It's old. Right, Fearghan?"

The boy nodded. "If these steps date from Fineleor's day, then nothing's happened here for nearly five thousand years. The chance that it'd happen today –"

"Oh," Tonlees sighed. "Good."

"Doesn't mean something *couldn't* happen now, of course," the Halfling shrugged. "With a fire-mount, you never know. And you three did unlock some rather spectacular magic just not." He shot a glance at Alainn. "Sorry. You *four.*"

"You talk too much," Toni groused.

After another hundred paces the light was bright enough that Alauda found herself blinking. The airborne scent had increased exponentially; she had to pause once more, overcome by a mind-numbing wave of throat-clenching exaltation. She felt like a grinding-stone spinning out of control, threatening to fly apart.

Desperate for some sort of distraction, she made a fist and smashed it into the wall. The jagged stone lacerated her knuckles – but the sharp, stabbing pain banished the scent of the trees from her thoughts, and the accompanying ache in her loins – at least for the moment.

"What're you doing?" Alacer exclaimed, seizing her hand.

"Trying to concentrate," she gasped. "Walk faster, before – before I –"

"Before you what?"

She tugged her hand from his grasp, unable to answer. Her mind was humming, bursting with impossibilities.

The stairs debouched at last into an enormous cavern. The light was as bright as day, now – and Alauda at last understood why. The cave was scores of paces across, but far, far taller – so tall, in fact, that its upper reaches were open to the air. A broad, bright eye of blue gleamed down at them from far above. After the long night and the shadows of the cavern, even the indirect light of the Lantern was almost blinding. "*Mons igneus*," she breathed.

Fearghan had been right; they were in a volcano. In the very throat of one, in fact.

"Hara's blood," Tonlees whispered. "Look there!"

Alauda followed her pointing finger. They were standing on a broad ledge above a vast, still pool. The water was as clear as crystal; so clear that in the light flooding down from above, she could see that it was essentially bottomless. She could feel warmth and life emanating from it, like the Lantern's noontide light upon her upturned face. *At least we know where the flood came from*, she mused.

On the far side of the cavern there was a ledge; an islet, almost, just above the level of the water. At this distance it looked small, but in truth, it had to be enormous. The ledge was almost entirely overgrown by roots. The roots knotted together, rising in a thick, knurled stump – and from there into a tall, straight tree, a tree with silver-grey bark and slender, reaching branches. The first hints of silvery leaves were just beginning to emerge from buds.

It was a Morbannen. And it was *huge*. Alauda blinked deliberately, trying to force her eyes to recognize what they were seeing. The scale of the cavern had deceived her; such a tree had to be hundreds of feet tall.

That explains the air, Alauda thought, a fragment of relief penetrating the mad whorl of her thoughts. *The buds, the flowers*...the cavern's depths were flooded with the scents of virile springtime. "That's it," she whispered. The silvery bark; the tiny, budding leaves; springtime.

No, she thought, bemused, *not springtime; Second Spring*. The time of the revel.

A fresh storm of desire overwhelmed her – but it was no longer a desire of the flesh. Before any of her companions could stop her, she sprinted for the edge of the platform. Without breaking stride, and forgetting that she was a terrible swimmer, she leapt, arcing far out into the air, plummeting to the water in a flawless dive. She speared the water cleanly – and was once again exalted. The crystalline fluid was like air, like fire, like pure, unadulterated life. She drew it into her lungs, laughing as the bubbles burst from her nostrils, floating happily in the most natural medium she had ever known.

WELCOME, CHILD OF THE GREEN!

Alauda spun in place as the voice echoed once more in every corner of her being. It came from all around her, suffusing everything, making the stones themselves vibrate in sympathy. Yet she saw nothing. Despite the light, the clarity of the pool, she saw *nothing*.

She tried to speak, but water makes no noise when flowing past mortal vocal chords; all she accomplished was a weak, inaudible gurgling. Instead, she closed her eyes, working her arms and legs lazily, and let her thoughts speak for her.

Who are you?

I am Kulkisari, the voice replied. **And this is my home. You are truly welcome, child of the Horned God – daughter of the Forest Mother. I have had few visitors these long years.**

I can't imagine why, Alauda thought. She realized belatedly that she could have no inner monologue; the being – Kulkisari, wherever, whoever he was – could hear her.

I can, the voice replied, confirming her suspicion. **This is not an easy place to find.**

Alauda winced. *You have that right.*

Come and greet me, thou Green-born, the shattering voice continued, **and learn my tale. There is a boon that I would beg of you.**

All the horses of the High Guard couldn't have stopped her from doing exactly that. There was only one problem. *Where are you?* she asked.

As it turned out, the answer to that was as obvious as her ears, as the elven saying went.

She emerged from the water near the isle against the far wall of the cavern. She'd found it by the simple expedient of following the roots. The instant she'd touched one of them, she'd known the truth: that *this* was Kulkisari.

The tree. The tree had spoken to her. She was so unsurprised by her discovery that her lack of astonishment flabbergasted her.

Her friends were shrieking at her, crying her name, but she couldn't be bothered to answer them; her mind was full of the echoing thunder of her host's voice. She did wave at them, to let them know that she was well. An instant later she heard a loud splash, and then several more. She didn't glance back; Alacer and Tonlees were both competent swimmers, and would be able to help anyone who faltered.

She clambered up onto the mound, her fingers stroking the smooth, rippling bark of the roots. The touch of the tree was ecstasy. It was like caressing captive skyfire; the power that infused the air, that invigorated the water, all came from here, from this one spot. It emanated from Kulkisari's being, from the ancient, limitlessly potent *sielu* that inhabited the vast and ancient tree.

When she reached the trunk she put her hands on it; and then, overcome by a glorious, numinous desire, she embraced it – or tried to. She could not encircle even the tenth part of its vast girth with her arms. *What are you?* she thought. *Are you one of the Powers of the Forest? A tree-warden, one of the great and glorious walkers in the woodlands?*

I am not, Kulkisari replied. *I am only what I am. What you see before you, and nothing more. I cannot move about, as they do.*

And then there were no more words; nothing but an endless series of images, of impressions. His existence had been an accident. A seed, plucked from a living tree by a mischievous bird, had fallen from its beak into the maw of the fire-mount, landing upon the islet; finding, entirely by chance, the only plot of fertile soil within the mountain's throat. The seed had sprouted, and a tree had grown there, stretching ever for the sky, waxing for an age; until at last it was discovered by a Presence, one with the gentle and loving touch of the Light, who had laid a hand upon his bark, awakening him to knowledge, and reason, and the spoken word.

More years had passed, until another master of the woodlands – Varinyr Orkarel, the duke whose tomb they had found above, who had later become *Centeng'rimba*, the Warden of the Woodlands – Varinyr had found and befriended him, making him a confidante...and a guardian. The duke had learned the tree's name. Kulkisari had been a companion to the Duke, who built a castle outside the mountain and named it after the ancient being that lay hidden within; and after Varinyr's passing, he had remained a friend to the Duke's family.

He had known Fineleor, Varinyr's descendent; known him well, and treasured the general's friendship. And he had known Anja, and had revered her fire and passion for the life of the woodlands.

Alauda found herself shaking with the raw joy of memory that surged through her. *He had known Anja!*

And then, after too brief a span, his friends were gone...and he was left alone. *Fineleor saw the way the world was turning*, the towering creature explained, *and the rising menace of the Ender. He feared that his land, his Realm, would fall. Far too many knew of my cavern – and as I am, I could not escape.* He paused. *The Ender's hordes so loved the burning of the trees. He hoped to spare me that fate.*

A vast clot of rage mingled with sorrow welled up in his thoughts, and Alauda found herself inexplicably weeping.

And so, Kulkisari continued, *he sealed me in. He put his second-greatest treasure in my charge, and he closed the doors, swearing that he would one day return, and that they would open again when he and his love were as one.* He caressed her with a thought. *And now you are here. You are not my beloved Anja, child of the Green – but you bear her blood. How can this be? How long has it been?*

Alauda heard splashing behind her, and turned; Alacer and

Tonlees were struggling out of the water, each of them holding a drenched and half-drowned Halfling by the collar. "What're you doing?" Alacer gasped, spitting and shaking the water from his eyes.

"Talking to our host," Alauda laughed through her tears. "Come and meet him."

She turned back to the tree, keeping her hands on the bark. It seemed to make her thoughts easier to hear. She didn't need the contact to make sense of Kulkisari's words; they echoed like thunder. "My name," she said, speaking aloud for the benefit of her comrades, "is Alauda Alyssa Antaíssin Volo. I am descended from the line of House Antaíssin."

Then they **did** *live!* the tree exclaimed. *And bore children! How marvellous!*

Alauda shook her head, almost choking with sorrow. She knew how her next words would wound the ancient being. "No," she whispered. "House Antaíssin lived on through Anja's younger sister's line." She swallowed heavily. "Fineleor and Anja met for the last time on the field of battle. Gryshgranax, the revenant fire-fiend who captained Bardan's hordes, surprised them near Arx Vespertinus, trapping their army in a pass. They remained behind, holding a narrow pass until their soldiers could escape. They…they fell together, in each others' arms." She slid down to sit on one of the roots, scrubbing tears from her cheeks with filthy hands.

But they saved their people, and their Realm?

"For a time," Alauda said hollowly. "For…for forty years. Then Bardan fell upon us at the Field of Oldarran, in the battle that the dragons call 'The Gloaming of the Wyrms'. He won. Yarchian, the High King, fell; and Jawartan, his companion, an argent dragon, bore his body back to the Vale of Skulls, to rest among the bones of the great wyrms. The ancient world ended, and darkness fell upon Anuru. Bræa and Bardan sealed the world beneath the Dome of the Firmament, and for two thousand years the exiled Dark Queen reigned over all."

She recited by rote, as if she were still a school-girl at lessons. "Then Olowartan – Jawartan's brother; gods, you - you might have known them, too." she added with a sudden shiver at the massive weight of history the ancient tree represented; "Olowartan and his companions brought the Book of the Powers to the Elvenking, and the Darkness ended. Twelve hundred years passed in peace. Then the Shadow King arose, and sundered the world. Seven hundred years have passed since then.

"I'm sorry, Kulkisari," she murmured, tears leaking from her eyes. "It's been a long time. Fineleor and Anja died almost four thousand years ago."

Of course they died, the tree said gently. *None of your kind could possibly still be alive after so long. It would be long even for a dragon –*

even for a tree! But death is not defeat. They were together. You opened the magicks with which we sealed this place, so you must know that that was all that he desired.

There was a long silence during which no one, not even the voluble Halflings, spoke; the ancient tree's placid grief was too obvious. It reverberated through the cavern like a dirge. Alauda's throat felt tight, and it was all that she could do not to sob. She let the tears run unheeded down her cheeks – not wallowing in their host's sorrow, but sharing it in silent respect.

At last, however, his voice echoed once more through the cavern – and Alauda could tell, from the startled looks on the faces of her companions, that he was speaking to all of them at once. *If Anja is dead*, he said, *then you, Alauda Alyssa Antaíssin, are her heir*.

"Eh?" Alauda exclaimed. "No! No, I'm not! House Antaíssin has a lady and a lord. I'm from House Volo. We're not even Duodeci anymore."

Fineleor, my mighty friend, laid a bond upon me, the tree rumbled. *He bade me guard his second greatest treasure, and deliver it only into the hands of his beloved lady of House Antaíssin when she came to claim it. In all the long years of my vigil, I have served his final purpose, anchoring the magic that we wove together. I have met none other of her name – and no others have met the conditions he imposed.*

There was decision in his voice. *You have answered my friend's intent, Green-born; you have passed the wards that we set upon this place, and opened the doors that were sealed to await the return of his love. Anja's dowry is yours.*

A groaning, crackling tremor shook the isle; several of the tightly intertwined roots shifted, revealing a pit. Fearghan was the first to reach it – and when he did, he whooped with glee. "It's a chest!" he cried. Before anyone could stop him, he leapt down into the pit, disappearing from view.

Alauda didn't follow. *Are you certain about this?* she thought, returning to silent conversation to conceal her words from her friends. She didn't know how the Halflings might react if they thought she was refusing the treasure. *I'm not who you want me to be, Kulkisari. I'm just...just a child.*

A child, yes, the vast voice mused. *But a true child of the Green, from the line of my greatest friend's greatest love. I have touched your heart, Alauda Alyssa Antaíssin Volo, and I know it to be true. Your doubts cannot unmake what you are. You are born of the same blood, and to the same kinship, as Fineleor, and Varinyr, and the Watchmen who came before them.*

You may not believe yourself a worthy successor to their duty and their love – but you **could be**.

Alauda didn't know what to say to that.

You fear the treasure! A sudden burst of amusement poured from the ancient tree. *You are wise beyond your years. Wealth is always to be feared. But you need not fear this bounty; your ancestor's bequest cannot be squandered or wasted. It is of value only to true hearts, like my friend Anja's. Like yours.*

Alauda froze. *I thought it was coin?*

Coin? The branches overhead rustled. *The World Made is awash in coin. Why would Fineleor entreat me to safeguard mere metal?*

Why indeed? Alauda, alarmed by the implications of that question, left the trunk and clambered over the tangled roots to the pit, following her companions.

Between the roots, Fearghan was kneeling before a peculiar object. It wasn't at all what Alauda had expected. Instead of iron-bound wood, the chest appeared to be made of porcelain. It was also enormous, a full pace in width, and nearly two-thirds that in breadth and height. The sides and top were as exquisitely crafted as any platter or tea-set that Alauda had ever seen, with subtle green and blue pigments worked into a cream-coloured base. The sheen of the glaze showed even through a thick layer of moss and miscellaneous rubbish – mostly shed bark.

Fearghan looked up, puzzled. "There's no latch or lock."

"Or hinges," Alainn added. He was examining the rear of the box.

Alauda could see the thin seam where the lid met the sides; it was obviously designed to be lifted off. She said so, and between them, Alainn and Fearghan tried, but to no avail; the top refused to budge.

She straightened. "Kulkisari," she frowned, "how does this open?"

How did you open the doors? the tree replied.

Her eyes flew instinctively to Alacer's; his were bulging. He sounded as if he were being strangled. "Does he mean that we – that we have to, to…"

Alauda didn't know whether to be amused or offended at her late lover's obvious discomfiture. "Shut up," she said, a little more harshly than she had intended. *Could you be more specific?* she asked.

Certainly, Kulkisari murmured. *Two joined by blood, to pass the wall; two joined in body, to pass the doors*. His branches swished softly. *To open the chest, child of the Green, and receive that which Fineleor wrought, requires two joined in spirit.*

Fearghan's brows knitted. "Wrought? What d'ye mean, wrought? Old Fineleor wasn't a coiner or a silversmith too, was he?"

Alauda ignored him. She was laughing weakly. "True love. Is that what you're saying, Kulkisari? It can only be opened by true love?!"

What can I say? the tree rustled, sounding amused. *My friend Fineleor was, as he himself put it, a 'hopeless romantic'.*

She shook her head. "Ridiculous," she sighed. "Pathetic." Putting a hand on a convenient root, she vaulted down into the pit, shoving Fearghan gently aside, and beckoning to Alacer. "Come on."

Alacer shot a nervous glance at Tonlees. The auburn-haired girl looked aghast; then her expression changed to something more neutral, and she merely shrugged. Alacer bit his lip, easing himself down into the pit.

Alauda took his hand with a hopeful smile. "Together at last, *heya*?" she quipped uneasily.

He didn't laugh. "What do I do?" he muttered.

"Try to remember how you feel about me." She laid his hand on the lid of the chest, and put her own beside it.

Nothing happened.

"Lift the lid," she commanded.

They did so in unison; still nothing.

She took a deep, shuddering breath. "Well," she said coolly, "I guess that's it, isn't it?"

He put a hand on her shoulder. "Ala –"

"Get away," she gulped. The tears were there, ready to overwhelm her; she forced them back with a savage curse. "Alainn?"

Alacer, red-faced, sidled out of the way, making room for the golden-eyed half-Halfling. Alainn took Alauda's proffered hand, and they repeated the experiment.

Nothing happened.

When Alainn tried to withdraw, she clenched his fingers, eliciting a wince, and held them in place. He looked white. "Alauda, I –"

"*Tacete!*" she whispered fiercely, throwing his hand aside. "So much for true love, *heya*?"She made a fist, pounding it on the chest, grinding her teeth in a desperate effort not to cry. "Br-Breaghan," she gasped at last, stepping away from Alainn, "maybe you ought to t-t-try."

Breaghan slid into the pit, not taking her eyes from the elf-girl. Her lip was split and bloody; Alauda had a vague, indistinct memory of striking her.

Breaghan took Alainn's hand, while Alauda's guts churned.

Nothing. Breaghan's eyes filled; when Alainn tried to remonstrate with her, the braided girl slapped him – twice. Hard. She scrambled out of the pit, weeping.

Alauda laughed to herself. A final test; a diabolical one. They'd breached every barrier, answered every challenge – but this one could well end with the lot of them murdering each other. She dug at her stinging eyes with her thumbs. "Fine," she grunted harshly, "F-f-fine. Toni, Alacer...your t-turn."

As her friends climbed down into the pit, Alauda leaned on the ancient vessel, her heart in tatters. The porcelain was at least cool and soothing under her fingers. She closed her eyes so she wouldn't have to watch what she knew was about to happen.

There was an interminable, agonizing pause...and then a soft, almost inaudible ringing as the spell on the chest shattered and died.

"That's it!" Fearghan crowed.

Alauda squeezed her fists until her nails scraped on the chest, until her knuckles cracked. *And to think,* she thought bleakly, *that I once wondered what a breaking heart sounds like.*

Now she knew; she knew. It sounded like nothing at all.

Or, if it was your own heart, she sighed to herself, it roared like crackling flame. It crashed and echoed like a winter storm upon the sea. It shattered, tinkling, like a dropped goblet. Like the soft ringing of a broken spell cast upon an ancient treasure, crumbling to nothing the moment its conditions were met.

And sometimes, a heart broke with a whisper.

When she opened her eyes, Tonlees was staring at her, a trembling smile distorting her delicate features. She was holding Alacer's hand, pressing it atop the chest. "I'm sorry, Ala," her auburn-haired friend whispered.

Alauda swallowed, struggling not to weep. "You promised," she said, her voice catching in her throat. "You promised that you wouldn't take him from me." She leaned against the wall of the pit, willing herself to keep calm, to show strength in the face of tragedy. "You *promised.*"

"I didn't take him, Ala. You let him go."

Alauda couldn't speak; she could only move her lips. *You promised.*

Tonlees turned away, putting her face in her hands.

Alacer, his mouth set in a frown, bent with Alainn and fumbled back the lid of the chest. They lifted it together and set it carefully on the ground.

There was a long, pregnant silence. Sîol was the first to speak. "What the Hells is all this?" she scowled.

Alauda glanced at their plunder, more to distract herself from her heartache than out of any real interest. The chest was filled not with coin or other valuables, but with...with..."Are those map cases?" she frowned.

Sîol had already pulled one of them out. It was a leather cylinder nearly two feet in length and a hand-span in diameter. One end was fixed; the other had a removable cap. A buckled strap connected the end-pieces, allowing it to be slung over the shoulder; that was why Alauda had assumed them to be for transporting maps. The leather, she could see, was ancient, but it wasn't cracked; only faded. Whatever magic had sealed the chest had also preserved the hide against the damp of the cavern, and the ravages of time.

The cases were all dark-hued, dyed different shades: black and blue, red and green and dirty, dusty white. "Where's the silver?" Fearghan fumed.

Sîol was gaping at the chest, making sputtering noises.

"It *is* a map case!" Alacer exclaimed. He tugged another from the chest. "The Chief Drover has one just like this!"

"Twenty-four map cases," Sîol muttered. She shook the cylinder, listening; all they could hear was a muted rustling. "Too light for metal. What kind of treasure *is* this?"

Toni wrinkled her nose, puzzled. "Fineleor Orkarel's second-greatest treasure," she mused. "I wonder what his greatest treasure was?"

Alauda threw her a sidelong glance. "Isn't it obvious?" she murmured. "He left his second-greatest treasure here, in the care of his oldest friend, and went off to see to the safety of his greatest treasure by himself; by the might of his steel, the power of his magic, and the strength of his arm."

Tonlees gaped. "Anja?"

"Anja," Alauda nodded dully. "What a thing it must be, to be cherished as the greatest treasure of a man like Fineleor Orkarel. Now *that*, friends – that was true love." She was carefully not looking at either Alacer or Toni.

"Bugger love!" Below them in the pit, Sîol prised the end off of one of the tubes. She reached in and extracted a thickly rolled cylinder of parchment. She spread the ancient, crackling hide open atop the remainder of the scroll-tubes. "It's writing. *Elvii*, but – but I think it's in your court dialect." She straightened up, obviously puzzled.

"Do you want me to read it?" Alauda asked quietly.

The read-head passed one of the sheets wordlessly up to her. Alauda scanned the first several lines –

– and burst out laughing. She was still weeping, but she couldn't help herself. It was too glorious. Too delicious.

"What is it?" Sîol demanded.

Alauda was giggling almost too forcefully to speak. "F-F-Fineleor's s-second-greatest t-t-treasure," she gasped. " 'Oh fair and f-foremost love, thou art / The f-faithful guardian of mine heart / And unto thee I p-pledge my troth / 'Till fate and Green unite us b-b-both –' "

She couldn't continue. She dropped the scroll, collapsing against the wall of the pit. She was gasping for breath like a lunatic, tears streaming down her face.

Tonlees, her brow furrowed, was looking at another sheet. " 'By the breadth of the sunlit sky above / In summer's warmth, or winter's chill / I'll walk together with my love / And all her careless dreams fulfill'...gods, it's...well, it's hardly Ceorlinus, is it?" She checked the back

of the parchment as well, shaking her head. The words continued there –
line after line after line of them.

Alauda chuckled. "Be fair to the man! Fineleor lived thirty-five
centuries before Ceorlinus. And he was a soldier, not a skald." What was it
Captain Rettik had said? "We should be grateful it's not all about...about
beer and bosoms!"

"Is it *all* the same?" Alacer said, wide-eyed. "All writing?"

Sîol had opened more of the tubes, and was pawing through sheet
after hand-written sheet. "Yes!" she shrieked. "All of it!" She scattered a
handful of pages angrily. "Are you telling me that the magnificent treasure
of Fineleor Orkarel is nothing but ream after ream of – of *bad poetry*?!"

"His *second*-greatest treasure, remember," Alauda gasped. "These
poems were meant for his lady-love, and he obviously valued that love
more highly than gold." The hysterical giggling threatened to overwhelm
her again. "M-m-maybe," she sniggered, "maybe you should've tried to f-
find h-h-his *third*-g-greatest –"

She couldn't go on. She bent at the waist, gasping for breath, and
hugging her aching ribs.

Sîol made a visible effort to calm herself. "Right," she said after a
moment. "If this rubbish is *that* old, then I suppose it might have some
value. Somebody ought to be glad to see it."

Her casual tone made Alauda sit upright, and helped her to
control her hilarity. "*Might* have some value?" she said, suddenly sober.
"Are you joking? This is the work of Fineleor! Fineleor, one of the most
storied heroes in the history of the Realm! He might not've been a poet, but
those are his words – his own words, his *only known* words, penned in his
own hand, to the love he perished with!" She snorted in amusement.
"Their deaths were renowned – one of the most celebrated endings in our
lore! They saved the Realm! They're our history! Gods, don't you people
know anything at all about elves?"

Sîol frowned. She slid the last of the scrolls back into its container.
"Apparently not," she grated. "What are you getting at, princess?"

"Hara's love!" Alauda cried, kicking at the elaborate box.
"Suppose this were full of silver. What then? How would we get it out of
here? And even if we did, who'd care? It's just money. Even the victory
coins minted by Yarchian, at the end of the day, are just money."

She stabbed a finger at the leather cases. "That – that's the stuff of
legend! It's the most marvellous piece of our cultural heritage to come to
light in centuries!" She was all but sputtering. "There's nothing – do you
understand, *nothing*! – that King Callaýian wouldn't pay for those!"

The redhead blinked. "Really?"

"Really!" Alauda said hotly. "And not just Callaýian! Any noble
house in the Realm would do the same. You don't understand; any high elf

worthy of the name would beggar himself just for the privilege of holding Fineleor's 'bad poetry' in his hand!"

"Hunh," Sîol said thoughtfully. "I suppose I really don't know elves after all. All right, then, friends; despite our best efforts, we appear to have done well. Let's pack it up and make for home." She glanced up at the vast maw of the volcano overhead. "Lantern's already up, and time's a-wasting. We need to be off."

She began parcelling out the map cases, handing four to each of the party members, exempting only Alauda. "No burdens for you, princess," she winked. "We might need you to get us out of trouble."

"That's a bad bet," Alauda snorted. "So far, I've only managed to get us into it."

"As far as I can see, you've done all right. You're owed," the redhead grinned. She glanced around. "Now, how do we get out of here? Without soaking our new-found riches?"

Alauda frowned.

"Kulkisari," Breaghan piped, looking nervous at the prospect of addressing the colossal tree directly, and wincing as speech made her split lip bleed afresh, "is there any way out of here that doesn't require swimming?"

Alauda wondered briefly why the waters that had healed her hand hadn't done the same for the Halfling girl's lip. She decided she didn't care.

The tree's branches rustled briefly. An instant later there was a subtle grinding noise…and then an ear-splitting *whoosh*. The level of water in the lake began to drop visibly.

I have just filled the chamber of the doors, Kulkisari said softly. *Look to the right of my islet*.

They looked. As the water fell a ledge appeared, following the wall of the chamber and circling the shore of the pond. At the far end, it joined a steeply-sloped set of stairs. Alauda was unsurprised that they hadn't noticed them before; they were lost in the shadows, and in any case led nowhere but down to the lake.

The four Halflings, along with Tonlees and Alacer, shouldered their burdens, making ready to depart. Alauda put her hand on the tree's trunk once more. *I don't want to say goodbye*, she murmured. *You've been alone for too long.*

I do miss my friends; but trees do not grow lonely, child of the Green, Kulkisari replied. *We do, however, resemble your kind in one way. We fear for our legacy; for that which we leave behind us.*

Your legacy is safe in our hands, Alauda assured the ancient being. *We'll see it safely home.*

I do not doubt it, the tree rustled. *But that is not the legacy of which I speak.*

On a branch far overhead, a bud burst newly into blossom. The blossom grew, producing the intoxicating fragrance that made the blood race, and that unlocked hearts – and the knees – of elves, and only of elves. With unnatural speed, the blossom gleamed, faded, and died, its petals first drooping, and then dropping free.

An instant later a seed fell from the dead bloom, plummeting to earth, and landing at Alauda's feet. She bent and picked it up, marvelling at its tight, silvery shell.

Plant it somewhere in the mountains, Kulkisari whispered. *Somewhere it will be warmed by the Lantern's light, and know what it is like to be touched by the blessing of Powers themselves.*

I will, Alauda promised. A sudden pang of emotion clogged her throat. *Kulkisari,* she said hesitantly, *who made you what you are? The very first time, back in the ancient days. You said that you were just a tree, once. Who awakened you?*

Bræa, he replied. The voice in her mind was distant, gentle – and overwhelmingly mighty. *Holy Bræa found me here, a lonely sapling far beneath the surface of the world, and She touched me. At Her touch I woke, and knew Her.*

It was She who told Duke Varinyr where to find me, and at her bidding he built his keep here, before my Well, upon the ruins of a fortress left by men. He introduced his grandson Fineleor to me, who in time became my friend. Fineleor made the fortress great and strong.

"You remember them," she whispered.

I do. I remember them, he mused distantly, while Alauda's eyes watered at the force of his recalling; *I remember them all.*

But of them all, he said softly, *I remember Holy Bræa best. Her touch, Her love, I will cherish always. It will stay with me, I think, even into the darkness. I shall remember Her even unto the sounding of the last horn, and the end in fire, and the breaking of the world.* His simple solemnity tore at her heart.

But, he went on, *I shall remember you also, child of the Green – distant daughter of my friend Anja. Plant my seed, and keep my secret. And cherish, too, the treasures you have this day won. See them safely home.*

"I will," Alauda promised. "Farewell, Kulkisari."

Farewell, Alauda Volo.

She turned and followed her friends, the silvery seed tingling in her fist.

◆

Nineteen

She stumbled down the last few steps, slipping between the great doors to find that Alacer and Tonlees were waiting for her. The last time she had been in the chamber of the rings, they had been unable to meet her gaze; now they embraced her, their eyes streaming.

Alauda stiffened, but only at first. There was no artifice, no deception in their relief and affection.

"I'm sorry," Tonlees was saying, struggling to force the words through her tears. "Ala, I'm so sorry! I should've told you."

"*We* should've told you," Alacer corrected. He looked grave, and a little sad, but unapologetic.

Alauda couldn't scream or shout. She couldn't scold, or even scowl. *And if I can't scowl*, she reasoned, *then why not smile*? So she did. Logic notwithstanding, it was the most difficult thing she had ever done. "I understand why you didn't," she murmured. "And Alacer, I'm –"

She raised her hand, and he winced reflexively; but he relaxed again when she did no more than touch his cheek. "*I'm* the one who's sorry. I shouldn't have dallied with Alainn, but...well, I'm not sure how much say I had in the matter. Second Spring, the trees, and all. But I most certainly shouldn't have expected you to wait for me to stop acting the fool."

Alacer caught her eyes. "Do you love him?"

Alauda swallowed. "A little, I think," she said thickly. "But I love you more. You and Toni both. And I loved you *first*. Both of you." She took his hand – and then Tonlees' hand as well. "If you have to throw me over, I'm glad it's for her."

"Thank you," Tonlees whispered.

"And I thank Wise Hara for settling this ungodly mess at last," the younger girl sighed. "I can't imagine what the rest of this trip would be like if we had to skulk around avoiding each other. I couldn't bear it." She nodded at the cases slung over their shoulders. "Do you want me to carry one of those?"

"No, there's nothing to them at all," Tonlees snorted. "Shouldn't you take your gown?" She pointed at a sad, sodden heap of fabric that lay crumpled against one wall.

Alauda knelt by the pile. "*Kak.*" She held up a filthy, sodden bit of cloth that might have been a sleeve. "There's no salvaging this. But if I show up in my shift after a night out, mother'll have the hide off of me for sure and certain." She laid the dripping mass over one arm. "Where are the others?"

"Waiting outside," Alacer said. "Sîol asked us to stay here and watch for you. She said she's got another way to get down."

"And thank Wise Hara for that, too," Alauda said with feeling. She'd not been looking forward to more mountain-climbing or amateur rope-work.

They mounted the steps together. Alauda's misgivings were fading; the air was cold, freezing even, but her heart was light. They'd accomplished a miracle, turning up a cache of ancient writings the likes of which even the Magisters of the College of Stars had never seen. Alauda couldn't imagine what their reward would be, but she was certain that they would be fêted for bringing such a trove to light – provided she survived returning to face her mother with her clothing in rags.

Might their reward be sufficient to restore House Volo to the ranks of the *Duodeci*? she wondered. Maybe; maybe. There would be wealth and influence at least; no more sheep and goats, no more stubborn oxen or stinking privies or slow-moving caravans. Her parents would be ennobled. She would have to go to Starmeadow, of course, and join the ranks of the *Ancillulae*, the so-called 'little slaves' of the Royal Palace – the white-gowned debutantes gathered from all of the great houses to study under the formidable Princess Ælyndarka, the King's sister, in her dreaded 'wife-works', serving both as ladies-in-waiting, and as hostages against their parents' good conduct. The 'Court Lilies' – so named for the white gowns that were their uniform – were derided by all during their tenure; but at the end of it they were desired by all, as the prized ladies of grace and perfection that they would in time become. Alauda had no desire to be trapped into so rigid and stultifying a class for the sixty years it would take her to pass without the walls; but she would do it. Doubtless there would be plenty to learn about the intrigues and plots of palace life. She might even manage to bring a touch of mischief to the place.

Such dreams preoccupied her as they left the Well, at least until the bright gleams of morning startled her back to reality. The light of the rising Lantern was blinding; it filled the tunnel, gilding the damp, vine-cloaked stone. The Halflings were waiting for them just inside the end of the passageway. Alauda caught Alainn's eye and waved happily.

To her surprise, he didn't respond. "All right," she said, glancing at Sîol. "How do we get out of here?"

The redhead stared at her, unblinking. "Magic, of course."

"Fair enough. What sort of magic?"

"This sort." Sîol smiled, set her jaw – and dragged a bare, calloused foot across the floor.

Hot, argent light exploded into the air, hissing and snapping, boiling up from the line of silver dust that Sîol had broken with her toe.

The force of the spell knocked both Alauda and the Halfling backward. Sîol collided with Fearghan, bearing both of them to the ground; Alacer caught Alauda. Her cheeks burned, as if she had leaned too close to a bonfire.

A high-pitched, penetrating shriek exploded through the night sky. It repeated itself over and over, clamouring like a tocsin.

"What are you doing?!" Tonlees shrieked. She reached toward the shimmering wall, and squealed as a tiny arc of skyfire leapt to her fingertip with a splintery *snap*.

Alauda thrust herself out of Alacer's arms. "Alainn!" she cried.

The boy looked at her, his heart in his eyes. "I'm sorry," he said, shouting so as to be heard over the crackling howl of the magical barrier. "You were right, my lady; this *was* a rite of passage." He held out one of the map cases. "But it was our rite, not yours."

Behind him, Sîol was standing next to the effigy of Anja, passing out small sticks. Each of the Halflings took one.

"You *dog*!" Alauda screamed. "You faithless *dog*!"

He spread his hands. "If you'll recall, I didn't took nothing from you; what we did was done at your bidding." His smile was crooked. "I'm not saying that I minded. In all honesty, my lady – my love – I wish it could've ended otherwise."

Alauda tore her attention away from him. "You swore!" she screamed. "Sîol, you swore! Before – before Cham's own face!"

"Have you ever seen Cham's face?" the Halfling asked with a deprecating smile.

Alauda was trembling with fury. "What's that got to do with it?"

"She's masked," Sîol laughed. "The goddess of thieves wears a hood, dearie, the better to deceive her marks. I made my vow by the trickster's hidden visage – and I meant every word of it. *Slan agus fhortan!*"

As she watched, Sîol snapped one of the sticks between her fingers. Then, to Alauda's shock, the redhead took a few quick steps, leapt from the ledge – and floated gently down and out of sight.

Fearghan immediately snapped his own stick. "What about Smuggy?" Alauda cried. "We left him on the mountainside!"

"He's already back at the camp," Fearghan replied. "He's smarter than the rest of us. No mucking about in old elfy ruins for him." His scowl deepened. "I like you, princess. You've got guts." He leapt, and floated away on the morning breeze.

"I'll see the colour of yours, you hairy-footed ditch rat!" Alauda screamed after him.

Alainn watched them go, a thoughtful look on his face. He turned back to the crackling wall. He was holding one of the parchment sheets gingerly in his fingers. "I saved this one for you," he shouted, bending to lay it gently on the ground. "A Fineleor original, to treasure forever."

"Keep it!" she shrieked. "You – you filthy –"

His expression didn't change. Alauda couldn't complete her curse; there was no breath left in her lungs. Tears ran freely down her face. *Oh, Alainn!*

There was something wistful in his smile. "It doesn't mean much, I know," he said, half-shouting over the crackling of the arcane wall, "but I am sorry. I wish I could've meant something to you, but I that's fanciful nonsense. The whole world knows how the Third House feels about half-bloods like me. I'll say this, though, and it's the truth: I might not be worthy of you, but I'll love you for as long as I live."

"That won't be long!" she screamed. Thrusting Alacer aside, she lunged for the sparkling, hissing plane. Fire scourged her fingers the instant she touched it. She ignored the pain, forcing her hands through the shimmering flame.

The shock contorted her fists, but she persevered. Tendrils of greenery, writhing with terrible force, exploded from her fingertips. They didn't reach him; the coruscating field flashed them instantly to flame. Scraps of ash fluttered to the floor of the cavern.

Alainn was standing frozen in place, a look of astonishment – and worry – on his face. She couldn't tell whether he was afraid for her, or *of* her.

By Hara's holy blood, I'll make it the latter, she swore to herself.

But she didn't; she couldn't. She was able to reach through the spell-wall up to the elbows before the strain of the power surging through her bones snuffed her wits out like a candle. Her eyes rolled back in her head, and she collapsed like an abandoned toy.

By the time she came to, the Halflings were gone. Tonlees was holding her head in her lap, stroking her forehead gently. Her skull was throbbing. Her hands, arms and shoulders were ached and cramping from the tearing agony of the magical wall that she had attempted to breach. The persistent screech of the magical claxon made her head ring.

She struggled to rise, but there was no strength in her arms; all she could feel from the shoulders down were pinpricks of pain in her hands. Her fingers were hooked, her fists clenched and wrists bent like the hands of a crone. She inspected her disobedient appendages clinically, as though from a distance, and was vaguely relieved to see that there was no obvious damage. The stiffness would pass.

Her throat knotted painfully. *Oh, Alainn!* And yet –

And yet, her eyes were dry. Tonlees helped her to sit up. Alacer was sitting nearby, fiddling idly with what remained of their plunder. The four map cases that they'd carried from the cavern were piled next to him, their caps removed. "How –" She managed an inarticulate croak, then cleared her throat. "How long?"

"Moments," Tonlees said soothingly. "Gods, you scared us, diving into the fire like that!"

"For all the good it did." She put her head in her numb, effectless hands. "They've all gone, I suppose?"

Tonlees nodded. "Yes. Alainn jumped off after them. He and Breaghan were holding hands. I think they're an item."

"Yes, I got that," Alauda grunted. Gods, her hands hurt!

Toni paused, then added somewhat irrelevantly, "Alainn waited until we were certain you we all right."

"How gentlemanly of him. The cases you were carrying were empty, of course." She recalled Sîol shuffling the sheets of parchment about.

"Of course," Alacer said. He looked glum, and winced periodically as the alarm shrieked into the night. "The halpies must have moved the scrolls before they gave these four to us."

Her fists were still stinging from the bite of the flux. She hammered them against the stone floor, livid with fury, anxious to feel something, *anything*, other than blind rage. Even pain was preferable to the impotent fury that burned within her breast.

"Are you going to be all right?" Tonlees asked, her face full of worry.

Alauda didn't know what to say. Hatred and sorrow, anger at her cupidity in trusting her heart, fury at Alainn's bald-faced duplicity, rage at having found and then lost a priceless treasure – and, too, the gut-wrenching knowledge that Alacer was no longer hers, all warred within her heart.

Wrath locked her throat; she choked, tasting bile, and could scarcely breathe. At last the tears came, like a storm after a long, stifling eve. She wept uncontrollably, grinding her teeth in effectless wrath.

Alacer watched, worried, but didn't attempt to touch her.

"Say something!" Tonlees pleaded.

Alauda swallowed thickly. "W-woe unto me," she whispered, "for mine innocence is sped, and my fair knight captived." She took a deep, shuddering breath, struggling to smile, but managed only a pathetic rictus. "Captived, by a beauteous treacher's false and...and f-f-faithless..."

She couldn't go on. Her head bowed to her lap, tears running freely down her cheeks. Tonlees goggled at her for a moment. Then she burst into sobs as well.

Alauda struggled to sit up. She put her arms about her sobbing friend, drawing her close. "There it is," she murmured tiredly. "That's what it sounds like."

She breathed deep, trying to draw the cavern's healing airs deep into her aching flesh. *That's what a breaking heart sounds like.*

Alacer sat back on the stone, exhausted, staring blankly as the two girls held each other.

While Tonlees wept hysterically, Alauda's eyes dried and grew distant. She was already thinking about what would come next – and making plans to meet it.

♦

Twenty

They were still sitting motionless, wondering what to do, when an echoing *crack* sounded beyond the hissing, shimmering barrier. The flux warped and bent, disgorging eight humans: an angry looking woman; an amused looking man; and an even half-dozen liveried soldiers with wide eyes, and drawn swords.

The woman spied the trio sitting despondent on the stone. She made a swift, imperious gesture, and the wall of hissing sparks crumbled into shards and gouts of powerless force. Tendrils of light leached into the stone and vanished. The screeching of the tocsin halted at the same instant.

Wizard, Alauda sighed. She knew the gesture; her mother had dismissed spells many times in her sight. She was certain who the newcomers were – who they *had* to be – and she wasn't looking forward to explaining her latest failure. But there was no virtue in attempting to postpone the inevitable.

She released Tonlees and struggled to her feet, sighing heavily. "My lord of Arx Cervus; my lady." She added a bow, less from politeness than as a sop to the smouldering ruins of her dignity.

<Children?> The well-dressed man turned to his lady, a quizzical smile on his face. <Elf-children? I thought you sealed this place, love. How'd they get in?>

They were speaking the travelling tongue. <This is not what I expected,> the woman replied, glowering down at Alauda and her friends.

<I shouldn't think so.> The man – the lord – shot his blade back into its scabbard and crossed his arms, scowling. "All right," he said, switching to *elvii*. "Let's hear it. Who are you? What are you doing here? And what, exactly, have you done?"

"And," the woman demanded, scowling fiercely, "how in Bardan's unholy name did you penetrate old Fineleor's wards!"

Their accents were good; that was a relief. Alauda was far too tired to struggle along in the travelling tongue. She was also encouraged by the fact that, thus far, no one had threatened to take their heads out of hand.

She offered introductions with as much gravity as their miserable circumstances allowed, then recounted the whole of their tale. She didn't bother prevaricating; if the lady of Arx Cervus was indeed a wizard of the College of the Eye, then she would have no difficulty ferreting out the truth.

Their tale took the better part of half a stick, throughout which she shivered uncontrollably in her wet boots and sodden shift. None of the glowering humans offered her so much as a kerchief. Neither Toni nor Alacer saw fit to interrupt; that was both a relief, and a worry.

By the time she finished, Lord Alfaric was smiling in bemusement. Alauda didn't know whether that augured for good or ill. "*Aiyah*, by Vara's mercy!" he exclaimed, using the colloquialisms of the elven tongue with the easy familiarity of someone who'd spent much of his life in diplomatic circles. He reminded Alauda a little of Lord Trivinako. "I'd like to meet somebody who knew Tior Magnus, even if he is only a tree." He paused, then said, "Tell me, who are you three again?"

Alauda repeated their names.

"And what exactly are you doing here?"

She reeled off the broad outlines of her story. By the end of the second telling, she was trembling with exhaustion as well as the cold.

"Right, well done," he nodded. "I was curious whether you'd be able to rattle off the same ridiculous tale twice."

"Then you're wasting your time, my lord, and ours," the elf-girl sighed. She pointed at Lady Nidlo. "She's been watching me like a hungry wolf, looking to sift fact from falsehood the whole time I've been talking."

The lady cocked an eyebrow. She was attractive enough, but her eyes were a little too large and too far apart for true beauty. Her hair and eyebrows, though, were as black as Alauda's, and her skin just as pale. "Not only watching, girl," she said. Her speech was oddly accented, reminding Alauda that she was reputed to hail not from the Empire, like her husband, but rather from its rival Gasparr, much further to the west. "I have been using the Art."

"My mother is a graduate of the College of Stars, my lady," Alauda said, not without a hint of irony. "Believe me, I can tell when someone is using magic to weigh my words. If you know that I'm telling the truth, then why aren't you chasing after them?"

"Chase after whom, girl?" Alfaric chuckled. "A handful of halpies, amid a whole blasted bother of them? If you're telling the truth, and this was so well planned that they brought magical knick-knacks with them so they could just...float away –" he joined his thumbs and made flapping motions with his fingers; Alauda coloured "– then surely they've thought of the certainty of their being followed. They'll have taken steps to conceal themselves, and we'll never find them.

"Whereas if you're lying," he shrugged, casting a glance at his wife "– no slight upon your skills as a truth-reader, my darling – then I'll end up spending the next several days rousting waist-high pick-pockets until my men don't have a farthing left between them. I'd have to pay'em double this month." He shrugged. "This is all assuming that I cared a rat's turd about a box of musty old elfy scribblings."

"You know that part's true, at least!" Alauda raged. She pointed at Lady Nidlo again. "She picked up the parchment that Alainn left outside."

"I did," the woman nodded. "I did indeed." She held the brittle scrap of hide by one corner. "A glorious treasure indeed. Would you like to know what is on it?"

Alauda's ire faltered, and she swallowed heavily. Alainn had left her that one, and that one alone. *And he said he loved me.* She nodded, not trusting herself to speak.

Nidlo held the parchment up. "*Dulcis amorem meum,*" she read, "*in carne vestra sentire cupiam, gustare dulcedinem tuam, et operuit os meum sentiat, facile telum –*"

Alacer's eyes bulged; Toni's hands went to her mouth.

"Stop!" Alauda cried, her face flaming, her fists clenched and shaking. "Hara's love, what – what was that?"

"An excellent question," Alfaric grinned. "A little spicy for a hero of the Realm, I'd say. Who knew old Fineleor had that kind of mouth on him?"

"Would you like it as a keep-sake?" Nidlo asked. "There's a drawing, too. It's a little crude, but at least it is…well, it's extremely crude, in fact. There's no honey-glazing this bit of smut, I fear." She dangled the parchment before Alauda's face. "Well done, all; you've recovered a truly wondrous memorial to the literary skill of Ancient Fineleor, Hero of the Realm; one that perhaps ought to –"

The elf-girl, livid with fury, flung up a hand; a hot, shimmering splash of green flame erupted from her fingertips. The bolt blasted the parchment from Nidlo's fingers, flinging it against the wall of the passage, where it smoked and smouldered…and stuck. The scrap of hide, and the stone around it, was splashed with errant gouts and gobbets of hissing, smoking verdure.

Before Alauda could expostulate in shock at what she'd done, Alfaric's sword was in his hand, levelled at her. Nidlo made a brief, clutching gesture, locking Alauda's arms to her sides, freezing even her jaw. So stiffly was she held that she could scarcely draw breath.

The lord, to her surprise, was still smiling. "What a dreadful temper, and quick with the Art to boot!" Alfaric chuckled. "She's a lot like you, my love."

"That is a matter of opinion," Nidlo snapped. "She has just destroyed a priceless historical artefact in a fit of pique. She does, however, have a point; we ought to be looking for the thieves." She stared at the three elves, her eyes narrow. "The competent ones, that is."

Toni and Alacer, Alauda noticed with relief, said nothing. Toni was still staring at her feet.

The wizard made the same brief, economical gesture she'd employed before, and Alauda felt the invisible bonds dissolve. She breathed more easily at once.

Alfaric was looking oddly at his mate. "Priceless? Really? That bit of *kak*?"

Nidlo nodded. "You must recall what elves of the Third House are like, at least when it comes to their heroes; you've served with them. I've no doubt that their king would give his last groat for a sheaf of old Fineleor's poems, *kak* or not. It would be a matter of honour. Yes?" she added, glancing at Alauda.

Alauda looked down at her boot-toes, miserable.

"But how would the halpies know *that*?" the lord wondered aloud.

Alauda sighed. "Because I told them. In the same words, more or less."

"Gods!" Alfaric stared at her. "You're quite the little idiot, aren't you?"

She ground her teeth, but managed to hold her silence. He wasn't wrong.

The lord turned back to his wife. "D'ye think there's even any point in looking for them?"

"How do you mean?"

"Well, they'll have to go to Starmeadow, won't they?" Alfaric reasoned. "They'll show up in the capital, trying to sell their spoils to King Callaýian. So long as I get this version of the story to the capital first, they'll be arrested at once."

Powers below! Alauda winced. The Halflings had even sworn that the treasure, all of it, would go to the Elvenking; they'd taken an oath on it. They'd been prepared for magical truth-detection, and had planned their lies, their deceptions, down to the last detail. Probably they'd planned to sell their expected haul of ancient silver to the throne; a colossal stash of Yarchian's victory coins would've been worth far more that way than as mere metal. The fact that Fineleor's hoard had turned out to be parchment instead of pennies had only worked in their favour.

But he was still wrong – and Alauda was too angry, and far too tired, for propriety. "Now who's the 'little idiot', my lord?"

Alfaric shot her a dangerous look. "I'm doing my best to maintain my composure amid these novel circumstances, young lady, but let me assure you that you're not out of the forest yet. You'd do well not to irritate me. I'd be well within my rights to decorate the parapets with your head, and those of your friends."

Toni and Alacer looked up in alarm. Alauda didn't; she crossed her arms, waiting.

Alfaric rolled his eyes. "Fine. What d'ye mean by that?"

"The halpies are far too clever to try to sell the scrolls to anyone of importance," Alauda pointed out. "Not directly, anyway. They're good; they're very good. They might look like children, but they're not. They even managed to fool me." *Not once or twice or even thrice*, she thought gloomily. They'd bought her wits at auction, and sold them again for a song. And the price had been nothing more than Alainn's smile.

"No offence," Alfaric said again, more drily this time, "but I really don't think it'd take much in the way of devilish cunning to wrong-foot you three."

"I can't argue with you on that score, my lord," Alauda allowed. "You're not exactly seeing us at our best. But if you'll take my advice, you'll ensure you're not anywhere near Starmeadow when the first half of a scroll shows up, along with an anonymous demand for ransom."

Nidlo's eyes narrowed. Her pale face darkened.

Alfaric frowned. "*Half* a scroll? What's that supposed to mean?"

His wife put a hand on his arm. "She means that the thieves are likely to tear the poems in half, and send them to the King one at a time, so that he will be forced to pay for the other half."

Alauda barked a laugh. "I told you, they're not stupid. They'll know that every exchange, every payment, will be an opportunity to get caught. No, they'll do it only once. And because they can only afford to send a single warning, they'll have to convince the King of their seriousness on the very first exchange." Her lip twitched. "If it were me, I'd send the King a scroll that'd been half-burned."

This time it was Nidlo's face that went white. "But that's your history, your...your past! You're Third House!"

"I'm also fond of keeping my head on my shoulders," Alauda countered. "With every failure to pay, every failure to meet a demand, another half-burned scroll will arrive at the gates of *Arx Magnificus* – and another priceless work of ancient lore will be lost forever. What do halpies care about such things, after all? But in Starmeadow, how long d'ye think the King will allow that to go on before he cries off and pays them whatever they ask? Especially if they make their deeds and demands public? How long would the King be allowed to ignore it? The royal council – all of the Duodeci houses, in fact – would rise up in revolt. And the Chanters' Guild would lay siege to the royal palace." The thought of an angry mob of skalds waving their shalms and mandols about and screaming their demands in multi-part harmony brought a momentary smile to her face.

"You think a bunch of halpies are clever enough to figure that out?" Alfaric wondered. "You think they'd destroy the scrolls? After all that they had to do to get in here in secret?"

"What have they to lose?" the elf-girl snorted. "What are Fineleor's verses to them but – how did you put it? 'Musty old elfy scribblings'?" She wrinkled her nose. "Actually, given the nature of the prize, if they're truly clever they'll send half-scrolls to all of the heads of the Duodeci houses; the wealthiest ones, anyway. Especially the Drýva, who hold no love or loyalty for King Callaýian. They could make a bidding war out of it. Any one of the noble houses would pay a prince's ransom for such pearls – and they'd *all* be willing to pay a premium for the chance to regain a fabulous treasure for the Realm, especially if they could contrive to humiliate the King and his family into the bargain."

"That's a little diabolical, isn't it?" Alfaric breathed. "How old are you, girl? You scheme like a chancellor!"

Alauda ignored the unflattering observation. "You've really no idea how bad this could get. If it were handled clumsily enough, it might ignite a war between the houses."

Nidlo was staring at her as though she were a poisonous snake. "In Gasparr – or in Ekhan – that would be deemed treason."

"It's only treason if you get caught," Alauda shrugged. "In the Realm, it's politics. And frankly, it's how *I'd* do it." She tugged at an ear, calculating. "It's also, I think, why you won't be bringing this little incident up with anyone. It simply wouldn't do for Starmeadow to find out that the reason our King has to pay – well, a king's ransom, I guess – is because you, my lord, a servant of the Empire charged with maintaining the defences of an ancient stronghold of the elves, somehow let Fineleor's second-greatest treasure slip through your fingers."

She clasped her hands solemnly at her waist. "I'm sure you've heard about the goings-on at Vitrafoss last week; how a warcaster of the Imperial Army had to put down a mutiny that'd been fomented by one of the daughters of a Duodeci house, and how he blasted her castle into rubble." *Artistic license*, she thought; Ring Castle was still standing, mostly. "The last thing Norkhan needs right now is more trouble with Starmeadow." She silently blessed Lord Trivinako for his incendiary ways.

Lady Nidlo's face had gone flat with white-lipped rage. "You arrogant little –"

"Enough," Alfaric interrupted. "Suppose you're right; suppose that I even agree with you. None of this is reason not to punish you three."

Alacer and Tonlees looked up from where they sat, their eyes wide.

"In fact," he growled, "the only reason I haven't done so yet is that I'm not convinced that you merit it. You look to me like a passel of fools, especially as you don't seem to have come away from this little endeavour with any plunder." He cocked an eyebrow at Alauda. "Or even much in the way of clothing, for that matter."

"Fortunes of war," Alauda said loftily. She didn't feel the arrogance she pretended, and folded her arms over her bosom, acutely conscious of how her damp shift clung to her body. "As for punishment, if there's to be any at all, then you'll have to deal with me and me alone, seeing as how I have the ill fortune to be captain of this sorry company.

But I can't imagine why you'd want to punish us at all."

Alacer frowned, glancing at Tonlees, who also looked puzzled.

"Can you not?" Alfaric mused aloud, tapping a finger on his sword's hilt. "You broke into my castle, slipped past my guards, and circumvented a claxon-spell that my lady wife had set to keep the curious out of here. After that, you breached a ward dating from the Age of Wisdom; managed to open doors that have been closed since the gods themselves walked the earth; and uncovered a treasure of incalculable value." He snorted. "To poetry-loving elves, anyway. And after all that, you let a pack of thieving halpies dupe you out of it!

"So tell me this, children: exactly why should I *not* hang the lot of you from the gatehouse parapet, as a warning to other light-fingered, brainless ne'er-do-wells?"

Alauda smiled. "Because we've made you a Count. Really, my lord, you ought to be thinking about how to reward us."

"Oh, I'm thinking about it," Alfaric glowered. "Trust me. But I'll play your game, little miss. A Count, eh? Talk."

"We know their names."

The soldier blinked. "Excuse me? Whose names? The thieves, you mean? That's all?"

"Isn't that enough?" she smiled. "Or perhaps I'm asking the wrong person." She turned to Lady Nidlo. "What do you say, *magistatrix*? Their names, how they look, the colour of their hair and eyes; their clothing, their possessions, the names of their parents and guardians..." she cleared her throat, "and other...er, distinguishing characteristics?" A momentary recollection of the frenzied moments in the chamber of the rings leapt up to trouble her anew; she shoved it back into the pits her memory. If nothing else, she could give the wizard a *very* detailed description of her late paramour. "Surely that ought to be enough for a mage of the College of the Eye." She cocked her head. "Aren't you meant to be the greatest masters of the arts of divination in all the World Made?"

Nidlo glowered down at her. "Perhaps. Go on."

"And I'm fairly certain," Alauda continued, still smiling, "that I just saw you leap the flux. Only the most powerful magi can do that. So if you could locate the halpies and their plunder, could you not just –" She snapped her fingers "– pop in with your good lord and a half-dozen armed men, and apprehend them? And then, having recovered the stolen treasure, you could present it to your lords in Norkhan. They'll be as dismissive as you, no doubt, about musty elven scribblings – at least until it occurs to them to return the scrolls to Starmeadow as a gift that will cost your king nothing, but that will put King Callaýian, and all of House Æyllian, forever in the Empire's debt."

Nidlo glanced at her mate, and dropped an eloquent shrug.

Alfaric nodded slowly. "Now, there's a notion," he said thoughtfully. "A count's coronet would look very well on my escutcheon. But why should I bargain? I could always just beat their names out of you."

"You could, eventually, assuming you're the sort of fellow to mistreat hapless ne'er-do-wells, and children at that," Alauda allowed. "But that sort of thing doesn't look at all good on anyone's escutcheon, my lord. It would also take time, and frankly I'm not sure how much time you have. If someone like me, who knows nothing of the flux, knows that they can be found with magic, then surely they'll have thought of it as well.

"Furthermore," she added a little more stiffly, "right now I'm feeling particularly ill-disposed toward our...our former associates. Consequently, I'm more likely to tell you the truth. Raise your hand against me and my friends, however, and I'll start feeling ill-disposed toward *you*. Do we understand one another?"

"I think we do," Alfaric nodded. "I must say, for all that you call yourselves children, you don't much act like it. Very well, then – the names of the thieves, and anything else you can recall, in exchange for your freedom and your silence, and you'll suffer no punishment at my hand. Accord – captain?"

"Accord, my lord." Alauda put out her hand, and Alfaric took it.

She spent the next few moments providing as fulsome a description of the Halflings as she could. Alacer and Tonlees filled in details. When they could recollect no more, Nidlo was already nodding. "With this, I can find them. Should I begin now?"

"In a little while, my dear," Alfaric chuckled. "Halpies have short legs; they won't get much further in an hour or two. And I'd still like to meet this tree who supposedly knew Mighty Tior."

"He knows Holy Bræa, too," Alauda murmured. She briefly considered mentioning the seed that the ancient tree had given her, but decided not to. That, she reasoned, had been a private request from Kulkisari to her.

"Does he?" the soldier breathed. "Does he indeed?"

The elf-girl nodded. "He said that she roused him herself, in the years after she first came to earth."

"Astonishing!"

"Indeed," Nidlo said coolly. "When you see this leafy prodigy, my love, please ask if I might beg a branch of him. Something long, thin, and suitably stiff." Her eyes glinted. "I am looking forward to treating our guests to the reward their deeds have earned them."

"Of course, my dear," Alfaric laughed. He trotted down the stairs, heading for the chamber of the rings.

Alauda's eyes widened. "That wasn't part of our agreement!" she objected.

"Your agreement was with my good lord," Nidlo said softly. "I have a different one to offer. My husband is soft-hearted, but I come from a different tradition, where errant brats are punished for their misdeeds. You can accept just chastisement, all of you; or I will surely give your parents an account of what you have been up to this night. Including all of the sordid details that my magic will reveal." She smiled unpleasantly. "There will be no need to mention any poems, ancient scrolls, or other nonsense; I'm certain that a simple tale of house-breaking, fumbling about beneath skirts, and outright fornication will be more than sufficient to appall them into dealing suitably with you. You folk of the Third House are so dreadfully sensitive about such things."

Alauda glanced at her friends. Alacer looked outraged; but Tonlees was obviously terrified. Alauda recalled her bragging that she had never once been switched.

She glowered at Lady Nidlo, opening her mouth to remonstrate. Before she could speak, however, the wizard held up a finger. "But I offer a special bargain to you, young captain: I shall take you up on your offer. I shall let the rest of your troupe go unmarked, if you as their chief will agree to bear with all good fortitude the entirety of your joint and just reward." Nidlo's smile was sweetly menacing. "Accord?"

"No!" Alacer cried.

Alauda threw him a stern but grateful glance. "Quiet," she said. Tonlees, she noticed, also tried to speak, but her tongue appeared to be paralyzed by fear.

She dragged her fingers through her matted hair, gritting her teeth at the innumerable tangles. So much for escaping the cane.

"Your answer, girl?" the wizard inquired.

Alauda bent her head and sighed. *You earned this, fool; accept it.* "Accord."

◆

Twenty-One

"For the love of all the Powers!" Alyssa barked. "Leave off fidgeting, child; I'm trying to read."

Alauda and her mother were sharing the bed of their wagon while her father managed the oxen. The vehicle was rocking only a little; east of Buckhill, the Great Road was well cared-for, and the ruts caused by the spring rain were already being filled in by teams of sweating men with shovels and picks. As far as the elf-girl was concerned, however, even the minimal swaying was torment; any motion at all exacerbated the throbbing, burning ache in her bottom. She was kneeling on a folded blanket, pretending to peruse her mother's book of magic, and silently blessing her father for having repaired the vehicle's leather springs.

"If you can't manage to be tranquil," her mother went on crossly, "then please feel free to sit with your sire, and leave me to my work."

"I'm sorry, mother," Alauda muttered. Sitting anywhere at all, let alone on the unyielding boards of the buck-seat, was out of the question. She resolved to remain on her knees, and to keep as still as her stinging backside permitted.

Kulkisari, to Alauda's vast disappointment, had ceded readily to Lady Nidlo's request, allowing Lord Alfaric to cut a long, slender branch with his compliments. The mage had made vigorous play with the peeled stick while Alauda, her teeth clamped firmly together, had knelt on the steps of the chamber of the doors, her shift bunched up about her waist. She'd lost count of the number of strokes, and by the time her chastisement was done, she hadn't been in any mood to ask her friends for a tally. Nidlo, it seemed, was an accomplished mistress of the rod, and had taken her time; and while she hadn't once broken the elf-girl's skin, she'd left behind such an appalling array of blue-black welts that Tonlees had been weeping openly by the time the mage had finally wearied and tossed the splintered switch aside. Alacer too had been forced to observe the whole affair, and it was with no little satisfaction that Alauda, through the dizzying haze of pain, had seen his fingers twitching for Nidlo's throat.

For her part, Alauda was gratified by the fact that she'd neither lost consciousness nor begged for surcease. She'd been weeping hot, silent tears by the end – but she hadn't cried out. Not so much as a squeak had escaped her clenched teeth. After such an utter fiasco of an evening, it was important to have some accomplishment of note in which to take pride – even if it was only the mundane sort of pride at having maintained a stoic silence through the most savage whipping of her life.

Her friends had been agreeably solicitous during the brief journey back to the wagons; they'd each taken one of her arms about their necks, supporting her when her own legs hadn't been up to the task. The journey itself had been a momentary wonder; Lady Nidlo, practised mage that she was, had simply ordered the three errant adolescents to join hands, and with a whisper had shunted them all through the glimmering, kaleidoscopic back-channels of the flux. They'd appeared with a subtle *crack* at the abandoned fair-grounds, not far from the dancing platform, beneath lowering clouds and the dim illumination of an early-morning Lantern. Alauda, who had never before leapt the flux, was so mesmerized that she even managed to forget about her throbbing posterior – for all of three breaths, anyway.

The Halflings' camp was empty. Every tent, every last wagon, was gone. They'd left behind nothing but tire-ruts and litter. And the tire-ruts, Alauda had remarked, went in every direction conceivable – including out into the Wastes.

"Clever," she'd muttered, clutching her damp and tattered gown to her bosom. They were so *damnably* clever. Try as she might, she couldn't hate them – not even Alainn O'Dell. The very thought of him – of his gentle hands, his soft lips, and his glorious, golden eyes – made her heart ache worse than her bottom. The horrid truth of it was that she couldn't even bring herself to regret having ceded her maidenhead to him. The memory of that single, glorious moment still filled her with incandescent bliss. Standing there in the darkness, shivering, her backside screaming imprecations at her, she *still* wanted him.

Her untrustworthy heart made her even more angry, though less at her absconded lover than at her own appalling cupidity. When she caught herself staring wistfully at the empty wagon-park, she snarled a blasphemy foul enough to blister paint. Her friends stared at her, startled. They didn't understand. They thought that she was cursing them, when in truth she was cursing herself.

Nidlo had gathered them with a glance. "No good can come from speaking of this night," she warned. "We keep to our accord: you know nothing of Arx Cervus, the speaking tree, or any ancient treasure. You will be safer so. My husband thinks like a knight of his empire, where faith and honour are said to bind all. But you three come from a land like my own. Like yours, my folk are not above the garrotte, the knife in the darkness, and the shallow grave. Your Elvenking would not scruple to seek vengeance on anyone responsible for placing him in an unenviable and costly position. *Anyone.* Do you comprehend?"

The three knew enough of the Realm's history and the rumours of cut-throat nature of palace politics to nod in mute unison. "*Bene,*" Nidlo said. "Then be off, and be well."

That unexpected sentiment had prompted Alauda to stare incredulously at the woman, who had replied with a narrow smile.

"Courage matters, girl," The wizard had observed, smiling at Alauda's perplexed gape. "Be grateful that you have it, and in abundance. It may save you when your lack of judgement tempts you once again down the path to folly."

And then, to the elf-girl's astonishment, she'd made a slight, negligent gesture...and the tattered, filthy gown beneath Alauda's arm had been once more dry, whole, and pristine. "Put that back on," Nidlo commanded. "It would not do to appear before your mother in such a sorry state. If she is truly worthy of her training, you will have difficulty enough deceiving her without returning home in naught but a soiled shift."

Alauda glanced down. The shift in question was no longer soiled. She very nearly thanked the woman, but her bruised posterior stopped her at the last moment.

With Tonlees' assistance, she struggled back into the snug gown, squealing when the fabric brushed her wounded backside. "This...helps," she grunted. "It might spare me a second hiding."

"I care naught for that," Nidlo sniffed. "No doubt it would be beneficial; meet sauce for your arrogance. Howbeit, as you are already well-marked by my hand, the mere act of raising your skirts would make your evening too difficult to explain. I suggest you lie, girl, and lie well."

"Oh, I will," Alauda snarled.

"She's good at it," Toni added, elbowing Alauda in a show of support.

"Excellent," Nidlo sniffed. "Lies are well; but silence is better. Remember that!" she cautioned harshly. "In this instance, the truth serves no one – you three least of all."

And with that final warning, she'd bent her fingers once more, and with a crackling *snap* of displaced air, was gone.

"What was *that* supposed to mean?" Tonlees had complained, hugging herself against the morning chill as they walked back to their own wagons.

"It means that we hold your tongues, now and forever," Alauda had replied firmly. "It means that if we're pressed, we lie until our lips turn black. Nothing about this little escapade – *nothing*; not a word, d'ye hear? – goes beyond we three. Are we agreed?"

Toni nodded dumbly.

"Alacer?"

"Agreed," the boy said, glancing down at his tunic. It too was spotless. "She sorted us all. I didn't even feel it!"

"She had to, for any lies to work," Alauda muttered. She turned immediately for home – but not before seeing Alacer take Tonlees in his arms and kiss her gently before going his own way. Toni at least had the decency to look guilty about it.

Her vision swam momentarily, and she swiped angrily at her eyes. If Nidlo's cane hadn't made her wail, her friends' betrayal certainly wouldn't. *Probably*, she corrected with a gulp; *probably* wouldn't.

"You enjoyed yourself last night, I hope?" Alyssa said suddenly, breaking into her daughter's reverie.

Alauda swallowed hard, willing her eyes to stay dry. "Yes," she replied. She wasn't trying to lie; she simply couldn't think of anything else to say. And besides, it was the truth; parts of the night had, after all, been *very* enjoyable.

"Good," her mother said complacently. "Did you dance with anyone besides Alacer?"

"Alainn," she replied without thinking. She felt her cheeks begin to redden, and fought the blush down fiercely.

Alyssa frowned. "I don't know the name. Is that Veronik's boy?"

Gods, Alauda despaired, *she's making conversation*. She shook her head. "He's a halpie. A Halfling. A half-Halfling, I mean. He's half-Halfling."

Her mother closed the book on her finger. "What in the World Made are you babbling about, girl?"

"He's only half a Halfling," Alauda insisted, cursing the vagaries of their tongue. "His mother was one of our people. Third House."

"I see." The wizard's cheek twitched. "However did you manage to dance with a halpie without straining your neck?"

"We're the same height, mother. He, uh…he had pretty eyes," she added, flushing again.

"I don't doubt it," Alyssa sniffed. "A woman of our folk, taking a Halfling to mate? That's a little unusual, *heya*?"

"*He* was a little unusual," Alauda muttered, shifting slightly; it was impossible to get comfortable. *I'll spend the next week sleeping on my belly*, she thought miserably. "Alainn said that they were wed because his father made his mother laugh."

To her surprise, her mother smiled. "Well, I suppose there are worse reasons for a mating. Did he make *you* laugh, this lad? Alainn?"

Tread carefully. "Yes," Alauda sighed. "Yes, that he did."

"I see." Alyssa wrinkled her nose. "And did you get a kiss from him?"

Alauda squelched a shiver, recalling the interlude between the wagons: Alainn's warm breath against her thighs, her fingers knotted in his hair, and the number of times he'd brought her to the very pinnacle of shuddering ecstasy. There was no way that she could lie – but it would've been utter madness to admit the truth. "Yes," she said as blandly as possible. She clenched her teeth, waiting for the inevitable explosion.

Once again, her mother wrong-footed her. "Was he any good at it?" Alyssa grinned.

Alauda blinked. Were they really talking about this? "Ah...not bad."

"That's all right then," Alyssa mused. "There are few things worse than a bad kisser. Well, good or bad, I don't suppose you'll see him again. They're gone now, you know. Hauled stakes and scampered, the whole scurrying, light-fingered pack of'em."

"I saw that," Alauda nodded at once, thanking her good luck for the change of topic. "When did they leave?"

"First light. They were packed and rolling early. Their harness-bells woke me." She glanced at her book once more, and then closed it with a snap and set it aside. "Speaking of which, you were home even later than that, little miss. Where were you? Lingering at your young man's lips, *heya*?"

Alauda wasn't fooled; she'd noted the page her mother had been reading, and had seen the minute, almost unnoticeable gestures. *She did it*, the girl realized, appalled. *She cast a spell*! The truth-finding spell, no doubt. Alauda had read through that one more than once, and knew that any lie that she told, no matter how minor, would be instantly revealed.

The suspicious old cow! Well, fine; two could play that game. It was simply a matter of calibrating her responses to remain outside of the bounds of strict falsehood. If she couldn't fool her mother, she wasn't worthy of her years. "I was with Alacer and Tonlees," she said firmly. "I spent the whole night with them. We were walking and talking."

"The whole night?" her mother demanded, dubious. "Just that? Walking and talking?"

"There was some climbing involved," Alauda shrugged. "We went for a hike along the river. It's rocky there."

"Did you?" Alyssa frowned. "And why is thy gown not a wreck, then? It looks like it's hardly been worn!"

"I tried to take care of it, mother," the girl said patiently. "You put a great deal of work into it, after all. I didn't want it to get ruined. I took it off when we went in the water."

"Water?!" her mother exclaimed. "You went swimming? In this cold?"

"We were warm from all the dancing," Alauda shrugged. "My hair was already ruined." She was grateful for the opportunity to work that particularly knotty fact into her excuse.

The older woman sat upright. "Warm, forsooth," she exclaimed. "Warm. Just how warm did'st thou get, may I ask?"

The girl frowned. "What exactly are you implying, mother?"

"Only this!" Alyssa said coldly. "Did'st thou lie with him? Did young Alacer spread your legs, little miss?"

Alauda felt the scream coming, but couldn't halt it. She didn't want to. "No!" she cried. "No, he didn't! He didn't, all right? But I...but I..." She put her face in her hands, feeling the tears streak down her cheeks. She'd been acting before, but no longer. "No," she moaned. "But I *wanted* him to. I *still* want him to!" There was no danger in admitting that fact; spell or no spell, it was the truth, and her mother knew it.

To her astonishment, Alyssa reached out and took her hand, nodding compassionately. "That was well done, child. I know how difficult this must be for you."

"Do you?" Alauda muttered. "I don't think so."

Her mother let that pass. "And Tonlees? Did she find anyone to dance with, and to give her a kiss or two?"

Alauda swallowed. She nodded, not trusting herself to speak.

"Well, that's good," her mother mused. "I like her; she's a sweet thing."

"I like her too," Alauda said. Her voice, like her heart, was empty. But it was true. She couldn't hate Toni. *I'd've done the same*, she realized dully. That too was the truth; and what was worse, she wouldn't have castigated herself over the betrayal. *At least Toni felt bad about what she did.*

There followed a pause. It was so artificial, so obviously contrived, that Alauda's innate caution immediately shrieked a warning at her. By the time her mother spoke again, the girl's nerves were vibrating, keyed to the acme of perception. "Is there anything else you ought to tell me?" her mother asked.

The girl crossed her arms, debating whether to go on the attack. She decided, for the moment, to rely on a stiff defence. "Like what, mother?" she demanded.

Alyssa regarded her daughter levelly. Then she turned and, from a basket, withdrew a small handful of white fabric. "I found these on our drying-line this morning," she said, tossing the thing to Alauda without expression. "Freshly washed. Care to explain?"

Alauda didn't need to untangle the tiny bundle. They were her smallclothes – the silky underthings she'd bought for herself (and for Tonlees), that she'd last seen disappearing into Alainn's pocket during their tryst betwixt the wagons. She'd completely forgotten about them.

Time for that attack, girl, she thought, summoning up her steel. "I shouldn't think I needed to explain this to you, mother," she said coldly. "My courses began last year. You know that as well as I." Neither the truth, nor a lie; *that* was how it was done.

"Oh," Alyssa said, blinking in surprise. "Ah. Well, do a better job of washing them next time; they smell sour."

Alauda stuffed the fabric into her apron pocket. She was in no mood to be discussing her underclothes with her mother.

"And what about this, then?" Alyssa spun a coin through the air.

Alauda had quick hands, and caught it reflexively. She examined it, and felt a chill ripple across her shoulders. It was one of the victory coins; the ancient silver *argentæ*, black with age, that the Halflings had shown her in the Lore-speaker's cart. She examined the face, with the lettering celebrating the victory of King Yarchian the Renewer over the fiendish usurper Mærglyn, daughter Biardath Ill-Born: *Yarchian, Deo Gratia Victor*. The obverse was just as she remembered it too, with its stylized dragon's head, and the stamped legend, *Jawartan Argentum*.

She'd kept one of them; as far as she knew (she didn't dare check) it was still in her crumena. "Where did you find this?" she murmured.

"On the ground, 'neath thy drying drawers," her mother said coolly. "I thought the one might be connected to the other."

Alauda clenched the coin in her fist, her knuckles whitening. "Very nice, mother," she muttered. "You, who only last night were teaching me how to unlock a man's knees with my lips – now you see fit not only to insinuate that I'm a whore, but to imply that I'm a cheap one to boot!"

She flung the coin back; her mother barely caught it before it struck her in the face. "Don't you think that a roll with your daughter – *your* daughter," the girl seethed, "ought to be worth more than a single *basztakt* argie?!"

"That's not an answer," the older woman snapped. "Thou'rt a wild thing, and there's little I'd put past thee!"

"Then ask me the question!" Alauda cried. "Go on, ask it of me! *I dare you!*"

Alyssa stared at her without speaking, red-faced and angry.

"*I didn't fuck Alacer!*" the girl hissed. "*I didn't!*" She was weeping again, and this time there was no artifice in her tears. She ground her teeth, rocking back and forth, heedless of the pain in her posterior, and begged the uncaring Powers: *Please, oh please; don't let her ask about Alainn!*

"Aye," Alyssa said at last, sighing audibly, "I'm sorry. I worry for you, child; that's all it is." She flicked the coin with a fingernail. "Where did this trinket come from, then?"

"You're the one who found it, not me," Alauda said dully, trying to remember not to say anything that wasn't literal truth. *This is what it's come to; I'm a creature of deceit, living by lies.* "I won some coins at the Halflings' games, the night before last. That one might've come from one of their wagons." Her cheek twitched; she knew, she *knew*, that Alainn had left it for her, just as he had left her drawers hanging on the drying-line. It was a message. "If so, then we should count ourselves lucky. The ones I won were fakes. Forgeries, I mean; brass washed with silver. But that looks to be a victory coin. It could worth hundreds of orries." She brushed away tears, and managed to feign a hopeful smile.

"Indeed?" Alyssa smiled. "Such wealth, and in our grasp! Tell me, how did you detect these forgeries, these counterfeit coins you speak of?"

Alauda blinked. "They were Ekhani shillings, stamped with the mark of the Imperial mint. But whoever made them had misspelled *imperialus*. A stupid mistake, but an easy one to make. They probably weren't native *elvii* speakers."

"Easy, aye; that's the truth." The older woman tossed the coin back. "Rub that against thine apron, chitling."

Frowning, Alauda complied. Her eyes widened as the corrosion vanished, leaving black smudges against the linen, and the silver glistening in her fingers. "What is this?" she whispered.

"*Acetum*," Alyssa smiled. "I could smell it – and you could too, were you not blinded by dreams of ancient treasure. A truly antique bit of silver would be black, aye – but the tarnish would not come off so readily. It takes hours of polishing.

"But there's a more obvious clue as well," the older woman snorted. "Look at the spade again, my duck."

Alauda stared at the dragon's head, trying to figure out what her mother was getting at. At last she shrugged. "I don't see what you mean."

"Do you not?" Alyssa chuckled. "Tell me once more: how did you know the brass coins were false?"

"Because the forgers had misspelled..."

Her voice trailed off. She stared at the coin, aghast, recalling the invisible bridge, and the waterfall; remembering the statue of the kneeling archer, the plinth – and the inscription upon it. A name, one of the most ancient and storied names in all of the history of the Realm: ANYA ANTAYYSSIN.

Not Anja; *Anya*.

Scripts change, she heard herself saying, as though from a great distance; *the texts from the Age of Wisdom are all like that*. The colour drained from her face.

Her mother's chuckle became an outright laugh. "Thou see'st it now, I ween!"

Alauda glared at the coin. "Jawartan," she murmured. "Jawartan! In the Age of Wisdom, when the victory coins were struck after Yarchian's triumph...there was no 'j'!"

"No 'j'," Alyssa nodded. "Had the Renewer lived to see our day, I'll wager he'd be known as 'Jarchian'. The 'j', my love, came later; thousands of years later. Every scrap of historical writ, every tome of magic – the oldest ones, anyway – they all call the old wyrm *Yawartan*, the name he bore when he carried Yarchian's standard at the Field of

Oldarran, and was one of the few to survive the Gloaming of the Wyrms."

She nodded at the coin in her daughter's fist. "Whoever knocked out that bit of mischief needs to go back to *schola*. No one in the Realm – no one with any education to speak of, at any rate – would be taken in by so obvious a sham."

"No," Alauda said weakly. "No, you'd have to be some kind of imbecile to be duped by...by something so obvious." She couldn't go on. She turned and, with a sigh, lifted the lid of the bench beneath which she stored her growing heap of possessions.

She'd intended to tuck the coin away; instead, she halted, frozen.

There, atop her precisely folded undergarments, her spare chemises, and her nightshirt, was the crystal rose. The rose that Alacer had bought for her, at Toni's urging. Now, *now* she knew why Toni had wanted him to give it to her – and why Toni had paid for it. And now she knew at last who had snatched it out of her hand.

They'd been watching her; the halpies. They'd been watching her from the first moment of her arrival in Buckhill. They'd known who she was, probably from contacts in Vitrafoss, contacts who'd heard about the elfy girl who'd gotten mixed up in plots between Third House nobles and Ekhani warlords. They'd known who she was, and that she was coming to Buckhill; and they'd plotted to inveigle themselves into her company. They'd refined their plot to suit her particular tastes, and had sprung it on her at the earliest opportunity.

And then last night, before leaving forever, Alainn – it *had* to have been Alainn – had snuck into the wagon lines, leaving her the coin, and the silkies she'd entrusted to his care...and the rose. The rose that had started it all. The three items were a message – that he and his comrades were more than common thieves. That they'd had no need of keepsakes or trinkets – or indeed of anything belonging to Alauda, anything at all that a competent mage might use to track them down.

Leaving the rose with her hadn't been sentiment on Alainn's part. It wasn't a gesture of love, or even fondness; it was common sense. It was part of his strategy for escape. He'd meant to leave not even the faintest of trails. He'd erased every footprint, save for the ones he'd left upon her heart.

She closed the bench seat. It took all of her self-control to do so gently; she was all but gagging on her rage.

It had been a trap. It had been a trap all along.

The Halflings had planned it all. They'd known all about Arx Cervus, and the legends, and the Well, and the wards placed upon it, both ancient and new. They'd known that they needed a high elf, a girl pure enough in the blood of the Third House to get past the force-wall unassisted – and that she had to be untouched in body, mimicking Anja, and also willing to give up her maidenhead to open the doors that ancient Fineleor had sealed. They'd needed a lover for her to boot – and so, after seeing them together and not trusting to her fickle relationship with Alacer, they'd put Alainn in her path.

Alainn, with his beautiful eyes, soft voice, gentle hands, and subtle, easy wit, had been the perfect bait. They'd set their snare, sweetening it with just enough enticement – false victory coins, ancient leather, a carefully-crafted urn engraved with just enough information to draw her in – but the key to the scheme had been the boy. The beautiful boy, gentle and kind, with a ready smile, and with the most important skills of all: a good voice, and a dab hand at the rebec, to inveigle her by her love of music. They'd dangled the perfect bait before her and she'd snapped it up with a will, giving up the prize for nothing more than a song. And the final part of the plan had been Second Spring: with the Morbannens in flower, Alauda would have needed a will of iron to avoid succumbing to Alainn's charms.

He hadn't just been a part of it; Alainn had been at the centre of it all. And he'd played his role to perfection. His deception had been a tour de force of treachery. She understood at last: the plot had been *his* rite of passage. She had been nothing more than a mark.

Flawless, she thought, both awed and appalled; *flawless*. A masterpiece of scheming. And she'd fallen right into their snare. They'd *played* her. They'd played *her*, the whole faithless, stinking lot of them, like a master skald upon a one-stringed lute. They'd marked their prize, and devised their plan, and then had waited at Buckhill for their cat's-paw to arrive.

That fact alone – the waiting – meant that the Bridle-bearer, *Sieur* Curmagh, as well as Mhaister Cloughsen had both been a part of the plot. Which meant in turn that *all* of the Halpies had been involved. She couldn't believe it, and yet it had to be true; their readiness for an immediate and deliberately scattered departure proved that much.

A whole camp, a whole *people*, comprised of wily, calculating tricksters? It was impossible to credit; no one would ever believe so paranoid an explanation. And yet, what other explanation could there be? The prize they'd sought had been beyond price. Clever thieves would stop at nothing to lay their hands upon it. The complexity of the plan required had certainly been no bar; Halflings, she knew, would be drawn to a plot, not deterred from it, by its complexity.

No one will ever find them, she realized with a start. Never. If they'd planned their strike to such perfection, they'd have left nothing to chance in planning their escape. That was why the wagon-tracks had led in every direction; it was only the first layer of deception. There would be more, many more. *Good luck to Lady Nidlo and her divinations*, she thought, appalled. Maybe a magistatrix of the College of the Eye would have a chance. But she doubted it.

I'll bet Alain O'Dell isn't even his real name, she thought, her heart giving a peculiar lurch. They wouldn't prepare so thoroughly, and then make so elementary a mistake, leaving behind one of the best possible clues for a diviner to search out.

Nidlo would never find them.

Even now, seething with the knowledge that she'd been hoodwinked as easily as a suckling infant, burning with fury at how comprehensively she'd been taken (in every sense of the word) – how thoroughly her heart had been broken, both by her friends and by the conniving swine to whom she'd surrendered her maidenhead – still, she couldn't bring herself to hate Alainn, or whatever his real name was. Bugger their schemes! What she'd felt in his arms had been real. The warmth of his hands, the lilt of his laughter, the joy of his heart, the pleasure that he'd given her, and that which she in her turn had given him…it had all been wonderfully, terribly real. The momentary magic of the Well had made it so. What they'd shared had to have been real; else Fineleor's ancient magic would still be intact.

She couldn't hate Alainn O'Dell. After all…he had made her laugh.

But she *could* be angry. It had *all* been a game; he'd told her as much. 'A rite of passage', he'd said. And his rite, tricking her into helping him and his confederates in pilfering a matchless treasure, had in the end been more important to him than hers; the common, every-day, yet far more rare and precious rite that they had shared together.

Well, then…fine, she thought, setting her jaw. If it was a game, then it wasn't over. She didn't have to hate him; she only had to beat him. It was her move, and she had all the time in the world to make it. He was only half a Halfling, after all; his mother had been an elf, and elves were extraordinarily long-lived. He couldn't escape her through old age and death; she could afford to take *years* to find and best him. Centuries, even.

And she *would* best him. She *would*. That – *that* was an oath that was worth taking a lifetime to fulfil.

Her resolve calmed her somewhat. She shifted her knees, struggling to find a less painful seat, wincing at the stinging agony of her wounded backside. "Still fidgeting, I see," Alyssa sighed. "What on earth is the matter with you, girl? Did'ye pick up fleas, dancing with the halpie-folk?"

"No," Alauda grated. The spell might still be active; she couldn't lie, and she certainly couldn't tell the truth. *Think, think…*"A, uh…tree-branch branch touched my bottom while I had my drawers off. After we were swimming. It must…it must have been something I've an aversion to. A serious aversion." She struggled to keep her face immobile; thus far, she'd spoken only honest fact.

Alyssa blinked. "Truly? You've a rash, or some such?"

"Something like that." She touched her backside gingerly. "I'm all over wheals."

She'd half-expected her mother to demand to inspect the area in question. That would've been the end of her deception; there was no way that anyone could mistake whip-welts for a rash.

But Hara in his infinite wisdom and mercy granted her a boon. Alyssa merely pursed her lips and shrugged. "Well…it can happen."

Alauda nearly fainted at the unanticipated reprieve.

"Here," the older woman went on, rummaging about in her herb-bag, and producing a small clay pot with a waxed wooden stopper. "Arnica and *somniferum* – Blood-Rose, aye? – with a little Golden-Mary and *khus*, all in goose grease. It'll ease any itch, and bring down the swelling."

The girl smiled in genuine relief. "Thank you, mother."

Alyssa dropped the vessel in her daughter's hand. "Rub it in, but gently. It'll feel better soon." She winked drolly. "It'd feel better even sooner if you were to ask your young man Alacer to do the rubbing for you, *heya*?"

Alauda's lip trembled; her smile slipped a notch. To her mother's surprised consternation, she burst into a flood of tears.

Alauda Volo's tale continues in *Lark's Kiss, Volume 5:*
The Iron Slaves

Map of Erutrei

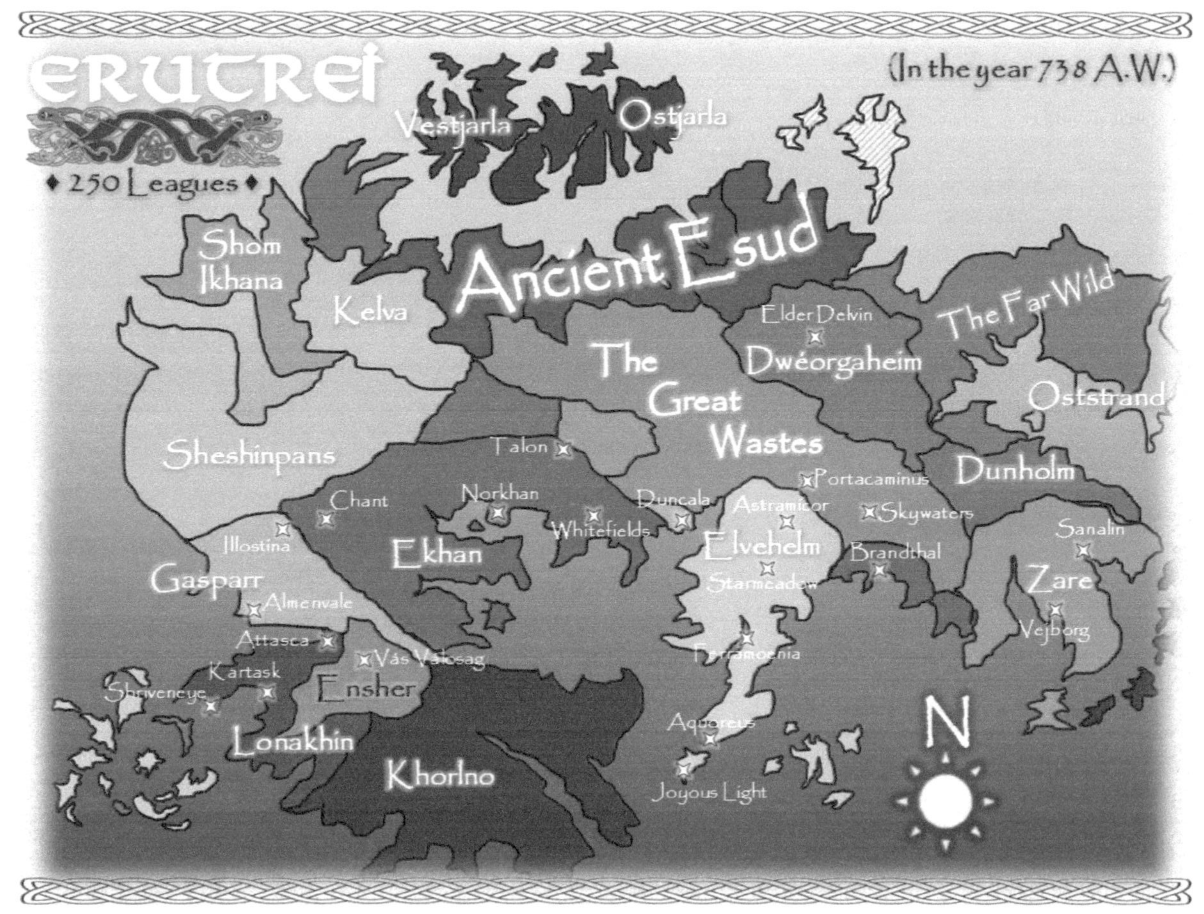

Map of The Realm, and northern environs

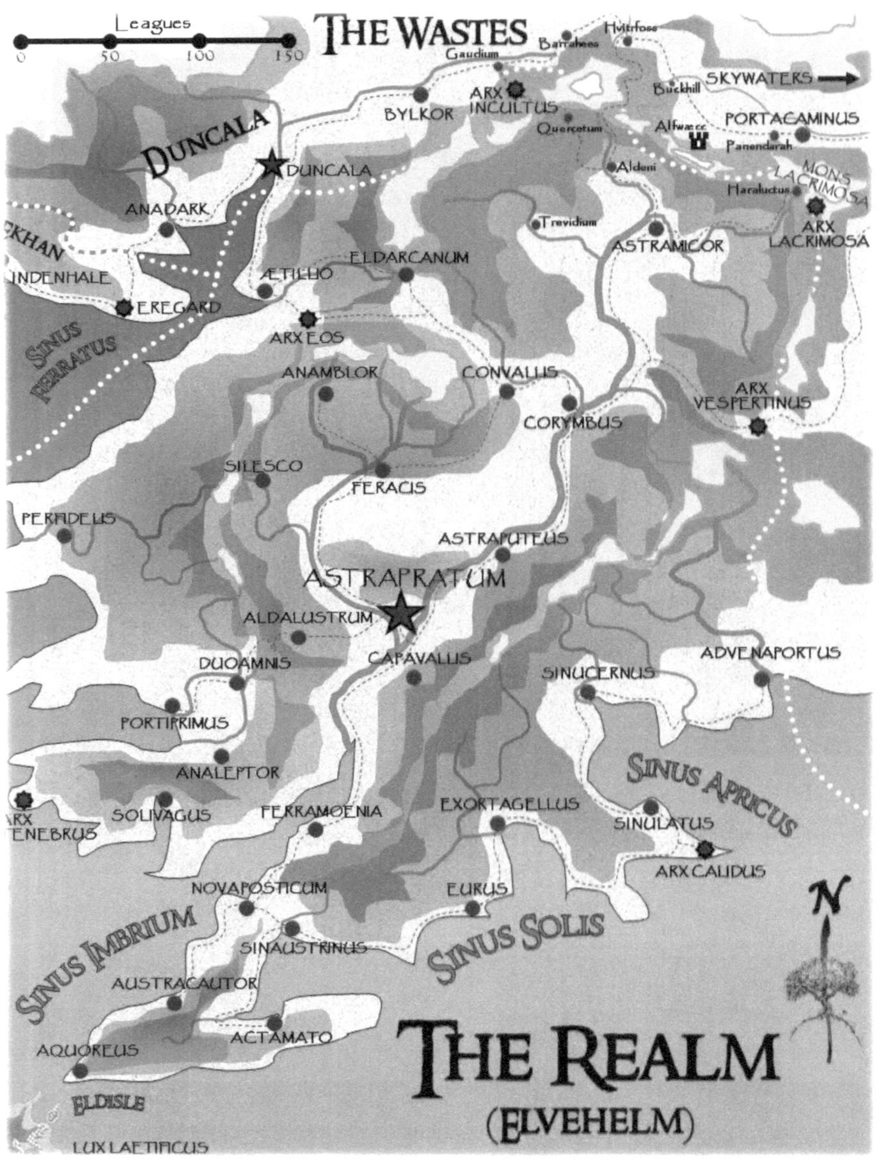

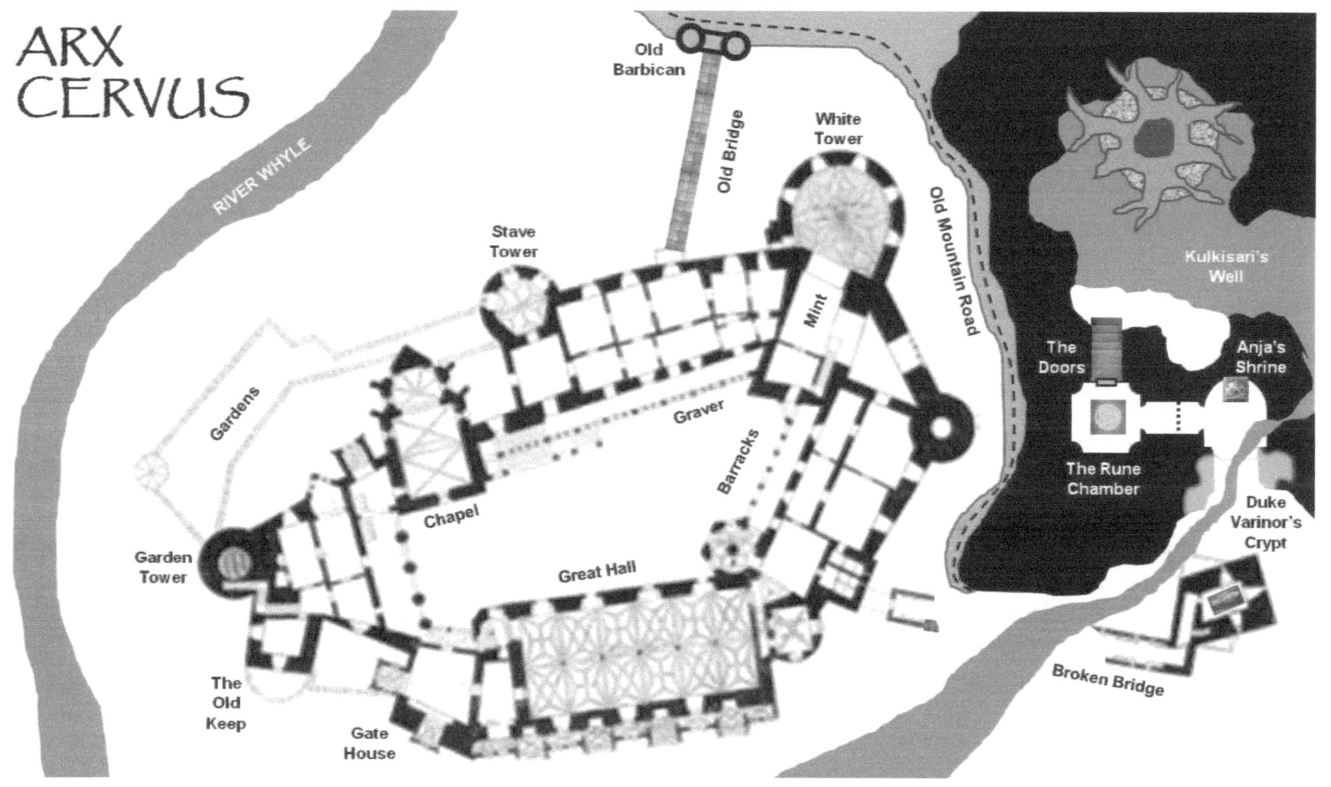

ARX CERVUS
RIVER WHYLE
Old Barbican
Old Bridge
White Tower
Old Mountain Road
Kulkisari's Well
Stave Tower
Mint
The Doors
Anja's Shrine
Gardens
Graver
Barracks
Chapel
The Rune Chamber
Duke Varinor's Crypt
Garden Tower
Great Hall
The Old Keep
Gate House
Broken Bridge

Glossary

Source languages

Ce.   The celestial tongue of the servants of the light, and the Anari

Dk.   The dark speech of fiends, fell folk, and the Uruqua

Dw.   *dwéorgaspræc* (dwarven)

El.   *elvii* (elven)

Es.   old Esudi (an ancient dialect derived from the *dwéorgaspræc*, no longer widely used. Esudi is the parent tongue to the *nordmannir* dialect (q.v.))

Fy.   Feyspeech; the tongue of the folk of the forest, and the Wild Elves

Gi.   The Giants' tongue

Hf.   The Halflings' speech

No.   *nordmannir* (a northern dialect peculiar to men. Derived from old Esudi as modified by the dwarven tongue during the Eon of Darkness, to become the language used by the empire of the Yonar'ri. Still spoken in the northlands, and as a patois by those southern nations that were colonized by the northlands. Original basis for much of the Travelling Tongue)

Or.   *Orkana*; Orkan. the tongue of the savage lands of Khorlno and Ensher; spoken also by the Wilders, the wild men of Semec, Celenora, and the Great Wastes

TT.   The travelling tongue; the *lingua franca* of the folk of Erutrei. Based on nordmannir speech, with words and phrases borrowed from the elves, the dwarves, the dragons, the giants, and even *Orkana*

Wy.   The dragons' tongue (wyrmspeech). It has a unique peculiarity: when spoken properly, it is impossible for the speaker to lie.

adlecto	(El.) enticement
aedes sacrum	(El.) holy place, place of worship, place of sacrifice, shrine
alacer	(El.) sprightly
alauda	(El.) lark
alaudalita	(El.) Little Lark, skylark
amator	(El.) darling, lover

Ancillulae	(El.) 'Little slaves'; girls of high social status who serve at the Palace in Starmeadow from the ages of 60 to when they 'pass without the walls' at 120. Usually trained and employed as handmaidens to the distaff members of the royal family, under the supervision of the senior lady of the royal household. Known colloquially as the 'Court Lilies' due to the white gowns they wear.
argies / argentæ	(TT./El.) Minted silver coin of the elven Realm.
arx	(El.) fortress, citadel
Arx Incultus	(El.) 'Desert Fortress' / 'Barbarian Citadel'
Arx Lacrimosa	(El.) 'Citadel of Tears'
Arx Vespertinus	(El.) 'Fortress of Twilight'
audax	(El.) audacious woman; hussy
Audite!	(El.) Listen (to me)!
auribus teneo lupum	(El.) 'I hold a wolf by the ears'; motto of House Volo. Derived from an ancient adage: 'When one holds a wolf by the ears, it is as dangerous to dismount as it is to ride on.'
basz-basz	(Or.) sexual intercourse (lit. 'fuck-fuck')
baszd makt!	(Or.) fuck this!
baszd meg!	(Or.) fuck off!
baszd-me!	(Or.) fuck me! (lit. 'copulate with me'; a common enticement shouted by the lowest caste of harlots to prospective clients)
basz-lyuk	(Or.) fuck-pit (vernacular term for a brothel)
basztakt	(Or.) fucking (adj.), fucked-up
bekakt	(Or.) lit. covered in shit; shitty
bene	(El.) good

| *blandior* | (El.) to praise; to caress |

chevauchée — (TT) a mounted ride through the countryside, usually in military force

chiliarch — (TT.) Commander of a Thousand (in the Imperial Army of Ekhan, this is equivalent to a general).

cicara — (El.) darling

civis — (El.) countryman, citizen

concedo — (El.) I concede, I surrender

Condelector — (El.) 'Delighted [to meet you.]'

coricularius — (El.) 'Counsellor of the heart'. A profession unique to the elven Realm, where relationships may last for centuries.

Cortina — (El.) 'Triangle'; a group of three Disciples of the Maiden, comprising one *præceptor/præceptrix*, one *senis*, and one *infima*

crown — (TT.) Minted gold coin of the Empire of Ekhan.

Cudorum Imperialis Ekhanium — (El.) Imperial Mint of Ekhan.

Custos Sylvanus — (El.) 'The Warden of the Green'

cupellatorium — (El.) smelter

dardy / dardies — (TT.) Colloquial term for a common soldier, a spearman. Derives from Or. *dárda*, meaning spear or pike.

Denuo! — (El.) 'One more time!' ('Encore!')

déorcísen — (Dw.) Darkiron. A type of iron that is *gandrfri* – 'magic-free' that can be used to block the arcane flux. Darkiron chains are often crafted specifically to imprison magi, especially blood-magi who do not require books and study to be able to cast spells.

Disciple — (TT). An adherent of the faith of Miyaga, the Maiden of Blinding Beauty.

| *Domina* | (El.) 'My Lady' |

Domina — (El.) 'My Lady'

Dominus — (El.) 'My Lord'

domus — (El.) house, i.e. family

Dos- — (El.) a prefix denoting a master craftsman

Dwéorgaheim — (Dw.) 'Dwarf-Home'; the Deeprealm

E vero? E vero! — (El.) exclamation; 'Is it true?'; 'It's true!'

Ensi Kuori! — (Wy.) lit. first shell; 'By the First Shell', oath or epithet

frikkies — (TT.) From the El. *frico*, to grind or rub; a derogatory term for the Disciples of the Maiden

Grimhorn (the) — (TT.) the common people's name for Cernunnor, the Horned God

groat — (TT.) Minted copper coin of the Empire of Ekhan.

heya — (TT.) A word used in most languages; origin unknown. May be a greeting ('*Heya!*', 'Hello!'). Also used as an interrogatory exclamation (e.g., 'Say *heya*?' = 'Do you agree?') or an exclamation of agreement (e.g., 'Say *heya*!' = 'Damned straight!', or 'Amen!'). Also as a terminal emphasis, where it means 'By golly!', 'By gum!' e.g., 'She's pretty, *heya*?'

infima — (El.) 'Student', the junior member of a Cortina of the Disciples of the Maiden

insitus — (El.) inborn; one whose magic comes from the blood, rather than books (pl: *insitii*)

invigilatrix — (El.) Guardian (female); compare *invigilator*.

ironweight — (TT.) The base coin of the dwarven monetary system.

kak — (Or., TT.) shit, crap

lente — (El.) slowly

lucum	(El.) grove. Usually *Lucum Sacrum*, sacred grove; a place of worship for followers of the Forest Gods (the Forest Mother, Hara Sophus, Larranel Sylvanus, Csæleyan the Wood-Maiden, and Cernunnor the Horned God).
megbasz	(Or.) copulate (lit. to fuck)
Miyaga / the Maiden (of Blinding Beauty)	(TT.) Miyaga is one of the lesser Uruqua, the Powers of Darkness. Her speciality is physical pleasure. She is the patron deity of the Disciples.
nec est	(El.) It's nothing; think nothing of it.
orries / *aureæ*	(TT./El.) Minted gold coin of the elven Realm.
Parati!	(El.) (I am) Ready!
Paska!	(Wy.) Crap!
pax	(El.) peace
pelice	(El.) a fur-lined out garment commonly worn in winter, under the cloak or cape
placet	(El.) agreed; lit. 'It pleases' (interrogatory: *Placet*? 'Agreed?')
pogue	(TT.) the prize (for a gang of thieves or pickpockets)
Promittimus	(El.) 'I promise', 'It's a promise', 'We promise'
præceptor/præceptrix	(El.) 'Teacher', the leader of a Cortina of the Disciples of the Maiden
Quod est necessarium non est iniuriam	(El.) 'What is necessary is never wrong' – the First Principle of the Art Magic.
rebec, *rebekken*	(TT.) (Dw.) A five-string bowed instrument, like a deep-bellied viol.
sal-petrum	(El.) 'salt-of-the-rock'; potassium nitrate.
Sanguinus Cælestis	(El.) 'Blood of the heavens'; the devise of House Cælestis, who claim descent from the *Sarvaloka*, the divine war-host that owes allegiance to the Powers of Light.

Satis est!	(El.) Enough of that!
scalpo	(El.) Colloquial term; a slender steel blade used to pick locks.
schola	(El.) elementary school (n.b. Elven children attend from age 15 [human equivalent 5-6] or so to age 60 [human equivalent 15-16], before beginning advanced schooling or trades/apprenticeship training, or joining the *Ancillulae*)
senis	(El.) 'Senior', the middle member of a Cortina of the Disciples of the Maiden
shilling	(TT.) Minted silver coin of the Empire of Ekhan.
shufty	(TT.) An 'affair'; a 'scuffle'; among gangs of thieves and pick-pockets, a 'shufty' means a scam, a set-up.
sielu	(Fy.) spirit, soul. pl: *sielli*
Slan agus fhortan	(Hf.) Farewell, and good luck.
solostratum	(El.) 'Sun-saddle'; a ladies' side-saddle fitted with supports for a sunshade. Expensive and impractical.
stingursteinn	(Dw.) A dwarven musical instrument designed to mimic the sound of picks upon stone.
stulta, stulto	(El.) moron, idiot, cretin
sulkakynsi	(Wy.) 'talon-quill'; a quill-pen designed to fit over a dragon's talon, to enable the creature to write on parchment.
sub-rosa	(El.) hidden, illegitimate
Suum cuique	(El.) To each his own.
Taceo	(El.) 'Shush' (gentle connotation)
Tacete!	(El.) 'Be silent!'; 'Shut up!' (harsh connotation)
taiva	(Wy.) blue dragon; short for *taivaansininen lohikäärme*
Te amo	(El.) I love you

Ut nihil!	(El.) Oh, fie! (mildest possible expression of annoyance in *elvii*)
Vara (White-Hands)	(TT.) One of the Anari, the Powers of Light; goddess of mercy, compassion, healing, and the waters of the world. Sister to Hara *Sophus*. Principle deity worshipped by the men of the Empire of Ekhan.
Venatrix/venator	(El.) 'Huntress/Hunter'
virga lætitia	(El.) A red sash worn by elven maidens to indicate their betrothal.
Vinarius	(El.) 'wine-seller'

◆

The Songs

Uxor Mihi ('The Mate for Me')

The mate for me has hair as black as night
And eyes of brilliant green
She'll keep her love for me alight
And be my happy little queen.

Ah coachman, why sit ye here pining?
Thy comrades are drinking and dining;
A beauteous mate can be thine,
And true love is better than wine!
<an arpeggio> *...yes, better than wine!*
<another arpeggio> *...much better than wine!*

♦

O Clara Lucerna ('O Lantern Bright')

O Lantern bright, who through the night
Reclines in silent leisure
While gold and silver moons above
Conspire thus in pleasure;
Their gleaming glow, to us below
Bequeaths an eve resplendent
And thus we know as, to and fro,
They rise in fire ascendant.

O show us, lamp of day, where hide the moons
Who light our loving night with star-shine strewn
O show us, lamp of day, where hide the moons
Who light our loving night with star-shine strewn

O silver moon, grant us this boon,
Who far below observe thee
We see thy love so far above,
And only wish to serve thee
The hour is late, and so thy mate
Arises swift to claim thee
With ardour hot, and so has got
No reason for to shame thee

O show us, lamp above, where silver shines
Thus followed by thy love, who for thee pines
O show us, lamp above, where silver shines
Thus followed by thy love, who for thee pines

O golden moon, we raise this tune
Unto thy gilt-edged glory
We know thy name, and blush for shame
To hear thee tell thy story
Thy silv'ry mate thy rich estate
Desires not to plunder
She rides above on wings of love
And fills the world with wonder

O tell us, lamp of gold, the reason why
Thou dost pursue thy love across the sky
O tell us, lamp of gold, the reason why
Thou dost pursue thy love across the sky

O heed my tunes, thou loving moons,
Who ply the sky above me
Perchance thy light, this darkling night
Shall find me one to love me
My aching heart must play its part,
For 'tis alone and tender
And waxing bright, in thy fair light,
Shall rise to nightly splendour!

O prithee tell me true, ye moons above –
Shall I have naught but thee to be my love?
O prithee tell me true, ye moons above;
Shall I have naught but thee to be my love?

♦

Cor Meum Inanis ('My Heart is Empty')

Fidelia: *My heart is empty, my heart is aching*
                 To know that love which life fulfills;

Trebax: *My heart is broken, my heart is longing*
                 For aught to mend its endless ills!

<table>
<tr><td>Both:</td><td>I live for love, that gift divine;
True love is sweet, as sweet as wine!
True love is sweet as the sweetest wine!</td></tr>
<tr><td>Fidelia:</td><td>The Lantern has set on my ambition,
No more do I long for a golden crown;</td></tr>
<tr><td>Trebax:</td><td>My mistress berates me; my master now hates me
I've no more use for a wedding gown –</td></tr>
<tr><td>Both:</td><td>There's nothing as sad as a loveless life;
And nothing noble as man and wife;
No, nothing noble as man and wife!</td></tr>
<tr><td>Fidelia:</td><td>And so in sorrow, I hasten whither
My love-lorn heart may heal for true;</td></tr>
<tr><td>Trebax:</td><td>While I, patient maiden, with heart heavy laden
Shall seek my blunders to undo.</td></tr>
<tr><td>Both:</td><td>With hopes of love blighted, and all uninvited
I'll make amends, and begin anew;
I'll make amends, and begin anew!</td></tr>
</table>

♦

O my love, won't you come lie with me?

In the dark night, 'neath the moons' light
We were dancing and singing
To the songs of our home far away
I was lying with my true love
With my heart nearly breaking
As he told me that he could not stay.

(Chorus) I remember that night, and the stars in his eyes
How they glimmered and glistened for me
He was gone upon the morrow
And my heart filled with sorrow
For the home that he'd never more see.
(O my love, won't you come lie with me?)

In the dark day, at the gateway
Of the wall where we waited

For some word of our comrades to hear
I was waiting for my true love
To return from his sortie
But no word came to gladden my ear.

(Chorus) I remember that day, and the bright clash of steel
What a terrible sight, you'll agree;
And I brought my fallen love in
With a green shroud above him
To the home that he'd never more see.
(Wait, my love, and I'll come lie with thee!)

◆◆◆

Other books by D. Alexander Neill

<u>**FICTION**</u>

The Chronicles of Anuru: *Kaunovalta*
Book I: The Running Girl
Book II: Dwéorgaheim
Book III: Daughter of Dragons
Kaunovalta: The Complete Series (comprises books I, II and III)

The Chronicles of Anuru: *Bjornssaga*
Book I: The Sea Dragon

The Chronicles of Anuru: Hallow's Heart
Book I: The Penitent
Book II: The Wizard's Eye

The Chronicles of Anuru: Lark's Kiss
Volume 1: The Horned God
Volume 2: The Huntress
Volume 3: The Mummers
Volume 4: The Sack of Arx Cervus

The Chronicles of Anuru: Tales of the Wyrm
(Anuru in Verse and Song)

♦

Other Works of Fiction

The Hero's Knot
Book I: Silviu the Thief

♦

<u>**NON-FICTION**</u>

NATO, Kosovo and Crisis Management
(by Donald A. Neill, CD, OMMM, Ph.D.)

♦

For more original art by J. Gagnon,
to purchase a print, or to request a commission,
contact **jgagnon999@gmail.com**

For more information about my writing,
including background, lore, and information on ongoing projects,
please visit:

...my Facebook page: **https://www.facebook.com/DAlexanderNeill/**

...my website: **http://www.alexanderneill.com/**

...or contact me at **dalexanderneill@gmail.ca**

And thanks for reading!

♦♦♦